"Violence may well be offered to anyone who tries to part you from this marvellous, dramatically intelligent novel. It shimmers with suspense, ambiguity and a deep, unholy joy." – *The Mail on Sunday*

"Search your thesaurus for superlatives to describe this new novel from the author of *The Ice House, The Sculptress* and *The Scold's Bridle*." – *The Halifax Daily News*

"Walters unfolds the dark complexities of Jinx's past with a master's hand, balancing sympathy and terror all the way." – *Kirkus Reviews*

"Minette Walters has emerged as one of the [mystery] genre's superior writers. Her novels are probing and intelligent, her characters riveting and her plots subtle and demanding." – *The Ottawa Citizen*

"Walters handles the juxtaposition of the physical and the psychological with immense fluency; she establishes a mood of fear and uncertainty from the start." – *The Times* of London

ALSO BY MINETTE WALTERS

The Ice House
The Sculptress
The Scold's Bridle

The Dark Room

MINETTE WALTERS

An M&S Paperback from
McClelland & Stewart Inc.
The Canadian Publishers

Published in association with Macmillan Publishers Ltd.

An M&S Paperback from McClelland & Stewart Inc.
Copyright © 1995 Minette Walters
First M&S Paperback edition June 1996
Cloth edition published 1995

Canadian Cataloguing in Publication Data

Walters, Minette
     The dark room

"An M&S paperback".
ISBN 0-7710-8778-0

I. Title.

PR 6073.A52D3 1996   823'.914   C96-930248-7

Cover photo by Tansy Spinks/
     Millennium Picture Library,
     with colour by George Snow
Cover design by Suzanne Dean

Typesetting by M&S, Toronto

Printed and bound in Canada

McClelland & Stewart Inc.
The Canadian Publishers
481 University Avenue
Toronto, Ontario
M5G 2E9

First published 1995 in
     Great Britain by
Macmillan, an imprint of
Macmillan Publishers Ltd.

First paperback edition
published 1996 in Great
Britain by Pan Books, an
imprint of Macmillan
Publishers Ltd.

1 2 3 4 5   00 99 98 97 96

For Colleen
&
In memory of my father

'And we forget because we must
and not because we will.'

Absence
MATTHEW ARNOLD (1822−88)

'The idea of the False Self was put forward by R.D. Laing,
adapting some theories of Jean-Paul Sartre. The false self
was an artificially created self-image designed to concur
with expectations, while the true self remained hidden and
protected.'

Killing for Company
BRIAN MASTERS

1994

MAY

S	M	T	W	T	F	S
1	2	3	4	5	6	7
8	9	10	11	12	13	14
15	16	17	18	19	20	21
22	23	24	25	26	27	28
29	30	31				

JUNE

S	M	T	W	T	F	S
			1	2	3	4
5	6	7	8	9	10	11
12	13	14	15	16	17	18
19	20	21	22	23	24	25
26	27	28	29	30		

Prologue

WITH HER SHARP little face set in lines of dissatisfaction, the twelve-year-old girl sat up and searched for her knickers among the forest leaves. It had finally begun to dawn on her that sex with Bobby Franklyn wasn't all it could be. She put on her shoes and kicked him hard. 'Get up, Bobby,' she snapped. 'It's your turn to find the bloody dog.'

He rolled over on to his back. 'In a minute,' he muttered sleepily.

'No, *now*. Mum'll skin me alive if Rex gets home before me again. She's not stupid, you know.' She stood up and dug the heel of her shoe into his naked thigh, twisting it back and forth in a childish desire to hurt. 'Get up.'

'OK, OK.' He rose sulkily to his feet, tugging at his trousers. 'But this is pissing me off, you know. It's hardly worth doing if we have to go looking for the dog every time.'

She moved away from him. 'It's not Rex that makes it hardly worth doing.' There were tears of angry humiliation in her eyes. 'I should have listened to Mum. She always says it takes a real man to do it properly.'

'Yeah, well,' he said, zipping his fly, 'it'd be a damn sight easier if I didn't have to pretend you were Julia Roberts. What would your sodding Mum know about it, anyway? It's years since anyone gave her a good shagging.' He had few feelings for these girls beyond the purely animal, but he grew to hate them very quickly when they gave him lip about his performance. The urge to smash their jeering little faces in was becoming irresistible.

The girl started to walk away. 'I *hate* you, Bobby. I really *hate* you, and I'm going to tell on you.' She tapped her watch. 'Three minutes. That's as long as you can keep it up. Three lousy minutes. Is that what you call a good shagging?' She gave a triumphant glance over her shoulder, saw something in his face that alerted her to the danger she was in, and took to her heels in sudden fear. 'REX!' she screamed. 'RE-EX! He'll *kill* you if you touch me,' she sobbed, her small wiry body darting through the trees.

But it was Bobby who was going to do the killing. His anger was out of control. He threw himself at her back and brought her crashing to the ground, breathing heavily as he tried to get astride her thrashing legs. 'Bitch!' he grunted. 'Bloody bitch!'

Fear lent her strength. She scrambled away from him, crying for her dog, slithering and sliding in a flurry of decomposing leaves into a broad ditch that scored the forest bed. She landed on her feet, only yards from the huge Alsatian, who stood, hackles up and growling. 'I'll set him on you, and he'll rip you to pieces. And I won't care, and I won't stop him.' She saw with satisfaction that Bobby had turned white to the gills. 'You're such a CREEP!' she yelled.

And then she saw that Rex was growling at her and not at Bobby, and that what had drained the colour from her boyfriend's face was not his fear of the dog but stunned horror at what the dog was guarding. She had a glimpse of something half-unearthed and repulsively human, before panic drove her up the slope again in sobbing, wide-eyed terror.

Chapter One

SHE CLUNG TO sleep tenaciously, wrapped in beguiling dreams. It was explained to her afterwards that they weren't dreams at all, only reality breaking through the days of confusion as she rose from deep unconsciousness to full awareness, but she found that difficult to accept. Reality was too depressing to give birth to such contentment. Her awakening was painful. They propped her on pillows and she caught glimpses of herself from time to time in the dressing-table mirror, a waxen-faced effigy with shaven head and bandaged eye – *hardly recognizable* – and she had an instinctive desire to withdraw from it and leave it to play its part alone. *It wasn't her.* A huge bear of a man with close-cropped hair and close-cropped beard leant over her and told her she'd been in a car accident. But he didn't tell her where or when. You're a lucky young woman, he said. She remembered that. Forgot everything else. She had a sense of time passing, of people talking to her, but she preferred to drowse in sleep where dreams beguiled.

She was aware. She saw. She heard. And she felt safe with the pleasant female voices that smoothed and soothed and petted. She answered them in her head but never out loud, for she clung to the spurious protection of intellectual absence. 'Are you with us today?' the nurses asked, pressing their faces up to hers. *I've been with you all along.* 'Here's your mother to see you, dear.' *I don't have a mother. I have a stepmother.* 'Come on, love, your eyes are open. We know you can hear us, so when are you going to talk to us?' *When I'm ready . . . when I'm ready . . . when I want to remember . . .*

ROAD TRAFFIC ACCIDENT:

Reported 21.45 approx 13.6.94 PCs Gregg
 and Hardy on scene at 22.04
Location: Disused airfield, Stoney Bassett,
 Hants
One vehicle involved. Black Rover Cabriolet
 automatic
Reg No: JIN 1X – vehicle written off
Driver: Miss Jane Imogen Nicola Kingsley
Unconscious and in need of emergency
 treatment
Driving licence gives date of birth: 26.09.59
 and registered address: 12 Glenavon
 Gdns, Richmond, Surrey

Property tycoon's daughter in mystery pile-up

It was reported late last night that Jane Kingsley, 34, the fashion photographer and only daughter of Adam Kingsley, 66, millionaire chairman of Franchise Holdings Ltd, was found unconscious following a mystery car crash on the disused airfield at Stoney Bassett, 15 miles south of Salisbury. Mr Andrew Wilson, 23, and his girlfriend, Miss Jenny Ragg, 19, happened upon the scene by chance at 9.45 p.m. and immediately summoned assistance for the unconscious woman.

'The car was a write-off,' said Mr Wilson. 'Miss Kingsley's very lucky to be alive. If she'd been in it when it hit the concrete pillar, she'd have been crushed to death in the wreck. I'm glad we were able to help.'

Police describe Miss Kingsley's escape as a miracle. The car, a black Rover Cabriolet automatic, had collided head-on with a solid concrete stanchion, which was once the corner support for a hangar. Police believe Miss Kingsley was thrown through the open door of her car shortly before the impact.

'That pillar is the only structure still standing on the airfield,' said PC Gavin Hardy, 'and we don't understand yet how she came to hit it. There was no one else in the car and no evidence of another vehicle being involved.'

Jane's stepmother, Mrs Betty Kingsley, 65, was shocked by the news, which comes only days after the surprise cancellation of her stepdaughter's wedding. At home this morning in Hellingdon Hall, where she and Mr Kingsley have lived for the last 15 years, she wept bitterly and said she would blame Miss Kingsley's fiancé, Leo Wallader, 35, if Miss Kingsley didn't recover. 'He's treated her so badly.'

Police admitted this morning that Miss Kingsley had been drinking prior to the accident. 'She had a high level of alcohol in her blood,' said a spokesman. Miss Kingsley is unconscious in Odstock Hospital, Salisbury.

Wessex Post – 14 June

Chapter Two

SHE AWOKE ONE night with fear sucking the breath from her lungs. She opened her eyes and strained them into the blackness. She was in a dark room – *her dark room?* – and she wasn't alone. Someone – *something?* – prowled the shadows beyond her vision.

WHAT?

Fear . . . fear . . . FEAR *. . .*

She sat bolt upright, sweat pouring down her back, screams issuing in a tumult of sound from her gaping mouth.

Light flooded the room. Comfort came in the shape of a woman's soft breasts, strong arms and sweet voice. 'There, there, Jane. It's all right. Come on, love, calm down. You had a nightmare.'

But she knew that was wrong. *Her terror was real. There was something in the dark room with her.* 'My name's Jinx,' she whispered. 'I'm a photographer, and this isn't my room.' She laid her shaven head against the starched white uniform and knew the bitterness of defeat. There would be no more sweet dreams. 'Where am I?' she asked. 'Who are you? Why am I here?'

'You're in the Nightingale Clinic in Salisbury,' said the nurse, 'and I'm Sister Gordon. You were in a car accident, but you're safe now. Let's see if we can get you back to sleep again.'

Jinx allowed herself to be tucked back under the sheets by a firm pair of hands. 'You won't turn the light off, will you?' she begged. 'I can't see in the dark.'

Query prosecution of

Miss J. Kingsley /driving

with 150mg per 100ml

Date: 22 June, 1994
From: Sergeant Geoff Halliwell

Miss Kingsley was thrown from her vehicle before it
impacted against a concrete stanchion in one corner of
the airfield. She was unconscious when she was found at
21.45 on Monday, 13 June, by Mr Andrew Wilson and
Miss Jenny Ragg. Miss Kingsley suffered severe concussion and bruising/laceration of her arms and face when
she was thrown from the car. She remained unconscious
for three days and was very confused when she finally
came round. She has no recollection of the accident and
claims not to know why she was at the airfield. Blood
samples taken at 00.23 (14.6.94) show 150mg per
100ml. Two empty wine bottles were recovered from the
floor of the car when it was examined the following day.

PCs Gregg and Hardy had one brief interview with
Miss Kingsley shortly after she regained consciousness,
but she was too confused to tell them anything other than
that she appeared to believe it was Saturday, 4 June, (i.e.
some 9 days before the incident on 13.6.94) and that
she was on her way from London to Hampshire. Since
the interview (5 days) she has remained dazed and
uncommunicative and visits have been suspended on
the advice of her doctors. They have diagnosed

post-traumatic amnesia, following concussion. Her parents report that she spent the week 4–10 June with them (though Miss Kingsley clearly has no memory of this) before returning to Richmond on the evening of Friday, 10 June, following a telephone call. They describe her as being in good spirits and looking forward to her forthcoming wedding on 2 July. She was expected at work on Monday, 13 June, but did not show. She runs her own photographic studio in Pimlico and her employees say they were concerned at her non-appearance. They left several messages on her answerphone on the 13th but received no reply.

Interviews by Richmond police with her neighbours in Glenavon Gdns, Colonel and Mrs Clancey, reveal that she made an attempt on her life on Sunday, 12 June. Col. Clancey, whose garage adjoins Miss Kingsley's, heard her car engine running with the door closed. When he went to investigate, he found her garage full of fumes and Miss Kingsley half-asleep at the wheel. He dragged her outside and revived her, but did not report the incident because Miss Kingsley asked him not to. He and his wife are deeply upset that she has 'tried to do it again'.

Both Col. and Mrs Clancey and Mr and Mrs Adam Kingsley made reference to a Mr Leo Wallader who was until recently Miss Kingsley's fiancé. It appears he left 12 Glenavon Gdns on Friday, 10 June, after telling Miss Kingsley he couldn't marry her because he had plans to marry her closest friend, Meg Harris, instead. Mr Wallader and Ms Harris are unavailable for interview at the moment. According to Sir Anthony Wallader (father) they are currently travelling in France but plan to return some time in July.

In view of a recent MOT certificate on Miss Kingsley's vehicle, which tends to rule out malfunction, and the fact that the chances of hitting the concrete stanchion by accident are virtually nil, it seems clear that she drove her car into it deliberately. Therefore, unless she recovers enough of her memory to give an explanation of the events leading up to the incident, Gregg and Hardy incline to the view that this was a second attempt at suicide after a drinking session in her car. Mr Adam Kingsley, her father, has offered to pay the costs of the emergency services, meanwhile Miss Kingsley has been transferred to the Nightingale Clinic where she is receiving treatment from Dr Alan Protheroe. Mr Kingsley's solicitor is pressing for a decision on whether or not we intend to proceed against Miss Kingsley. My view is to do nothing in view of her father's willingness to pick up the tab, her disturbed state of mind and the fact that she chose such a deserted location. Please advise.

Chapter Three

Wednesday, 22 June, Nightingale Clinic, Salisbury,
Wiltshire – 8.30 a.m.

HOW DRAB REALITY was. Even the sun shining through her windows was less vivid than her dreams. Perhaps it had something to do with the bandage over her right eye, but she didn't think so. Consciousness itself was leaden and dull, and so restrictive that she felt only a terrible depression. The big bear of a doctor came in as she toyed with her breakfast, told her again that she'd been in an accident and said the police would like to talk to her. She shrugged. 'I'm not going anywhere.' She would have added that she despised policemen if he'd stayed to listen, but he went away again before she could put the thought into words.

She had no memory of the first police interview at Odstock Hospital and politely denied ever having met the two uniformed constables who came to her room. She explained that she could not remember the accident, indeed could remember nothing at all since leaving her house and her fiancé in London the previous morning. The policemen resembled each other, tall, stolid men with sandy hair and florid complexions, who showed their discomfort at her answers by turning their caps in unison between their fingers. She labelled them Tweedledum and

Tweedledee and chuckled silently because they were so much more amusing than her sore head, bandaged eye and hideously bruised arms. They asked her where she had been going, and she replied that she was on her way to stay with her parents at Hellingdon Hall. 'I have to help my step-mother with wedding preparations,' she explained. 'I'm getting married on the second of July.' She heard herself announce the fact with pleasure, while the voice of cynicism murmured in her brain. *Leo will run a mile before he hitches himself to a bald, one-eyed bride.*

They thanked her and left.

Two hours later, her stepmother dissolved into tears at her bedside, blurted out that the wedding was off, it was Wednesday, the twenty-second of June, Leo had left her for Meg twelve days previously and she had, to all intents and purposes, driven her car at a concrete pillar four days later in a deliberate attempt to kill herself.

Jinx stared at her ugly, scarred hands. 'Didn't I say goodbye to Leo yesterday?'

'You were unconscious for three days and very confused afterwards. You were in the hospital until Friday, and I went to see you, but you didn't know who I was. I've come here twice and you've looked at me, but you didn't want to talk to me. This is the first time you've recognized me. Daddy's that upset about it.' Her mouth wobbled rather pathetically. 'We were so afraid we'd lost you.'

'I've come to stay with you. That's why I'm here. You and I are going to confirm the arrangements for the wedding.' *If she said it slowly and clearly enough, Betty must believe her. But no, Betty was a fool. Betty had always been a fool.* 'The

15

week beginning the fourth of June. It's been in the diary for months . . .'

Mrs Kingsley's tears poured down her plump cheeks, scoring tiny pink rivulets in her over-powdered face. 'You've already been, my darling. You came down a fortnight and a half ago, spent the week with Daddy and me, did all the things you were supposed to do, and then went home to find Leo packing his bags. Don't you remember? He's gone to live with Meg. Oh, I could murder him, Jinx, I really could.' She wrung her hands. 'I always told you he wasn't a nice man, but you wouldn't listen. And your father was just as bad. "He's a Wallader, Elizabeth . . ."' She rambled on, her huge chest heaving tragically inside a woollen dress that was far too tight.

The idea that nearly three weeks had passed without her being able to recollect a single day was so far beyond Jinx's comprehension that she fixed her attention on what was real. Red carnations and white lilies in a vase on her bedside table. French windows looking out on to a flag-stoned terrace, with a carefully tended garden beyond. Television in the corner. Leather armchairs on either side of a coffee table – walnut, she decided, and a walnut dressing table. Bathroom to her left. Door to the corridor on her right. *Where had Adam put her this time?* Somewhere very expensive, she thought. The Nightingale Clinic, the nurse had told her. In Salisbury. *But why Salisbury when she lived in London?*

Betty's plaintive wailing broke into her thoughts. 'I wish it hadn't upset you so much, my darling. You've no idea how badly Daddy's taken it all. He sees it as an insult to him, you know. He never thought anyone could make his little girl do something so' – she cast about for a word – 'silly.'

Little girl? What on earth was Betty talking about? She had never been Adam's little girl – his performing puppet perhaps – never his little girl. She felt very tired suddenly. 'I don't understand.'

'You got drunk and tried to kill yourself, my poor baby. Your car's been written off.' Mrs Kingsley fished a newspaper photograph out of her handbag and pressed it into her stepdaughter's lap. 'That's what it looked like afterwards. It's a mercy you survived, it really is.' She pointed to the date in the top left-hand corner of the clipping. 'The fourteenth of June, the day after the accident. And today's date' – she pushed forward another newspaper – 'there, you see, the twenty-second, a whole week later.'

Jinx examined the picture curiously. The writhing mass of twisted metal, backlit by police arc lights, had the fantastic quality of surrealist art. It was a stark silhouette and, in the distortions of the chassis and the oblique angle from which the photographer had taken his shot, it appeared to portray a gleaming metal gauntlet clasped about the raised sword of the pillar. It was a great picture, she thought, and wondered who had taken it.

'This isn't my car.'

Her stepmother took her hand and stroked it gently. 'Leo's not going to marry you, Jinx. Daddy and I have had to send out notices to everyone saying the wedding's been cancelled. He wants to marry Meg instead.'

She watched a tear drip from the powdered chin on to her own upturned palm. 'Meg?' she echoed. 'You mean Meg

Harris?' Why would Leo want to marry Meg? Meg was a whore. You whore . . . you whore . . . YOU WHORE! Some horror – *what?* – lurched through her mind, and she clamped a hand to her mouth as bile rose in her throat.

'She's been out for what she can get as long as you've known her, and now she's taken your husband. You always were too trusting, baby. I never liked her.'

Jinx dragged her wide-eyed stare back to her step-mother. That wasn't true. Betty had always adored Meg, largely because Meg was so uncritical in her affections. It made no difference to her if Betty Kingsley was drunk or sober. 'At least Meg thinks I've something sensible to say,' was her stepmother's aggressive refrain whenever she was deep in her cups and being ignored by everybody else. The irony was that Meg couldn't tolerate her own strait-laced mother for more than a couple of hours. 'You and I should swap,' she often said. 'At least Betty doesn't play the martyr all the time.'

'When was this decided?' Jinx managed at last. 'After the accident?'

'No, dear. Before. You went back to London a week ago last Friday after Leo phoned you during the afternoon. Horrible, horrible man. He called every day, pretending he still loved you, then dropped the bombshell on the Friday night. I don't suppose he was at all kind in the way he did it either.' She held the handkerchief to her eyes again. 'Then on the Sunday, Colonel Clancey from next door rescued you from your garage before you could gas yourself, but didn't have the sense to ring us and tell us you needed help.' She swallowed painfully. 'But you were so cool about it all on the Saturday when you phoned home to tell Daddy the

18

wedding was off that it never occurred to us you were going to do something silly.'

Perhaps she'd been lying ... Jinx always lied ... lying was second nature to her ... Jinx looked down at the newspaper clipping again and noticed amidst the wreckage in the photograph the JIN of the personalized number plate that her father had given her for her twenty-first birthday present. J.I.N. Kingsley. *Jane Imogen Nicola – her mother's names – the most hated names in the world.* JINXED! She had to accept it was her car featured there. *You got drunk ... Colonel Clancey rescued you ...* 'There's no gas in my garage,' Jinx said, fixing on something she could understand. 'No one has gas in their garage.'

Mrs Kingsley sobbed loudly. 'You were running your car engine with the doors closed. If the Colonel hadn't heard it, you'd have died on the Sunday.' She plucked at the girl's hand again, her warm fat fingers seeking the very comfort she was trying to impart. 'You promised him you wouldn't do it again and now he wishes he'd reported it to somebody. Don't be angry with me, Jinx.' The tears rolled on relentlessly in rivers of grief, and Jinx wondered, basely, how genuine they were. Betty had always reserved her affections for her own two sons and never for the self-contained little girl who was the product of Adam's first wife. 'Someone had to tell you, and Dr Protheroe thought it should be me. Poor Daddy's been knocked sideways by it all. You've broken his heart. "Why did she do it, Elizabeth?" he keeps asking me.'

But Jinx had no answer to that. *For she knew Betty was lying. No one, least of all Leo, could drive her to kill herself.* Instead she dwelt on the incongruities of life. Why did she call her father Adam while his wife of twenty-seven years called him Daddy? For some reason it had never seemed significant before. She stared past her stepmother's head to her reflection in the dressing-table mirror and wondered suddenly why she felt so very little about so very much.

A young man came into her room uninvited, a tall gangling creature with shoulder-length ginger hair and spots. 'Hi,' he said, wandering aimlessly to the french windows and flicking the handle up and down, before abandoning it to throw himself into one of the armchairs in the bay. 'What are you on?'

'I don't know.'

'Heroin, crack, coke, MDMA? What?'

She stared at him blankly. 'Am I in a drug rehabilitation centre?'

He frowned at her. 'Don't you know?'

She shook her head.

'You're in the Nightingale Clinic where therapy costs four hundred quid a day and everyone leaves with their heads screwed on straight.'

Oh, but her anger was COLOSSAL. It wheeled around her brain like a huge bird of prey, waiting to strike. 'So who runs this place?' she asked calmly.

'Dr Protheroe.'

'Is he the man with the beard?'

'Yeah.' He stood up abruptly. 'Do you want to go for a walk? I need to keep moving or I go mad.'

'No thanks.'

'OK.' He paused by the door. 'I found a fox in a trap once.

He was so scared he was trying to bite his leg off to free himself. He had eyes like yours.'

'Did you rescue him?'

'He wouldn't let me. He was more afraid of me than he was of the trap.'

'What happened to him?'

'I watched him die.'

Some time afterwards, Dr Protheroe returned.

'Do you remember talking to me before?' he asked her, pulling up one of the armchairs and sitting in it.

'Once. You told me I was lucky.'

'In fact we've talked a few times. You've been conscious for several days but somewhat unwilling to communicate.' He smiled encouragement. 'Do you remember talking to me yesterday, for example?'

How many yesterdays were there when she had functioned without any awareness of what she was doing? 'No, I don't. I'm sorry. Are you a psychiatrist?'

'No.'

'What are you then?'

'I'm a doctor.'

The waxen image in the mirror smiled politely. *He was lying.* 'Am I allowed to smoke?' He nodded and she plucked a cigarette from one of the packets Betty had brought in, lighting it with clumsy inefficiency because it was hard to focus with one eye. 'May I ask you something?'

'Of course.'

'Wouldn't it have been courteous to tell me before I spoke to the policemen that the accident happened several days ago?' He had a rather charming face, she thought, a little weary, but lived in and comfortable. Like his sports jacket, which had seen better days, and the cavalry twill trousers that drooped at the hem where his heel had caught it. He was the sort of man whom, in other circumstances, she might have chosen for a friend because he seemed careless of convention. But she was afraid of him and sought refuge in pomposity.

He balanced his fountain pen between his forefingers. 'In the circumstances, I thought it better to let you speak the truth as you understood it.'

'What circumstances'

'You had almost twice the legal limit of alcohol in your blood when you crashed your car. The police are considering whether to charge you but I think they may let the matter drop after this morning. They tend to be somewhat sceptical of a doctor's diagnosis, less so of the patients themselves. I could see no harm in wringing a little sympathy out of PCs Gregg and Hardy.'

Her reflection smiled at him in the mirror. 'That was a kind thought.' *She had never been drunk in her life because she had watched Betty stagger about the house too often to want to emulate her.* 'Could you pass me the ashtray?' *'You got drunk and tried to kill yourself . . .'* 'Thank you.' She placed it on the bed in front of her. 'What exactly has happened to me, Dr Protheroe?'

He leaned forward, clamping his large hands between his knees. 'In a nutshell, you left a car travelling at approximately forty miles per hour, gave yourself the sort of knock-out blow that would have felled an ox, then continued under your own impetus, grazing your scalp, eye and arms as you did so. The first miracle is that you're here at all, the second miracle is that you didn't fracture anything in the process and the third miracle is that you'll be as good as new before you know it. Once your hair grows back over the flaps of skin that had to be stitched, no one will know you've had an accident. The price you paid for all that, however, was concussion, one symptom of which is post-traumatic amnesia. You have been conscious but deeply confused for the last five days, and that confusion may persist on and off for some time to come. Think of your brain as a computer. Any memory that is safely filed has a good chance of reinstatement, but memories that you were too confused to store properly may never return. So, for example, despite the fact you were conscious, you're unlikely to recollect your transfer here from Odstock Hospital, or indeed your first interview with the police.'

She looked past him towards the gardens that lay beyond her window. 'And is pre-traumatic amnesia equally normal?' she asked him. 'I have no memory of the accident or what led up to it.'

'Don't be confused by the term "post". That's simply referring to amnesia after trauma. But with regard to what you don't remember before the accident, that's usually referred to as retrograde amnesia. It's not uncommon and seems to depend on the severity of the head injury. We talk about loss of memory,' he went on, 'when we should talk about *temporary* loss. Bit by bit you'll remember events before the accident, though it may take a little while to understand how the pieces fit together because you may not remember them in chronological order. You may also, although it's less likely, remember things that never happened, simply because your memory will have stored plans of future events and you may recollect the plans as real. The trick is to avoid worrying about it. Your brain, like the rest of your body, has taken a knock and needs time to heal itself. That's all this amnesia is.'

'I understand. Does that mean I can go home quite soon?'

'To your parents?' he asked.

'No. To London.'

'Is there anyone there who can look after you?'

She was about to say Leo before she remembered that, according to her stepmother, he wasn't there any more. *Do me a favour, said the intrusive voice of cynicism,* Leo *look after you? Ha! Ha! Ha!* Instead, she said nothing and continued to stare out of the window. She resented the way this man called her Jinx, as if he and she were well acquainted, when her entire knowledge of him resided in an avuncular chat about a condition that was rocking her to her very foundations. And she resented his assumption that she was a willing participant in this conversation, when the only emotion she felt was a seething anger.

'Your father's keen for you to remain here where he feels you'll be properly looked after. However, it's entirely your choice and, if you think you'll be happier in London, then we can arrange to transfer you as long as you understand that you do need to be looked after. In the short term anyway.'

Her reflection examined him. 'Is Adam paying you?'

He nodded. 'This is a private clinic.'

'But not a hospital?'

'No. We specialize in addiction therapy,' he told her. 'But we do offer convalescent care as well.'

'I'm not addicted to anything.' '*You got drunk . . .*'

'No one's suggesting you are.'

She drew on her cigarette. 'Then why is my father paying four hundred pounds a day for me to be here?' she asked evenly. 'I could have convalescent care in a nursing home for a fraction of that.'

He studied her as she sat like a dignified, one-eyed Buddha upon her bed. 'How did you know it costs four hundred pounds a day?'

'My stepmother told me,' she lied. 'I know my father very well, Dr Protheroe, so, predictably, it was the first thing I asked her.'

'He did warn me you'd take nothing for granted.'

The reflection smiled at him. 'I certainly don't like being lied to,' she murmured. 'My stepmother told me I tried to commit suicide.' She watched him for a reaction, but there was none. 'I don't believe it,' she went on dispassionately, 'but I do believe that Adam would pay a psychiatrist to straighten me out if *he* believed it. So what sort of therapy is he buying for me?'

'No one's lying to you, Jinx. Your father was very concerned that you should be in an environment where you could recover at your own speed and in your own way. Certainly we have psychiatrists on the premises, and certainly we offer therapy to those who want it, but I am precisely what I said I was, a doctor pure and simple. My role is largely administrative, but I also take an interest in our convalescent patients. There is nothing sinister about your being here.'

Was that right? It didn't feel right. Even the woman in the mirror found that one hard to swallow. 'Did Adam tell you I am very hostile to psychiatrists and psychiatry?'

'Yes he did.'

'Why does he think I tried to kill myself?'

'Because that's the conclusion the police have reached after their investigation into your crash.'

'They're wrong,' she said tightly. 'I would never commit suicide.'

'OK,' Protheroe said easily. 'I'm not arguing with you.'

She closed her eye. 'Why would I suddenly want to kill myself when I've never wanted to before?' Anger roared in her ears.

He didn't say anything.

'Please,' she said harshly. 'I would like to know what's being said about me.'

'All right, if you accept that there's a good deal of physical evidence to support the police theory, then the rationale behind it seems to be that you were upset by your broken engagement. Your last real memory is saying goodbye to Leo when you left London two and a half weeks ago to stay with your parents at Hellingdon Hall. You probably don't remember doing it, but you've repeated that memory several times – to the police and to my colleagues at Odstock Hospital – and they have concluded, possibly wrongly, that it's important to you to preserve a happy memory over the memory of the night a week later when Leo told you he was leaving you for your friend, Meg Harris.'

She considered this in silence for a long time. 'Then they're saying my amnesia isn't entirely physical. There's an element of face-saving in it. Because I can't bear to think of Leo rejecting me, I've wiped his shabbiness out of my mind and then gone on to forget my own weakness in being unable to face life without him.'

Her choice of words was fascinating. 'In substance, that's what your father's been told.'

'All right' – he saw tears glistening on her lashes – 'if I was so distraught about Leo deserting me two weeks ago that I had to wipe the whole thing out of my memory, then why am I not equally distraught learning about it all over again?'

'I don't know. It's interesting, isn't it? How would *you* explain it?'

She looked away. 'I was having too many problems adjusting to the whole idea of marriage. The only thing I feel now is relief that I don't have to go through with it. I'd say I wasn't distraught the first time.'

He nodded. 'I'm prepared to accept that. So, let's talk about it. Was the wedding your idea or Leo's?'

'The wedding was my father's idea, but if you're asking me whose idea it was to get married, then that was Leo's. He sprang it on me out of the blue a couple of months ago, and I said yes because at the time I thought it was what I wanted.'

'But you changed your mind.'

'Yes.'

'Did you tell anyone?'

'I don't think so.' She felt his scepticism as strongly as if he'd reached out and touched her with it. *Oh God, what a bloody awful situation this was.* 'But I'm sure Leo must have known,' she said quickly. 'Does he say I was unhappy about him leaving?'

Dr Protheroe shook his head. 'I don't know.'

She looked at the telephone on her bedside table. 'I know Meg's home number. We could phone him and ask him.' *But did she want to do that? Would Leo ever admit that it was she who didn't want to marry him?*

'At the moment he's not available. The police have tried. He's out of the country for a few weeks.'

Not available. She already knew that. *How?* She licked her lips nervously. 'What about Meg?'

'She's with him. I'm told they've gone to France.' He watched her hands writhe in her lap and wondered what complicated emotions had driven the other two to betray her. 'You were telling me why you changed your mind,' he prompted her. 'What happened? Was it a sudden decision or something that developed gradually?'

She struggled to remember. 'I came to realize that the only reason he wanted to marry me was because I'm Adam Kingsley's daughter and Adam's not poor.' *But was that true? Wasn't it Russell who had wanted to marry her for her money?* She fell silent and thought about what she'd said. '"He that diggeth a pit shall fall into it," she murmured.

'Why do you say that?'

'Because you're going to ask me if Meg Harris's family is wealthy.'

He didn't say anything.

'They're not. Her father earns a pittance as a rural vicar.' She ground her cigarette into the ashtray and fixed a smile to her lips. 'So presumably Leo has discovered true love at last.'

'Are you angry with Meg? Your stepmother tells me you've known her a long time.'

'We were at Oxford together.' She looked up. 'And no, I'm not, as a matter of fact, but that's only because I'm finding it all rather difficult to believe at the moment. I only have Betty's word for it.'

'Don't you believe her?'

'Not often, but that's not an indication of an Electra complex. She's the only mother I've ever known and I'm very fond of her.'

He raised an amused eyebrow. 'What did you read at Oxford? Classics?'

She nodded. 'And a complete waste of time they were, too, for someone who was only ever interested in photography. I can do crosswords and decipher the roots of words, but apart from that my education was wasted.'

'What is that?' He gave his beard a thoughtful scratch. 'A defence mechanism against anyone who thinks you're over-privileged?'

'Just habit,' she said dismissively. 'My father finds my qualifications rather more impressive than anyone else does.'

'I see.'

She doubted that very much. Adam's pride in his only daughter bordered on the obsessional, which was why there was so little love lost between any of the inhabitants of Hellingdon Hall. How much did this doctor know? she wondered. Had he met Adam? Did he understand the tyranny under which they lived?

'Look,' she said abruptly, 'why don't I make this easy for you? I mean, I know this routine off by heart. How old were you when your mother died? Two. How old were you when Adam remarried? Seven. Did your stepmother resent you?

29

I've no idea, I was too young to notice. Did you resent her? I've no idea, I was too young to know what resentment was. Have you any brothers or sisters? Two half-brothers, Miles and Fergus. Do you resent them? No. Do *they* resent *you*? No. How old are they? Twenty-six and twenty-four. Are they married? No, they still live at home. Do you love your father? Yes. Does he love you? Yes.'

Protheroe's laugh, a great booming sound that would bring reluctant smiles whenever she heard it, bounced around the room. 'My God,' he said, 'what do you do for an encore? Bite psychiatrists' heads off? I came to find out if you were comfortable, Jinx. As far as possible, I would like your stay here to be a happy one.'

She lit another cigarette. *He knew nothing.* 'I'm sure it will be. Adam wouldn't pay four hundred pounds a day unless he'd checked you out very thoroughly.'

'You're the one who'll be calling the shots, not your father.'

She flicked him a sideways glance. 'I wouldn't count on that if I were you,' she said quietly. 'Adam hasn't made his millions by sitting idly by while other people express themselves. He's a very manipulative man.'

Protheroe shrugged. 'He certainly seems to have your best interests at heart.'

She blew a smoke ring into the air. 'Show me his heart, Dr Protheroe, and I might believe you.'

Chapter Four

Wednesday, 22 June, 53 Lansing Road,
Salisbury – 8.05 p.m.

THE YOUNG MAN was in no hurry to get up. He lay on the bed, his limbs sprawled in satiated contentment upon the rumpled bedclothes, watching the woman button her blouse in front of the mirror. Her reflected eyes stared warily back at him. Despite his airs and graces, and his liberal use of 'please' and 'thank you', she knew exactly what she was dealing with here, and it terrified her. She'd seen every type there was to see – or thought she had – but this one was in a class of his own. This one was mad.

'You'll have to go now,' she said, trying to hide her nervousness. 'I've another customer due in a minute.'

'So? Tell him to go away. I'll pay you double.'

'I can't do that, love. He's a regular.'

'You're lying,' he said lazily.

'No, love, honestly.' She forced a smile to her sore lips. 'Look, I've really enjoyed this. It's years since I've come with a client. You wouldn't believe that, would you? A pro like me and it takes a man like you to give her something to remember.' She offered her raddled face to the mirror and applied eyeliner to her lids, watching him carefully while she did it. 'But it's a tough old world and I need my income just like any other girl. If I tell him to bugger off, he won't come again' – she gave a wretched giggle – 'in every sense of the word. Know what I mean? So do us a favour, love, and leave me to my regular. He's not a patch on you, and that's God's honest truth, but he pays me weekly and he pays me handsome. OK?'

'Did I really make you come?'

'Sure you did, love.'

'You fat slag,' he said, surging off the bed with terrifying speed and hooking his arm about her neck. 'It'd take a bloody bulldozer to make an impression on you.' He levered his arm closed. 'I hate slags who lie to me. Tell me you're a lying whore.'

But she'd been on the game long enough to learn that you never told psychopaths the truth. She reached for his penis instead and set about rearousing him, knowing that if she came out of this alive, she'd be lucky. So far, his only real pleasure had been to beat her about the face while he reached his climax, and she knew he was going to do it again.

As he twisted his hand in her hair and yanked her backwards on to the bed, she had time to reflect on the awful irony of it all. She was so used to servicing old and inadequate men that when the voice on the phone had translated itself into an Adonis at her door, she couldn't believe her luck. God, but she was a stupid bitch!

Nightingale Clinic, Salisbury – 8.20 p.m.

The phone rang beside Jinx's bed, setting her nerves jangling with its insistent summons to a world outside that she wasn't sure she was ready to face. She was tempted to leave it until it occurred to her that it might be an internal call. *If she didn't answer it*, said the voice of paranoia inside her head, *then a little black mark would go down in a book somewhere and her mental equilibrium would be called into question*. She lifted the receiver and held it against her ear on the pillow. 'Jinx Kingsley,' she said guardedly.

'Thank God,' said a man's voice. 'I've had the devil's own job trying to find you. It's Josh Hennessey. I finally got through to your stepmother, who gave me this number. She says you're OK to talk but that you've lost bits of your memory.'

'Josh Hennessey?' she echoed in surprise. 'As in Harris and Hennessey? You sound so close. Where are you?'

He gave a rumble of laughter at the other end. 'The very same, except that it's all Hennessey at the moment and remarkably little Harris. She's buggered off to France and left me nursing the office. I'm in a call-box in Piccadilly.' He paused briefly and she heard the sound of traffic in the background. 'I'm damn glad the memory loss doesn't extend to your mates. There's a few of us eating our hearts out over this.' He paused again. 'We were really sorry to hear about your accident, Jinx, but your stepma says you're progressing well.'

She smiled weakly. Typical Josh, she thought. Always we and never I. 'I'm not sure I'd agree with her. I feel like something the dog threw up. I suppose you know about Leo and Meg?'

He didn't say anything.

'It's all right, you don't have to spare my feelings. Matter of fact, I'm quite glad Leo found a good home.' *Was she telling the truth?* 'They're welcome to each other.'

33

'Well, if it's of any consolation to you, I can't see it lasting. You know Meg and her brief enthusiasms. She'll have some French guy in tow by the time she comes back, and poor old Leo will be on the scrap heap along with all the others. She's a two-timing bitch, Jinx. I've always said so.'

Liar, she thought. You adore her. 'She hasn't changed just because Leo prefers her to me,' she said. 'I don't bear any grudges, so why should you?'

He cleared his throat. 'How are you coping after the – well, you know?'

'You mean my suicide attempt? I don't remember it, so I'm fine.'

There was a short silence.

'Good, well, listen, the reason I phoned is that I've been trying to get hold of Meg for the last eight days and I'm getting zilch response from her answerphone. She swore on her sainted granny's grave that she'd call in for her messages every day but, if she's doing it, then she sure as hell isn't replying to any of them, and I'm going slowly ape-shit with all the work that's piling up. I've tried her brother and a few of her other friends to see if they know where she and Leo went, but they're as much in the dark as I am. You're my last hope, Jinx. Have you any ideas at all how I can contact her? Believe me, I wouldn't ask if I wasn't desperate. I've got a sodding contract here that needs her signature and I've got to fax it through post-haste.' He gave an angry grunt. 'I tell you, the way I feel at the moment, I could wring her neck. And Leo's, too.'

Jinx jabbed her fingers against the vein above her eye that was pounding and rushing like a swollen river. A strangely murky image had floated into her mind as he

34

spoke, a meaningless, dark negative that relayed nothing to her at all except an intense frustration. She sought to hold on to it but, like a drowning man, it slipped away and left her cheated. 'Well, if it's France,' she said slowly, 'then they've probably gone to Leo's house in Brittany, but I'm afraid I can't remember the phone number, Josh, and I doubt he's got a fax either.'

'That doesn't matter. Do you know the address?'

She dug deep into her memory. 'I think so. It's Les Hirondelles, rue St Jacques, Trinité-sur-mer.'

'You're a brick, Jinx. Remind me to take you out to dinner one day.'

She gave a shaky laugh. 'It's a date,' she told him. 'Assuming I can remember to remind you.' She paused. 'Did you really want Meg's address?'

He avoided an answer. 'I could come and see you at the weekend,' he suggested. 'Or are you hibernating?'

'Sort of,' she said, unsure if she wanted to see anyone. 'I'm vegetating.'

'Is that a yes or a no?'

The vein above her eye throbbed mercilessly. 'It's a yes. I'd love to see you,' she lied.

For fifteen minutes paranoia held Jinx's hand. Ten times she had reached it out towards the telephone on the bedside table and ten times she had withdrawn it again. Her nerve had abandoned her along with her memory. She was afraid of eavesdroppers listening in. And what could she say that wouldn't sound foolish? At eight-thirty, as credits rolled on the television in the corner, she muted the sound, seized the telephone with sudden decision and dialled a number.

'Hello?' said a brisk voice that belied its eighty-three years.

'Colonel Clancey?'

'Yes.'

'It's Jinx Kingsley. I wondered – are you busy or can I talk to you for a moment?'

'My dear girl, of course you can talk. How are you?'

'Fine. You?'

'Worried,' he barked. 'Damned worried, if I'm honest. I feel responsible, Jinx. Daphne, too. We should have done more. Hold on a minute while I close the door. Bloody television's going full blast. Usual old rubbish, of course, but Daphne likes it.' She heard the receiver clatter on to their hall table, followed by the slam of a door and the distant yapping of Goebbels, their mild-mannered Yorkshire terrier. 'You still there?' he said a moment or two later.

She felt tears of affection pricking at the back of her eyelids. He made himself out to be so much more ferocious than his funny little dog and, in her mind, he was always Colonel Goebbels and the dog was Clancey. 'Yes. It's nice to hear you.' She paused a moment, unsure what to say. 'How's Goebbels?' She wondered why they'd called their dog that. *Was it something she knew and had forgotten, or was it something she had simply accepted as she had accepted all their other eccentricities?*

'Flea-ridden as usual. Daphne gave him a bath and he's looking like a mohair sweater. Absurd creature.'

She wondered if he was referring to the dog or to his wife. 'I'm worried about my plants,' she said, seeking neutral territory and remembering the Clanceys had her spare key.

'Would it be an awful bore for you or Mrs C to water them for me?'

'We go in every day, Jinx. Assumed it's what you'd want. Plants are fine, bit of cleaning up done. It's all ready for you as soon as you're well enough to come home.'

'That's very kind. Thank you.'

'Least we could do in the circumstances.'

There was an awkward pause while she sought for something more to say. 'Let me give you my phone number. I'm at the Nightingale Clinic in Salisbury.' She squinted at the dial. 'I don't know the code but the number's two-two-one-four-two-zero. Just in case anything unexpected crops up.'

'Got it,' he told her. 'And you say you're fine. Glad to hear it. Looking after you all right then, are they?'

'Yes.'

'Well, you sound cheerful enough.'

Another awkward pause. They spoke together.

'Best be going then —'

'Colonel —'

'Yes?'

'Please don't go, not yet.' She rushed her words. 'My stepmother said you rescued me from my garage. Is that true? She said I had the car engine running and you found me before I could – well – finish myself off.'

His voice grew gruff with emotion. 'Don't you remember?'

'No.' She swallowed painfully. 'I'm really sorry, but I don't. I don't remember anything – at least – not since I left to stay with my parents two weeks ago. Is Leo really not there any more? I don't know who else to ask – and I'm so, so sorry if it's embarrassing but I do need to be sure. They keep telling me . . . things . . . that don't make sense. They say I've got amnesia – that I got drunk and tried to kill myself. But – I just – oh, God . . .' She clamped her hand over her mouth because tears were flooding her throat. *Hang up, you stupid woman.*

'There, there,' said his comforting elderly voice, 'no need for embarrassment. Good lord, I've had six-foot-tall men weep on my shoulder before now. Clear answers, eh, that's what you want. Your stepmother's a nice enough woman, I expect, but, if she's anything like Daphne, she'll have managed to confuse the message somehow. Not that I know all that much,' he warned. 'Never been one to poke my nose in where it's not wanted, as you know.'

'Quite. Best sort of neighbour always.' Odd, she thought, how she picked up his shorthand when she spoke to him. Perhaps everyone did.

'Leo's been gone over a week, Jinx. Left the night you came home from Hampshire. Hope it's not an imperti-nence, but I'd say you're well shot of him. Never did like the cut of his jib much. You were far too good for him. Funny thing is, I spoke to you on the Saturday and you didn't turn a hair. "The bastard's jilted me, Colonel," you said, "and the only bugger is he beat me to it."' He chortled at the memory. 'And then, on the Sunday, there you were in your garage with the engine running. Fact is, it was Goebbels who spotted something was up. Parked himself in front of your garage door and barked his little head off.' He paused for a moment and she could picture him, fluffing his moustache and squaring his shoulders. 'Upshot was, pulled you out

PDQ and got some fresh air into you. Should have done more, though. Called a doctor, got a friend round. Rather upset about that, to tell you the truth.'

'I wish you wouldn't be. Did I say anything? I mean, explain or something?' Her fingers tightened involuntarily around the handset. 'I just don't believe – well, you know. Not over Leo . . .'

'Matter of fact, I agree with you. Personally, thought it was an accident, garage doors slammed after you started the engine, that sort of thing. Not as though you had a hose pipe attached to the exhaust, is it? Truth is, you weren't feeling too clever afterwards, not surprising in the circumstances. But you can't have been in there very long. Back to normal in no time, cracking jokes and telling Daphne not to fuss. Even made a phone call to some friends you were off to see. The old girl was all for a doctor but you wouldn't have it. "I'm perfectly all right, Mrs C," you said, "and if I don't get going I'll be late." Worst thing was, thought you were going to squash poor Goebbels, the way you hugged and petted him.' He gave a gravelly laugh. 'Hah! You said dogs were the only things worth having in your bed from then on.'

She dabbed at her cheeks. 'Then why does Betty think I was trying to kill myself?' Her voice was remarkably steady.

'On the principle that one swallow doesn't make a summer but two probably do, dear girl. Dare say it's our fault. Bobbies turned up a week ago, telling us you'd driven your car at a wall in what looked like a deliberate attempt at suicide, and did we know of any other attempts? So Daphne piped up about the garage and how you promised you'd be more careful in future, then told them what a rat

Leo had been and, hey presto, conclusions being drawn all over the place. Silly old woman,' he said fondly. 'Practically ga-ga, though, let's face it, and awfully worried about you. Matter of fact, I did try to stem the breach by pointing out you weren't the type, but I might have been banging my head against the proverbial wall for all the good it did.' He cleared his throat. 'Must say, Jinx, talking to you now, more inclined than ever to think it's all nonsense. Never struck me as the type to throw in the towel.'

She couldn't speak for a moment. 'Thank you,' she managed. 'I don't think I am either. Will you give Mrs C and Goebbels a hug from me?'

'Certainly will. Coming home soon, I trust?'

'I'd like to but I'm bandaged to the hilt at the moment. You should see me, Colonel. I look like Boris Karloff in *The Mummy*.'

'Hah!' he harrumphed again. 'Kept your sense of humour, I see. Visitors keeping you chirpy, dare say.'

'No,' she said honestly. 'It's talking to you that's cheered me up. Thank you for getting me out of my car. I'll ring you the minute I'm demobbed and give you my ETA.'

'We'll be waiting for you, dear girl. Meanwhile chin up and best foot forward, eh?'

'Will do. Goodbye, Colonel.'

Jinx cut the line but held the receiver to her chest for several minutes as if, by doing so, she could maintain the link with him, for the comfort that the conversation had given her was all too ephemeral. Depression swept in behind it like an engulfing tide when it occurred to her that, of all the people she knew, the only one she had felt able to telephone was a man whose first name she was too shy to use. *Had she felt as lonely as this a week ago? Could she have done it? God help her if she had . . .*

'Your brother's come to see you, Miss Kingsley,' said a black nurse, pushing wide the half-open door. 'I've told him ten minutes. Visitors out by nine o'clock, that's the rule, but as it's your brother and he's come all the way from Fordingbridge, well – just so long as you don't make too much noise.' She noticed Jinx's pallor suddenly and clicked her tongue anxiously. 'Are you all right, my lovely? You look as if you've seen a ghost.'

'I'm fine.'

'OK,' she said cheerfully. 'Not too much noise, then, or my job will be on the line.'

Miles, exuding his usual boyish charm, took the nurse's hand in his and smiled into her face. 'I really appreciate this, Amy. Thank you.'

Her dark skin blushed. 'That's all right. I'd best be getting back to the desk.' She withdrew her fingers from his with clear reluctance and closed the door behind her.

'God,' he said, flopping into the armchair, 'she really thought I fancied her.' He eyed Jinx. 'Ma tells me you're back in the land of the living, so I thought I'd come and check for myself. You look bloody awful, but I expect you know that.'

She reached for her cigarettes. 'I'd hate to disappoint you, Miles.'

'She says you can't remember anything since the fourth. Is that true?'

She didn't answer.

'Which means it is.' He giggled suddenly. 'So you don't remember the week you spent at the Hall?'

She eyed him coldly as she felt for her lighter.

'You borrowed two hundred quid off me that week, Jinxy, and I want it back.'

'Bog off, Miles.'

He grinned. 'You sound pretty on the ball to me. So what's with this amnesia crap? You trying to get yourself off the hook with Dad?'

'What hook?'

'Whatever it is you've done that you shouldn't have done.'

'I don't know what you're talking about.'

He shrugged indifferently. 'Then why did you try to top yourself? Dad's been worse than usual this last week. You might have thought of that before you started playing silly buggers.'

She ignored him and lit a cigarette.

'Are you going to talk to me or have I wasted my time coming here?'

'I doubt you've wasted your time,' she said evenly, 'as I imagine seeing me was the last thing on your list.' She was watching his face, saw the flash of intense amusement in his eyes, and knew she was right. 'You must be mad,' she continued. 'Adam wasn't bluffing when he said you'd be out on your ear the next time. Why on earth do you do it?'

'You think you know everything, don't you?'

'When it comes to you, Miles, I do.'

He grinned. 'OK then, it gives me a buzz. Come on, Jinxy, a couple of hands of poker in a hotel bedroom, it's hardly major gambling. And who's going to tell Dad anyway? You certainly won't and neither will I.' He giggled again. 'I scored' – he tapped his jacket pocket – 'so no lectures, all right? I'm not planning to run up any more debts. The old bastard's made it clear enough he won't bail me out again.'

He was more hyped up than usual, she thought, and wondered how much he'd won. She changed the subject. 'How's Fergus?'

'About as pissed off as I am. A couple of days ago, Dad reduced him to tears. You know what my guess is? The worm'll turn when Dad least expects it and then it'll be your precious Adam who gets the thrashing.' He was fidgeting with the lapels of his jacket, brushing them, smoothing them. 'Why did you do it? He hates you now, hates us, hates everyone. Poor old Ma most of all.'

Jinx lay back and stared at the ceiling. 'You know as well as I do what the solution is,' she said.

'Oh, God, not more bloody lectures. Anyone would think you were forty-four not thirty-four.' He raised his voice to a falsetto, mimicking her. 'You're old enough to stand on your own two feet, Miles. You can't expect your mother to give you Porsches all your life. It's time to move out, find your own place, start a family.'

'I don't understand why you don't want to.'

'Because Dad refuses to ante-up, that's why. You know the score. If we want to live in reasonable comfort we stay at home where he can keep his eye on us. If we want out, we do it the hard way and graft for ourselves.'

'Then welcome to the human race,' she said scathingly. 'What the hell do you think the rest of us do?'

His voice rose again, but this time in anger. 'You damn well never had to graft. You stepped straight into Russell's money without lifting a finger. Jesus, you're so bloody patronizing. "Welcome to the human race, Miles." You piss me off, Jinx, you really do.'

She was dog-tired. Why didn't the nurse come back to rescue her? She stubbed out her cigarette and turned to look at him. 'Surely anything has to be better than letting Adam treat you like dirt. When did he last beat you?' There was something wrong with him, she thought. He was like an addict waiting for a fix, twitched, unable to sit still, fidgeting, fingering, eyes overbright. *Oh, God, not drugs . . . not drugs . . .* But as she fell asleep, she was thinking that, yes, of course it was drugs, because self-indulgence was the one thing Miles was good at. If nothing else, his father had taught him that.

Odstock Hospital, Salisbury – 9.00 p.m.

The Casualty doctor was barely out of medical school and nothing in his training had prepared him for this. He smiled tentatively at the woman in the cubicle. It was worse than the Elephant Man, he was thinking, as he took his place beside the nurse whose hand the wretched woman was clutching. Her face was so swollen that she looked barely recognizable as a human being. She had given her name as Mrs Hale. 'You've been in the wars,' he said vacuously.

'My husband – belt . . .' she croaked through lips that could hardly move.

He looked at the bruising on her throat where the marks of someone's fingers were clearly visible. 'Is it just your face that's been hurt?'

She shook her head and, with a pathetic gesture of apology, raised her skirt and revealed knickers saturated with blood. 'He' – tears squeezed between her swollen lids – 'cut me.'

Three hours later, a sympathetic policewoman tried to persuade her to make a statement before she was transferred to the operating theatre for surgery to her rectum. 'Look, Mrs Hale, we know your husband didn't do this. We've checked and he's currently serving eighteen months in Winchester for handling stolen property. We also know you're on the game, so the chances are that the animal responsible was one of your customers. Now, we're not interested in how you make your money. We're only interested in stopping this bastard doing the same thing to some other poor girl. Will you help us?'

She shook her head.

'But he could kill next time. Do you want that on your conscience? All we need is a description.'

A faint laugh croaked in her throat. 'Do me a favour, love.'

'You've got two fractured cheekbones, severe bruising of the throat and larynx, a dislocated wrist, and internal bleeding from having a hairbrush rammed up your back passage,' said the policewoman brutally. 'You're lucky to be alive. The next woman he attacks may not be so lucky.'

'Too right. It'll be yours bloody truly if I open my mouth. He swore he'd come back.' She closed her eyes. 'The hospital shouldn't have called you. I never gave them leave, and I'm not pressing no charges.'

'Will you think about it at least?'

'No point. You'll never pin it on him and I'm not running scared for the rest of my life.'

'Why won't we pin it on him?'

She gave another croak of laughter. 'Because it'll be my word against his, love, and I'm a fat old slag and he's little Lord Fauntleroy.'

Thursday, 23 June, Nightingale Clinic,
Salisbury – 3.30 a.m.

As he did every night at about this time, the security guard emerged from the front door of the Nightingale Clinic and strolled towards a bench on the moonlit lawn. It was a little treat he gave himself halfway through his shift, a quiet smoke away from the nagging lectures of the nursing staff. He wiped the seat with a large handkerchief then lowered himself with a sigh of contentment. As he fished his cigarettes from his jacket pocket he had the distinct impression that someone was behind him. Startled, he glanced round, then lumbered awkwardly to his feet and went to investigate the trees bordering the driveway. There was no one there, but he couldn't rid himself of a sense that he was being watched.

He was a phlegmatic man, and put the experience down to the cheese he'd eaten at supper. As his wife always said: Too much cheese isn't good for anyone. But he didn't linger over his smoke that night.

Jane Kingsley was floating in dark water, eyes open, straining for the sunlight that dappled the surface above her. She wanted to swim, but the desire was all in her mind and she was too weary to make it happen. A terrible hand was upon her, pulling her down to the weeds below – insistent, persuasive, compelling – she opened her mouth to let death in . . .

She burst out of sleep in a threshing frenzy, sweat pouring down her back. *She was drowning . . . Oh, Jesus, sweet Jesus, somebody help her!* The moon beamed through a gap in her curtains, lighting a path through the room. *Where was she? She didn't know this place.* She stared in terror from one dark shadow to the other until she saw the lilies beside her, gleaming white and pure against the black of the carnations. Memory returned. *Jane was her mother . . . she was Jinx . . . Jane was her mother . . . she was Jinx . . .*

With shaking fingers, she switched on her bedside light and looked on things she recognized. The door to the bathroom, television in the corner, mirror against the wall, armchair, flowers – but it was a long time before the thudding of her heart slowed. She slid slowly down between the sheets again, as rigid and as wide-eyed as a painted wooden doll, and tried to stem the fear that grew inside her. But it was a vain attempt because she couldn't put a name to what she was afraid of.

Two miles away, in another hospital bed, her terror had its haunting echo in the battered face of a prostitute who had supped with the devil.

A case of 'caveat investor'?

If anyone needed a reminder that investments can go down as well as up, they received it yesterday when Franchise Holdings (FH), the property development group, suffered a temporary drop in the value of its shares, following a rumour that Adam Kingsley, 66, founder and chairman, was about to resign. FH has been a rare success story amidst the spectacular property group failures of the nineties.

The rumour was apparently generated by a remark made by Kingsley in a BBC interview on Tuesday night. Referring to his daughter Jane's recent car accident, he said: 'There are always times in one's life when one asks, has it all been worth it?' But Kingsley, nicknamed the Great White when he snapped up Charford Gordon Associates eight years ago, has now sunk his jaws into the BBC.

It is his policy to make private tape-recordings of interviews, and he has issued a typescript of the one on Tuesday. This includes a follow-up sentence which was edited out of the broadcast. 'This is not one of those times,' he went on to say. The matter is under investigation by the Broadcasting Complaints Commission.

However, the extraordinary episode has highlighted City fears about the long-term future of Franchise Holdings. As one analyst said: 'Adam Kingsley is a master juggler. No one knows how many balls there are in the air at any one time. Frankly, it's difficult to imagine who will catch them safely when he finally leaves the stage.'

Daily Telegraph – 23 June

Chapter Five

'LITTLE LORD FAUNTLEROY,' echoed a sceptical sergeant the next morning. 'You think that's relevant, do you?'

'Yes,' said WPC Blake stoutly. 'I reckon he's a lot younger than she is and probably quite well spoken, otherwise why would she have chosen that analogy? She obviously thinks he'd make a far better impression in court than she would.'

'It's not much to go on.'

'I know. So I thought – if I went through the files, I might find someone else. The chances are high he's done it before. If I could get two of them to support each other' – she shrugged – 'they might find the confidence to talk to us and give us a description. You should see her, Guv.'

He nodded. He'd read the report. 'You'll be doing it in your own time, Blake,' he warned, 'because there's no way I'm going to explain to them upstairs why you're shirking your other responsibilities to chase a prosecution that doesn't exist.' He winked at her. 'Still, have a go and see how you get on. I've been nicking Flossie's old man for years. She never bears grudges. She's a good old soul.'

Nightingale Clinic, Salisbury – 10.30 a.m.

Jinx had been abandoned in an armchair by the window. 'Time you were up and about, dear,' coaxed a terrifying nurse with the hair of Margaret Thatcher and the nose of Joseph Stalin. 'You need to get some of those muscles working again.'

Jinx smiled falsely and promised to have a little walk later, then lapsed into quiet contemplation of the garden when the bossy woman had gone. Her ginger-haired visitor of yesterday – he of the fox obsession – made signs to her from a bench on the lawn, but she moved her head to stare in a different direction and he abandoned his half-hearted attempts at communication. She could see a wing of the building, projecting out at the far end of the terrace, and she guessed she was in a Georgian mansion, built for some wealthy family of two centuries earlier. What had become of them? she wondered. Had they, like the family who had built and inhabited Hellingdon Hall, simply faded away?

'Hello, Jinx,' said a quiet voice from the open doorway into the corridor. 'Can you stand a visitor, or should I make polite excuses and leave?'

Her shock was so extreme that her heart surged into frantic activity.

Fear . . . fear . . . FEAR! But what was there to be afraid of?

She recognized the voice and turned away from the window. 'Oh, God, Simon,' she said angrily, 'you gave me such a fright. Why on earth would I want you to leave?' She held a hand to her chest. 'I can't breathe. I think I'm having a panic attack. Don't you ever dare do that to me again.'

'I'd better call someone.'

'No!' She waved him inside and took deep breaths. 'I'm OK.' She leaned back, drawing the air into her lungs. 'I don't know why, but I'm really on edge at the moment. I keep thinking – no, forget it – it doesn't matter. How are you?'

Simon Harris stood half-in and half-out of the doorway, looking irresolutely down the corridor. 'Let me call someone, Jinx. I really think I should. You don't look at all well.' He had the fine-boned, rather ascetic face of the clergyman he was, and he was as different from his sister as chalk was from cheese. Meg would have told her: 'Sod it, sweetheart, be it on your own head. Don't blame me if you die.' Simon could only peer through his glasses with well-meant but impotent concern.

'Sit down, Simon,' she said wearily. *She wanted to scream.* 'I'm OK. Why wouldn't I want to see you?'

Reluctantly, he abandoned the doorway and made his way to the other chair. 'Because it struck me as I was walking along the corridor that I had deliberately shut my eyes to the potential embarrassment my visit might cause.'

Why do you always have to be so pompous, Simon? 'To you or to me?'

'To you,' he said. 'I'm more angry than embarrassed. I still can't believe my sister would steal her best friend's fiancé.'

'Well, I'm neither embarrassed nor angry, just very lethargic and rather sore.' She eyed his dog-collar and cassock with disfavour. 'Mind you,' she grumbled, 'I don't go a bundle on the uniform. Couldn't you have worn jeans and a T-shirt like everyone else? They all think I'm suicidal as it is, so having a vicar visit me will destroy any credibility I've managed to salvage.'

He smiled, reassured by her feeble attempts at humour. 'No choice, I'm afraid. I'm doing an official stint in the Cathedral in approximately two hours so, if I wanted to visit you as well, I wasn't going to have time to change.'

'How did you know I was here?'

'Josh Hennessey told me,' he said, squeezing his knees with bony fingers. 'I managed to get through to Betty once during the week but she hung up as soon as I said who it was. The name Harris is *nomen non gratis* at Hellingdon Hall at the moment,' he finished ruefully, 'and I can't say I'm altogether surprised.'

'Then how did Josh persuade her? She knows quite well he's Meg's partner not mine.'

Simon pulled a face. 'He got the same treatment I did until he realized deception was the better part of valour. He lied, said he was Dean Jarrett and needed to talk to you urgently on business.'

Dean was Jinx's number two at the photographic studio and he played his homosexuality for all it was worth because it amused him. Jinx massaged her aching head. 'She must have been drunk as a skunk to fall for that. Josh doesn't sound anything like Dean.'

'*In vino* absolutely, but don't be too harsh on her. Josh says she sounded genuinely upset for you.'

Sudden irritation seethed in Jinx's soul. *Why shouldn't she be harsh on the silly woman? By what right did anyone suggest that she temper her scorn?* 'You will never speak about your stepmother like that again,' her father had said, when, at the age of ten, she had pointed out with genuine anxiety that Betty was so stupid she thought the moon orbited the sun and that Vietnam shared a border with America, which was why they were fighting a war there. 'She does nothing but paint her fingernails and go shopping,' she had told him severely.

But all she said now was: 'She was very sweet to me yesterday,' before plucking a cigarette from the packet on the arm of her chair and lighting it. 'So has Josh managed to track down Meg? I gather he's pretty annoyed with her for leaving him in the lurch.'

Simon shook his head. 'Not as far as I know, but I haven't spoken to him since last night.'

She studied his face through the smoke from her cigarette and saw he'd been lying when he said he wasn't embarrassed. He looked deeply uncomfortable – *almost as drained and wretched as she felt herself* – with his thin fingers smoothing and pleating the black serge of his cassock and his eyes looking anywhere but at her. Her irritation mounted. 'I couldn't give a toss about Leo,' she said harshly. 'If you want the truth, he was beginning to get on my nerves.' A tear glittered along her lashes. 'The only thing that's upsetting me is the embarrassment of everyone thinking I tried to kill myself over him.' She gave a hollow laugh. 'I don't envy Meg at all. Believe me, Leo will be absolutely insufferable if he thinks I couldn't bear to lose him.' *Oh, stupid, stupid woman! No one will believe the grapes weren't sour.*

Simon sighed. 'Dad and Mum don't know which way to turn. They felt badly enough before your accident, but afterwards – well . . .' He lapsed into silence. 'I don't know what to say to you, Jinx, except that I've never felt angrier with Meg than I do at the moment. God knows, she's no angel, but none of us thought she'd do something like this.'

'Like what?' She took quick nervous drags on her cigarette. 'All I've been told is that Leo said he wanted to marry her and that they then left for France. But does Meg want to marry *him*? If so, it'll be a first. She's never wanted to marry anyone else.'

'You really don't remember anything about it?'

'No,' she said grimly. 'I've made a prize arse of myself by telling everyone I'd be prancing up the aisle on July the second.' Tears threatened again. 'Look, it's not important. Tell me what's been happening in the world in the last week. Is everyone still killing each other in Bosnia? Is the Queen still on the throne?'

He ignored this and addressed himself to what she really wanted to know. 'Meg phoned Mum and Dad a week ago last Saturday and sprang on them that she and your fiancé had been having an affair for some time, that he wanted to marry her instead and that they were off to France until the fuss died down because they thought it would be more tactful.' He pulled a rueful face over the word 'tactful'. 'Rather predictably, she and Dad had a flaming row about it. He accused *her* of being shameless, and she accused *him* of being holier than thou as per usual. Result, they hung up on each other. Mum threw an almighty wobbly, screamed at poor old Dad that it was his fault because he would insist on preaching at her, then phoned me. My view was that if Leo was prepared to jilt *you* so unceremoniously, then he was probably a scoundrel and would abandon Meg just as unceremoniously, and Mum got on the blower to her and said she wasn't to go anywhere until they'd met him. Meg told her she was worrying unnecessarily and that she'd bring Leo down the minute they got back from France. And that's all we knew until we read about your attempted suicide.'

She flinched at the word 'suicide' but let it go. 'He wasn't a scoundrel, Simon. You're not old enough to use words like "scoundrel". He was a fucking scumbag.'

'I'm a vicar, Jinx.'

'So? I'm a millionaire's daughter who went to public school.' She rubbed her hands over her shaven scalp. 'Look, I don't care. They can shag each other to death as far as I'm concerned.' Tears flooded her throat. 'It's no big deal. I'd hate to lose Meg because of it. She's my friend, Simon.'

He felt ashamed in the face of such generosity, and as usual rushed to condemn his sister. Would Meg, he wondered, in the same circumstances, be as unjudgemental of the woman who had stolen her fiancé? 'Does it help if I say I don't believe you tried to kill yourself? Is that what's worrying you? What people are thinking?'

Jinx fished the newspaper clipping that Betty had given her from her pocket and stared at it. 'Except that it doesn't look like an accident, does it?' she said slowly, offering him the picture. 'They say it's a miracle I escaped.'

'Miracles do happen, you know.'

Not in her philosophy they didn't. 'Apparently I was drunk when it happened.'

'Does that matter?'

'Yes,' she said flatly, 'it does. To me, anyway.'

'Because of Betty's problems?'

'Partly.' She paused. 'No, it's more to do with my own

self-esteem. I refuse to believe that I'd need to get drunk in order to kill myself.' She smiled faintly. 'You see, I'm a very proud woman, which makes me doubt I'd have given anyone, least of all Leo, the satisfaction of knowing I cared *that* much.'

'I believe you,' he said.

Tears flooded her eyes again, and she jabbed at them with the palm of her hand. 'Look, don't take any notice, OK? I'm tired, I'm pissed off and I wish to hell I was back in London.' She took deep breaths to bring her sorrow under control. 'Will you do me a favour? Tell Meg I'm happy for her, and that I don't bear any grudges. And tell your parents that I'm not about to end a damn good friendship because a bastard like Leo swaps horses mid-stream. Truly, Simon, I don't care.'

He nodded. 'I'll tell them,' he promised. 'You're very generous, Jinx.'

She listened to the screams of frustration that echoed off the walls of her mind. 'I wouldn't say it if it wasn't true,' she said carefully, glancing sideways at him. 'There's no generosity involved.'

He leaned forward, staring at the floor. 'You think you know a person and then something like this happens. She wasn't even remotely apologetic, just said these are the facts, stick them in your pipe and smoke them. It's caused the most unbelievable bitterness between the folks. Mum's blaming Dad for trying to force religion down Meg's throat for years, and he's blaming her for her frigidity.' He sighed. 'He's more upset than Mum is but I think that's because he's always been so fond of you. He can't understand why Meg would want to hurt you. I can't either for that matter.'

'I'm sorry,' she said inadequately, 'but I don't expect she meant to hurt anybody. You know Meg. *Carpe diem* and leave tomorrow to look after itself. She's always been the same.' She rubbed the side of her head where it was hurting. *Why did memories of Russell keep flooding her mind?* 'Your father must be very angry if he's saying things like that to your mother.' *Russell and Meg . . . Meg and Leo . . .*

'They're just words,' he said, 'he doesn't mean anything by them, any more than poor old Mum means anything by striking out at religion.'

But in a way they're both right, you know.' She felt very tired suddenly. 'Meg's never been comfortable in the role of vicar's daughter, and she's far too raunchy for your mother.' Her eyelid drooped in exhaustion as memories whirled effortlessly across her mind. 'It's your fault as much as anyone's.'

Russell dying . . . she had an affair with Russell, too, you know . . . you got drunk and tried to kill yourself . . .

His voice came across vast stretches of space. 'Why?'

'She couldn't compete with a saint, Simon, so she became a sinner . . .'

She lurched out of sleep with a sickening jolt and opened her eyes on Alan Protheroe. He was bending over her, and Jinx's immediate thought was that he must be Simon until relieved recognition told her he wasn't. She looked around rather vaguely. 'I was smoking a cigarette.'

He pointed to the butt in the ashtray. 'I put it out.'

'I had a visitor.'

'I know. Father Simon Harris. I gave him his marching orders. I was afraid he'd upset you.'

'He wouldn't dare,' she said with a twisted smile. 'He's an Anglo-Catholic priest.'

'And Meg's brother,' he said, taking the other chair. 'Do you like him, Jinx?'

She could feel the inevitable sweat drenching her back again. 'He's a sanctimonious prig like his father and mother, and he made his sister into a whore.' Her face turned towards this huge amiable man who was doing his best to care for her, and she felt an incredible urge to reach out and touch him. She wanted to curl in his lap, feel his arms about her, shelter, childlike, inside the protection of his strong embrace. Instead she withdrew to the other corner of her chair and wrapped her thin arms about her chest. 'I'm not sure why I said that.'

'Because you're angrier with her than you think you are.'

'Simon came to apologize.'

'For his sister's behaviour?'

'I suppose so.' She fell silent.

'Is he older or younger than she is?'

'He's a year younger.'

'Does Meg look like him?'

'Not really. She's very beautiful.'

'Do you like her, Jinx?'

'Yes.'

He nodded. 'You were dreaming just now, and they didn't look very happy dreams. Do you want to tell me about them?'

She didn't – *couldn't?* – answer. Even after ten years, the wound was still raw and she shrank instinctively from anything that might re-open it. Yet, there was an extraordinary need within her to convince someone – *anyone* – of how little Leo had really mattered to her. Do you like her? *Yes. Yes.* YES. *But why did it hurt so much to say it?*

'I was dreaming about a man I knew,' she said abruptly. 'He was beaten to death ten years ago, and I was the one who found him. He had an art gallery in Chelsea. The police think he disturbed some burglars because the place had been ransacked and several of the paintings stolen. We were supposed to be having dinner but he never turned up, so I went to the gallery to find him. There was blood everywhere. I found him in the store room at the back, but I didn't recognize him . . .' Her voice faltered and she held her fingers to her lips. 'He was still alive, but he couldn't say anything because his jaw had been smashed. So he tried to use his eyes to talk to me, but – I – couldn't understand what he wanted.' She lived the terrible scene again in her mind, her shock, her revulsion, her inadequacy in the face of the bludgeoned bleeding mask that had once been Russell. 'And there was nothing I could do except call an ambulance, and watch him . . . I watched him die.' She fell silent. *Had Russell been in a trap, too?*

Protheroe didn't press her to go on. He was content to let her tell the story at her own speed, realizing perhaps that because it was so rarely told it was bound to lack fluency.

'I had nightmares about it for ages, so Adam packed me off to a hypnotherapist. But that just made everything worse. The man was a quack. He encouraged me to confront what disturbed me most about the incident and then put it into perspective, but all he actually succeeded in doing was exacerbating every feeling of guilt I had.' She fell silent again, and this time her face took on an introspective look as if she were revisiting rooms long closed.

Protheroe was more interested in what she hadn't said than what she had. He knew the details of the story already, both from what her father had told him over the phone and from reading the notes made by her psychiatrist. Why hadn't she mentioned, for example, that she and Russell Landy had been married? Or that the murder of her husband had caused her to miscarry at thirteen weeks? Why did she talk about being referred to a hypnotherapist when she had, in fact, been admitted to hospital in a state of near starvation, weighing under six stone, and with very severe depression? He ran his thumb down his jawline and pondered this last thought. She had referred to the therapist as 'he', yet the notes he had in his office were written by a woman.

He waited for another minute or two, then prompted her gently when it became clear she was lost in self-absorption. 'Did the psychiatrist at Queen Mary's Hospital help you at all, Jinx?'

'You mean the second one, Stephanie Fellowes?'

'Yes.'

She seemed to find her position uncomfortable and unlocked her arms to reach for the inevitable cigarette. 'When am I going to be allowed outside?' she demanded suddenly, flicking the lighter to the tip and eyeing him through the smoke.

'The sooner the better. We could go now if you like. I've a pretty good arm for leaning on and we can find ourselves a bench away from the madding crowd.'

She smiled faintly. 'No thank you. I'll wait till I can manage it alone.' She nodded towards her bathroom door. 'I've been to the loo a couple of times and had to crawl most of the way, so I'll practise in private for a bit. I'm not particularly keen to have you laugh at me.'

'Why would I want to do that?'

She shrugged. 'Not in front of me, perhaps, but I'm sure you could work it up into a good story for the golf club.' She mimicked his lower register. 'I say, chaps, have I told you the one about my pet hysteric who drove her car at a concrete pillar, survived by a miracle, then fell flat on her face when she tried to stand up?'

'Do you always ascribe such base motives to the people who care for you?'

'Stephanie Fellowes certainly thought so.' *But then I didn't trust her.* She blew smoke rings into the air. 'You see, I'm not a willing guinea pig. I'd rather live with all my fears, depressions and obsessions than have clumsy people in hobnailed boots trampling about in my head.' She smiled without hostility. 'I presume she or my father has told you that I became so depressed I was starving myself?' She looked at him enquiringly and he nodded. 'Which one, as a matter of interest? Stephanie or Adam?'

He showed no hesitation about answering. 'Both. Stephanie sent me a copy of the notes she took at the time. Your father told me when you first came here.'

'Have you met him?'

'No. We spoke on the telephone.'

She nodded. 'That's how he does business. Technology, particularly the impersonal fax, was invented for Adam. He knows how intimidating it is to deal with somebody you never meet. I'd keep it that way if I were you.'

'Why?'

'No particular reason.'

'He seemed pleasant enough, and he's very concerned for you.'

She smiled to herself, and he wondered if she realized how provocative that smile was. As a character she was fascinating. She was determined to wean him away from her father, but in the most subtle of fashions – through innuendo rather than fact, through sympathy rather than honesty. And he knew he wasn't immune. There was something infinitely appealing about the combination of incisive intellect and physical weakness. Particularly for him, although she couldn't know that.

'So concerned that he hasn't been near me,' she pointed out.

'Then phone him and find out why not,' he suggested.

She shook her head. 'Adam and I never ask each other personal questions, Dr Protheroe.'

'Yet you always call him Adam. I assumed that meant you saw each other as equals.'

But that was clearly something she didn't want to discuss. 'We were talking about my alleged depression,' she said abruptly. '*Alleged* being the operative word.'

He abandoned the subject. 'You wanted to know whether it was Stephanie or Adam who told me you became so depressed that you were starving yourself,' he reminded her, 'and I said they both had. Shall we go on from there?'

'It happened the other way round. The depression developed because I wasn't eating, so when they took me into hospital and started feeding me I began to feel better.'

He thought it more likely that her improvement was due to anti-depressants, but he had no intention of arguing about it. 'Do you know why you weren't eating?'

'Yes.'

He waited for a moment. 'Are you going to tell me?'

'Maybe. If you tell me what Stephanie put in her notes.'

She would be satisfied with nothing less than the truth, he thought, although whether she would believe that what he told her *was* the truth was another matter altogether. 'The notes are in my office,' he said, 'so I can't quote her verbatim but I can give you the gist of what she wrote. You were admitted with severe reactive depression, following the murder of your husband and the loss of your baby. Your symptoms were extreme – in particular, loss of appetite and persistent insomnia. It was clear to Dr Fellowes that you were very disturbed and that your malnutrition was due not so much to a loss of appetite as a refusal to eat, and she diagnosed you a potential suicide. Your treatment consisted of a combination of drug and psychotherapy and, while she admits that you were extremely hostile to the psychotherapy, your condition began to improve quite markedly after three to four weeks. As far as I recall you were discharged fit after six weeks and, although you have consistently refused to have your progress monitored at out-patient attendances, Dr Fellowes regards you as one of her successes.' He paused briefly. 'Or she did until I requested your notes.'

Jinx frowned. 'I hadn't realized she thought I was doing it deliberately.' She took a thoughtful puff of her cigarette. 'It explains why you're all assuming suicide now. *Pardus maculas non deponit.* The leopard doesn't change his spots,' she translated idly, her eyes drifting towards the window where a man was wandering across the lawn. Fair hair, green sweater, brown cords. For a fraction of a second she thought it was Leo, and her heart lurched violently.

'If you weren't starving yourself for a reason, then why were you doing it?'

She waited a moment before she answered. 'Because the quack I saw first used hypnosis to unlock my nightmares, and turned me into a psychotic wreck in the process.' She shrugged and stubbed out her cigarette. 'But a nightmare isn't so bad. Most of the time you don't remember details, and the relief of waking always outweighs the fears.' She used her fingertips to sweep the arm of the chair, something she would do again and again during the next few minutes. 'I wasn't getting very much sleep admittedly, but, other than that, I was coping pretty well in view of everything that had happened. At which point, enter my father.' She shook her head. 'You have to understand that he'd always loathed Russell, partly because we got married without telling him, but mostly because Russell was twenty years older than I was and had been one of my dons at Oxford. If my father referred to him at all it was always as "the twisted paedophile".' She dwelt on that for a moment. 'Anyway, about a week after the miscarriage, Adam had an attack of conscience – at least I assume that's what it was – and paid this extremely expensive therapist to counsel me through my double bereavement.' She took out another cigarette. 'If I hadn't been so shocked by it all, I might have realized he was a charlatan, but you don't think straight in situations like that. Do you know what flooding is?' She flung the question at him as she bent to the lighter.

Protheroe was taken by surprise. 'In psychiatric terms? Well, yes, it's a drastic method of dealing with fear. You force a patient to confront the thing he's afraid of, often without warning and usually with no means of escape. It's risky and not always successful, but when it works it's spectacular. It has its place in the treatment of phobias.'

'Do you use it here?'

'No.'

'Do you use hypnosis?'

He shook his head.

'Then what *do* you use, Dr Protheroe?'

'Nothing.' He smiled at her expression of disbelief. 'No tricks, anyway, and no short-cuts. We simply concentrate on restoring self-esteem, and most of the people who come here are halfway to winning the battle before they even walk through the door because they've already made up their minds they want to be free of whatever disturbs them.'

'One of your patients came in yesterday. He wanted to know whether I was on heroin or cocaine, so I presume he's a drug addict himself. He didn't strike me as being halfway to winning anything.'

'What did he look like?'

'Tall, skinny, long ginger hair.'

He looked pleased. 'Matthew Cornell. Well, that's an improvement. At least he's beginning to notice a world beyond smack, poppers and MDMA.'

'Is that why he came to my room uninvited, because you encourage your patients to notice each other?'

'I rely entirely on human nature,' he told her without a hint of guile. 'In the end, curiosity usually wins out. You're our newest resident, therefore you're of interest. I'm quite pleased Matthew found the courage to defy the restrictions.'

'What restrictions?'

'There's a huge notice outside your door saying Do Not Disturb.'

'I didn't know.'

'You should have looked.'

'If it's there, why did Simon Harris ignore it?'

He shrugged. 'Are you sure he did?'

'He came in.'

'Uninvited?'

'No, he asked me if he should make polite excuses and leave, but I could hardly say I didn't want to see him when he'd come all this way.'

'Why not?'

Because no one ever taught me how to say piss off. 'I won't be psychoanalysed, Dr Protheroe. I won't do group therapy. I won't join in. I won't play games.'

'Is anyone saying you must?'

'I know how it works.'

'I wonder if you do.'

'You were asking me about the hypnotherapist,' she said, ignoring this. 'He treated me for a phobia that I didn't have. All I had were feelings of guilt about letting Russell down. There was so much blood, and his face was completely raw and pulpy.' She pressed a hand to her bandaged eye, which had begun to ache. 'He wanted me to kiss him,' she said flatly, mechanically even, 'but I couldn't. And then I lost the baby, and there was more blood.' She paused. 'All I needed was a little time.'

He let her sit in silence for several minutes, relentlessly sweeping the chair arm and drawing on her cigarette. 'What did the therapist do?' he prompted finally.

She looked at him in surprise as if she thought he would have guessed. 'He put a raw steak on my face while I was in a trance and then woke me. It smelt of blood and dead meat, and I thought it was Russell come back from the grave for his kiss. It was an awfully long time before I could eat something without being sick.'

'Good God!' He was genuinely shocked. 'Who was this man?'

She stared at him blankly for a moment. 'I don't remember his name.'

'Where was his office?'

But she couldn't remember that either. 'Somewhere in London,' she told him.

'OK, it doesn't matter.'

'You don't believe me, do you?'

'I've no reason not to.'

'How could I remember something so awful if it never happened?'

He didn't say anything.

'You think I've invented it,' she accused him. 'But why would I want to invent something that never happened?'

Perhaps because nobody's ever been charged with Russell's murder, he thought, for her guilt seemed rooted in a far more powerful anguish than her very natural reluctance to kiss the mutilated face of her dying husband.

Bodies found in Ardingly Woods

The remains of a man and a woman were discovered yesterday in Ardingly Woods in Hampshire. Cause of death has yet to be revealed but police are not ruling out foul play. 'We are asking for help in trying to establish their identities,' said a spokesman. 'Death is believed to have taken place ten to twelve days ago, but no one matching their descriptions has been reported missing.'

The man is described as 6'1", medium build, aged between 30–40, with straight blond hair. He was wearing fawn cotton slacks, a checked shirt and dark green ribbed jumper. The woman was 5'4", slim build, aged between 30–40, with short dark hair. She was wearing blue denim jeans and a navy blue T-shirt.

Police admit to being puzzled as to how the bodies came there. 'There are no reports of a car being abandoned in the area,' said the spokesman, 'and the woods are not on a bus route. We believe someone must have driven them there, and we are asking anyone who gave a lift to a couple answering these descriptions to come forward. It is possible that they hitched a ride from outside the county.'

Police have not ruled out a suicide pact, although they are concerned that neither body carries any form of identification. 'This is unusual,' said the spokesman. 'We would have expected to find a wallet or a handbag.' The woods continue to be searched for further evidence.

Mrs Mary Hughes, 73, who discovered the bodies with Pepita, her Jack Russell, is recovering at home, following a slight heart attack. She ran over a mile to the nearest telephone to alert police, and blames the attack on shock and over-exertion. 'I should have walked,' she said. 'I'm an old woman now and those bodies weren't going anywhere. There's no fool like an old fool.'

Chapter Six

THE REVEREND CHARLES Harris watched from his study window as the white Rolls-Royce – registration number KIN6 – pulled in through the vicarage gates and parked by the front door. The number plate said it all. By the strategic placing of a yellow-headed screw to break the six and turn it into a G, the word KING screamed out from both ends of the ostentatious vehicle. Not for the first time, he wondered how Jinx had remained so apparently unaffected by her vulgar family and, not for the first time either, he berated himself for being uncharitable.

His dismay grew when the chauffeur opened the back door and assisted Betty Kingsley out. Adam he might have coped with, but Betty was a different matter altogether, particularly when, as was clearly the case now, she had been hitting the bottle hard during the journey. With a sigh, he opened the door of his study and called to his wife. 'Caroline, we have a visitor. Betty Kingsley has just driven in.'

His wife appeared in the kitchen doorway, a look of apprehension on her thin face. 'I don't want to see her,' she said. 'I can't stand it, Charles. It was bad enough talking to her on the phone. She'll just start screaming at me again.'

'I don't think we have a choice.'

'Of course we do,' she snapped, frayed nerves getting the better of her. 'There's no law that says we have to answer the door. We can hardly be blamed because Leo preferred our daughter.' The doorbell rang. 'Just ignore it,' she hissed at him. 'I won't be harangued by a common fishwife in my own home.'

But he was an old-fashioned man with old-fashioned manners. He shook his head in gentle admonishment and crossed the hall to open the front door. 'Hello, Betty,' he said kindly. She stank of gin and her lipstick was smeared at one corner. There was something infinitely sad, he thought, about the worn face covered in make-up and the plump body squeezed into a girlish dress. Growing old would always be something to fear because drink had addled whatever wisdom she had, and now there was nothing left to make her interesting.

She pushed past him belligerently to confront Caroline, bumping into a walnut card table as she did so and slopping water from the vase of flowers on to the polished surface. 'It's your slut of a daughter drove Jinx to kill herself, not me or her Daddy,' she grunted, jabbing her finger at the other woman. 'She'd never need to kill herself because of us. You've got me that riled, Mrs High-and-Bloody-Mighty. You think you can say what you like about me and mine, when the truth is it's your precious Meg deserves the blame.'

Caroline Harris glanced helplessly towards her husband. This is your fault, said her expression, so do something about it, but he gave an unhappy shrug and left her to fight the battle alone. 'I really can't see the point of discussing this,' she said in a voice that was pitched too high. 'Far too much dirt has been peddled already.'

'Yes, well, Meg always said you were a tight-arsed bitch who'd rather see everything swept under the carpet than have it aired in public.' She clutched at the table with a meaty fist and affected a classy accent. '"Oh, I say, I can't see the point of discussing this."' She took a deep breath. 'But you fucking well discuss it when it suits you. "Now, now, Betty, don't go blaming Meg for your own failings. Jinx needs a mother to talk to."' She slammed the table and set the vase rocking alarmingly. 'Well, she's got a bloody mother. Me.'

'But probably not the one she wants,' said Caroline icily. 'You were very offensive over the telephone, Betty. You called us murderers before you even knew if Jinx was dead. What did you expect me to do? Agree with you? Charles and I barely had time to digest the news that Leo had left Jinx for Meg before you were on the phone screaming abuse. It's been a terrible shock for all of us.'

'Where's the apology? The apology's what I'm after, missus, or perhaps you're too grand for that?' Tears welled in the heavily mascara'd eyes. 'You know what's being said? The wedding's off because Sir Anthony Wallader wouldn't have his son marry a Kingsley. And why? Because we're too bloody common.' She gulped her tears. 'But there's only one rotten apple in the barrel and I've a mind to make that public. Your Meg, who couldn't keep her knickers on if she was paid.'

Caroline Harris's lips thinned to an unattractive horse-shoe but, before she could say anything, the vicar intervened. He placed a hand on Betty Kingsley's arm and drew her round to face him. 'Is this true, Betty?' He smiled apologetically. 'We know so little, you see. Only what Meg told us over the phone and, in all conscience, that wasn't very much. Just that Leo preferred her to Jinx and they were leaving for a holiday in France.'

The woman's thick lips worked aggressively. 'Why should me and the boys take the blame for your daughter's screwing?' she slurred drunkenly. 'Adam says we've ruined Jinx's chances with our goings-on, but I can't see it myself. Leo's a right bastard – like his father – but we did nothing to upset the apple cart.' She took a deep breath. 'Not our fault,' she resumed after a moment. 'Meg's jealous, always has been. Sets out to bed anyone Jinx likes. Common is as common does. Bedded Russell, in case you didn't know.'

Charles turned a shocked face towards his wife but Caroline looked away and refused to meet his eyes. 'I didn't know,' he said. 'I'm sorry.'

Friday, 24 June, HO Forensic Lab,
Hampshire – 11.30 a.m.

Dr Robert Clarke, the Home Office pathologist, took pity on the three policemen and herded them out of the laboratory and into his office, peeling off his gloves and his mask as he did so. 'Not a pretty sight,' he agreed, opening his window to allow in the sweeter-smelling air of the busy road outside, 'but sealing both caboodles in body bags and spraying with Nuvanstykil is the only way to kill the maggots off and make what's left presentable enough to examine. Coffee?' he suggested.

The three men swallowed convulsively, and wondered

how he could consider taking anything into his mouth after what they had glimpsed going on inside the bags. The stench of putrefaction still lined their throats, as it had done since yesterday when they had stood beside the ditch and stared in gagging repulsion at the pulsating white mass that had seethed turbulently amongst the pieces of clothing and decomposing body parts that lay there. They shook their heads vigorously.

'No thanks, Bob,' said Detective Superintendent Frank Cheever, wiping his lips with a handkerchief. He was older than the other two policemen, a fine-boned, rather studious-looking man with grey hair and pale blue eyes which he fixed unnervingly on the person he was talking to. He was something of a dandy and caused much amusement amongst his officers over what they considered his fetish for silk. He wore silk bow-ties, tucked matching silk handkerchiefs into his jacket breast pocket, and kept his expensive silk socks at permanent stretch by the use of sock suspenders. Rumour had it that he also wore silk underwear. 'But don't mind us,' he murmured, looking unhappily at the empty coffee mug on the desk, 'you go ahead.'

'I will.' The doctor stuck his head round the door, waved the mug in the air and asked his secretary to bring him a black coffee. 'It takes the taste away,' he said insensitively as he settled himself behind his desk and waved them towards some empty chairs. 'Now, let's see what we've got.' He consulted some typed notes in front of him. 'I won't bore you with the life history of *Calliphora erythrocephalus*, which is the bluebottle we're dealing with here, but in essence the time lapse in warm weather between the laying of the eggs and the pupal stage is some ten to eleven days. We found no pupa cases, and the larvae at the time of the discovery were on the way to being mature third-stage maggots, which would suggest the eggs were laid some eight or nine days before.' He tapped a calendar. 'Yesterday was the twenty-third, so we're looking at the fourteenth or fifteenth as likely dates for laying. Add another day or two for *Calliphora erythrocephalus* to find the bodies and my estimate for when death occurred would be the twelfth, thirteenth or fourteenth, with Monday the thirteenth as my first choice.' He beamed at his secretary who came in with his coffee and a plate of chocolate biscuits. 'Sure you won't join me, gentlemen?'

They became visibly paler. It occurred to Detective Inspector Maddocks, a tall heavy-set man in his mid-forties with a permanent scowl on his face, that Bob Clarke was doing this on purpose, a kind of trial of strength between the hard man of pathology and the hard men of CID. He'd always suspected the little bugger – Clarke was a miserable five feet six inches – of having a chip on his shoulder. Now he was sure. There was a horrible similarity between this cocky little scientist and the maths teacher who was the cause of his pending third divorce. *God, how he loathed arrogant little men!*

'All right, Jenny. Thank you.' Clarke dunked a biscuit into the cup and munched on it with pleasure. 'Their hands and feet were tied, as you know, so we've got two people quite unable to defend themselves. Cause of death was ferocious bludgeoning with a blunt instrument.' He pushed some X-ray photographs in Superintendent Cheever's direction with the flick of a finger. 'We took these before we put them in the bags. You see how both skulls have been fractured in several places. This one, in particular, shows a clear rounded depression in the woman's parietal bone. A long-handled club or sledgehammer would be my bet, certainly something very substantial. Notice the break in the man's right clavicle which would imply a missed shot' – he made a downward swing with his hand – 'possibly glanced off the side of his head and landed with the force of a two-ton truck on the poor wretch's shoulder.' He shook his head. 'What we're looking at is two people on their knees with hands tied behind their backs and a maniac using them for target practice with something very heavy indeed. I think we can assume the first blows were delivered from behind because those are downward sweeps, and the blows that shattered the jaws and cheekbones were done after the bodies had toppled on to their sides. Imagine our maniac holding his hammer like a golf club and driving at both faces when they were on the ground. That should give you a good idea of what probably occurred.'

Cheever dabbed at his lips again as he examined the photographs. 'Where do you think it happened? In the ditch itself or at the top of the bank?'

'My guess would be on the bank. The sort of blows I envisage would have been harder to achieve in a confined space. No, I see him killing them at the top of the slope, then pushing the bodies over. It's not very pleasant to dwell on' – he dunked another biscuit in his coffee – 'but the golf-swing blows may have been his method of driving the corpses into a roll. Not that it would have worked very well,' he said thoughtfully. 'He'd have had to lay them out straight and give them a heave around their middles to really get them going.'

'What about those slide marks we found five yards down?'

Bob Clarke sorted out another photograph. 'Very interesting,' he said. 'Clearly made with a thin, hard heel. See here, quite deeply scored as if the wearer was sliding on one side with the heel digging in as a brake. But it's no more than an inch wide so I'd suggest it was a woman's shoe.'

'The female corpse was wearing trainers,' said Cheever.

'Yes. She couldn't have made marks like this, and neither could our male corpse. His heels are a good four inches wide. They weren't done all that recently either – you can see where the grass has started to sprout again in places – so the chances are there was either a woman present while the murder took place or someone else, who didn't report it, found the bodies before your old lady did.'

'If that's true,' said Cheever pensively, 'then it's conceivable they may be our wallet thief. The logical assumption is that the murderer removed anything that could identify them, but it's not beyond the bounds of possibility that someone else did the business.' He glanced towards his colleagues. 'What do you think?'

Gareth Maddocks gave a non-committal shrug, his narrowed eyes, sunk in folds of thick flesh, watching the pathologist's biscuit-dunking routine with disgust. 'You said it meant a woman might have been present during the murder,' he reminded him. 'Does that mean a woman could have delivered blows like this, or that she was there only as a witness to a man delivering them?'

Apparently oblivious to the other man's distaste, Clarke rubbed biscuit crumbs from his fingers and started in on his coffee. 'Assuming she had two people, incapacitated, on their knees in front of her and assuming a sledge- or club-hammer with a reasonable length handle, then any woman with the strength to swing the thing several times could inflict this sort of damage. But it's an unlikely *modus operandi* for a woman acting alone.'

'Not impossible, though?'

'Nothing's impossible, but, frankly, statistics and psychology are against you. It was a very physical crime, requiring energy and extreme savagery, neither of which are typical of female murderers. That's not to say there aren't some extremely savage and dangerous women about, but, in my experience, they prefer to conduct their murders within the four walls of a house, using a pillow over the face, poison, guns and knives even. I'd plump for a man or men, if I were you, with the possibility of a woman in tow who witnessed the whole event. It really is a pity there's been so little rain recently. A nice piece of soggy ground and I could have told you how many people were there, what they weighed and probably how tall they were.' He paused briefly. 'Of course you realize there'll have been a great deal of blood, and that's a brute to clean off, as you know. Your killer will probably have left bloodstains in the car he drove away in. I certainly feel those are areas worth concentrating on.'

'Tell us about the victims,' said Frank Cheever. 'We've got height, build and colouring. Anything else? What do their clothes say?'

'Ah, well, Jerry's having a field day with them.' Clarke pulled out another set of notes. 'It'll be a while before he can give you a full analysis but this is what he's come up with so far. These people weren't poor, quite the reverse in fact, Jerry says look at the wealthier end of the market. The woman first. Not much help from the jeans, which are stone-washed men's Levi 501s, but the T-shirt is American, made by a company called Arizona, and imported into this country by the Birmingham-based Interwear. Preliminary talks with them indicate that these T-shirts retail at fifty-five pounds from only ten stores throughout the country, all of which are centred in London, Birmingham or Glasgow. We're expecting a faxed list this afternoon, and Jerry will send it through to you as soon as it arrives, with precise details of the size, colour code and style that she was wearing.' He followed the notes with his finger. 'Her trainers are a Nike brand, retailing at eighty-five pounds, and her underwear, again not too helpful, is top-of-the-range Marks and Spencer. The point is, nothing that she was wearing was what you or I would call cheap, considering all her clothes are of the casual type.

'Now, the man. He's the better bet, by a long chalk. The pullover is dark green, Army-style with leather-patched elbows, designed by Capability Brown and retailing only through Harrods at a price of one hundred and three pounds.' He smiled at Frank Cheever's grunt of excitement. 'That's only the beginning, my friend. The shirt is a casual green/brown check from Hilditch and Keys in Jermyn Street, retailing at eighty-five pounds. Trousers by Capability Brown again, one hundred per cent lined cotton, with pleated front and button detail, colour described as taupe, and retailing out of Harrods for two hundred and fifty pounds. Socks by Marks and Spencer, shoes probably purchased in Italy because Jerry has no record of an importer who deals in that particular brand, but he's working on it.

His best advice is that our chap has an account with Harrods and probably one with Hilditch and Keys as well. He has located some interesting fibres on both sets of garments which he believes are from the same carpet, probably a thick-pile, off-white Chinese rug, and some hairs which he suggests tentatively are cat hairs, but give him a few more days and he claims he'll be able to describe the room these two were in before they were taken to Ardingly Woods.'

'Anything else?' asked Cheever.

Clarke chuckled. 'Isn't that enough to be getting on with? Good God, man, we've had them less than twenty-four hours. What else are you expecting?'

'Some reasonable fingerprint impressions,' he said. 'You were doubtful yesterday, but perhaps you've had new thoughts today? If either of them have previous records, that's got to be the quickest route to identification.'

'Yes, well, I'll be in a better position to judge that when we've got them out of the bags.'

'What about the green nylon twine that was used to tie their hands and feet? Anything useful to say about that?'

'Not really. It's available in most garden centres, DIY stores and supermarkets. Impossible to break and takes years and years to wear through. The knots were standard grannies, repeated several times to stop them slipping, and they were very tight, so presumably the victims struggled to get out of them. That's an avenue worth exploring. How does one man tie up two healthy adults? And when did he do it? Before he transported them to Ardingly or after he got them there? If it was before, how did he get them to the middle of the forest? If it was after, why didn't one of them run away while the other was being trussed? I really think the most likely scenario is that you should be looking for two or more suspects.'

DI Maddocks rubbed his jaw in thought. 'Are you sure it was a hammer and not a heavy branch? If it was a branch, we could be looking at a rather more spontaneous attack. Our maniac – and I use the word advisedly – stumbles on a sleeping couple in the wood, renders them unconscious, ties them up and then bludgeons them to death before absconding with their money. Could it have happened like that?'

'Not with a branch,' said Dr Clarke amiably. 'Whatever made that neat hole in the woman's skull was cleanly and symmetrically shaped, very hard and heavy, and was probably at right angles to its shaft to penetrate so deeply. I wouldn't put my life on a sledgehammer, but I'd certainly put my savings on it.'

The third policeman, Detective Sergeant Sean Fraser, who was leaning against the wall by the open window, stirred into life. 'With respect, Guv'nor,' he said to Maddocks, 'if it had been a spontaneous killing, we'd have found a car somewhere. A guy who buys his clothes at Harrods isn't going to hitch a lift to Ardingly Woods for a snooze with his bird.' He crossed his arms and tapped his fingers against his leather jacket sleeve. 'It's interesting listening to the doctor's description of how it happened. Pick any war you like, and you'll have seen film footage of victims kneeling in front of open graves before they're dispatched with a shot in the back of the head to topple forward into the pit. I'd say it's a fair bet these two were executed.'

The others digested this in silence for a moment.

'What sort of execution are we talking about?' asked

Superintendent Cheever finally. 'If it was a professional contract killing, we'd be looking at X-rays of bullet holes. You said yourself, a shot in the back of the head. I can't see a pro using a sledgehammer.'

'I've known gangs take each other apart with baseball bats, sir,' said Fraser, 'but, looking at what we've got, a man and a woman, mid-thirties to forties, I'd say it's a jealous husband we should be after. An execution of passion, that's my guess.'

Cheever punted the idea about his head. 'I still don't understand why no one's reported them missing. Well-dressed people don't vanish for two weeks without anyone noticing.'

'Unless it's their families who've done away with them,' said Maddocks. 'Perhaps we've got a Menendez situation on our hands – wealthy parents slaughtered by teenage sons out of greed for money or revenge for prolonged sexual abuse, depending on who you believe. It happens far too often for comfort. There was Jeremy Bamber – remember him? – did away with his entire family for the house and money and then tried to blame it all on his dead sister. Makes you wonder why any of us bothers to lumber ourselves with the next generation.'

Dr Clarke consulted his watch and stood up. 'Well, unlike you chaps, I don't earn enough to make it worth my children's while. A little kudos now and then for getting it right, that's my only real satisfaction for all the hours I put in on your behalf. Look for the bloodstains. Your individual, or more likely your duo or trio, will have had quantities of bright red haemoglobin splattered across their fronts. Someone, somewhere will have seen it and said: Ah!'

'Assuming Joe Public notices anything beyond his stomach and his prick,' said Maddocks sourly.

'All being well,' went on Clarke, opening the door, 'I should be able to pin-point their ages a little better for you by the end of the day, probably get some usable finger-prints and, in addition, tell you if the woman has ever given birth.' He ushered them into the corridor. 'But first I'll have to unzip those charming bags. Care to lend a hand, any of you?' He was chortling to himself as he headed for the lab.

'He's a miserable old fraud,' said Superintendent Cheever to the others. 'He earns twice as much as I do and puts in half the hours.'

The smell of death issued from the lab as the patholo-gist opened the door and went inside.

'I suppose you noticed,' said Maddocks, grinning at his boss while nodding towards the young sergeant, whose face had taken on an unhealthy hue under its thatch of blond hair, 'that the good doctor ate his biscuits without washing his hands.'

Nightingale Clinic, Salisbury – midday.

Jinx was standing in her bay window, leaning against the back of a chair for support. She was aware of the ginger head poked around her door for a long time before she said anything. 'Why don't you come in?' she said finally to the pane of glass in front of her.

'You talking to me?'

'There's no one else here.'

Matthew eased his thin frame through the gap in the door and joined her in her study of the garden. He found it impossible to stand still for very long and, out of the corner of her eye, she watched his nervous twitching with amusement. *God, he was unattractive.*

'Are you religious?' he asked bluntly.

'Why do you ask?'

'You had a vicar in here yesterday. Thought you might be one of the God squad.'

She flicked him a sideways glance, saw he was busy picking at the spots on his chin, and resumed her own scrutiny of the sunlit lawn and the people on it. 'He's the brother of a friend of mine. Came to see how I was. Nothing more sinister than that.'

He gestured towards a man on the right. 'See the guy in the checked shirt and blue trousers? Recognize him? Singer with Black Night. Used to shoot smack every two hours. Now look at him. And the guy next to him. Owns a freight company, but couldn't do the business unless he downed two bottles of whisky a day. Now he's dry.'

'How do you know?'

'I've done group therapy with them.'

'Did Dr Protheroe ask you to come and see me?' she asked cynically. 'Is this group therapy by the back door?'

'Do me a favour. The Doc never asks anyone to do anything, just sits back and rakes in the loot.' He kicked his toe at the carpet. 'The way I see it, the less he does, the longer we're here, and the better he's pleased. It's money for old rope, this lark.'

'He's obviously doing something right,' Jinx pointed out, 'or none of the patients would improve.'

Matthew ran a shaky hand around his stubble. 'Just keeps us away from temptation, that's all. There's no booze here, no drugs, but my guess is everyone looks for a hit the minute they leave. I'm sure as hell going to. Jesus, it's a bloody morgue this place. No excitement, no bloody fun, death by boredom. I'd fix myself now if I could lay my hands on something.'

She was suddenly tired of him. 'Then why don't you?'

'I just said, there are no drugs on the premises.'

'There must be some. I was offered a sleeping pill last night. Why don't you dissolve a few and shoot them?' she said evenly. 'It'd be a hit of sorts, wouldn't it?'

'Not the sort I want and where'd I get a syringe from?'

She glanced at him again. 'Then walk out. Go into town. Or are we prisoners here?'

'No,' he muttered, rubbing his arms as if he were cold, 'but someone would see. This place is crawling with security officers in case the proles get at the rich and famous. Anyway, what would I use for money? They take it off you when you first come in.'

Which presumably explained why she didn't have her handbag. There were a few clothes in her wardrobe, but no handbag. She had assumed it'd been lost in the crash.

'Well,' she said with idle sarcasm, 'if I was as desperate as you seem to be, then I'd go and mug some poor old woman for the money. I can't see what's stopping you.'

'You're just like everybody else,' he said angrily. 'Go and knock down old ladies, beat the shit out of a bank manager, steal some kid's piggy bank. Jesus, I'm not a criminal. All I want is one bloody hit. You should listen to the Doc some time. What's keeping you here, Matthew? You're over twenty-one, you know what you're doing, so go walkabout, phone your supplier, get him to bring you something. I bloody rang my old man and told him, the Doc's not trying to cure me, he's trying to encourage me, and this is what you're paying for.'

'What did your father say?'

'He said: "No one's stopping you, Matthew, so go ahead and do it." I don't know what the hell's wrong with everyone. How about that walk then? Do you fancy a walk?'

'I can't,' she said rather curtly. 'My legs aren't strong enough yet.'

'Yeah, I forgot. You tried to top yourself. OK, I'll get a wheelchair, then.'

'I suppose Dr Protheroe told you I was suicidal?' she said bitterly.

'Shit, no. Like I said, he doesn't do a damn thing. Everyone knows about you. You've been in the papers. Millionaire's daughter who tried to kill herself.'

'I didn't try to kill myself.'

'How would you know? The word is you can't remember a thing.'

She turned on him. 'You bloody little shit,' she said. 'What the fuck would *you* know about anything?'

He touched a surprisingly soft finger to the tears on her cheek. 'I've been there,' he said.

She was still standing in front of the window twenty minutes later, propped against the chair, when Alan Protheroe came in. 'I have a message for you from Matthew,' he told her. 'It goes something like this: "Tell the bird in number twelve that I've found a wheelchair but it's so filthy that I'm having to clean it. She probably wouldn't say no to some sodding lunch in the garden, so I've laid it on for her under the beech tree."' His amiable face broke into a grin. 'Does that charming invitation appeal at all, Jinx, or should I tell him I've ordered you back to bed? As before, he totally ignored the Do Not Disturb sign outside your door, so, in my view, he hasn't earned your company for lunch, and the chances are he'll bore you solid with constant reiterations of his urge to shoot smack. However, it's an entirely free choice.'

She smiled rather cynically back at him. 'I'm beginning to understand how you operate, Dr Protheroe.'

'Are you?'

'Yes. You work on the principle that people always do the opposite of what the figure in authority is telling them to do.'

'Not necessarily,' he said. 'I'm interested in encouraging each individual to establish his own set of values, and it's remarkably unimportant what triggers that process off.'

'Then you force us to make choices all the time.'

'I don't force anyone to do anything, Jinx.'

She frowned. 'Well, what am I supposed to do? Have lunch with Matthew or tell him to shove his head in a bucket. I mean, he's a patient, too. I wouldn't want to do the wrong thing.'

He shrugged. 'It's nothing to do with me. He'll clean the wheelchair till it shines, because he's made up his mind you're worth it. His brain's a bit one-tracked at the moment, because he's been doing drugs for years, but his father's a barrister and his mother's in advertising, and ten years ago he got three A-levels, so he can't be entirely stupid. It's a free choice, Jinx.'

'I wish you wouldn't keep saying that. In my philosophy,

there's no such thing as a free choice, any more than there are free lunches. You always pay in the end.' She allowed him to see her dislike. 'And, as a matter of interest, if you're prepared to tell me so much about Matthew, then what have you told him about me?'

He arched an amused eyebrow. 'I said the bird in number twelve is streets brighter than you, went to Oxford to read Classics, and probably thinks you're a greasy-haired git who hasn't got the balls to go out and knock down an old lady for the sake of a hit. Which is pretty close to the truth, isn't it? He related most of the conversation you had with him.'

'Spot on,' she said tightly. 'I couldn't have put it better myself.'

'So, what do I tell him? That you'd like to have lunch with him in a wheelchair, or that you wouldn't?'

'You know I wouldn't.'

He tipped a finger at her. 'Then that's what I'll tell him.' With the briefest of waves he disappeared through the door.

'NO!' she shouted. 'COME BACK!' But he didn't come back, and, more angry than she could ever remember, she set off across the floor and thrust herself out of her own doorway. 'DR PROTHEROE!' she screamed at his retreating figure. 'DON'T YOU DARE SAY A WORD, YOU BLOODY SODDING BASTARD!'

He turned round and started to walk back. 'You *do* want to have lunch with Matthew?'

She waited until he had reached her. 'Not particularly,' she said quietly, 'but I will.'

'Why?' he asked curiously. 'Why do something you don't want to do?'

'Because you won't tell him "no" kindly. You'll tell him exactly what I told you, and I don't want you to do that. He's been nicer to me than anyone else and I think you might hurt him.'

'You're right on every count, Jinx.'

She gave a bored sigh. 'Oh, for God's sake. Look, I know what you're doing and I know why you're doing it. You're no different from Stephanie Fellowes. You want me to get out of this room, you want me to stop feeling sorry for myself, and you want me to start mixing again. But why can't you just say: Do it, please, Jinx, because it's good for you? Why involve that wretched boy in your silly games? He's not responsible for what's happened to me.'

Why couldn't she see that the room he wanted her to leave was the one in her mind? What was keeping her there?

'I agree, but I didn't involve him, he involved himself.' He tapped the Do Not Disturb notice that was taped to the wall beside her door. 'Don't you think it's a little patronizing to refer to him as a wretched boy, Jinx? He's twenty-eight and doesn't require protection from me or from you.' He grinned broadly. 'And one last point: as a matter of policy, I never instruct anyone to do anything. You either do things willingly, or you don't do them at all. My credibility's at stake here. I can't have people refusing. It would undermine everything I stand for.'

'Then please tell Matthew, thank you very much and, yes, I'd love to have lunch with him.' She reached up, tore off the notice, scrumpled it into a ball and threw it at him. 'As a good existentialist, Dr Protheroe, I'm sure you know why I did that.'

His thundering laugh boomed along the corridor as he

walked away, tossing the ball into the air and catching it again. 'Because you enjoyed it,' he said over his shoulder.

She was wheeled around the gardens like a highly prized pig in a wheelbarrow, with her lanky escort showing her off with pride to anyone who was interested. She loathed every minute of it, spent the entire time chain-smoking and grinding her teeth at what she regarded as a Protheroe-inspired hijack. She perked up when, at the end of a tour of the boundary wall, they came to the main gate and paused by the gatekeeper's box. He glanced at them briefly through the window, then resumed his reading of the newspaper. Jinx gestured towards the unrestricted exit. 'Why don't we just keep going?' she suggested. 'You can get some smack and I can take a taxi home.'

'Sure,' said Matthew. 'You take it over then.'

She squinted up at him. 'Take over what?'

He made pushing motions with his hands. 'The wheels. It's no skin off my nose if you want to scarper. You're not my responsibility.' He squatted down beside her. 'But if you want out, why don't you just tell the Doc and phone for a taxi from your room?'

She shrugged. 'Probably for the same reason you don't.'

'Yeah,' he said. 'Reckon the guy from the band's got it about right. What he says is, when you've flung yourself into the ultimate abyss and you're still alive when you reach the bottom, it's probably worth asking yourself what the hell you're doing down there. So, do you want lunch? Or do you want out?'

'Both,' said Jinx, 'but I'll settle for lunch. You're not a rebel at all, are you?'

Matthew grinned. 'That depends,' he said.

'On what?'

'*Cui bono?* If it's me who gains, then I might be interested. What's the deal?'

'I don't know yet,' she said thoughtfully, 'but I'll tell you this for free. If you ever manage to kick the habit, you could make millions. You're even more manipulative than my father.'

'It takes one to recognize one,' he said, spinning her round. 'You're not exactly backward in that direction yourself. Hold tight now. Let's see how fast this contraption will go.' He bent down to press her back into the seat and, as he did so, she turned her head to smile at him.

The shock of *déjà vu* was so extreme that she flung her hand out instinctively and caught him a glancing blow across the face. *Meg and Russell . . . Meg and Leo . . .* BLOOD *. . . whore . . . whore . . .* WHORE *. . .*

Chapter Seven

AT THE OUTSET Bobby Franklyn had been careful with the four stolen credit cards, all of which carried the flamboyant signature that was so easy to copy. He had started in a modest way with purchases under thirty pounds to avoid incurring the inevitable telephoned checks, but after two days he was seduced by a leather jacket at one hundred and fifty pounds and caution gave way to greed. He sweated under the beady eye of the shop manager while the call for authorization was made, only to hit an adrenalin high when the jacket was handed to him and he knew that the cards had still not been reported missing. In the next five days, using each in turn, he bought goods to the value of six thousand pounds without, apparently, ever reaching any of the credit ceilings. He had yet to touch the woman's cards.

Of course, he grew careless. It was the nature of the beast to proclaim his cleverness and flaunt his new-found wealth, for there was no forward-thinking in Bobby's intellectual make-up, merely a childlike need to gratify immediate appetites and demonstrate that he was a cut above his peers. He strutted his stuff with increasing arrogance, provoking jealousy and resentment, and was grassed up by an old school-friend, turned police informant, for a smoke and the price of a beer.

Friday, 24 June, Romsey Road Police Station,
Winchester, Hampshire – 12.15 p.m.

At about the same time that Jinx was considering absconding, DS Sean Fraser tapped on the open door of DI Maddocks's office. 'You remember what the Super said about a third party nicking our couple's IDs and money? Well, I took a look at the charge sheets for the last week and came up with a cracker. It's too bloody neat to be coincidence, Guv'nor. A lad by the name of Bobby Franklyn was brought in this morning by the uniformed boys. He lives on the Hawtree Estate, single-parent family, five kids all running wild. He's the eldest. Seems he's been using stolen credit cards to buy electrical goods and clothes to the tune of six thousand quid in five days. When they prised up the floorboards in his bedroom they found four cards in the name of Mr Leo Wallader and two in the name of Miss M. S. Harris. He claims he found them in a carrier bag in the High Street, but when Ted Garrety phoned through to find out when they'd been reported missing he was told that, as far as the companies who issued them are concerned, they're still kosher. Ted's been trying to contact the two cardholders. Wallader's registered address is 12 Glenavon Gardens, Richmond, and Harris's is 43a Shoebury Terrace, Hammersmith. Two London numbers with no answer at either end. What do you reckon?'

The permanent scowl on Maddocks's heavy face smoothed into alert interest. 'Is Franklyn still here?'

Fraser nodded. 'He's a nasty piece of work. Seventeen years old, and knows his rights. We've hauled him in before but this is the first time he's been old enough and bad enough to charge. According to Garrety, he had five televisions, half a dozen stereo systems still in their boxes beside his bed, and a quantity of brand new flashy clothing in his cupboard.'

'Does he have a brief with him?'

'A young woman from Hicks and Hicks. She's advised him to keep his mouth shut.'

The scowl returned. 'Miranda Jones, I suppose. If women stuck to what they're good at instead of muscling in on the male preserves, the world would be a better place.' He flicked a lazy glance at the young sergeant's prudish face. 'You'd agree with that, wouldn't you, Sean?' he goaded him, knowing that Fraser hadn't got the balls to contradict a superior officer.

Fraser stared at a spot on the wall above the Inspector's head and toyed briefly with the idea of thumping the bastard. He really hated Maddocks. He suspected the man's misogyny was pathological and put it down to the fact that Maddocks was in the middle of his third divorce. But it was no excuse, any more than it was an excuse for his apparent willingness to abandon the six children he had had along the way. 'She's better than some of the men they send, Guv.'

'OK, let's take a look at him,' said Maddocks, abandoning his sport to push his chair back and stand up. 'No chance he's our murderer, I suppose?'

Fraser stood aside to let him pass. 'I wouldn't think so, Guv. According to Ted Garrety, he has a reputation for liking little girls. A thirteen-year-old accused him of rape a couple of years back but no charges were ever brought because her mother removed her very speedily when it emerged how many other boys her daughter had slept with. The view is that Franklyn has all the makings of a paedophile, and give it another two to three years and we'll be banging the little sod up on a regular basis for child molestation. A type like that is deeply inadequate, so he'd probably rob two mature dead adults without a qualm, but I doubt very much he'd have the bottle to abduct them while they were alive.'

Which was a fair summary, thought Maddocks, as he examined the depressingly low-grade young man in the interview room who couldn't open his mouth without uttering obscenities and who fingered his crotch from beginning to end of the interview, apparently unaware he was doing it. He appeared unhealthy and unwashed with pinched, sharp features, eyes that looked anywhere but at the person to whom he was talking, and a sullen cast to his mouth. At times like this, the Fascist in Gareth Maddocks wondered why society tolerated such weasels within its midst.

'We have something of a problem here,' he murmured after Franklyn had replied 'no fucking comment' to the first three questions. 'I'm going to deal this one straight, Bobby, so that you know where I'm coming from. I think, then, you might decide to give me some answers. I'm not interested in your credit card fraud. As far as I'm concerned that's a separate issue. What I am interested in are the two people named on the cards, Mr Leo Wallader and Miss M. S. Harris, and the reason I'm interested is because I have two corpses I can't identify who were found in Ardingly

Woods yesterday afternoon. Now, guesswork tells DS Fraser and myself that our couple could very well be Mr Wallader and Miss Harris and it would save us a great deal of time and effort if you could confirm that for us, Bobby. We think the chances are you stumbled on the bodies a week or so ago and did what any normal red-blooded male would do, and removed their wallets.' He smiled amiably. 'What the hell, eh? They were dead, not by your hand, no question about that, but they weren't going to need their credit cards any more, were they? How about giving us a break on this one? It really would help us to know who they are.'

'Sod off,' said Bobby. 'No fucking comment.'

Maddocks glanced towards the young solicitor. 'What say the Sergeant and I leave the room for five minutes and you discuss options with your client? It's worth pointing out, I think, that we might very well decide to bring additional charges against Mr Franklyn if and when we identify our dead couple as Wallader and Harris, and I should add that perverting the course of justice will be the least of them.'

Fraser watched Bobby's involuntary masturbation with marked distaste. 'If we're forced to go house to house on the Hawtree Estate, I wonder if we'll turn up someone else, a young girl perhaps, who was in the woods with Bobby.'

'There weren't no one wiv me,' said Franklyn in a rush, ignoring his solicitor's warning hand on his arm. *Shit, if they ever found out he'd screwed a twelve-year-old.*

'OK, OK, so I did find them two bodies and, Jesus, they were sodding 'orrible. Smashed bloody faces and bluebottles everywhere, but I was on me own. D'you fink I'd 'ave been able to lift them cards if I'd 'ad someone wiv me?

Use yer fucking brains. They'd 'ave wanted an in on the goods, wouldn't they? But it was like you said, them two was dead and they wasn't gonna use their sodding cards again. Couldn't see no 'arm in taking them and doin' a bit of business.'

'You had a duty to report it, Bobby,' said Maddocks mildly, his habitual aggression cloaked in an encouraging smile which said: Don't worry about it, lad, we're men of the world, you and I, and we both know rules are made to be broken.

'Fuck that! It weren't none of my business. If I were a bit keener on you lot, then maybe, but you've never done me no favours so why should I do one for you? They was so bloody dead, you wouldn't believe. Couldn't see what difference it'd make to them if they was found a week ago or if they was found today. They'd still be dead, wouldn't they?'

Maddocks couldn't argue with that. 'Are you sure you were on your own, Bobby? If you had a girl with you we need to know now. It is important.' He was thinking of the skid marks on the bank, made by a woman's heel.

'Yeah, I'm sure.' He pondered for a moment. 'I'll tell you this for free. If a girl 'ad seen what I saw, she'd still be puking all over the sodding shop. I'm not thinking about it too much meself.' His skin grew even more unhealthy-looking. 'I 'ad to 'old me breath to search them. It was that bloody disgusting. Reckon there was a million bluebottles in that ditch. You gonna charge me? It weren't me what did them in. I don't do that kind of stuff.'

Maddocks glanced at Fraser, who shrugged. The lad's story certainly had the ring of truth. 'No,' said the DI, standing up. 'At the moment I don't intend to add any charges to those you're already facing, but we will want to talk to you again, Bobby, so I advise you very strongly to make yourself available. Neither DS Fraser nor I want the trouble of having to look for you.' He paused at the door. 'Just one last thing. Had there been any attempt made to bury the bodies?'

'You mean in a grave?'

'No, I mean had they been covered over with anything?'

'Only wiv leaves.'

'Well covered?'

'Yeah. Pretty well.'

'Then how did you know they were there?'

Franklyn's sharp little eyes shifted nervously. 'Because somethink 'ad been at the guy,' he said. 'A fox, maybe. The 'ead and top 'alf of 'is body 'ad been dug out, least that's what it looked like. I didn't know the woman was there till I started taking the leaves off 'im and found 'er 'ead beside 'is sodding legs. To tell you the truth,' he said, 'I wish I'd never seen them now.' He wiped his hands on his trousers. 'It's got me in bother and I'm not sure I cleaned myself properly afterwards. I've been worrying about that.'

Nightingale Clinic, Salisbury – 6.30 p.m.

Alan Protheroe looked in on Jinx later that afternoon and found her walking with gritty determination about her room. 'I'm not going out in a wheelchair again,' she told him angrily. 'I hadn't realized quite how sensitive I am to being stared at. It was a deeply humiliating experience.' She jabbed a finger at her bandages. 'When's this idiotic thing coming off my eye?'

'Probably tomorrow morning,' he said, wondering if it was only humiliation that had sparked her anger. It would be a while, he thought, before she felt confident enough to admit she remembered anything. 'You've an appointment at Odstock Hospital for nine-thirty. All being well, it'll be removed then.'

She came to a halt beside her dressing table. 'Thank God for that. I feel like Frankenstein's monster at the moment.'

His amiable face creased into a smile. 'You don't look like him.'

There was a short silence.

'Are you married, Dr Protheroe?'

'I was. My wife died of breast cancer four years ago.'

'I'm sorry.'

'Why did you want to know?' he asked her.

Straightforward curiosity. You're too nice to be running around free and most of your shirts have buttons missing. 'Because it's six-thirty on a Friday evening in June and I was wondering why you were still here. Do you live in?'

He nodded. 'In a flat upstairs.'

'Children?'

'One daughter at university, who's nineteen and very strong-minded.'

'I'm not surprised. You've probably been using her as a guinea pig for your theories on individual responsibility since she was knee-high to a grasshopper.'

'Something like that.'

She eyed him curiously. 'As a matter of interest, what happens when one of your patients chooses a wrong set of values? Acts in bad faith, in other words. I can't believe they all toe the existentialist Protheroe line. It's a statistical impossibility.'

He lowered himself into one of the chairs, stretched his long legs in front of him and clasped his hands behind his head. 'That's an extraordinarily loaded question but I'll have a stab at an answer. By "wrong" you presumably mean that they leave the clinic with the same problems they came in with? In other words, their time here hasn't persuaded them that another *modus vivendi* might be worth considering?'

'That's a very simplistic way of putting it, but it'll do, I suppose.'

He lifted an amused eyebrow. 'Then the simplistic answer is that my methods haven't worked for them, and they either remain as they are or seek alternative therapy. But they're usually the ones who discharge themselves within forty-eight hours because they didn't want to be here in the first place.'

Like me, she thought. 'You must have your share of backsliders, though. I can't see Matthew sticking to the straight and narrow once he's away from here.'

'I think you're underestimating him. He's only been here two weeks, you know. Give him another month and then tell me he won't make it.'

She looked appalled. 'A month? How long am I supposed to stay here then?'

'As long or as short as you like.'

'That's not an answer. How long does my father expect you to keep me?'

'This isn't a prison, Jinx. I don't *keep* anyone.'

'Then I can leave tomorrow after the bandages have been removed?'

'Of course you can, subject to what I told you on Wednesday. You're still not physically fit, so I'd feel duty bound to inform your father that you'd discharged yourself.'

She smiled faintly. 'Does that mean I'm mentally fit?'

He shrugged. 'My impression, for what it's worth, is that you're as tough as old boots.' He leaned forward and studied her face closely. 'I'm having some difficulty squaring this rugged self-reliance of yours with the picture the police gave me of a heartbroken, vulnerable woman who drove her car at a wall.'

She pressed a fingertip to her eyelid to hide the awful rush of tears. 'So am I,' she said after a moment, 'but I've read the piece in the newspaper over and over again and I can't come up with another explanation.' She lowered her hand to look at him. 'I phoned Meg's answer-machine today. I thought if I could only talk to her and Leo, they could at least tell everyone that I wasn't upset about him going.'

'Is that something you can remember?'

'You mean, not being upset?' He nodded and she shook her head. 'No, I'm just so certain that it wouldn't have worried me.'

'Why?'

Because it didn't worry me last time. 'Because,' she said out loud, 'I didn't want Leo myself.' She looked away from him, fearful perhaps of seeing his disbelief. 'I know it sounds like sour grapes but I'm relieved I don't have to marry him. I can remember hanging around the studio till all hours just to avoid going home and spending cosy evenings with him, and I don't think it was cold feet about the wedding. I was beginning to actively dislike him.' She gave a hollow laugh. 'So much for rugged self-reliance. Why was I marrying someone I didn't like? It doesn't make sense.' She lapsed into a brief silence. 'It wouldn't be so bad,' she said suddenly, 'if I didn't have to keep shoring up my defences.'

'Against what?'

She pressed her fingertips to her good eye again to shut him out. 'Fear,' she said.

He waited a moment. 'What is there to fear?'

'I don't know,' she murmured. 'I can't remember.'

Romsey Road Police Station,
Winchester, Hampshire – 7.00 p.m.

Events moved extraordinarily quickly once the bodies were given tentative names and addresses. A telephone call to the Richmond police uncovered the interesting information that 12 Glenavon Gardens had attracted the attention of another branch of the Hampshire police some ten days previously, following a road traffic accident involving Miss Jane Kingsley, the owner/occupier.

'You want to speak to a Sergeant Halliwell at Fording-bridge,' said the voice at the other end to Fraser. 'He asked us to make some enquiries about Kingsley because it looked to them like the RTA was a deliberate attempt to kill herself. The gist is, she was engaged to Leo Wallader, who lived with her in Glenavon Gardens for about two months before buggering off on the night of Friday, the tenth of June, three weeks before the wedding, to shack up with Kingsley's best friend. We talked to Kingsley's neighbours who mentioned another suicide attempt on the Sunday, the twelfth, and also to Wallader's parents by phone. The information we were given is that Wallader and his new girlfriend have scarpered to the continent until the fuss over the cancelled wedding has died down.'

'Any idea what the name of the girlfriend is?' Fraser held his breath.

'Harris. Meg Harris.'

Bull's-eye! 'Do you have an address for Wallader's parents?'

'Let's see, now. The father's Sir Anthony Wallader. Address: Downton Court, Ashwell, near Guildford.'

'What about Meg Harris's parents?'

'Sorry. She only came into it as the new girlfriend. We've nothing on her at all except her name.'

'OK, can you fax me everything you've got on this?' He read out the number. 'Within the next five minutes, if possible.'

'Will do. What's the story then?'

'Not sure yet, but we've got two bodies here that we think are Wallader and Harris. You'd better warn your chaps to expect us some time tomorrow. Cheers.'

He cut the line, flipped through a police directory and dialled Fordingbridge. 'Is Sergeant Halliwell still there?' he asked. 'Yes, I know it's late.' He drummed his fingers on the desk. 'OK, well this is urgent. Can you find him and ask him to call either DI Maddocks or DS Fraser in the Ardingly Woods incident room.' He rattled off the number. 'And make that a priority please.'

He gathered his notes together and made his way down

the corridor to the fax machine, which was already print-ing the first of two pages being transmitted down the wire from Richmond. He skimmed both sheets before shoulder-ing his way into Maddocks's office. 'Here's the Hampshire connection, Guv'nor. Leo Wallader was engaged to a Miss Jane Kingsley up until a couple of weeks ago. They were supposed to be getting married on the second of July, but Leo jilted her on the tenth of June for her best friend, Meg Harris.' He looked up. 'Miss Kingsley's father is Adam Kingsley of Franchise Holdings and the wedding was sup-posed to be taking place at Hellingdon Hall, which is where Kingsley Senior lives. It's a mansion to the north of Fordingbridge.' He handed Maddocks the sheets of paper. 'I've asked for a Sergeant Halliwell at Fordingbridge to give us a call. He's the one who requested this information when his guys hauled Miss Kingsley out of her car on the thir-teenth of June, unconscious and drunk as a skunk. A suicide attempt, they reckon, following a previous one on the twelfth of June.' He tapped the Ordnance Survey map on the wall. 'According to the guy I spoke to in Richmond, the RTA was at Stoney Bassett airfield, which is' – he spread his hand across the map – 'two-thirds of the way between Ardingly Woods and Hellingdon Hall, say fifteen miles from the woods to the airfield and another seven from the airfield to the Hall. I've a real gut feeling about this one, Guv'nor. The geography's right, we've got skid marks on the bank made by a woman's shoe, and the Doc said a woman could have done it.'

Maddocks was an older and warier hand. 'Let's wait to hear from Halliwell,' he said.

Half an hour later they transferred to the Superintendent's office and brought him up to date on what they knew. 'I accept there's a remote chance that Wallader and Harris are sunning themselves on the Riviera,' finished Maddocks, 'either because Franklyn's lying to us or because our two bodies nicked the credit cards only to have them nicked again by Franklyn, but it's so damned unlikely that it's not worth considering. It explains why no one's reported them missing. According to Halliwell, Leo's family said they ran away to France to avoid the embarrassment of the cancelled wedding. So what do we do? Tell Sir Anthony Wallader we think his son's in the bath at the lab and ask him to make an identification? Or wait till we're sure the ID's accurate before we tell the families? We can probably lift some fingerprints from Harris's flat in Hammersmith, but Richmond say there's no way they can go back into Glenavon Gardens without alerting Jane Kingsley to the fact that something's up. Which could be a bad move if she's involved.'

Frank Cheever steepled his fingers on his desk and gazed thoughtfully out of the window. 'Did I ever tell you,' he said at last, 'that I began my career as a beat-bobby in London's Mile End?'

Maddocks and Fraser stared straight ahead. If he'd told them once, he'd told them a hundred times. Maddocks prepared to be bored. There was no merit in the old fool's reminiscences, beyond the one undeniably interesting fact that Cheever had been born a bastard to an East London prostitute. Even Maddocks had to admit that to work his way up through various police forces, while remaining married to the same woman for thirty-eight years, was an achievement for a boy who began life in the gutter.

'I was barely out of school,' he mused, 'and one of the first bodies I picked off the street was a black fellow who'd been bludgeoned within an inch of his life.' He thought about that for a moment. 'It turned out the poor wretch was engaged to the sister of an East End gangland boss and there was circumstantial evidence to show the future brother-in-law had done his dirty work himself. All my guv'nor needed was confirmation of identity but when the victim came round, he refused to co-operate and we had to drop it. I've never seen anyone look so scared. He was black as the ace of spades but he went white every time we mentioned a prosecution.' He looked from one to the other. 'The bastard who bludgeoned him was called Adam Kingsley. He wasn't prepared to have black blood in his family.' He fixed his pale eyes on Maddocks. 'But he got it anyway. The black fellow had more guts than Kingsley credited him with. He married the sister a week later, and went up the aisle on crutches to do it.'

Maddocks whistled. 'The same guy? This girl's father?'

Cheever nodded. 'He made a fortune out of buying up cheap properties with sitting tenants, then sending in his heavies to evict the wretched people in order to flog off the properties with vacant possession. He turned respectable in the sixties, probably about the time his daughter was born.' He stared out of his window into the darkness. 'All right,' he said, 'I suggest we tread carefully on this one. You and I, Fraser, are going to visit Sir Anthony Wallader tomorrow morning. We'll leave at eight sharp to be with him between nine and nine-thirty, and I want you to warn Dr Clarke that we may be bringing him back with us.' He turned to Maddocks. 'Meanwhile, Gareth, I suggest you split your team in two – half to concentrate on Meg Harris, the other half on Jane Kingsley. I want to know where they met, how long they've known each other, what sort of personalities they are. In particular I want to know about the relationship between Jane Kingsley and her father. OK? See what you can come up with by the time we get back.'

'But we don't approach Kingsley himself, presumably?'

'No.'

'What about the daughter? Halliwell says she's in the Nightingale Clinic in Salisbury suffering from the effects of concussion. Do we leave her alone as well? She has a drink-driving charge hanging over her head so we could get away with interviewing her on that without too much difficulty.'

'You think so, do you?' said Cheever dryly. 'Listen, my friend, this isn't the Samaritans we're dealing with, and you make damn sure Kingsley doesn't get a sniff of the questions you're asking. Understood? No one makes a move on that family until we know exactly where we are and what we're doing. If Jane is anything like her father, you handle her as delicately as you'd handle a snake. Of course you leave her alone. You leave them *all* alone.'

Saturday, 25 June, Downton Court, Near Guildford, Surrey – 9.30 a.m.

Sir Anthony Wallader ushered the two sombre-looking policemen into the drawing room of his house and waved them towards empty chairs with a perplexed frown creasing his forehead. 'To tell you the truth, gentlemen, I've had it up to here' – he raised his hand to the side of his neck – 'with that wretched girl and her suicide attempts. I don't say I applaud my son in what he's done, but I do object to the way Philippa and I keep being dragged into something that is, frankly, none of our business. You do realize how long I've spent on the telephone to your colleagues round the country, not to mention the appalling conversation poor Philippa had with Jinx's stepmother. Philippa would insist on doing the right thing and sending her best wishes for Jinx's recovery, but Betty was as rude and offensive as one would expect from someone of her class and background.' He gave a shudder of distaste. 'She's the most objectionable creature, little better than the lowest East End tart, if I'm honest. God knows, we're well out of that family entanglement.'

Fraser, who knew Cheever's background, writhed quietly on behalf of his boss. The Superintendent merely nodded. 'It's not an easy situation, sir.'

'You're right, of course. And why should we be made to feel responsible for a grown woman's inability to deal with her emotions? Is this really so important that you can't wait for Leo to get back?' He sank on to the sofa and crossed one neat leg over the other, every inch the aristocrat. In different circumstances, Fraser might have been tempted to kick his arse. There was no sincerity, he felt, in Sir Anthony Wallader. 'Philippa and I barely know Jinx. Leo brought her down for the odd weekend but not enough for us to feel comfortable with her. She's a very clever girl, of course, but rather too modern for our taste.'

'In fact, we'd very much like to talk to your son,' said Frank Cheever evenly. 'Do you have an address or telephone number where we can contact him?'

Sir Anthony shook his head. 'We haven't heard a word since they left. Not surprising really. They're embarrassed.' He clasped his hands over his knee. 'Us, too. We've been keeping our heads well down, as you can probably imagine. Not the done thing, jilting the bride four weeks before the wedding, but the trouble is we can't criticize him for doing it. Embarrassment tempered with relief is probably the best description of how we feel at the moment. She was quite wrong for him, took everything far too seriously, as amply demonstrated by these suicide attempts.'

Fraser was examining some family photographs on the table beside him. 'Is this your son, sir?' he asked, pointing to one of a tall, fair-haired man leaning against a Mercedes convertible with his arms crossed and a broad smile on his face. The family resemblance was strong. He had the same wide forehead as Sir Anthony, the same thick hair, the same elegant tilt to his patrician head.

'Yes, that's Leo.'

'Where exactly did he and Miss Harris say they were going, Sir Anthony?'

'They didn't. They just said they were taking the car across the Channel until the flak stopped flying.'

'You spoke to them in person?'

'Not face to face. Leo phoned on the Saturday morning to say the wedding was off, and that the best thing he and Meg could do was make themselves scarce.'

'Saturday being the eleventh of June?'

'That's right. Two weeks ago today.'

'And you haven't heard from him or Meg since?'

'No.' He swept his trousers with the palm of his hand. 'But I have to say that I can't see why any of this is important. It's hardly a hanging offence if your erstwhile fiancée makes an attempt on her life. Or is it now? I'm afraid the law makes less and less sense to me as I get older.'

Frank Cheever removed a folded piece of paper from his inside breast pocket and spread it out on his knees before passing it across to Sir Anthony. It was a photocopied montage of the credit cards that had been in Bobby Franklyn's possession. 'Do you recognize either of the signatures on this page, sir?'

Sir Anthony held it at arm's length. 'Yes,' he said after a moment, 'the top four are Leo's.' He half-closed his eyes. 'The bottom two are M. S. Harris, so presumably Meg's.' He shifted his gaze to the Superintendent. 'I don't understand.'

'I regret this very much, Sir Anthony, but we have reason to be very concerned for your son and Miss Harris. We came here because we hoped you could give us some idea of where they were and so assure us they were still alive.' He nodded towards the piece of paper. 'A seventeen-year-old boy was charged yesterday in Winchester with credit card fraud, and those six cards were in his possession. He informs us that he stole them a week ago from two bodies he found in Ardingly Woods, some two miles to the west of Winchester. It is my very sad duty to tell you that it is our belief the bodies are those of your son, Leo Wallader, and his friend, Meg Harris.'

Perhaps the information was too shocking to take in, perhaps, quite simply, it didn't make sense. Sir Anthony gave a surprised laugh. 'Don't be absurd, man. I've already told you. They're on the continent somewhere. What is this? Some sort of practical joke?' His brows snapped together angrily. 'That wretched man Kingsley's doing, I suppose.'

'No, sir,' said Cheever gently, 'not a practical joke, although for your sake I wish it were. We do have two unidentified bodies' – he glanced towards the smiling photograph – 'one male, aged between thirty and forty, six feet one inch in height with blond hair, and one female, aged between thirty and forty, five feet four inches in height, with short dark hair. While there is still a chance that the boy lied to us about how he came by the credit cards, I must warn you that it's very remote. Certainly the description of the male seems to fit your son, although we have still to compare the female with Miss Harris. As yet we have no description of her.'

Sir Anthony shook his head in denial. 'There must be some mistake,' he said firmly. 'Leo's in France.'

'Perhaps you can give us a description of Meg,' suggested Fraser.

'She came here once,' said the older man slowly, 'dropped in for lunch on her way back to London when Leo and Jinx were down for the weekend. Philippa took to her immediately. She was a nice girl, clearly besotted with Leo, a far better prospect in every way than Jinx. Good family, decent background. Philippa and I were pleased as punch when the boy phoned to say he was planning to marry Meg instead. The family comes from Wiltshire, I believe. A pretty girl, dark hair, slim, always smiling.' He lapsed into silence.

'What sort of age —' began Fraser, but Cheever glanced across at him and made a damping motion with his hand.

Despair settled on Sir Anthony's face. 'This will destroy my poor wife, you know. Leo was the only one. We tried for more, but it wasn't to be.' He pressed a thumb and forefinger to his eyelids to hold back the tears. 'What was it? Some sort of accident?'

Cheever cleared his throat. 'We don't think so, no. The pathologist's view is that they were murdered.' He clamped his hands between his knees. 'I'm so sorry, Sir Anthony.'

He shook his head again angrily. 'No, no, this is outrageous.'

There was another long silence.

He raised a trembling hand to his forehead. 'Who would want to murder them?'

'We don't know, sir,' said Cheever quietly. 'They've been dead some time, perhaps as long as two weeks. At the moment we're looking at the thirteenth of June as the most likely date for when it happened.'

'That would be the day Jinx tried to kill herself,' he said flatly.

'So we understand.'

Sir Anthony's mouth worked. 'I suppose you know her husband was murdered?' he said harshly.

Frank Cheever leaned forward with a frown. 'You mean Miss Kingsley's husband?' This was news to him.

The other man nodded. 'She was Mrs Landy then. It was nine or ten years ago. Her husband's name was Russell Landy. He was an art dealer in Chelsea.' He fixed Frank with a penetrating stare. 'He was clubbed to death with a hammer but his murderer was never found. Landy was so badly beaten that his face was unrecognizable. The news-papers described it as one of the most brutal killings anyone

could remember. How was my son murdered, Superintendent? Will I be able to recognize him?' He saw the brief
hesitation in the policeman's eyes, a shutter close on something horrific. 'Was he clubbed to death like Landy?'

Frank wiped a weary hand across his face. Good God,
he was thinking. Could it be this easy? 'Death is never
pretty, Sir Anthony, less so when several days have elapsed.'

'But was he clubbed to death like Landy?' There was
anger in Wallader's voice.

'At this stage,' said Frank carefully, 'nothing has been
ruled in or out. The pathologist hasn't had time to finish
his examination and, until he does, it would be wrong to
speculate, but I give you my personal assurance that I will
pass on his conclusions to you as soon as possible after they
have been reported to us.'

Whatever spark had fired Sir Anthony's anger extin-
guished itself as rapidly as it had ignited. He looked lost
suddenly, as if the fact of his son's death had only just
dawned upon him. 'I suppose you need me to identify the
body.' He started to get up.

'There's no hurry, sir. I'd like you to take as much time
as you need to talk it through with your wife. Please don't
feel this is something you have to do immediately.'

'But it is,' he said abruptly, pushing himself from his
chair. 'Philippa's out for the day doing her voluntary stint
in the hospital so she won't even know I've gone. You
talked about a remote chance,' he reminded the policeman with tears in his eyes. 'For my poor girl's sake, I'm
praying for that.'

HO Forensic Lab, Hampshire – 11.45 a.m.

He stood, dry-eyed, over what was left of his son, now transferred to a clinically clean table, his torso discreetly veiled by white cotton sheeting. The hair, as thick and blond as it had been in life, was unmistakably Leo's and, dreadful though it was, there was still enough of the facial structure left for recognition.

His eyes sought out Dr Clarke. 'What should I tell my wife?' he asked him. 'I don't even know how to begin.'

Clarke looked down at the poor dead body. 'She'll need comfort, Sir Anthony, not truth. Tell her how peaceful he looked.'

Art Dealer Murdered

The battered body of Russell Landy, 44, was found in the stock room of his art gallery in Chelsea last night by his wife Jane Landy, 24. He was still alive when the ambulance reached him but died on the way to hospital. Mrs Landy, who is three months pregnant, is said to be deeply shocked. She had waited over an hour for him at Le Gavroche, where they were to have dinner together, but when he didn't arrive, took a taxi to the gallery to look for him. She was alone when she found him. Doctors say he had probably been attacked some 1–2 hours previously and might have survived had he been discovered sooner.

The gallery was ransacked and several of the more valuable paintings stolen. Police believe Mr Landy may have disturbed the robbers. A sledgehammer was recovered from the scene. Russell Landy was a relative newcomer to the art world. His gallery, Impressions, opened less than four years ago and specialized in the minimalist work of young painters such as Michael Paggia and Janet Hopkins.

Daily Telegraph – 2 February, 1984

Jane Landy Loses Baby

Two weeks after the murder of her art dealer husband, Russell Landy, Jane Landy has suffered a second tragedy. It was announced yesterday that she has lost the baby she was expecting. She is said to be distraught. Police are no nearer finding the murderer of her husband.

Daily Telegraph – 18 February, 1984

Landy Murder Mystery

Police admit to being puzzled about the murder of art dealer Russell Landy, 44, whose battered body was found two nights ago by his wife, Jane. 'The premises were broken into,' said a police spokesman, 'and some paintings were stolen, but we cannot account for the frenzied attack on Mr Landy. This sort of specialist robbery isn't normally associated with extreme and savage violence. Art thieves pride themselves on their professionalism.'

The police are asking dealers and collectors to watch out for the stolen paintings. 'If we can establish that robbery was the motive,' said the spokesman, 'it will assist us in our enquiries. At this stage, it is not clear whether the sledgehammer used to murder Mr Landy was already on the premises or was brought there by his attacker. Clearly we have to consider that murder may have been the intention all along.'

Jane Landy, 24, is the only daughter of Adam Kingsley, millionaire chairman of Franchise Holdings Ltd. He is said to be deeply upset by his son-in-law's death, despite declaring publicly after the wedding that Russell Landy was little better than 'a gold-digging cradle-snatcher'. Kingsley has two sons by his second marriage, Miles and Fergus, aged 16 and 14.

Friends of the Landys say Russell was a popular man with no enemies. 'He was an intellectual with a wonderful sense of humour,' said a close friend. 'I cannot understand why anyone would want to kill him.'

The stolen paintings have been valued at £250,000 but police believe they will be difficult to sell. Michael Paggia's work is well known in minimalist art circles but his appeal has a narrow base. His most famous work, Brown & Yellow, two large brown canvases on either side of a smaller yellow canvas, is currently on display at the Tate. It caused a furore when it was bought. One critic described it as: 'S**T & P**S'.

'It is very unclear,' said the police spokesman, 'why thieves would bother to steal paintings like this. Who would want to buy them?'

Daily Telegraph – 3 February, 1984

MEMORANDUM

To: ACC Hendry
From: Superintendent Fisher
Date: 9 August 1984
Re: Murder of Russell Landy – 1.2.84

Following our conversation of yesterday, I have asked Andrews and Meredith to put together a summary of the case for you. The salient points are these:

- None of the stolen paintings have materialized. Andrews' and Meredith's view, which I share, is that robbery was never the motive. Extensive enquiries have produced no witnesses to the break-in. (NB: Mrs Landy has made an insurance claim for compensation. The paintings were valued at £200,000 plus.)

- Landy's movements were traced for the three months prior to the murder but there is no evidence of anything remotely untoward in his background. His business was solvent, as were his personal finances, and bar some indications that he was an occasional cannabis smoker, he did not engage in any illegal activities. Despite questioning of friends, colleagues and relations, there is no evidence of a secret liaison. It seems highly unlikely, therefore, that he was killed by a jealous rival.

- He had several gay friends but extensive questioning

of the gay community has convinced Andrews and
Meredith that he himself was not an active homo-
sexual and that this was not a 'gay' killing.

- He was on good terms with his wife. Friends describe
  him as 'overly possessive of her' but there is no evidence of domestic violence or cruelty. Her alibi for the
  afternoon and evening of 1 February is solid. The only
  time she was alone from midday onwards was when
  she paid off the taxi which took her from the restaurant
  to the gallery and entered the premises. She was
  alone when she found Landy. Andrews and Meredith
  have taken several opinions on the forensic evidence,
  all of which support the original theory that Landy had
  been attacked a minimum of one hour before she
  arrived at 21.05. With the cab-driver's evidence of the
  time he dropped her, and the logged 999 ambulance
  call, there is no question of her having committed the
  assault herself.

- Her movements have also been traced for the three
  months prior to the murder. Andrews and Meredith
  looked specifically for evidence of an affair, but found
  none. They also looked for evidence of a contract
  between her and a third party to eliminate her
  husband but, again, found none. Nor, it must be said,
  could they discover a reason why she would want him
  eliminated. Over a hundred friends and colleagues
  have been interviewed and they all speak of an amicable relationship between the two. There is some indication that Mr Landy suffered periodic bouts of

jealousy but this was put down to the fact that he was twenty years older than she was and not to any infidelity on her part.

- There remains a continuing doubt over the role played by Mrs Landy's father, Adam Kingsley. All the evidence points to extreme hostility between him and Mr Landy. It is clear that he opposed the relationship from the outset and was deeply angry when the marriage took place without his knowledge. He refused ever to speak to his son-in-law, however phoned and was phoned by his daughter on a regular basis. Friends of hers say she was upset by the gulf between them, but refused to pander to either man's 'jealousy' and continued to relate to both on surprisingly easy terms. Her only proviso was that she would never talk about one to the other.

- After a prolonged investigation into Kingsley's movements in the weeks leading up to the murder and on the day of the murder itself, Andrews and Meredith have concluded that while it was not impossible for Kingsley to have committed the crime himself (he was in London that day and could have gone to Chelsea between a meeting in Knightsbridge which ended at 4.30 p.m. and another in the Edgware Road which began at 6.30 p.m.) they believe it to be unlikely. Kingsley refuses to give an account of his whereabouts between those two times, but independent enquiries, based on his movements in the preceding weeks, have elicited three witness statements which confirm he was with a prostitute in Shepherd's Market.

This is a regular occurrence, and has been going on for many years.

- In the absence of any other explanation, Andrews and Meredith incline to the view that Kingsley took out a contract on his son-in-law's life. However, they have been unable to substantiate this view and, without any firm evidence to support it, see no way to proceed. Their suspicions are grounded in an analysis of Kingsley's character and background, which is briefly as follows:

1: He is known to have had extensive contacts with the London underworld since his early career. Born and brought up in and around the Docks in the 30s and 40s. Founded his fortune on black market racketeering during and after the war. Progressed to property scams in the 50s and 60s before 'legitimizing' his business under Franchise Holdings and expanding into full-scale development of office sites.

2: Began to amass an enormous fortune in the early 70s during the property boom. He has always had a reputation (unproven) for dishonest business practices but has twice won out-of-court settlements against newspapers who were foolhardy enough to suggest it.

3: Since Thatcher came to power he has been acquiring tracts of London's Docklands at deflated prices. To do this, he is known to be using his contacts in the underworld.

4: He has been married twice. His first wife, the mother
   of Jane Landy, died in 1962 of septicaemia. She was
   a middle-class doctor's daughter who was educated at
   private school, and Kingsley is said to have adored
   her. He remarried in 1967. His present wife, Elizabeth
   Kingsley, came from his own background and was a
   girlhood friend of his sister. It is thought he was
   engaged to Elizabeth in 1958 but broke the engagement to marry his first wife. The second marriage has
   not been a success. Mrs Kingsley has a drink problem
   and the two sons from the marriage have been cautioned for petty thieving, vandalism and car theft. The
   boys have been educated privately at Hellingdon Hall
   since their expulsion from Marlborough for possession
   of drugs. Kingsley is known to adore his daughter.

In conclusion, I endorse Andrews' and Meredith's analysis. Kingsley remains the prime suspect, although it is
extremely unlikely that he will have committed the
offence himself. In the absence of any witnesses to the
break-in or the murder, or indeed the stolen paintings
coming to light, it is difficult to see how we can proceed.
Even were we given leave to search Kingsley's numer-
ous accounts for evidence of a contract payment, it is
very doubtful we would find it.

John

Chapter Eight

DI MADDOCKS AND his team had put together a substantial amount of information about Jane Kingsley in the
short time they'd had, but had discovered nothing about
Meg Harris or her parents. 'At the time of Miss Kingsley's
car crash, a couple of PCs went out to talk to her parents,'
he told Cheever. 'The stepmother, Mrs Elizabeth Kingsley,
was tipsy and offered some vitriolic comments about Leo
and Meg: They were both bastards but Meg was a snake in
the grass and had set out to steal Jane's boyfriends since they
were at Oxford together.' He looked up. 'BT can't help us.
At a rough estimate, Wiltshire has over five thousand families called Harris living in it. If we had the father's initial
it might help, or a profession even, but you say Sir Anthony
doesn't know what her father was called.'

'No,' said Frank Cheever with rather more cynicism than
was his wont. 'Despite his enthusiasm for her as an alternative daughter-in-law, he seems to know remarkably little
about her.'

Maddocks eyed him curiously. Well, well, well, he
thought, times they are a-changing. 'I've put two of our

121

guys on to tracing Meg's next-of-kin through the university,' he went on, 'but then there's the other problem that Harris may not be her maiden name. I still say our quickest route is via the flat in Hammersmith, so Fraser and I are going up there this afternoon.'

'Understood. What about Jane Kingsley?'

'OK, first the Landy murder.' He pointed to some papers on the Superintendent's desk. 'That's as much as we've managed to get hold of on the case. It seems pretty comprehensive and there's a phone number you can call for an up-date. I guess you missed the Kingsley connection because she was calling herself Jane Landy in those days. Anyway, within weeks of her discharge from hospital following her treatment for depression, she negotiated an extremely favourable sale of his gallery and invested the lot in a photographic studio in Pimlico. She bought it out, lock, stock and barrel – premises, equipment and good-will. Until then, she'd been working part-time as a stand-in photographer when regulars didn't show.' His voice took on a note of reluctant admiration. 'She appears to have turned it into a success. Under the old management it was a run-of-the-mill enterprise, dealing in portraits of the local big-wigs' families, friends and pets. Under Miss Kingsley's management it's become a favoured studio for promotional work – actors, pop stars, fashion models, magazines. She's earned quite a name for herself in the trade.'

'Who's running it at the moment?'

Maddocks consulted his notes. 'A chap called Dean Jarrett. He's been with her from the beginning. She recruited him through an ad in the newspapers, asking for samples of work with a view to employment. She had over one thousand applications, interviewed fifty and selected one. The word amongst the professionals is he's brilliant and devoted. I got Mandy Barry to phone through and ask whether appointments and bookings were being honoured with Miss Kingsley in hospital, and the receptionist, one Angelica, was bullish and convincing about the studio's continued commitment. Loyalty to the boss was deeply felt and not feigned, according to Mandy.'

Cheever nodded. 'What else?'

'The house in Richmond was bought by Landy in eighty-one with an endowment mortgage of thirty thousand. On his death, the endowment paid off the mortgage and the house became Miss Kingsley's. She has shown no inclination to sell it. She gets on well with Colonel and Mrs Clancey who live next door and is well regarded by other people in the road. She lives quietly and unostentatiously and, bar the odd appearance of her father's Rolls-Royce, does not draw attention to herself. Interestingly, nobody referred to Landy at the time of Miss Kingsley's traffic accident, although some of them must have remembered him, but they were very ready to talk about Leo Wallader. The general view is that no one liked him very much and that he behaved badly, but Richmond police were left with the impression that her neighbours were more put out about missing a wedding at Hellingdon Hall than they were about Leo's shenanigans.'

'What about other boyfriends between Landy and Wallader?'

'Only what we've gleaned from the gossip columnists. There've been two or three, but nothing lasting more than six months. Mind you, Wallader didn't make six months either. She met him in February and he was dead by June. Bit of a whirlwind romance, considering the marriage was scheduled for July.'

'What was the attraction?'

Maddocks shrugged. 'No idea, but Colonel Clancey said it was very clear to him and his wife that Jane was having cold feet about the wedding even if it was Leo who called it off. Claims he can't understand why she would want to top herself when he left.'

'Any ideas?'

'Only the obvious – that she killed them herself or witnessed the killing and then suffered a similar breakdown to the one she had at the time of Landy's death. She's pretty damn weird, that's for sure. I mean, according to what we've found out, her favourite backgrounds for photographic shoots are cemeteries, derelict factories and graffitied subway walls.' He took a folded page that had been ripped out of a magazine from his pocket. 'If you're interested, that's her most famous photograph to date. It's that black supermodel standing in front of a filthy tiled wall with every obscenity you can imagine scrawled all over it.'

Cheever spread the sheet on his desk and examined it. 'Fascinating,' he said. 'She's quite an artist.'

'Well, I think it sucks, sir. Why put a beautiful woman against crap like that?'

'Where would you have put her, Gareth?' asked the other man tartly. 'On a bed?'

'Why not? Somewhere a bit more glamorous, anyway.'

The Superintendent frowned. 'It's a statement. I think it's saying that real beauty is incorruptible, never mind how profane or ugly the setting.' He pinched the end of his nose. 'Which is interesting, don't you think, in view of the ugliness of Landy's death? I wonder when she started using backgrounds like this in her work. There's something rather moving about the triumph of fragile human perfection over a wasteland of mindless filth.'

Maddocks decided the old man was going ga-ga. It was only a creased fashion photograph, not the *Mona Lisa*.

Hellingdon Hall, Near Fordingbridge,
Hampshire – 12.30 p.m.

Miles Kingsley shook his mother angrily then pushed her back on to the sofa. 'I don't believe it. My God, you're such a stupid cow. Why can't you keep your bloody great mouth shut? Who else have you told?' He glared across at his brother, who was skulking at the far end of the drawing room, feigning an interest in the leather-bound books his father had bought by the yard when they'd first moved into the Hall. 'Your neck's on the line, too, you little shit, so I suggest you wipe that smirk off your face before I slap it off.'

'Sod off, Miles,' said Fergus. 'If I had any sense I'd never have listened to you in the first place.' He kicked a Chippendale chair. 'It was your idea, for Christ's sake. Foolproof, you said. What can possibly go wrong?'

'Nothing *has* gone wrong. You'll see. Just a little more time, and we'll be free and clear with a sodding fortune.'

'That's what you said last time.'

Romsey Road Police Station, Winchester – 12.45 p.m.

Frank read the documents on his desk relating to the Landy murder, then dialled the contact number Maddocks had given him. DCI Andrews had been involved from the outset.

'The case was effectively closed at the end of eighty-five,' he said down the wire from Scotland Yard, 'when Jason Phelps was put away for the Docherty murders. Remember him? Clubbed an entire family to death for twenty grand on the instructions of Docherty's nephew. They both got four life sentences. We tried to persuade Phelps to confess to the Landy killing because it was a carbon copy of the Docherty murders, but we never got a result. There was no question he did it, though, and if we could have got him to spill the works, we'd have nailed Kingsley. *He* was the one we wanted.'

'Tell me about the daughter,' prompted Frank. 'What was she like?'

'I rather took to her, as a matter of fact. She was a good kid, deeply shocked, of course, and suffered a nervous break-down afterwards. She kept saying it was all her fault but we never believed she had anything to do with it. Meredith put it to her that she was afraid her father was responsible but she said no. A day or two later she lost her baby.'

'Did she ever suggest who might have done it?'

'An unknown artist whose work Landy had rejected. She said he could be very cruel in what he said and she was insistent that he'd told her a few days before the murder that he was being watched by some creep who'd come to the gallery. She didn't think anything of it at the time, because

126

he treated it as a joke, but it certainly preyed on her mind afterwards. We checked it out, but there was no substance to it and we took the view that, if the watcher existed at all, it was as likely to be Kingsley's contract killer as an embittered artist.'

Cheever pondered for a moment. 'Still, it's something of a minefield. The only contact I've had with Kingsley was years ago when he beat his future brother-in-law to a pulp to warn him off the wedding. Now you're telling me he pulped his son-in-law *afterwards*? Why didn't he do it before?'

'That was his daughter's argument. She claimed Kingsley had done his best to get rid of Landy three years previously by having him sacked from his job, but had long since accepted defeat on the matter. Our view was that the pregnancy changed things. She admitted that she and Landy had been going through a rocky patch but that the baby had brought them together again, and we didn't think it was coincidence that the wretched man was murdered a week after she told her parents she was expecting. We guessed Kingsley was relying on the marriage failing and when he was presented with evidence that it wasn't, he signed Landy's death warrant.'

Cheever tapped one of the pieces of paper in front of him. 'According to the memo you faxed through, you and Meredith believed Kingsley adored his daughter. But we're talking about something much sicker than adoration, surely? I could understand it if Landy had been treating her badly and Kingsley wanted him punished, but from what you've said he acted out of jealous rage. There'd have to be a pretty powerful sexual motive behind actions like that.'

'In a nutshell, that's what we thought it was all about. Look, the man was very highly sexed, he was visiting the Shepherd's Market prostitute every week. The second marriage was a disaster because the poor creature he settled on wasn't a patch on the first wife and took to the bottle within a couple of years. Her sons never matched up to the first wife's daughter who, to make matters worse, is the spitting image of her dead mother. There's no evidence that Kingsley abused the child, but they lived alone together for five years before he married again, and we estimated the chances were high that he did. We had his psychological profile drawn up based on what was known of him, and it was very revealing. There was a heavy emphasis on his need to control through ruthless manipulation of people and events, and it was thought very unlikely that his daughter could have escaped unscathed.'

'Did you suggest it to her?'

'Yes' – a hesitation – 'more's the pity. We gave her the profile to read, and the next thing we knew, she was under the care of a psychiatrist with severe anorexia and suicidal depression. We felt rather bad about it, to be honest.'

'Mind you,' murmured Frank thoughtfully, 'it's a typical reaction of an abused child who's suddenly forced to come to terms with a buried past.'

43a Shoebury Terrace, Hammersmith,
London – 3.30 p.m.

Later that afternoon, Maddocks and Fraser entered Meg Harris's flat in Hammersmith. They were met at the door by two Metropolitan policemen and a locksmith, but dispensed with the services of the latter in favour of the spare key which a stout middle-aged neighbour produced when she saw the congregation through her window and issued forth to quiz them about what they were doing. 'But Meg's in France,' she said, countering their sympathetic assertion that they had reason to believe Miss Harris was dead. 'I saw her off.' She wrung her hands in distress. 'I've been looking after her cat.'

The men nodded gravely. 'Can you remember when she left?' asked Maddocks.

'Oh, lord, now you're asking me. Two weeks ago or thereabouts. The Monday, maybe.'

Fraser consulted his diary. 'Monday, June the thirteenth?' he asked her.

'That sounds about right, but I couldn't say for certain.'

'Have you heard from her since?'

'No,' she admitted, 'but I wouldn't expect to.' She looked put out. 'I can't believe she's dead. Was it a car accident?'

DI Maddocks avoided a direct answer. 'We've very few details at the moment, Mrs – er . . . ?'

'Helms,' said the woman helpfully.

'Mrs Helms. Do you know anything about Miss Harris's boyfriend?'

'You mean Leo. He's hardly a boyfriend, too old to be a boyfriend, Meg said. She always called him her partner.'

'Did he live here?'

'On and off. I think he's married and only comes to Meg when his wife's away.' She caught up with Maddocks's use of the past tense. 'Did?' she asked him. 'Is Leo dead too?'

He nodded. 'I'm afraid so, Mrs Helms. Would you have a contact address or telephone number for Miss Harris's parents, by any chance? We'd very much like to talk to them.'

She shook her head. 'She gave me the vet's number last year in case the cat fell ill, but that's all. As far as I remember her family lives in Wiltshire somewhere. She used to go down there two or three times a year for a long weekend. But how awful!' She looked shocked. 'You mean she's dead and her parents don't even know?'

'I'm sure we'll find something in the flat to help us.' Maddocks thanked her for the key and led the way down the stone steps to the basement flat, which was marked 43a and had terracotta pots, alive with busy Lizzies, cluttered about the doorway. He inserted the key into the lock and pondered the elusive nature of Meg's family. Even Sir Anthony Wallader, who claimed to know something about the Harrises, had no idea which part of Wiltshire they came from or what Meg's father did by way of a job. 'You'll have to ask Jinx Kingsley,' he told them. 'She's the only one left who knows.'

But, in the circumstances, the Hampshire police had preferred the more tortuous route of arriving at Wiltshire via Hammersmith.

A tortoiseshell cat greeted them with undisguised pleasure as they let themselves into the narrow hallway, rubbing its sleek head and ears against their legs, purring ecstatically at the thought of food. Fraser nudged it gently with the toe of his shoe. 'I hate to be the one to tell you, old son, but you're an orphan now. Mummy's dead.'

'Jesus, Fraser,' said Maddocks crossly, 'it's a cat, for Christ's sake.' He opened the door into what was obviously the living room and took stock of the off-white Chinese rug with its embroidered floral pattern of pale blues and pinks which covered the varnished floorboards in front of the fireplace. 'A cat and an off-white rug,' he murmured. 'The boffins will be even more unbearable after this.' He went inside, took a pen from his jacket pocket and manipulated the buttons on the answerphone.

'*Hello darling,*' said a light female voice. '*I presume you're going to phone in for your messages so ring me as soon as you can. I read in the newspaper today that Jinx was in a car accident. I'm very worried about what to do. Should I try and phone her? I'd like to. You were such friends after all, and it seems churlish to ignore her just because . . . well, well, enough said . . . no more rows, we promised . . . Ring me the minute you get this message and we'll talk about it. Goodbye, darling.*'

'*Hi, Meg, where the hell are you?*' A man's belligerent voice. '*You swore on your honour you'd come into the office before you left. Damn it, it's Wednesday, there's a mound of sodding messages here and I can't make head nor tail of them. Who the fuck's Bill Riley? Most of them are from him. Ring me before you ring anyone else. This is urgent.*'

'*Meg.*' The same man's voice. '*Ring me. Immediately. Damn it, I'm so angry I feel like belting you one. Do you realize Jinx has tried to kill herself? I've had your wretched parents on the phone every day asking for news. They feel bloody about this and so do I. Phone, for Christ's sake. It's Friday, seventeenth of June, eight-sodding-thirty, no breakfast and I haven't slept a wink. I knew Wallader would be nothing but trouble.*'

'*It's Simon.*' A different, cooler man's voice. '*Look, Mum and Dad are going spare. You can't just bury your head in the sand and pretend nothing's wrong. I'm sure you know Jinx has*' *tried to kill herself. It's been in all the newspapers. Mum says you're refusing to answer your messages, but at least ring me if you won't ring her. I'm going to visit Jinx, see how she's coping. One of us ought to show some interest.'*

'Darling, it's Mummy again. Please, please ring. I really am awfully concerned about Jinx. They say she tried to commit suicide. I can't bear to think of her being so unhappy because of you and Leo. Someone should talk to her. Don't forget how ill she was after Russell was killed. Please ring. I'm so worried. I do hope you're all right. You're usually so good about phoning.'

'For your information, Bill Riley is now planning to sue us. He claims we're in breach of contract. Why the hell did you agree to work with him if you weren't prepared to see it through? Message timed at nine-thirty p.m., Thursday, June twenty-third. If I don't hear from you in the next twenty-four hours, consider our partnership terminated. I'm pissed off with this, Meg, I really am.'

'Hello, Meg.' A deeper woman's voice. *'It's Jinx. Look, I know this is probably politically incorrect'* – a low laugh – *'I ought to be ripping your first editions to pieces or something – but I really would like to talk to you. Things are a bit complicated this end – well, you've probably heard about it . . .'* A pause. *'They say I drove my car at a concrete post – deliberately. Can you believe that? The bugger is I've lost my memory, can't remember anything since Saturday the fourth, so everyone's jumping to the conclusion that I was upset about you and Leo.'* Another laugh, rather more forced this time. *'It's the pits, old thing, which is why I need to talk to you both. You may not believe me, but I swear to God I am not harbouring grudges, so if you can bear the embarrassment, ring me on*

Salisbury two-two-one-four-two-zero. It's a nutters' hospital and I'm shit-scared of going round the bend here. Please ring.'

The rest of the tape was blank.

Maddocks raised an eyebrow at Fraser. 'Genuine?' he asked. 'Or planted for the police to hear after they found the bodies?'

'You mean hers?' Fraser shrugged. 'I'd guess genuine. The pissed-off partner made his last call two days ago, so hers must have been pretty recent.'

'How does that make it genuine?'

'Because she couldn't know when the bodies would be found. If it was a bluff, she'd have phoned sooner to make sure we got the message.'

Maddocks was more sceptical. 'Unless she's been following the newspapers.' He turned to a bookcase along the wall and plucked a book at random from the shelves. 'The reference to first editions was genuine. Look at this. A signed Graham Greene.' He ran his finger along the spines. 'Daphne du Maurier, Dorothy L. Sayers, Ruth Rendell, Colin Dexter, P.D. James, John le Carré. She's even got an Ian Fleming. I wonder who she's left them to.'

'Probably her friend Jane Kingsley,' said Fraser, opening a door to the right of the fireplace and disclosing a neat white kitchen with slate-grey worktops and pale grey units. He turned to the two London policemen. 'Do you fancy tackling this? Chances are there'll be papers in some of these drawers. I'll take her bedroom.'

He moved across the hallway to a door on the other side, clicked it open and surveyed the room. Like the rest of the flat, it was clean and meticulously tidy – so tidy, in fact, that he decided it was a spare bedroom and went to the only door he hadn't yet opened and found the bath-room. Apart from a pair of fluffy white towels that were folded with measured precision over the rail, there was nothing to indicate that the room had ever been used – no sponge, no soap, no toothpaste. He lifted the latch on the cabinet above the basin and stared thoughtfully at the meagre contents. A bottle of disinfectant, a packet of Disprin and a clean tooth mug. Meg Harris was unreal, he thought. No one was this tidy, not even when they went away on holiday. And where was Leo's presence? Surely something should remain to show a man had lived there on and off. He lifted the lid of the laundry basket, but it was empty.

He retreated into the hall again where he noticed the cat's bed beneath a small radiator and wondered why Meg had bothered to keep a companion when she was clearly so house-proud that its movements had to be thoroughly restricted whenever she was absent. Tidiness appeared to be an obsession with her. Back in the bedroom, he opened the wardrobe and sorted through the few clothes hanging there. Only women's, he noted, no men's. The same was true of all the drawers. He searched for anything that might give a clue to the woman's personality, but it was like searching a hotel bedroom where a guest was staying just one night. Her clothes were neatly folded away, some odds and ends of costume jewellery and make-up lay in ordered rows in her dressing-table drawer, a small bowl of potpourri on the bedside table gave off a faint scent. But if there had ever been anything of a personal nature in that room she had taken it with her.

Maddocks looked up from a book as Fraser rejoined him. 'Last year's diary,' he said, 'but there's not a single phone number or address in it. Any luck your end?'

Fraser shook his head. 'Nothing. Just a few clothes. It looks as if she took everything that mattered to her, which is odd if she was only going away for a couple of weeks. I couldn't find any suitcases.'

Maddocks abandoned the diary and stared about the living room with a frown. 'I don't get it. It's so damn clinical. Have you noticed there aren't any photographs about? I've been looking for an album but I can't find one. You'd think there'd be at least one photograph of her family, wouldn't you?'

'What about papers?' suggested Fraser. 'House insurance, mortgage details, a will? Where are they?'

Maddocks jerked his head towards a pine bureau in the corner. 'In there for what it's worth, but there's no will, just one folder with "house insurance" written across the front. There aren't even any letters, no indication at all who her friends were or what the family address is. It's bizarre. Most people have a few letters littered about the place.' He moved across to the kitchen door. 'What about you two? Have *you* found anything?'

The older man shook his head. 'Tell you what, sir, it reminds me of those cottages you rent in the summer. There's cutlery and crockery here and it's all clean, but there's no food anywhere, the fridge is empty, dishwasher's empty, new plastic bag in the pedal bin. Either she rented it and was about to move out or she was planning to move out and let it to somebody else.' He gestured towards a peg board on the wall. 'Even her notice board's empty but you don't do that when you're off on holiday. I'd say she's got another place somewhere.'

Fraser agreed with him. 'That's got to be it, Guv. It doesn't make sense otherwise. Have you ever seen a flat as devoid of personality as this one is?'

'Why did she leave her first editions behind?'

'Because the insurance policy here probably specifies and covers the collection, which would make this the most sensible place to leave them unattended. What's the betting she moved all her personal stuff before the holiday, left the cat behind because she had a neighbour who would feed it, and was planning to come back for the books, the rest of her clothes and the cat on her return? She was moving in with Leo – it's the only logical scenario.'

'Goddammit,' said Maddocks ferociously, 'everything points to him moving in with *her*. If he had a place of his own, why the hell was he shacked up in Glenavon Gardens with the Kingsley woman? Frank'll go mad over this. It's my guess Jane Kingsley's the only person who knows anything.'

Nightingale Clinic, Salisbury – 3.30 p.m.

Minus her bandage and dressed in black jumper and trousers, Jinx sat on a bench in the shade of a weeping beech tree and studied the comings and goings on the gravel sweep in front of the clinic. She felt herself to be comfortably anonymous behind a pair of mirrored glasses, and for the first time in several days she allowed her tired body to relax.

The memory that she *had* known about Leo and Meg's

affair pierced her brain like a needle. *My God!* Leo himself had told her in the drawing room of his parents' house with Anthony and Philippa there as silent, horrified witnesses. She had screamed at them all – *why had she been screaming?* – and Leo had said: I'm going to marry Meg – *and she had been so, so shocked. Meg and Leo . . . Meg and Russell . . .* But when? When had Leo told her?

She wrestled with the memory, desperate to hold on to it but, like a dream, it started to fragment and fade and, in confusion, she took the bunch of flowers that was being pressed on to her lap and heard Josh Hennessey saying: 'Jinxy, love, are you all right?'

She had forgotten he was coming and stared up at his anxious face, smiling automatically while she knitted back the fabric of her subconscious and let the memory go. 'I'm fine,' she heard herself saying. 'Sorry, I was miles away. How are you?' *But, oh God, she'd been so angry . . . she could remember her anger . . .*

He squatted in front of her, his hands resting lightly on her knees, his eyes examining every inch of her face. 'Pretty bloody depressed if I'm honest. How about you?' He seemed to be looking for a reaction and was disappointed – *surprised?* – when he didn't get it.

She held a thin hand to her chest where her heart was beating frantically. *Something else had happened.* The knowledge weighed on her like a ton weight. *Something else had happened . . . something so terrible that she was too frightened to search her memory for it . . .* 'I'd describe myself as being in a state of suspended animation,' she said, breathing in jerky, shallow breaths. 'I exist, therefore I am, but as I can't think straight it's a fairly meaningless existence.' She thought how unattractive he looked, with fear and worry pinching his nose and mouth. 'I suppose if you're depressed, it means you haven't got hold of Meg.'

He shook his head, and she saw with dismay that there were tears in his eyes.

'I'm sorry.' She fingered the flowers on her lap, then laid them beside her. 'It was kind of you to bring these.'

He lowered himself to the ground and withdrew his hands. 'I feel so awful about this. Couldn't you have phoned, told me you were in trouble? You know I'd have come.'

'You sound like Simon,' she said lightly.

He ruffled his hair and glanced away from her gaunt, bruised face and shaven head. 'Simon's been on the phone almost every day. His parents are devastated, blaming each other, blaming Meg, wanting to do something to make up . . . Well, I'm sure you can imagine how they feel. Simon tried phoning the Hall to find out where you were and got a mouthful of abuse. It's understandable, of course, but it didn't make things any easier.'

'I'm sorry,' she said again, 'but, oddly enough, Josh, it doesn't make it any easier for me either, to have everyone blaming themselves because I drove at a brick wall.'

He flicked her a quick glance but didn't say anything.

'Not that I did it deliberately,' she said through gritted teeth. 'That car cost me a fortune, and I can think of a hundred better ways of killing myself than writing off a perfectly good Rover.'

He plucked at a blade of grass. 'I spoke to Dean last night,' he said uncomfortably. 'The poor chap was in tears, said if I managed to get hold of you, I was to tell you business is fine but please call him the minute you feel up to it.

I gave him the number here, but he's afraid to call himself in case you're too unhappy to talk to him.'

It was hopeless. 'I'm not unhappy,' she said with a forced smile. 'I feel great. I'm looking forward to going home.' *Why was sympathy so unbearable?* 'Look, let's put these flowers in my room and then go for a walk.' *Stupid woman! Fifty yards would see her on her knees.*

'Are you sure you're up to it?' he asked, pushing himself to his feet.

'Oh, yes,' she said briskly. 'I keep telling you, I'm fine.' She set off ahead of him so he wouldn't see her face. 'Believe me, I don't intend to stay here very long. They've already said I'm mentally fit to go home, now all I need to do is prove I'm physically fit.' *Who the hell did she think she was kidding?* 'It's in here,' she said, putting one groggy leg over the sill of the french windows and hauling herself towards a chair.

The flowers slipped from her fingers on to the floor. She felt Josh's arms closing about her and saw murky images floating on the swollen river of her memory.

43 Shoebury Terrace, Hammersmith,
London – 4.00 p.m.

Fraser rang the doorbell of number forty-three and asked Mrs Helms if Meg had given any indication that she intended to vacate her flat after her holiday.

'Not in so many words,' said the stout woman thoughtfully, 'but, now you come to mention it, there was a lot of coming and going shortly before they left. I remember saying to my Henry, it wouldn't surprise me if there was a change in that direction. Then she asked me to feed

Marmaduke and it rather went out of my mind, except that she was insistent the poor creature shouldn't go into any of the rooms. Keep him in the hall, Mrs H, she said, thrusting a tin of cat food at me. What's going to happen to him now? Henry won't have him anywhere near, but then he's not well, you know.'

'We'll do our best to sort something out,' said Fraser, 'but in the meantime perhaps you could go on feeding the cat?'

'I won't let him starve,' she said grudgingly, 'but something ought to be done before too long. That stuffy hallway's no place to keep an animal.'

He agreed with her. 'You wouldn't happen to know what Miss Harris did for a job, would you, Mrs Helms?'

'Seems to me you know very little about her, Sergeant. Are you sure you've got the right person?'

He nodded. 'Her job?' he prompted.

'She called herself a headhunter. Used to be with a big consultancy firm in the City, then set up on her own about five years ago.' She spread her hand and made a rocking gesture with it. 'But it wasn't going too well from what I could gather. People are scared to give notice because of the recession, and you can't hunt heads when there are no vacancies to fill.'

'Any idea what her company is called?'

'No. We talked about Marmaduke and the milkman from time to time but other than that' – she shrugged – 'we were just neighbours. Nothing special. Nothing close. I'm sorry she's gone, though. She never gave us any trouble.'

Fraser found himself dwelling on that last sentence as he walked the few yards to the DI's car. 'She never gave us any trouble' was the most depressing epitaph he had ever heard.

Nightingale Clinic, Salisbury – 4.00 p.m.

'What's the problem?' asked Alan Protheroe, reaching for Jinx's wrist and feeling for a pulse. He wondered who this man was and why he'd started so violently at the sound of the voice behind him.

'Well, look at her for God's sake,' said Josh in desperation, laying her slack head on the pillow and lowering her gently on to the bed. 'I think she's dying.'

'No chance. Built like a tank this one.' He let the wrist go. 'She's asleep.' He looked at the man's pinched nostrils and frightened eyes. 'You look in worse shape than she is.'

'I thought she was dying.' He leaned his hands on the side of the bed to steady himself. 'Now I feel sick. Jesus, I'm not sure I can take much more of this. I haven't slept in days, not since Simon Harris phoned to say Jinx was dead.'

'Why did he do that?'

'Because Betty Kingsley got rat-arsed and phoned Meg's mother. Told the poor woman her daughter was a murderer.'

Alan gestured towards the terraced area beyond the windows. 'Let's go and sit outside. I'm Dr Protheroe.' He took the man's arm and supported him.

'Josh Hennessey.' He allowed Alan to lead him through the windows. 'One minute she said she was fine, the next her eyes rolled up and – wham!' He slumped on to a wooden bench and buried his face in his hands. 'I wish to hell she wouldn't keep pretending she's OK when she's not. She was the same when Russell was murdered. Kept saying: I'm fine, and then ended up in hospital.'

'You've known her a long time?'

He nodded. 'Twelve years. As long as I've known Meg. I'm Meg Harris's partner,' he explained. 'We run a recruitment consultancy.' He bunched his fists angrily. 'Or we did until she buggered off and left me high and dry with a bank manager baying for blood and work in progress with people I've never even heard of.'

Alan could feel the stress flowing off him in waves of anger and nerves. 'I see.'

'Do you? I sure as hell don't. Presumably you know Meg's hijacked Jinx's fiancé? I mean, have you any idea what that's doing to Meg's parents? First they get a phone call out of the blue to say Leo's jilted Jinx for her, then the next thing they hear is that Jinx has killed herself. Jesus! And on top of all that, I'm left in the bloody lurch, trying to run an office on my own, while Meg's farting about in France with a prize bastard.' His voice broke. 'I don't know what the hell's going on.' He rubbed his eyes. 'I'm so fucking tired.'

Alan watched him sympathetically for a moment or two. 'If it makes you feel any better, I think you're worrying unnecessarily on Jinx's account. All things considered, she's doing well.'

'Simon warned me she looked ill, but I wasn't expecting this.' He jerked his head towards her room. 'She's much worse than I thought she was going to be.'

'She probably isn't, you know. Look, she took a heck of a crack on the head and she's forgotten a couple of weeks out of her life, but that's all. She's a tough lady. Give her another week or two and she'll be good as new. It's only a matter of time.'

Josh stared at his hands. 'You've probably never seen her with hair. She's a bit of a stunner. Very Italian looking.' He touched a hand to his shoulder. 'Thick black hair to here, and dark eyes. I've always thought it's crazy her being on the business end of the camera when she should have been in the frame.' He fell silent.

'You sound fond of her.'

'I am, but my timing's lousy. When I was free, she was married. When she was free, I was married.' He looked away towards the trees bordering the lawn. 'Then I got divorced and Leo muscled in on the act. Do you reckon she still loves him?'

'She says she doesn't.'

Josh twisted his head to examine the older man's face. 'Do you believe her?'

'I do, yes.'

'Why?'

Alan shrugged. 'She isn't angry enough with Meg.' But *you* certainly are, he was thinking.

The Vicarage, Littleton Mary, Wiltshire – 4.00 p.m.

Charles Harris laid down his pen and folded his hands across the sermon he was writing. 'This has to stop, Caroline. You're working yourself into hysterics over nothing. Meg will phone when she's ready. And let's face it,' he added rather dryly, '"when Meg is ready" are the operative words. Judging by the frequency of her calls and visits in the past, you and I could go to hell and back without her even being aware of it. She's always been far more interested in whichever man she has in tow than she's ever been in us.'

Caroline looked at him with dislike. 'That's what you hate, isn't it? The men.'

'Don't be absurd,' he snapped. There were times when he had to restrain himself from hitting her. 'Must we go through this again?' he said, picking up his pen and returning to his sermon. 'I do have work to do.' He made a note in the margin.

'It shocked you to hear about her and Russell, didn't it?' she said spitefully.

'Yes, it did.'

'Your little Meggy in the arms of a man old enough to be her father. She loved him, you know.'

He kept his eyes on the page but found he couldn't write anything because his hand was shaking.

'Does it offend you to think of your daughter enjoying sex with old men when she can't even bear to be in the same house with you?'

'No,' he said quietly, 'what offends me is her shabbiness towards her best friend. Between us, you and I created a monster, Caroline.'

Chapter Nine

JINX HAD RESUMED her vantage point under the beech tree, dark glasses firmly in place, anonymity restored. To observers, she was an object of curiosity, this thin, gaunt woman who sat alone and used the protective fronds of the hanging branches to hide behind. Almost, thought Alan Protheroe, watching her from the french window in his office, like a bird in a cage, for it was her loneliness that impressed him most. He wondered if it was advisable or possible to unlock the iron control that she exercised upon her emotions, for he was doubtful that happiness was a condition to which Jinx aspired. She couldn't bear to be so vulnerable.

'I'm relieved,' she said when he'd asked her if she was happy that her bandages had been removed. 'Only children know how to be happy.'

'And were you happy as a child, Jinx?'

'I must have been. The smell of baking bread always puts me in a good mood.' She smiled slightly at his frown of puzzlement. 'My father wasn't always a rich man. I remember being a small child and living in a two-up, two-down in London somewhere. My mother did all her own cooking and baked all her own bread, and I can't smell warm bread now without wanting to turn somersaults.'

'Which mother was that? Your real mother or your stepmother?'

She looked confused suddenly. 'I suppose it was my stepmother. I was too young to remember anything my mother did.'

'Not necessarily. We begin to store emotions at a very young age, so there's no reason why you shouldn't remember happiness from when you were a toddler, particularly if it was followed by a period of unhappiness.'

She looked away. 'Why should it have been?'

'Your mother died, Jinx. That must have been an unhappy time for you and your father.'

She shrugged. 'If it was, I don't remember it. Which is sad in itself. Death should make an impact, don't you think? It's awful how quickly we forget and move on to something new.'

'But very important that we do,' he replied, 'otherwise we become like Miss Havisham in *Great Expectations* and sit for ever at an empty table.'

She smiled. 'If I remember my Dickens, poor old Miss Havisham was jilted by her fiancé on her wedding day and spent the rest of her life in her bridal gown with the remains of the banquet all around her. Hardly the most tactful parallel you could have drawn. In the circumstances, wedding plans are not a subject I particularly want to dwell on.'

'Then let's talk about something you *would* like to dwell on. What makes you feel alive?'

She shook her head. 'Nothing. I prefer the peacefulness

of feeling nothing. For every up there's a down and I hate the sadness of disappointment.'

'Relationships don't have to be disappointing, Jinx. Far more often than not, they represent the sort of fulfilment most of us long for. Do you not think that's a goal worth pursuing?'

'Are we talking marriage and children, Dr Protheroe?' she asked suspiciously. 'Did Josh Hennessey tell you he fancied me?'

He chuckled. 'Not in so many words, but he seems fond of you.'

'He's far fonder of Meg than he is of me,' she said dismissively. 'Too fond, really. She treats him like a brother because business and pleasure don't mix, when all *he* wants to do is fuck her. Also, he was fond of his wife when he married her,' she added tartly, 'but he walked out on her four years later because he claimed she was boring. Is that the kind of fulfilling relationship you want me to have?'

'I doubt he'd find you boring, Jinx, but in any case, that's a side issue. What I think we're talking about is contentment.'

She gave a low laugh. 'Well, I'm a good photographer, and that makes me content. If I'm remembered for just one photograph, then that will be immortality enough. I don't need any other. It's a birth of sorts, you know. Your creation emerges from the darkness of the developing room with a similar sense of achievement as a baby emerging from the womb.'

'Does it?'

She shrugged again. 'I think so. Admittedly the only birth I can compare it with was a rather messy business in the lavatory, but I imagine going to term and producing a living child is somewhat more rewarding. Yes, I'd say the sense of achievement in those circumstances is not dissimilar.' Her face was devoid of expression. 'By the same token, I imagine there's the same sense of disappointment when the result of your hard work is less than you'd hoped for. Works of art, be they children or photographs, can never be perfect.' She hesitated a moment. 'I suppose if you're lucky, they might be interesting.'

After that she had excused herself politely and walked outside, leaving Protheroe to wonder if she was talking about her own hopes of the child she had lost or her father's hopes of her. Although perhaps she was talking about neither. He reflected on the two unmarried brothers who still lived at home and who, if Jinx's closed expression when their names were mentioned was any guide, had little love for their intellectually gifted sister.

He was about to turn away from the office window and his contemplation of her seated, solitary figure when he noticed a man approaching across the lawn. *Now where the hell had he come from?* For no obvious reason, other than that he was responsible for Jinx's safety and she was clearly unaware that anyone was behind her, he felt a sense of imminent danger and, with a flick of his long fingers, turned the key in the lock and thrust the door wide. With farther to travel than the other, he raised his voice in a bluff bellow. 'There you are, Jinx!' he called. 'I've been looking for you.'

Startled, she turned her head, saw her younger brother first, then looked beyond him to Protheroe. 'God, you gave me a shock,' she said accusingly as they both drew close. 'Hello, Fergus.' She nodded a welcome. 'Have you two met?

Fergus Kingsley, my brother – Dr Alan Protheroe, my existentialist shrink. You're a very bad liar,' she told Alan. 'You've been watching me for the last ten minutes, so why the sudden panic?'

He shook Fergus by the hand. 'Because I take my responsibilities seriously, Jinx, and for all I knew your brother was a stranger to you.' He folded his arms across his chest. 'As a matter of interest,' he said without hostility, 'which way did you come in? It's a rule of the Nightingale Clinic that visitors seek permission at the front desk before approaching our guests. It's a simple courtesy but an important one, as I'm sure you'll agree.'

Fergus reddened under the older man's stare. 'I'm sorry.' He looked very young. 'I didn't realize.' He gestured behind him to the other side of the lawn. 'I parked by the gate at the bottom and walked up.' He looked sullenly towards Jinx. 'Actually, I was going to do the thing properly, then I saw you under the tree.'

Jinx removed her dark glasses and squinted up at Protheroe with one blackened eye closed against the evening sunlight. 'I don't recall my consent being sought before. It's a perverse rule that operates at the whim of the director.'

He smiled affably. 'But a rule, nevertheless. I shall have to make sure it's properly enforced in future.' He nodded to them both. 'Enjoy your visit. If you want some tea, your brother can order it from the desk and have it sent out.' He raised a hand in farewell, then walked briskly back to his office.

Jinx stared after him. 'I think he's madder than some of his patients,' she said.

Fergus followed her gaze. 'He fancies you,' he said bluntly.

She gave a splutter of laughter. 'Don't be an oaf! The man's not blind, and they do let me look in a mirror from time to time.' She sobered suddenly and her eyes narrowed. 'Actually, I hate the way he's always watching me. It makes me feel like a prisoner.'

'Do you like him?'

'Yes.'

'Is he married?'

'He's a widower.' She frowned. 'Why so interested?'

He shrugged. 'You know what they say about psychiatrists and their patients. I was just wondering if he was going to be the next one in the Kingsley marriage stakes.'

'Do me a favour, Fergus,' she said crossly. 'I don't intend to stay here long enough to develop anything more than a passing acquaintanceship with the man.'

He leaned against the tree trunk. 'So you're planning to come home?'

'*Go* home,' she corrected him. 'Back to Richmond and back to the studio. Sitting around and doing nothing isn't what I'm best at.'

'Is that supposed to be a dig at me?'

'No,' she said mildly. 'Oddly enough, Fergus, I am more interested in my own problems at the moment than I am in yours.' She studied his sullen face, which was so like Miles's to look at, but which lacked the charm that his older brother could switch on and off at will. 'Did you have a reason for coming?'

He scuffed the grass with his foot. 'I wondered how you were, that's all. Miles said you weren't too hot when he came, said you passed out when he was talking to you.'

'It's just tiredness.' She replaced her dark glasses so that he couldn't read the expression in her eyes. 'Miles told me Adam made you cry. Is that true?'

He reddened again. 'Miles is a bastard. He swore he wouldn't tell anyone. You know, sometimes I don't know who I hate more, him or Dad. They're such shits both of them. I wish they'd drop dead. Everything would be OK if they were both dead.'

It was the same childish whine she'd heard from him since he was five years old. Only the register of his voice was different. 'Presumably he belted you again. So what did you do to make Adam angry?'

'It wasn't me who made him angry. It's you being in this place.' He slid his back down the tree trunk to squat at the foot of it. 'He just went overboard and started screaming and yelling at everyone. Miles cowered in the corner, as per bloody usual, and Mum sat and blubbered. Well, you know what it's like. You don't need me to tell you.'

'But you must have done something,' she said. 'He might be angry about me and' – she gestured towards the building – 'all this, but he's never belted you without good reason. So what did you do?'

'I borrowed twenty pounds,' he muttered. 'You'd think it was a hanging offence the way he carried on.'

She sighed. 'Who from this time?'

'Does it matter?' he said angrily. 'You're as bad as bloody Dad. I was going to pay it back.' His mouth thinned unattractively. 'What nobody ever seems to recognize is that I wouldn't have to borrow money if Dad treated me like a human being instead of a slave. It's really degrading having to admit you're the son of Adam Kingsley when everyone knows you're earning peanuts. I keep telling him, if he'd only pay me a decent whack, I wouldn't have to resort to borrowing. I'm the boss's son. That should stand for something. Why do Miles and I have to start at the bottom?'

'You know,' she said with sudden impatience, 'if you called a spade a spade occasionally, you'd be halfway to earning Adam's respect. It's the lies that you and Miles tell that really fire him up. Can't you see that? You're a thief' – she fixed him with a scornful stare – 'and everybody knows it, so why bother with this garbage about borrowing? Who did you steal from this time?'

'Jenkins,' he muttered. 'But I was going to pay him back.'

'Then I'm not surprised Adam belted you,' she said tiredly. 'I wouldn't enjoy having to apologize to my gardener after my twenty-four-year-old son had stolen money from him. I suppose you thought Jenkins wouldn't have the nerve to say anything and that you'd get away with it. That's almost worse than stealing from him in the first place.'

'Oh, leave it out, Jinxy. I've had all this from Dad, and you're both wrong, anyway. I really was going to pay him back. If he'd had a word with me, I'd have sorted it out, but, oh no, he had to go running to the old man and make a bloody mountain out of a molehill.'

Something fundamental snapped inside Jinx's head. She would always think of it afterwards as the blood bond that had tied her physically to a family that in any other circumstance she would have avoided like the plague. Suddenly, she found herself free to acknowledge that she didn't like them. More, she had only contempt for them. Ultimately, in fact, she agreed with what everyone knew Adam thought but had never put into words: Miles and Fergus were their mother's sons and, like Betty, saw Adam Kingsley only in terms of their meal ticket.

She smiled savagely. 'I'm going to tell you things that I've never told a soul in my life. First, I despise your mother. I always have done from the minute she came into our house. She's a fat drunk with an extraordinarily low IQ. Second, she married my father because she wanted to be a lady, and she had enough cunning to persuade him that, while she could never fill my mother's shoes, she could at least be a comfortable slipper for him at the end of a long day. He was lonely and he fell for it, but what he actually saddled himself with was a vulgar, money-grabbing tart.' She held up three fingers. 'Third, it might not have been so bad if she hadn't lumbered him with you and Miles. Even your names are an embarrassment. Adam wanted to call you something straightforward, like David or Michael, but Elizabeth wanted something befitting the sons of a rich lady.'

Her voice took on the accent of her stepmother. 'It has to be something posh, Daddy, and David and Michael are so common.' She drew an angry breath. 'Fourth, Adam finds himself father to two of the laziest, most unintelligent, most dishonest sons a man could have. Every gene you have has come to you straight from your mother. You are incapable, both of you, of contributing anything worthwhile to your family. Instead, you are only interested in bringing Adam and me down to your own shabby levels. Fifth, how the hell can you begin to justify stealing off a gardener who works day in day out to fund his very modest house and his very modest car while you, you little bastard' – she spat at him – 'swan around in your swank Porsche so that you can pick up any little tart who's stupid enough to think the Kingsley name means something? Will you explain that to me? *Can* you explain it to me?'

He stared at her. It was a shock to see his father mirrored in the set of her chin and the fury in her voice, but he had spent years playing on her conscience and, like Miles, he was a master at it. 'We've always known you were a snobbish bitch, Jinx,' he said idly. 'What the hell do you suppose it was like for Mum moving into a house with the perfect child already in residence and pictures of her perfect mother all over the walls? She says you were so condescending she wanted to slap you. I wish she had, as a matter of fact. If you'd been treated the way Dad's treated us, then maybe things would have been better for us all.'

'He didn't treat you any differently at the beginning from the way he treated me,' she said coldly. 'I can remember the first time he belted you because it was the first time you and Miles were reported for stealing. You were nine years old and Miles was eleven, and you stole money from the till in the village shop. Adam paid over a hundred pounds to Mrs Davies to hush the whole thing up, then took a strap to the pair of you to remind you what would happen if you ever did it again.' She shook her head. 'But it didn't work. You just went on doing it and he went on beating you, and it was me who had to try and calm him down because Betty was always drunk. Do you think I enjoyed any of that?'

He shrugged. 'I couldn't care less whether you did or not, and anyway you're exaggerating. Most of the time you were either at school or bloody Oxford, playing the family genius while Miles and I were being treated like Neanderthals. You should put yourself in our shoes once in a while. You know damn well he's always hated us. We only took that money from the shop because we thought he might notice us instead of mooning over his precious Jane.' His mouth took on a sullen cast. 'You don't know what it was like. When you were home for the holidays he was only interested in you and what you were doing, and when you were away he used to shut himself in his office with those bloody photographs of your mother.'

She saw that for what it was, the manipulative emotional blackmail of a selfish, twisted mind, but the habits of a lifetime die very hard and, as usual, she foundered on the hard certainty of Adam's obsession with her mother and herself. 'But why will you never help yourselves?' she asked him. 'Why do you go on doing what you know he hates? Why do you stay there and give him the opportunity to despise you? I just don't understand that.'

'Because it's my home as much as his and I don't see why he should push me out,' he said. 'It's all right for you. You got Russell's money. You were lucky.'

She experienced the strange sensation of a door slamming shut on a memory. For the briefest second, she had a glimpse of something remembered but it was as transient as a puff of wind on a summer's day and the memory was lost. *Had they had this conversation before?* 'You have some very warped ideas, Fergus. How can you regard anything to do with Russell's murder as lucky?' *Why did Russell keep intruding into every conversation? She had banned him from her thoughts for so long, but now she was being forced into thinking about him all the time.*

'Leave it out, Jinx. You weren't that fond of him and you

ended up with all the loot.' But it was said without conviction, because he, like she, had lost the energy to continue an argument that was going nowhere. Where trust had been sacrificed, knowledge was all, and it mattered very little whether thoughts were spoken or unspoken when everyone knew where they stood. *Except . . .* 'You're wrong to slag off poor old Mum,' he said with a half-hearted show of belligerence. 'She's gone out and batted for you, which is more than Dad's done since you've been in here. She's given the Walladers and the Harrises a pasting for the way Leo and Meg have treated you. She called Sir Anthony "a boil on the bum of society" and Caroline Harris "a tight-arsed bitch".'

Jinx lowered her head abruptly so that he wouldn't see the laughter in her eyes.

'OK, she was drunk,' said Fergus sulkily, 'but she meant well. Actually, Miles and me thought it was quite funny.'

So did Jinx . . . She had called Anthony a 'parasite' but how much more astute was Betty's judgement . . .

Romsey Road Police Station, Winchester – 7.30 p.m.

'You're going to have to let me talk to Miss Kingsley,' said Gareth Maddocks, dropping wearily into a chair. 'Seriously, sir, bar sitting by Miss Harris's phone and waiting for the damn thing to ring, I can't see how we're going to find out where her parents live.'

'Did you try Sir Anthony again?'

Maddocks nodded. 'He just keeps bleating Wiltshire at us. All this guff he gave you about what a relief it was when Leo took up with a nice girl like Meg amounts to sweet FA.

The only thing she had going for her, as far as I can make out, was that she wasn't Jane Kingsley. The impression I get is that if Leo had turned up with some old slag from the local pub and announced his intention of marrying *her*, the Walladers would have jumped for joy.'

'Can't say I blame them,' said the Superintendent dryly. 'I wouldn't want Adam Kingsley for an in-law either.'

'Well, for what it's worth, his daughter sounds fairly reasonable. She left a message on the answerphone. Nice voice, sense of humour, says she doesn't bear any grudges and wanted Meg to phone her.'

Frank raised an eyebrow. 'Have you got it with you?'

The DI reached into his pocket and took out a tape-cassette. 'We made copies at the Hammersmith nick, then took the original back to the flat.' He put it on the desk in front of him. 'Hers is the last message. I've listened to it several times now and I'm inclined to agree with Fraser that she has no idea Leo and Meg are dead.'

Cheever fingered the cassette for a moment, then picked it up, swivelled in his chair and pushed it into a tape-deck on the shelf behind him. He sat with bowed head, listening to the recorded messages, only stirring when Jinx's ended. He pressed *Rewind*, listened to hers again, then rubbed his jaw thoughtfully as he pressed *Stop*. 'She says she can't remember anything since June the fourth,' he pointed out.

'Which tallies with the Fordingbridge report,' said Maddocks. 'According to that, the concussion after the accident left her with amnesia.'

'Agreed, but it doesn't mean she didn't know about the deaths. Do you follow what I'm saying? She could have wiped the knowledge from her memory.' He tapped a finger on the desk. 'I think it would be extremely foolish to assume anything on the basis of this one recording.'

'I'm not arguing with you, sir, but it strikes me this is our best opportunity to question her without raising anyone's hackles, least of all her father's.' He leaned forward. 'Look, we are simply trying to trace the whereabouts of Miss Harris. Her credit cards have come into the possession of the police after the arrest of a thief, but repeated attempts to contact her at her address in London have failed to produce a response. Hammersmith police, concerned for her welfare, have entered the flat in order to trace her family and friends, only to discover that the flat has been cleared out. The one lead they came up with is Miss Kingsley because she was the only caller who left her telephone number. We have been asked by Hammersmith to interview Miss Kingsley with a view to tracing Miss Harris.' He spread his hands. 'Are you going to give me a shot at her on that basis? It's a legitimate approach.'

The Superintendent steepled his fingers on the desk in front of him and stared the other man down. 'You do realize I'll have your hide if you make a mess of it.'

Maddocks grinned. 'Trust me, sir.'

His eyes narrowed. 'I hate people who say that. Just make sure you get the consent of her doctor before you talk to her. In fact, you can go further, and ask him to be present while you put your questions. I do not want this force accused of bullying a sick young woman.'

'Do me a favour, sir,' said Maddocks plaintively, 'I wouldn't know how to begin. I like women.'

Frank's eyebrows beetled into a ferocious frown. It was

common knowledge that Maddocks had been the subject of sexual harassment complaints by three different female officers, although, predictably, nothing had come of them. 'You've been warned,' was all he said.

Canning Road Police Station, Salisbury – 8.00 p.m.

WPC Blake stuffed a photocopy under the nose of the sergeant, as she came in at the end of her shift, and shook it vigorously. 'Read that, Sarge. It's a dead ringer for Flossie Hale's experience. Same MO, same refusal to talk, same injuries.'

He took it in both hands and placed it squarely on his desk. 'It may come as a surprise to you, Blake, but I have A-one vision. As yet, I do not require documents to be held half an inch from my eyes in order to read them.' He then scanned the page.

Incident report
Officers attending: PC Hughes and PC Anderson.
23.3.94. Disturbance reported 23.10 at 54 Paradise Avenue.
Woman banging on neighbour's door and causing a nuisance.
On investigation, woman found to be in need of urgent medical treatment. Severe bruising to the face and lacerations of the rectum.
Name: Samantha Garrison. Known local prostitute.
Claimed assailant was her husband but believed to be lying.
Refused to co-operate further.

'Have you followed this up with Hughes and Anderson?' he asked.

'Not yet.'

'Talk to them tomorrow.' He spread a broad palm across the sheet. 'Then have a word with Samantha, assuming you can find her, and keep me posted. Good girl. I think you could be on to something. Let's see you nail this bastard.'

Blake flushed a rosy-red. At twenty-one, she was still untouched by cynicism, so other people's approbation mattered.

Nightingale Clinic, Salisbury – 11.30 p.m.

Time had no relevance. An hour spent reading a book passed in a minute. A minute of agony lasted an hour. Only fear was eternal for fear fed itself. *Whose fear? Yours? Theirs? Ours? Mine? His? Hers? Everyone's.*

Even the dark was fearful.

Confusion . . . confusion . . . confusion . . .

Forget . . . forget . . . forget . . .

A moment of clarity.

Why am I here? What am I doing?

MEG WAS A WHORE! booms the great voice of reason. *My father made me evil.*

Chapter Ten

Sunday, 26 June, Wiltshire – 2.10 p.m.

FOR VARIOUS REASONS, DS Sean Fraser was none too happy about accompanying Maddocks to the interview with Jane Kingsley, and he sat in gloomy silence in the passenger seat as the car headed for Salisbury. He had made himself a hostage to fortune by rashly promising his wife and two young daughters that he would take them to the beach at Studland that Sunday, and their tears and recriminations at the cancelled treat lay heavily on his conscience. His gloom was exacerbated by Maddocks's disgusting cheerfulness at the thought of a possible collar which he chose to express through a tuneless and repetitive rendering of 'The sun has got his hat on, Hip-hip-hip-Hooray . . .'

'Give over, Guv,' he said at last. 'It's worse than having a tooth extracted.'

'You're a miserable creature, Fraser. What's eating you, anyway?'

'It's a Sunday, Guv, so it's going to be a waste of time. You realize her entire family will probably be there visiting her, which means we won't get a look in, not unless we want Kingsley on our backs as well.'

'Nn-nn.' Maddocks gave a self-satisfied grunt. 'I sent

Mandy Barry over to chat up the nurses this morning and find out who's been visiting Jane and when. According to her, Kingsley hasn't been near his daughter since she was admitted, the stepmother's been in once and doesn't look like showing again, and the two brothers came independently and left in sulks. The word is there's no love lost between any of them, so the chances of them giving up their Sunday for her are nonexistent.'

'You're round the flaming bend,' said Fraser angrily, seeing himself cast as co-conspirator in Maddocks's unorthodox methods. 'By the book, the Super said. He'll flip if he finds out you've had Mandy sneaking around behind people's backs.'

'Who's going to tell him?' said Maddocks carelessly. 'I'd be even more round the bend if I went in cold.' He swung the car on to the main road and accelerated up the hill. 'Look, lad, you've got to find some backbone from somewhere. You'll never get anywhere in this business if you can't act on your own initiative occasionally.' He broke into his tuneless dirge again.

Fraser turned away to gaze out of the passenger window. What really riled him about Maddocks was that the bastard was more often right than he was wrong. Initiative in Maddocks's vocabulary meant taking short-cuts and using methods that wouldn't stand scrutiny for a minute under the Police and Criminal Evidence Act, but he got away with it because, in his own terminology, 'he could smell guilt'. Privately, Fraser put this down to the fact that the Inspector was as ethically bankrupt as the people he arrested – he had heard more than one whisper that Maddocks had taken bribes in the past – but this raised troubling questions about the effectiveness of policemen and, as Fraser was a thoughtful man, the whole issue worried him. For there was an intrinsic absurdity about forcing the police to follow every rule, when criminal behaviour, which was dedicated to rule-breaking, remained unchanged.

Nightingale Clinic, Salisbury – 2.30 p.m.

Alan Protheroe listened to what the two detectives had to say with a frown creasing his amiable face. 'Presumably there's more to this than meets the eye,' he suggested. 'If the Hammersmith police only wanted the address of Miss Harris's parents, why didn't they telephone Miss Kingsley and ask her for it?'

'Because, in the message she left on Harris's answerphone, she refers to this clinic as a nutters' hospital,' said Maddocks easily, 'and, as I'm sure you know, there are rules governing the police in the way they question the mentally disturbed. So, before they approached her direct, Hammersmith asked us to find out why she was here, and we discovered very quickly from our colleagues in Fordingbridge that she had been admitted following a suicide attempt after her fiancé deserted her for Miss Harris. We have no desire to upset her unnecessarily, so it was felt that any questions should be asked by plainclothes policemen.'

Alan took exception to his references to 'nutters' and 'the mentally disturbed'. More, he took exception to Maddocks himself, disliking the man's over-powering personality which thrust into the room like a bad smell. 'Why didn't you ring *me*?' he said suspiciously. 'I would have been happy to ask the questions for you.'

Maddocks spread his hands in a gesture of surrender. 'All right, I'll be honest with you, sir. The problem is not Miss Kingsley but Miss Kingsley's father. The orders from above are very clear. Do not give Adam Kingsley any excuse to sue the Hampshire police for alleged insensitivity towards his sick daughter. We haven't a clue what her reaction will be to questions about the woman who seduced her fiancé. For all we know, the mere mention of Meg Harris's name will have her climbing the walls, and we have enough difficulty paying our policemen without squandering the budget on court battles with a tetchy millionaire who's already worried about his daughter's state of mind.' He turned his hands palms down. 'And with good reason, it would seem. By her own admission, she's in a nutter's hospital and she's shit-scared she's going round the bend. Her words, sir, not mine.'

Fraser had to admire Maddocks's psychology. Whatever Protheroe's suspicions about their motives for being there, he was side-tracked into defending his clinic and his patient. 'I would prefer it, Inspector, if you ceased referring to the Nightingale Clinic as a nutters' hospital,' he said tartly. 'Jinx has a healthy cynicism about everything, coupled with a dry sense of humour. She was clearly joking. I have no concerns at all about her mental equilibrium. Nor, I am sure, has she. She has limited loss of memory following her accident, but is otherwise mentally acute.'

'Well, that's a relief,' said Maddocks. 'It'll be all right for us to talk to her then?'

'Assuming she agrees, then, yes, I see no reason why not.' He stood up and led the way to the door, noticing with interest that Sergeant Fraser appeared to find Detective

Inspector Maddocks as uncongenial as he did. The body language spoke volumes, principally in the younger man's attempts to keep daylight between himself and his superior. He took them down the corridor. 'I think it would be better if I remained during the interview,' he said, tapping on the door of number twelve.

'I see no reason why not, sir, assuming Miss Kingsley agrees,' said Maddocks with derisory emphasis.

Jinx, in her turn, listened to the Inspector's explanation for being there. She sat in the chair by the window and, bar wishing the two policemen 'good afternoon' when they came in, said nothing until Maddocks had finished. Even then she didn't answer immediately, but eyed him in silence for a moment or two with curiously little expression on her pale face. 'Meg's parents live in a village near Warminster called Littleton Mary,' she said finally. 'Her father's the vicar there. I'm afraid I can't give you the telephone number because it's in my address book and I don't have that with me, but I should imagine it's in the book. Her father's initial is C for Charles and he and Meg's mother live in the vicarage.'

She reached towards the cigarette packet on the table, then changed her mind and left it where it was. She found herself reluctant suddenly to draw attention to the tremors in her hands, and doubted her ability to hold the flame steady long enough to light a cigarette. 'But Meg won't be there,' she continued in her deep voice. 'She's on holiday in France at the moment.'

'Well, that would explain why we've had difficulty contacting her,' said Maddocks, as if hearing this information for the first time. He glanced towards Alan Protheroe. 'In fact, Doctor, I really don't think we need keep you, not unless Miss Kingsley feels nervous at being left on her own.' He smiled down at her. 'Do you, Miss Kingsley?'

She shrugged indifferently. 'Not in the least.'

'Then thank you very much, sir. We won't be long.' Maddocks stood by the open door.

Alan frowned at him angrily, well aware that he was being rail-roaded. 'I'd rather stay, Jinx,' he said. 'I'm sure your father would expect me to.'

She gave her low laugh. 'I'm sure you're right, but as you keep trying to persuade me, Dr Protheroe, I call the shots, not my father. Thank you anyway. I think I can manage a few questions on my own.'

'Well, you know where I am if you need me.' He allowed himself to be closed out by Maddocks's firm hand on the door, but he wished he knew what the hell was going on. It was obvious that Jinx was as reluctant as the policemen to let him listen in on the conversation.

Inside the room, Maddocks beamed encouragingly at Jinx. 'Any idea which part of France, Miss Kingsley?'

She shook her head. 'No, but I can probably guess. I know the man she's gone with. His name's Leo Wallader and he has a cottage on the south coast of Brittany. The address is Les Hirondelles, rue St Jacques, Trinité-sur-mer. There is a telephone, but again' – she gave a small shrug – 'the number's in my address book.'

Maddocks nodded. 'But if you know she's in France,' he said with a puzzled frown, 'why did you telephone her London number?'

Jinx looked at him for a moment, then picked up her

cigarette packet and tapped a cigarette into her fingers. Nicotine was more important than pride. She reached for the lighter but Fraser was there before her, holding the flame steady beneath the wavering tip. She thanked him with a smile. 'Meg can ring her answerphone and listen to her messages,' she said. 'I assumed that's what she'd do.'

'Who told you she was in France?'

'Her partner, Josh Hennessey.' She gazed at him through the smoke. 'He phoned me on Wednesday.'

Maddocks glanced towards Fraser to see if he'd written that down. 'And has Meg called you back, Miss Kingsley?'

'Not yet, no.'

'Is this Mr Hennessey in contact with her?'

'Not as far as I know. She didn't give him a contact number.'

He made a play of consulting his notebook. 'In fact we know about Mr Leo Wallader. He came up in connection with your car accident. I believe he was your fiancé until a couple of weeks ago?'

She blew a stream of smoke into the air and watched it ripple towards the ceiling. 'That's right,' she said evenly.

'But he preferred your friend Meg Harris and left you for her.'

She smiled slightly. 'Right again, Inspector.'

'So perhaps Miss Harris is embarrassed to phone you,' he suggested, 'despite your insistence in your message that you don't bear grudges.'

She tapped ash into the ashtray. 'To tell you the truth,' she said slowly, 'I can't really remember what I said.' She looked at him with an enquiring expression in her dark eyes.

'You talked about political incorrectness, said you ought to be ripping her first editions to pieces, told her you'd lost your memory after driving at a concrete post and asked her to phone you here if she could stand the embarrassment of talking to you. Does that ring any bells?'

'Only alarm ones,' she murmured. 'You were very precise in your introductory spiel. You said that Hammersmith police had listened to her messages, taken down this phone number and then asked you to contact me here for her parents' address. You made no mention of listening to the tape yourself.' She pressed the palm of her hand against the side of her head where a pain was beginning. 'So either you were there when they listened, or they made a copy which they sent on to you.'

'They faxed us a transcript,' said Maddocks. 'Why does that alarm you?'

'May I see the fax?'

He glanced at Fraser again. 'Did we bring it with us, Sergeant? The last time I saw it, it was on your desk.'

The young man shook his head. 'Sorry, Guv. I didn't think we'd need it.' He turned to prop his notebook against the wall, hoping that his anger and unease were less obvious than they felt.

Jinx watched him for a moment. He was a poor liar, she thought, but then his complexion was against him. He was fair, like Fergus, and the blood ran too easily to his face. She felt a twinge of sympathy for him. He had a bully for a boss and she knew better than anyone that it took a peculiar kind of courage to stand up to bullies. 'As a matter of interest,' she said calmly, 'why didn't you phone Meg's business number and ask Josh these questions?'

'Because Hammersmith have been unable to locate it,' said Maddocks. 'As I explained at the beginning, she appears to be in the process of moving out. According to them, there's nothing left except a few first editions, some clothes and the cat.'

She turned to Fraser. 'So who's looking after Marmaduke?'

'The neighbour, Mrs Helms,' he answered obligingly.

There was a long silence.

'What exactly has happened to Meg?' asked Jinx quietly. 'I can't believe that Winchester CID would go all the way to London to search someone's flat just because her credit cards have been stolen.'

Maddocks, controlling an urge to show Fraser what a pillock he thought him, perched instead on the edge of Jinx's bed and leaned forward, hands clamped between his knees. 'It wasn't only hers that were stolen,' he admitted gravely, 'but Mr Wallader's as well. The registered address for his cards is 12 Glenavon Gardens, Richmond, which was already in the Hampshire police file as a result of your accident. Richmond police were able to give us the address and telephone number of Leo's parents because they retrieved that information from your house following the crash. However, when we contacted Sir Anthony to discover where Leo and Meg have gone he couldn't tell us anything. And that worried us, because we couldn't understand why neither of them had notified the credit companies that their cards had been stolen. If they're in a cottage in Brittany, then perhaps that explains it, but I don't understand why Sir Anthony couldn't give us the address.'

She drew away from him into the back of her chair and

tried to control the panic in her heart. *Something else had happened . . . something so terrible that she was too frightened to search her memory for it . . .* 'He doesn't know it,' she said in an uneven voice which came back to her through the thudding, racing blood in her ears. 'He knows very little about his son. Philippa, too.'

Maddocks's heavy face drew closer, his shrewd little eyes fixed on hers. 'Are you all right, Miss Kingsley?'

'Yes, thank you.' *Something else had happened . . . forget . . . forget . . . FORGET!* 'As far as they're concerned,' she went on more steadily, 'his only capital assets are a few stocks and shares, when in fact he has the cottage in Brittany, a house in London, which he rents out to anyone who can afford it, and a condominium in Florida. There could be a great deal more, for all I know. Those are the three he told me about.'

'Do you know the address of the London house?'

They'd had a row . . . Anthony and Philippa had been there . . . I want to marry Meg . . . Meg's a whore . . . She flicked her gaze back to Maddocks's face. 'Only that it's in Chelsea somewhere,' she said, licking her lips nervously. 'His solicitor could tell you. His name's Maurice Bloom and he has an office somewhere off Fleet Street. I'm sure you can find him through the Law Society.'

Maddocks checked to see that Fraser had taken down the name. 'Is there a good reason why he doesn't want his parents to know about his properties?' he asked her.

She thought about that. 'It depends on your definition of good. Yes, he has a reason and, personally, I think it stinks, but it makes sense to Leo.' She paused. 'I can't really tell you what it is without sounding bitter.'

'I think we need to know,' said the Inspector.

Did they? She was finding it hard to concentrate. *I said goodbye to Leo at breakfast . . . we're getting married on the second of July . . .* 'They're a type, not Philippa so much perhaps, but Anthony and Leo certainly.' Her voice sounded strangely remote again. 'You never pay for anything if you can get someone else to pay for you, you use other people's expertise to help you up the ladder, and you plead poverty all the time while making snide remarks about how wealthy everyone else is. It becomes very wearing very quickly for the person who's being bled, particularly when you know that the parasite you're supporting is rolling in it.' *Was she mad? These were the last people who should be hearing her confession. Talk to the doctor . . . he wants your stay here to be comfortable . . . it's a free choice . . .*

Maddocks watched her eyes grow huge in a face made tiny by her lack of hair. He felt the pull of their attraction even while he was thinking: Got you, you murdering bitch. You really hated the poor bastard. 'And Leo did this to you?' he asked gently.

'Not immediately. He wasn't so crass. Actually, he was quite generous at the beginning. It was only when he moved into Glenavon Gardens that I realized what I'd saddled myself with.' She took deep breaths.

'There's no hurry, Miss Kingsley. Take your time.'

Memories of Russell's murder flooded her mind. *Take your time . . . there's no hurry . . . we know your father hated him enough to kill him . . . we know your father's a psychopath . . .* 'He's a believer in the what's-yours-is-mine principle,' she said in a rush to drown out the voices in her head, 'but without the reciprocity. He was just as secretive with me as he was with his parents. I only found out about his

171

properties when Maurice Bloom phoned him at my house one day, and it was clear from his end of the conversation that he owned something in Florida. I was angry enough to make him tell me about it, because he had given me the impression he was in financial difficulties.' *So much so that, like Fergus, he had borrowed money from her handbag. God, she remembered now. It was the meanness that had finally got to her, the tax dodges, the obsessive secrecy surrounding his bank and credit card statements, the me-me-me of his lifestyle.*

'What sort of job did he have?'

She noted the past tense but let it pass. 'He called himself a stock broker but, as he never mentioned clients by name, I guessed he was playing the markets for himself.'

'Did he go out to work each day?'

He certainly went somewhere each day. 'He spends his time in the City.' *I want to marry Meg . . .* 'Keeping his finger on the pulse, as he calls it.'

'What sort of financial difficulties did he say he was in?'

'He said he'd lost everything on some bad investments but I think he was lying. He was always complaining about how badly off he was compared with me. He used to do the same with his father.'

'Yet you said his father's the same.'

She had let rip the day she decided to end it, told them all what she thought of them, called them over-privileged leeches whose only claim to respectability was that one of their ancestors had had the brains and the balls to earn a title. 'Anthony's certainly very mean. He never pays bills until the final demand arrives in the hopes the business may have gone under before he has to write the cheque.'

'If I understood you right, Miss Kingsley, you're saying Leo touches his father for money.'

She nodded but didn't say anything. *God, but they'd hated her for it. And triumphant Leo had told her he'd been having an affair with Meg, and that she was the one he wanted to marry. And the shock had been* ENORMOUS! *She remembered it all. Anthony's loathing . . . 'You're the daughter of a barrow boy . . . we never wanted you in this family . . .' Philippa's distress. 'Do stop . . . do stop . . . words can't be taken back . . .' Leo's sulk . . . 'I want to marry Meg . . . I want to marry Meg . . .'*

'Which is why he's never told him about these properties he owns?' Maddocks suggested. 'He doesn't want his father to know what he's actually worth.'

She nodded again. 'He was – *is*,' she corrected herself, 'obsessive about money. They both are.' She called her thoughts back from the past. 'One thing I can absolutely guarantee is that Leo would have his credit cards stopped the minute he realized they were stolen. And he certainly wouldn't leave for France without them.'

'So what are you saying?'

I'm saying Leo's dead. A picture flashed out of nowhere into her tired brain. A lightning image, sharply defined, but so brief that it was gone again before she could register what it was. *Meg's a whore . . . Meg's a whore . . . too many secrets . . . déjà vu . . . this has happened before . . .* 'God,' she said, pressing a bruised hand to her chest, 'I thought – just for a moment, I thought . . .' She looked blankly at Maddocks. 'What did you ask me?'

He hadn't missed the flicker of astonishment that swept across her face. 'I was wondering what conclusions you've drawn from the fact that Leo hasn't had his cards stopped?'

She pressed trembling fingers to her forehead. 'I feel awful,' she said abruptly. 'I think I'm going to be sick.'

Fraser bent down to look into her face. 'I'll get the doctor to you,' he said.

'The name of Miss Harris's company, that's the only other thing we need,' pressed Maddocks, getting to his feet. 'We can take it from there. You said her partner was Josh Hennessey. What's the name of her company?'

'Leave it out, Guv, for Christ's sake,' said Fraser angrily, pressing the bell beside the bed. 'Can't you see she's not well?'

'Harris and Hennessey,' she murmured. 'The number's in the book beneath Meg's home number. M. S. Harris first, then Harris and Hennessey. I don't understand why you didn't call it before coming here.'

'Well?' demanded Maddocks of Fraser as he unlocked his car door. 'Why the hell didn't we?'

'Don't ask me, Guv. I went to Downton Court, remember. My recollection is that the Super instructed *you* to find out what you could about Meg Harris.'

'It's bloody Hammersmith's fault,' said Maddocks irritably. 'Goddammit, they've got the fucking telephone books in front of them.' He slid behind the wheel. 'What did you make of her?'

Fraser folded himself into the passenger seat and pulled the door shut. 'I felt sorry for her. She looks really ill.'

'Hmm, well, it didn't stop her running rings around you, did it?' He fired the engine.

'Or you,' said Fraser curtly. 'You set the alarm bells ringing, not me.'

But Maddocks wasn't listening. He thrust the car into gear and swung the wheel. 'I'll tell you something, she certainly didn't like Leo very much, or the parents either. You've met Sir Anthony. Would you say her description of him was accurate?'

'You can't tell much about a man when he's in shock. He's not poor, that's for sure.' He thought back. 'Matter of fact, I did think he was a bit of a pseud, but the poor bastard was about to be hit with his son's death, so I didn't analyse over much.'

'It's odd, though,' said Maddocks thoughtfully. 'If she despised them all as much as she claims she did, then why was she going through with the wedding? I mean, it was Leo who called it off, not her, and if he was so obsessive about money, why did he get shot of a Kingsley in order to hitch himself to a vicar's daughter? It doesn't ring true to me.' He gave Fraser a friendly punch on the shoulder. 'Well done, lad. Looks like you were right all along. She's our villain, no question about it. Now all we have to do is nail the bitch.'

Fraser had his doubts. She'd looked so damn good on paper, but the person, predictably, was a different matter. Could someone so frail have committed so physical a crime? 'She's not strong enough, Guv. There were two of them and Leo was over six feet.'

Maddocks slowed at the clinic gates. 'She's sharp as a tack. She used deception to kill them, not strength.' He pulled on to the road. 'And don't be seduced by that feeble-little-girl act either. Christ, I've never met such a calculating woman. She was one step ahead of us most of the time, and if she's suffering from amnesia I'll eat my hat.'

The Ragged Staff, Salisbury – 6.30 p.m.

WPC Blake, comfortably unobtrusive in jeans and a T-shirt, finally tracked Samantha Garrison to earth in a city centre pub. She was alone at the bar, a rather pathetic sight in a tight black strapless sheath that showed every one of her middle-aged bulges and encouraged her underarm fat to flow like soft lard over the sequined border. Limp hair hung like a damp curtain about her heavily made-up face and cheap scent rose in a thick miasma from her warm pores.

'Samantha Garrison?' she asked, slipping on to the neighbouring stool.

'Oh, Jesus,' sighed the woman, 'tell me you're not the filth, there's a love. I just don't need the aggro at the moment. I'm having a quiet drink in my local, all right? Do you see any customers because I sure as hell don't. Chance'd be a fine thing on a Sunday night in this miserable hell-hole.'

'I'm not here for aggro,' said Blake, catching the barman's eye. 'What are you drinking?'

Samantha eyed the half-pint of bitter that she'd been spinning out for the last forty minutes. 'Double rum and Coke,' she said.

Blake ordered a gin and tonic for herself, waited for the drinks to arrive, then suggested they adjourn to an isolated table in the window.

'You said no aggro,' Samantha reminded her. 'What do you want to say to me over there that you can't say here?'

'I want to talk about what happened to you on the twenty-third of March. I thought it would be less embarrassing if we were a little more private.'

A bleak expression settled over the painted face. 'I knew that one would come back to haunt me. What if I say I don't want to talk about it?'

'Then I'll be conducting a one-sided conversation which everyone will hear.' She glanced towards the barman. 'I'm trying to make things easy for you, Samantha. If you'd rather, we can go back to your house.'

'Gawd no. D'you think I want my kids reminding what happened?' She eased off the stool. 'Get your arse over here then but I'm not making no promises. It still gives me the sweats just thinking about it. I suppose it's what happened to that other girl that's got you on my back again.'

Blake took the chair opposite and leaned forward, elbows on the table. 'Which other girl's that?'

'The word is another one got done same as me.'

'It certainly looks like it.'

'Is she talking?'

'Not at the moment. She's too scared.'

Samantha took a huge swallow of her rum and Coke. 'Not bloody surprised.'

Blake nodded. 'We need one of you to help us. We're worried that if he does it again he might kill the next girl.' She examined the woman's face closely. 'Girl,' she thought, was quite the wrong expression. Flossie had given her age as forty-six and Samantha would never see forty again. There were other similarities, too. They were both plump, both blonde and both extremely heavy-handed with near-white face powder. 'How did he contact you, Samantha.

Did he pick you up off the street, or do you advertise somewhere?'

'Listen, love, I said I wouldn't make no promises and I meant it.'

'Flossie called me "love". You call me "love". Look, please don't take offence, but you and she are very alike. I'd describe you both as "motherly". She paused to collect her thoughts. 'The only reference Flossie made to her attacker was to call him Little Lord Fauntleroy, so I'm guessing he's much younger than both of you, probably well spoken and probably handsome, and I'm guessing, too, that he didn't choose either of you by accident. Judging by the fact that you and Flossie are of similar age and similar appearance, he was clearly looking for a specific kind of prostitute. Which means he must have picked you up off the street or he wouldn't have known what you looked like. Am I right?'

'I'm long past walking the streets, love.' Samantha sighed again. 'Look, get me another double rum and Coke, then maybe – just maybe – I'll tell you.'

'I'm not shelling out again unless it's a definite maybe,' said Blake firmly. 'This isn't official, you know, it's my own hard-earned money I'm using.'

'More fool you, dear. No one thanks you for anything these days.'

'How much did he pay you to keep quiet?'

'Forty,' said Samantha, 'but it's not the money, love. It was him. He promised me another going over if I opened my mouth, and I believed him. Still do, if it's of any inter-est to you. He was mad as a bloody hatter.'

'Forty,' Blake echoed in genuine astonishment. 'Christ! He must have money to burn. What do you normally charge? Ten?' No answer. 'So he's a *rich*, well-spoken, handsome young man?' Again no answer. 'Come on, Samantha, how did he know what you looked like? Tell me that at least. It means I can put the word out among the other girls to be careful in future.'

The woman nudged her glass towards the WPC. 'I reckon you've got it back to front, love. I reckon he was expecting something young and pretty, and found a fat old slag instead. All I know is, he rang me on the number on my card – and the card's in that many shop windows I wouldn't know which one he saw – made an appointment to visit, climbed on to my sodding bed and went berserk. Claimed I was old enough to be his mother and that I'd no business to be advertising under false pretences. Now give us a fill-up, there's a good girl.'

Blake took the glass and stood up. 'So you think he's a regular round the prostitutes but only lashes out at the older ones?'

The heavy shoulders rose in a shrug. 'Thinking's never been my strong point, dear. If it had, I'd have been a brain surgeon. Mind, I reckon his father beats up on his ma. "Tell 'em your old man did it," he said, "and they'll believe you."'

Chapter Eleven

Sunday, 26 June, Nightingale Clinic,
Salisbury – 7.00 p.m.

THERE WAS NO pattern to Jinx's thoughts. Bits of remembered conversation plagued her weary brain. *Do your brothers resent you?* Yes, yes, YES! *You were so condescending she wanted to slap you . . .* She had been seven years old. A baby, still . . . *the perfect child already in residence with pictures of her perfect mother all over the walls . . .* Was it her fault that her father had begun to despise his second wife within months of the wedding? *Relationships don't have to be disappointing, Jinx . . .* She had never known one that wasn't. She had married Russell because she felt sorry for him and discovered too late that pity is a bad basis for marriage. Yet, without the wisdom to predict events before they happened, could anyone in her shoes have done better? *So what are you saying?* I don't know, I don't know, I DON'T KNOW! *Something terrible happened . . . Russell's dead . . .*

Dr Protheroe looked in on her at seven o'clock. 'How's it going?'

She was propped up on her pillows. 'I'm a mess,' she said honestly, feeling again that ridiculous urge to be plucked from the bed and held in the comfort of his arms. *Oh, God, she had never felt so alone.*

He leant over her and she could smell the soap on his hands. 'You told me the police hadn't upset you when the Sergeant called me in, but I think you were lying. What did they really want to talk to you about?'

She fixed on the hairs that were sprouting from his shirt where the button was missing, funny little black tendrils that poked out wickedly and made a mockery of his position as clinic director. Adam would have fired him a long time ago *pour encourager les autres*, but then Adam rated presentation above content, and Adam was a bully. 'They just wanted a few details about Meg,' she said. 'And they didn't upset me. I'm just very tired at the moment.'

He pulled the chair forward and sat in it. 'OK. So what's this mess you're in? Physical? Mental?'

A tear glittered along her lid. 'Life,' she said. 'I've made a mess of life, and I don't know how to put it right.'

What a very seductive combination it was, he thought, this switch from tough-minded independence in the company of policemen to tearful vulnerability when alone with her doctor. He wished he felt more confident that the tear was genuine. As Veronica Gordon, one of the nursing sisters, had said to him that morning: 'She has a way with her, Alan. I think it's those extraordinary eyes. They say one thing and her voice says another.'

'What do the eyes say?' he'd asked her.

'Help,' she'd said succinctly, 'but it's the one thing she never asks for.'

'Perhaps life has made a mess of you,' he suggested now.

'No,' said Jinx flatly. 'That's the excuse I've always used, but it's not true. I allow things to happen instead of controlling them. Like this place, for example. I don't want to be here, but I am. And the only reason I stay is because my father will pursue me to London and put pressure on me to go home with him, and I want that even less than I want this.' She raised the sheet to her eyes to wipe away her tears. 'I'm only just beginning to realize how passive I am.'

'Why? Because you don't want to do battle with your father?'

'Among other things.' She sat up and linked her arms around her raised knees. 'Do you know that the only man I have ever been able to talk to on an equal basis is my next-door neighbour in Richmond, and he's in his eighties. I've been trying to remember all afternoon whether there's ever been anyone else and I haven't come up with a single person.'

'What about your people at the studio? Dean and Angelica. Surely you talk to them on an equal basis. As a matter of interest, have you called either of them since you arrived?'

He knew she hadn't. There had been only two calls out. And neither had been to her studio.

'There'd be no point. We only ever talk about work and I trust them to get on with it. Besides, I don't find it easy discussing my private life.'

He'd noticed. 'Josh? Can't you talk to him?'

She pulled a face. 'When I see him, which isn't very often. In any case, I usually end up apologizing for being Meg's friend. God knows why he ever went into business with her. She can be very unreliable at times.'

For the moment, he let Meg go. 'What about Russell?'

She stared beyond him out of the window. 'He was like my father. He was possessive, he was jealous and he thought I was wonderful.' She fell silent, lost in the past somewhere.

He was about to prompt her again, when she continued of her own accord. 'It was a classic case of out of the frying pan and into the fire. The odd thing is, he was fine as long as we weren't married. It was ownership that changed him. He became like my father.'

'Why do you feel your father owns you, Jinx?'

'I don't. That's how Adam sees it. He thinks he can control us all.' She glanced at him. 'You, too, Dr Protheroe.'

He frowned. 'Because he's paying this clinic to look after you? That's hardly control.'

She smiled. 'But if push came to shove, whose interests would you put first? Your own and your daughter's, or mine and the other patients'?'

He found that amusing and gave a short bark of laughter. 'That's like asking me if I'd rather be the Archbishop of Canterbury or Jack the Ripper. Why should I be faced with such a dramatic choice?'

'Because if you do something my father doesn't like, you'll probably find yourself out of a job,' she said bluntly. 'Why do you think that, at the age of forty, Russell suddenly left a comfortable well-paid career in Oxford to buy a down-at-heel art gallery in London? Not through choice, believe me.' She smiled grimly. 'To coin a phrase, my father made him an offer he couldn't refuse.'

Interesting use of words, he thought. 'What was the offer?'

'Leave voluntarily, or leave in disgrace.'

'You'll have to explain, I'm afraid.'

'Adam doesn't play by civilized rules. He uses information to destroy people who get in his way.' She shrugged. 'He paid fifty thousand pounds for the information on

Russell, and that's discounting what he paid his team of investigators to unearth the fact that it existed at all. He doesn't mess about.'

He hid his scepticism. 'Am I allowed to know what this piece of information was?'

She looked at him. 'You don't believe me, do you?' She could see that he didn't. 'Then it'll be your funeral, Dr Protheroe. Everybody underestimates Adam. He encourages people to believe they're dealing with a gentleman, when they're not. You see, he's not like Betty. You can't tell his origins by looking at him or speaking to him. He's far too clever for that.'

Protheroe felt he was being drawn once again towards a choice between her and her father, and chose to side-step the issue. 'I neither believe nor disbelieve,' he said. 'I am merely wondering what Russell could have done that was so bad. Even ten years ago, and particularly at a liberal university like Oxford, leaving in disgrace seems a somewhat old-fashioned concept.'

'Not if you go to jail, it isn't.' She sighed. 'Russell went to Europe every summer on lecture tours. When he came back he'd bring upwards of fifty kilos of cannabis packed into the chassis of his car. It was a straightforward transaction. He made the collection in Italy and was paid on delivery in England. He used the money to fund his art collection. He had no conscience about it. His view was that cannabis was less dangerous than alcohol or cigarettes and that the Government was mad to criminalize its use. But the penalty for smuggling is prison. Adam offered him resignation or prosecution. Russell chose resignation.'

'Did you know he was smuggling drugs?'

She shook her head. 'Not till afterwards.'

'How did Adam find out?'

'According to Russell, he traced the contact in Italy and bought him off. Adam works on the principle that everyone has a chink in his armour, and if he keeps going long enough, he'll find it. I think what probably happened is that his people calculated the value of Russell's collection, realized he couldn't have afforded it on his salary, and started digging into the trips abroad.'

'Presumably it was Russell who told you about it, not your father.'

'Yes.'

'Did he explain why your father wanted him to leave Oxford?'

'To get him away from me.'

'Then why did Russell marry you, Jinx? Why didn't the blackmail hold good after he'd left? Presumably he was no keener to go to prison afterwards than he was before.'

She gave a hollow laugh. 'You sound as though you think I'm making this up.'

'Not at all. I'm just trying to understand.'

Again, she didn't believe him. 'I've told you before, Dr Protheroe. We got married without my father's knowledge. I persuaded Russell that Adam would back off the minute I became Mrs Landy because, whatever he might want to do to Russell, Adam would never drag me in the mud. And I was right. He didn't.'

Alan pondered over that for a moment, thinking that far from being passive, Jinx was describing herself as a consummate manipulator. 'Didn't it ever occur to you that your father would react the way he did?'

She frowned, but didn't say anything.

'If my maths is correct, Russell was only twelve years his junior. Did you seriously think Adam would welcome him as a son-in-law?'

'Of course not, but at the time Adam found out about us there was no question of my marrying Russell. Look, we were having a quiet little affair which was nobody's business but our own.' She stared wretchedly at her hands.

'Who told him?'

'My brothers.'

'And how did they know?'

She smoothed the sheet across her lap. 'Russell used to write to me during vacations, and they opened one of his letters and showed it to Adam. I should have expected it, really. They were always looking for my clay feet.' She paused. 'The irony is, my father's hated them for it ever since. I think he knows that nothing would have come of the affair if they hadn't drawn it to his attention.'

'Are you saying you wouldn't have married Russell if you hadn't felt guilty about what your father did?'

She gave her faint smile. 'He was thoroughly miserable so, yes, Reader, I married him. Actually I was pretty miserable, too. I had another year at Oxford after he'd gone and it was just a series of tearful phone calls. I thought we'd both be happier if we made the thing official.'

'But you weren't?'

She didn't answer.

'How long were you married?' asked Protheroe.

She looked at him. 'Three years.'

'And you didn't enjoy it?' he persisted.

'I found it very stifling. He was afraid I was going to leave him for a younger man, and became jealous of everyone.' She seemed to think she was being disloyal. 'Look, it wasn't that bad. He was very funny when he was on form, and when I think of him now it's with affection. On the whole, the good times far outweighed the bad.'

Quite unconsciously, Alan echoed Fraser's thoughts of the day before. What a dismal epitaph on a dead husband. 'When I think of him now it's with affection.' But how clear it was to Alan that she tried not to think of him at all.

'As a matter of interest,' he asked curiously, 'did you approve of his smuggling?'

She picked at her fingernails. 'I shared his views on the idiocy of criminalizing cannabis. Or any drugs in fact. Black markets always undermine social orders. But I thought he was a fool to have done it. Someone was bound to find out about it sooner or later.'

'What sort of a lover was he?'

She gave a snort of laughter. 'I wondered when we'd get round to that. Sigmund Freud has a lot to answer for. Why do you give so much credence to the fantastic theories of a cocaine addict? I've never understood that.'

He smiled. 'I don't think we do any more, or not to the extent you're suggesting. Freud has his place in history.' He leaned back in the chair and crossed his legs, deliberately extending the space between them. 'But wouldn't you agree that the sexual relationship between a man and a woman is an integral part of the whole relationship?'

'No. I don't have sex with Eric Clancey and I get on better with him than anyone else.'

'He being your elderly neighbour?' She nodded. 'Yes, well, I was referring to relationships where there is a sexual content.'

'And you've had my answer. In my experience the best relationships have no sexual content whatsoever.' She reached for her cigarettes. 'In fact, Russell was a good lover. He knew which buttons to press – and when – and he was considerate and not overly demanding. Bed was one of the few places where we could communicate on a level playing field because it was only there that Russell could put aside his jealousy.' She lit a cigarette. 'There was no telephone in our bedroom so Adam couldn't reach me.'

Adam again. 'Was there any basis for his jealousy? Were you attracted to other men?'

'Of course,' she said honestly. 'In my shoes, so would you have been. The grass looked a great deal greener on the other side of the marital fence, but I never did anything about it.' She drew deeply on her cigarette. 'It was my father he was really jealous of. He recognized that Adam was as possessive as he was, and it frightened him. He was sure Adam would win in the end.'

'You told me the other day that you loved your father. Was that true or were you telling me what you thought I wanted to hear?'

'It was partly true.' She eyed him with sudden amusement. 'I never know whether I want to sit on his lap and be hugged by him, or dance a jig of freedom on his grave. I expect Freud would have found me fascinating.'

'Does he ever hug you?'

She shook her head. 'He hates demonstrations of affection. I kiss him on the cheek sometimes if I catch him unawares, but most of the time he won't even touch me.'

'Does he hug your stepmother?'

'No.'

'Your brothers?'

'No.'

'Do they hug their mother?'

'No. We're a very undemonstrative family.'

'Is there any love at all in that house, Jinx?'

'There's passion,' she said. 'They all fight like cat and dog for Adam's approval.'

'But you don't join in?'

'I don't need to,' she said dismissively. 'I already have it. Adam paid good money to transform his most intelligent child into something he could be proud of. The fact that I am incapable of making sensible decisions about my personal life is a minor irritation.' Angrily, she turned away from him, propping her chin on her hand and staring into the mirror. 'He made a lady out of me and he's besotted with her.'

'Is that why you call him Adam? To prove you aren't a lady?'

'I don't follow.'

'I assume it's a statement of equality. "You and I are no different, Adam. If you can't behave like a gentleman, then I can't be a lady." Something like that?'

She continued to stare into the mirror. 'You really do assume far too much, you know. In normal circumstances, I hardly think of Adam at all, and never in such analytical terms.'

'You said earlier that the best relationships were the ones without a sexual content,' he reminded her, 'yet you clearly don't have a good relationship with your father. Should I infer from that that you and he have had a sexual relationship?'

'No,' she said calmly, 'you should not infer any such thing. I will not allow you to foist some tacky child abuse theory on to me because it happens to be in vogue at the moment. Anyway, what would you know about any of this? I thought you said you weren't a psychiatrist.'

He could feel her anger. 'Why so defensive? Is it because you recognize that, but for his self-control, you and he might have had a sexual relationship? Perhaps the desire wasn't all one-sided.'

She closed her eyes suddenly. 'I really do urge you to remember what my father does to people he doesn't like, Dr Protheroe. You'd be quite mad to make an enemy of him.'

Now why, he wondered, did he get the feeling she was talking about herself?

With an effort of concentration she remembered Dean Jarrett's home telephone number. 'Dean?' she said when he picked up the receiver at the other end. 'Look, I'm really sorry to bother you at home —'

'Who is it?'

'It's Jinx.'

'Oh, my God!' screamed his well-remembered voice. She could picture him so clearly. The telephone was in the sitting room, an art deco excrescence, amongst all the other art deco excrescences in his vibrant and colourful living space. He would be lying on the *chaise-longue*, she thought, his peroxided silver head propped against the ornate tracery at the end of it, receiver in one hand, glass of champagne in the other. Dean performed even when he was alone, and she loved him for it because she couldn't do it herself.

'We've been worried sick,' he rattled on. 'I said to Angelica, Angelica sweetheart, supposing we've lost her? We didn't know what to do. Face the dread prospect of phoning that awful man who passes for your father and puts the fear of God into us, or sit tight and rely on you to come round eventually. You know he phoned and spoke to Angie, and he was most fearfully rude, all but called her a nigger, but he wouldn't say where you were. Just said you were unconscious in hospital and told us to get on with what we were paid to do. Then the fuzz came rushing round asking questions, and we nearly *died* of shock.' He floundered to a halt. 'Business is fine,' he went on more calmly after a moment. 'Don't you worry about the studio. Thank God, people have enough faith in yours truly to stay with us.'

She smiled. 'I know, that's why I haven't been worried.'

'You should have phoned,' he said. 'We've been that upset. We wanted to send you some flowers. Angelica's been sobbing her heart out, said someone ought to be visiting you.'

'I'm sorry. The trouble is' – she paused – 'well, to be honest, I'm only firing on about half a cylinder at the moment. I gave myself a hell of a crack on the head and ended up with galloping amnesia.' She forced a laugh. 'Can't remember much about the last three or four weeks. Silly, isn't it? Look, I'll give you the details of where I am, then you can get in touch when you want to.' She gave him the address and telephone number of the clinic. 'But I don't intend to stay here much longer,' she went on. 'As soon as I can find the energy, I'm hopping on the first train back to London.'

He clucked like a mother hen. 'Stay as long as you need. No sense in coming back before you're ready. Everything's tickety-boo this end, or it will be when I pass on the good news that I've spoken to you. Actually, my darling, you sound great even if the memory is a bit dicky. Is it worrying you?'

'Yes.' She took a deep breath. 'Have I spoken to either of you between the fourth of June, when I left for Hampshire, and now? Can you remember? I mean, did I phone you at all while I was with my parents or did I come in to work on the Monday after I got back? That would be the thirteenth.'

'No,' he said apologetically. 'That's what the police kept asking when they came to the studio. Had we seen you? Had we spoken to you? Did we know why you'd gone back to Hampshire on the Monday? And we told them the truth. Not a cheep out of you since Friday the third. Angelica phoned over and over again on the thirteenth when you didn't come in to work, and all she got was your answerphone. We were girding our loins to contact Hell Hall on the Tuesday morning when the devil himself phoned with the awful news that you were unconscious. Since which time we've been tearing our collective hair out.' He was silent for a moment. 'Do you really not remember anything since the fourth?'

She heard the note of concern in his voice. 'No, but it's all right,' she said with a light laugh. 'I've been told the important stuff, like the wedding's off, Leo's scarpered with Meg, and I tried to kill myself. I just don't remember any of it.'

'Well, for what it's worth, dear, neither of us believes the crash was deliberate. You were making it clear as crystal for a good week before you set off for the Hall that you'd made up your mind not to go through with the wedding. Angie and I assumed you were going to break the news to the old devil then, and call the whole thing quits. It came as a bit of a shock to find you hadn't.'

She stared at her reflection. 'Did I say I wasn't going through with it?'

'Not in so many words, but you were back to your old sunny self again, and I said to Angie, well, thank God for small mercies, she's come to her senses and told Leo to get stuffed, and Angie agreed with me. Well, you know we never liked him. He's very pretty, of course, but he wasn't for *you*, Jinx. Far too interested in number one, and you want someone who cares for you, sweetheart. Let's face it, we all do.'

She laughed. 'How's George?'

'Unmentionable. He's left me for a Filipino chef.'

'I'm sorry. Are you surviving?'

'Of course. Don't I always? Now, tell me why you rang. I feel in my bones there was a reason, and it wasn't just to hear my dulcet tones.'

She raised her knees and propped her elbows on them. 'I want you to phone Leo's parents and say you need to contact Leo or Meg Harris as a matter of urgency.'

'With reference to what?'

Something terrible . . . 'Can you invent an excuse? Say you're an old school-friend of Leo's, that you're only in the country for a week and that you want to meet up with him. He went to Eton if they ask. I just want you to try and find

193

out where they are without letting on you know me. Is that OK with you? I want to be able to talk to them and show there are no hard feelings. Could you do that for me?'

'Sure. What's his parents' number?'

'I don't know, but you can get it through Directory Enquiries because I did it myself once. It's A. Wallader, Downton Court, Ashwell, Guildford, and if *he* answers it's Sir Anthony and if *she* answers it's Lady Wallader. And Dean, whatever they say, you must ring me back tonight. Please. I don't care what they tell you, you must ring me back. OK?'

'No problem,' he said breezily.

The phone rang twenty minutes later. Jinx picked it up with trembling hands and cradled it against her face. 'Jinx Kingsley.'

'It's Dean,' he said carefully.

'They're dead, aren't they?'

There was a short silence. 'Why did you get me to make the call if you already knew?'

'But I didn't,' she said quietly. 'I guessed. Oh, God – and I was so hoping I was wrong. I'm sorry. I'm really sorry. I didn't know who else to ask. Who did you speak to?'

'His father. He was pretty upset.'

She rushed into self-justification. 'The police came this afternoon and asked me questions about them, but they wouldn't say why. And I thought, my God, they're dead and no one's telling me.' She chewed her lower lip. 'Did Anthony say what happened to them?'

There was another silence. 'Look, love, half an hour ago I thought you were unconscious, then I find you aren't. I don't know what to do. I phoned back because I promised I would, but let me talk to your doctor in the morning. It'd make me a damn sight happier, it really would.'

'No,' she said coldly. 'Tell me now.' She thought she heard his nervous finger rattle the receiver rest. 'And don't hang up on me, Dean, because I swear to God you'll be out of a job if you do.' *Oh Jesus! She sounded like her father . . . No matter how much she tried to deny it, his tyranny and passion were in her, too . . .*

'You don't have to threaten me,' he said in mild reproof. 'I'm only trying to do what's best.'

'I know and I'm sorry, but I'm slowly going mad here. I must know what's happened.' She waited but he didn't respond. 'OK,' she said abruptly, 'then I'm calling in your debts.' Her eyes narrowed. 'Just remember that the only reason anyone feels confident about you running the studio in my absence is because I've encouraged you to make a name for yourself along with me. I didn't have to do that. I could have done what everybody else does and put your work out under the studio's name. You owe me for that at least.'

'I owe you a great deal more, Jinx, which is why I'm shitting bricks this end. I don't want to make things worse for you.' He heard her indrawn breath. 'OK, take it easy, I will tell you, but you must promise me you won't do anything silly afterwards.'

'Do you mean try and kill myself?'

'Yes.'

'I promise,' she said wearily. 'But if I was desperate enough to want to do it, then giving my word in advance wouldn't stop me. It's only fair you should know that.'

Perversely, he found this honesty more reassuring than the pledge. 'Sir Anthony said Leo and his girlfriend had been murdered. Their bodies were found last Thursday in a wood near Winchester but the police think they were killed the week before.'

She clenched her fist against her heart. 'Which day the week before?'

'The Monday, according to Sir Anthony, but I'm not sure he knows. He really was very upset.'

Ice settled in a frozen block inside her. 'What else did he say?'

'Nothing much.'

'Did he mention me?'

He didn't answer.

'Please, Dean.'

'He said Leo had been engaged to a woman whose husband died the same way.'

She stared at her terrible image in the mirror.

'Are you still there?'

'Yes,' she said. 'I'm sorry I made you do it. It wasn't fair.'

'Don't worry about it.' But the line had gone dead and his words fell on deaf ears.

The Nightingale Clinic, Laverstock, Salisbury, Wiltshire

one page sent via fax (handwritten) to:
>*Adam Kingsley*
>*Hellingdon Hall*
>*Nr Fordingbridge, HAMPSHIRE*

Date: Sunday, 26 June 1994
Time: 20.30
Dear Mr Kingsley,

Is there any chance of your coming to the clinic tomorrow morning or afternoon for an informal chat about Jinx's progress? She is, as I am sure you are aware, a private person, and finds it difficult to talk about herself, but it would be helpful for me to have a clearer picture of her history and background. I have some problems understanding what compelled her to make an attempt on her life when she presents herself as a self-reliant and, in the circumstances of her tragic widowhood, well-adjusted personality. I would welcome your views on this. One idea I'd like to discuss is the possibility of a joint session where, under my guidance, you and Jinx can explore any rifts that may have developed between you. She is clearly fond of you, but retains a certain ambivalence following the death of her husband. I have tried telephoning but, in the absence of a reply, may I suggest that you call first thing tomorrow with a convenient time? Please be assured that I know how busy you are and wouldn't trouble you if I didn't believe it to be important.

With best wishes,

Alan Protheroe

**HELLINGDON HALL
NR FORDINGBRIDGE
HAMPSHIRE**

facsimile: 27.6.1994   09.45   * one page sent

Dear Dr Protheroe,

If the brief you were given is beyond your capabilities, please advise me immediately. I understood my daughter would be allowed to recover at her own speed and in her own time.

Yours sincerely,

Adam Kingsley

Chapter Twelve

THE REVEREND CHARLES Harris and his wife came to view the remains of their daughter together, but it was a more harrowing identification than Leo's because Mrs Harris was present. Frank Cheever had done his best to persuade her to remain at home in the company of a police-woman, but she had insisted on seeing Meg for herself. She had worn her grief with calm composure throughout the car journey but, faced with the terrible sight of her daugh-ter, she broke down. 'This is Jinx Kingsley's doing,' she cried. 'I warned Meg what would happen if she took Leo away from her.'

'Hush, Caroline,' said her husband, putting his arm about her shoulders. 'I'm sure this has nothing to do with Jinx.'

Her anger was immediate and terrible. 'You stupid man!' she screamed, thrusting him from her. 'This is your baby lying here, not some parishioner's child. Look at her, Charles. Your Meggy, your darling, reduced to *this*.' She held a fluttering hand to her lips. 'Oh, GOD!' The word exploded from her with hatred. 'How can you be so blind?

First Russell. Now Leo and Meg.' She rounded on Super-intendent Cheever. 'I've been so worried. From the moment she said Leo had left Jinx for her, I've been so worried. She's a murderer. She and her beastly father. They're both murderers.'

Calmly, Dr Clarke pulled the shroud over Meg's head, then took the mother's hand and tucked it into the crook of his arm. 'We have to leave now, Mrs Harris,' he said gently. 'Would you like to say goodbye to Meg before we go?'

She stared at him with drowned eyes. 'Meg's dead.'

'I know.' He smiled into the sad face. 'But this isn't a bad place. God is here, too.'

'Yes,' she said, 'you're right.' She turned and took a final look at the shrouded corpse. 'God bless you, my darling,' she whispered through her tears. 'God bless you.'

Frank Cheever watched Bob usher the wretched woman through the doors, and it crossed his mind that perhaps pathologists earned their salaries after all. He gestured awkwardly to Meg's father. 'I'm not as good at this as Dr Clarke,' he said apologetically, 'but if you'd like some privacy with your daughter . . .' He broke off.

'No,' said the vicar. 'God and Meg both know what's in my heart. I can't say any more to her than I've said already.' He led the way to the doors, then faltered. 'You really mustn't pay any attention to what Caroline said, Superintendent. Jinx would never have done anything to harm Meg.'

'Are you sure about that, sir?'

'Yes,' he said simply. 'She's rather a fine person, you know. I've always admired her courage.'

Nightingale Clinic, Salisbury – 10.00 a.m.

The telephone rang in Jinx's room, fraying her nerves with its jangling peal. She pushed herself out of the chair and reached reluctantly for the receiver. 'Hello,' she said.

'It's your father, Jane. I'm sending the car to collect you.'

Fear ripped through her like burning acid. *What did he know?* There'd been no mention of Meg and Leo in the papers or on the television news. Her fingers clenched involuntarily round the receiver, knuckles whitening under the strain, but her voice was calm.

'Fine,' she said, 'send the car by all means, it's no skin off my nose. I never wanted to be here in the first place. But I'm not coming home, Adam. I'll tell the driver to take me back to Richmond and, if he refuses to do that, then I'll call a taxi and go to the station. Is that what you intended to achieve by this phone call?'

There was an ominous silence at the other end.

'Leave things as they are or I promise I'll discharge myself.' Her voice hardened. 'And this time, you'll lose me for good. Do you understand, Adam? I'll take out an injunction to prevent you coming within a mile of my house.' She slammed the receiver down with unnecessary force, and sank on to the edge of the bed as the strength seeped like sawdust from her knees and thighs. She felt the beginnings of a headache sawing away behind her eyes, and squeezed her temples tightly with shaking fingers.

The flash of memory that burst in her brain was blinding in its clarity. *Meg on her knees, begging . . . please . . . please . . . please . . .* She looked in confusion on her friend's terrified face, felt a corresponding rush of terror drive her own heart into a frenzy, before nausea sent her staggering into the bathroom to retch in agony into the lavatory. Shaking violently, she lowered herself to the tiled floor and, as she laid her cheek on the cold ceramic, she clung in desperation to the fact that, despite all her friend's faults, she had loved Meg Harris.

But it was an hour before the shaking stopped.

The White Hart Hotel, Winchester – 10.10 a.m.

'We know very little about your daughter,' said Superintendent Cheever to the Reverend Harris and his wife. 'As I explained, we had some difficulty finding you. There is almost nothing of a personal nature in Meg's flat, and we can only presume she was in the process of moving out of it.'

He had baulked at driving them to the police station and the sterility of an interview room, opting instead for a small upstairs parlour in a hotel near the mortuary, where Fraser and a WPC could sit unobtrusively in the background taking notes. He had abandoned the flamboyance of silk bow-tie and silk handkerchief in favour of sombre black, and he looked to be what he really was – an ordinary man in ordinary surroundings, unthreatening and rather kind. Mrs Harris sat hunched in an armchair beside the half-open window, a cup of tea, untouched, on the table next to her. Her husband sat on a hard chair next to her, clearly unsure whether to comfort her or leave her to come to terms with her grief alone, holding his own grief in check for fear of making things worse for her. Cheever felt sorry for both of them, but he reserved his deepest sympathy for

Meg's father. Why was it, he wondered, that men were expected to disguise their feelings?

'She was going on holiday with Leo,' said Charles quietly, 'but she didn't say anything about moving out of her flat. Not to me anyway.' He looked irresolutely at his wife.

'She didn't tell you anything, Charles, because she knew you'd disapprove.' Caroline mopped her red-rimmed eyes. 'She had an abortion ten years ago. She didn't tell you about that either, did she? And why not? Because you'd have ruined her life for her.' She crumpled the handkerchief between her palms. 'Well, it's ruined anyway, but it might not have been if she'd been able to talk to you as a father instead of a priest. Everything had to be kept secret in case you preached at her.'

Her husband stared at her, the planes of his face bleached white with shock. 'I didn't know,' he murmured. 'I'm sorry.'

'Of course you're sorry. Now,' she added bitterly. 'I'm sorry, too. Sorry for her, sorry for the baby, sorry for me. I'd like to have been a grandmother.' Her voice broke on a sob. 'It's such a waste. It's *all* such a waste.' She turned to the Superintendent. 'We have a son, but he's never wanted to marry. He wanted to be ordained like his father.' Her eyes filled again. 'It's such a terrible waste.'

Cheever waited while she fought for control. 'You implied that you knew Meg was moving out of her flat, Mrs Harris,' he said at last. 'Could you tell us about that? Where was she going?'

'To live with Leo. He had a house. It made more sense for her to move in with him.'

'Do you know where the house is?'

'Somewhere in Chelsea. Meg was going to give me the address when she came back from France. Don't Leo's parents know?'

Frank side-stepped the question. 'They're very shocked at the moment.'

There was a painful silence.

'Have you met Sir Anthony and Lady Wallader?' Cheever asked next.

Caroline's mouth puckered tragically. 'We never even met Leo,' she said. 'How could we have met his parents? It was all so quick. We had an invitation to Jinx's wedding sitting on the mantelpiece, and then Meg phoned to say Leo wanted to marry her instead.' She shook her head in disbelief.

Charles stirred on his chair. 'She rang on the Saturday morning,' he murmured quietly, 'the eleventh, I believe, and I was rather upset by the news. I wondered what sort of a man Leo was to abandon his fiancée so close to the wedding in order to take up with her best friend.' He lifted his hands in resignation. 'She told me that she'd known Leo far longer than Jinx had, and that he'd only proposed to Jinx because of some silly row they'd had. "He wanted to spite me," she said.' He paused for a moment. 'I forget sometimes that she's a grown woman – was a grown woman,' he corrected himself, 'and, yes, I can see now that I tended to preach, but it was so clear to me that this man was not to be relied upon, and I'm afraid we had a terrible argument about him. I said his behaviour was neither mature nor honourable, and that if he was prepared to treat Jinx so shabbily then Meg would be wise to have nothing more to do with him.' His voice faltered slightly. 'I'm afraid she hung up on me and we never spoke again, although I believe Caroline tried later the same day.' He turned to his wife. 'That's right, isn't it?'

She wrapped her arms about her thin body and hugged herself tightly. 'You know it is. You were listening.' She gave a shuddering sigh. 'She wouldn't hear me out either, but at least we didn't scream at each other. I said, why had she never mentioned him before if she'd known him so long, and she said there were a million things she'd never mentioned. It was her life and there was no rule that compelled children to tell their parents everything. I blame her father,' she said in a drained voice, turning her shoulder to freeze Charles out. 'She couldn't leave home quick enough to get away from him, so of course there were things we would never know.'

The Superintendent absorbed this in silence, careful to keep his face neutral. 'When did she tell you she was moving in with Leo?' he asked after a moment.

'During that telephone call. "We're going to live together until we get married," she said. "Leo has a house in Chelsea and I'm moving my stuff in now, but I don't want you to tell Dad because I can't take any more lectures." Then she said they were going to France until the fuss died down and that she'd phone her answer-machine regularly for messages.' She fingered her handkerchief, pulling out the crumples. 'She said we'd stop worrying once we met Leo, and promised to bring him down as soon as they came home. And I said, what about poor Jinx? And Meg said Jinx would survive because she always has. Then we said goodbye.' She held the handkerchief to her eyes.

To Frank's ears, this description of Meg was an unflattering one and he wondered if Mrs Harris was aware of the picture she was painting. 'Tell me about Meg,' he invited. 'What was she like?'

Her sad face brightened. 'She was a beautiful person. Kind, thoughtful, very loving. "Don't worry, Mummy, I'll always be here," that's what she used to say.' The tears welled again. 'She was so intelligent. She could do anything she set her mind to. "I'm going places," she always told me. Everyone adored her.'

Frank turned to the vicar. 'Is that how you saw her, sir?'

Charles glanced at his wife's rigid back. 'She had faults, Superintendent, we all do. She was a little self-centred, perhaps, rather too careless of other people's feelings, but, yes, she was a popular girl.' He folded his hands in his lap. 'Our son Simon could give you a better idea of what she was like. He's worked in various London parishes over the years and saw far more of her than we did. As Caroline told you, we effectively lost her when she went to university. She used to come down two or three times a year, but other than that we had very little contact.'

'Is he still in London, sir?'

'No, he was given a parish of his own two years ago. It's a village called Frampton, ten miles to the north-east of Southampton.' He lifted the cuff of his cassock to look at his watch. 'But he'll be at the vicarage in Littleton Mary by now. I thought it would be easier for us if he came up.'

'Easier for you, you mean,' said Caroline unsteadily, swinging round to face him. 'You think he's going to take your side.'

Charles shook his head. 'There's no question of anyone taking sides, Caroline. I hoped we could support each other.'

Her cheeks blazed suddenly. 'There's been too much secrecy. I can't stand it any more.' She reached out a claw to clutch at the Superintendent's sleeve. 'I knew we'd lost her,' she said. 'I prayed we'd only lost her to Leo, but in my heart of hearts, I knew she was dead. I kept asking myself why Jinx had tried to kill herself.' Her eyes rolled alarmingly, and Frank glanced towards the WPC for assistance, but Caroline went on in an unsteady voice: 'She did the same thing after Russell was murdered, you know, but that time she tried to starve herself to death. If it hadn't been for her father, she'd have succeeded. This is Jinx's doing, Superintendent. She won't have her men taken away from her.'

'You're talking nonsense, Caroline,' said her husband severely.

'Oh, am I?' she snapped. 'Well, at least I'm not a hypocrite. You know the truth as well as I do. We're talking about jealousy over Meg, Charles, something you know all about.'

He pressed his hands to his face and breathed deeply for several seconds. 'I really don't think I can continue, Superintendent,' he said unexpectedly. 'I do apologize. Can I urge you to talk to Simon? I'm sure he's the best person to give you an objective view of this sorry business.'

Fraser, who was sitting a few yards apart, looked up and caught Cheever's eye. 'Sorry business' was a peculiarly cold-blooded way to describe a brutal murder, but then it hadn't occurred to either of them at that stage how much the Reverend Charles Harris had disliked his daughter.

Nightingale Clinic, Salisbury – 1.00 p.m.

'Are you busy, Dr Protheroe?'

He glanced up from his desk to find Jinx hovering, poised for flight in the doorway, a look of indecision in her dark eyes. 'We're very informal here, you know. You can call me Alan if you want.'

The idea of anything so intimate appalled her. 'I'd rather stick with Dr Protheroe, if you don't mind.'

'Fine,' he said indifferently. 'Come in then.'

She stayed where she was. 'It's not important. I can come back later.'

He gestured towards a vacant armchair. 'Come in,' he said again. 'I could do with a break from the paperwork.' He stood up and walked around the desk, ushering her in and shutting the door behind her. 'What's up?'

With her escape route barred, Jinx accepted that the die was cast. She crossed the parquet flooring but, instead of sitting down, took up a position by the window and gazed out across the garden. 'My father phoned to say he wants me out of here. I wondered why. Do you know?'

'No,' he said, resuming his seat and swinging round to look at her back.

'Did you phone him about the police visit?'

'No.'

She turned round to study his face closely, then nodded in relief. 'Then I don't understand,' she said. 'Why does he want me to leave?'

'I suppose it may have something to do with the fax I sent him.' He reached inside his top drawer and removed both the fax in question and the reply he had received that morning. 'Read them,' he invited. 'My extraordinarily anodyne letter is typical of a hundred more on file, so why should your father find it threatening?'

She perched on the edge of the armchair and read both pieces of paper before handing them back to him. 'What was your brief?' She chewed nervously on the side of her thumb.

'What he says. To let you recover at your own speed. He didn't want psychiatrists meddling.'

Why not? What was there to fear from psychiatrists this time? What did Adam think she could tell them? What could she tell them? 'Then it must be your invitation to talk about Russell's death,' she said slowly. 'Wild horses wouldn't make him do that, and certainly not with me present.'

'What's he afraid of?'

'Nothing.'

Why did she keep lying to him? he wondered. And why this need to protect her father when it was so very clear she thought he'd murdered her husband? 'There must be something, Jinx, or it wouldn't require wild horses to drag it out of him,' he said reasonably.

'There's nothing,' she insisted. 'It's just that, as far as Adam's concerned, Russell didn't exist. His name's never mentioned. The episode is forgotten history.'

Protheroe mulled this over. 'You obviously think your father views your tragedy as a "forgotten episode",' he said thoughtfully. 'But is that how you see it, too?'

She didn't answer.

'Tell me about your father's background,' he suggested next. 'Where did he come from?'

She spoke in quick, jerky sentences. 'I only know what

Betty's told me. Adam never talks about his past. He was born in the East End of London. He was the third of five children. His father and two older brothers were merchant seamen – and all died when their ships were sunk in the North Atlantic. His younger brother and sister were evacuated to Devon while he remained with his mother to face the blitz. His education was minimal. He learnt more from the black marketeers working out of the docks than he ever learnt in school. By the end of the war he had amassed a list of contacts abroad and enough money to set up as an importer. The first goods he shipped in were silks, cottons and cosmetics – they arrived on his seventeenth birthday. He doubled his money overnight by flogging the lot on the black market, and he's never looked back. He began life as a crook – knew the Kray twins very well. That's all I know.'

He believed her. If Adam Kingsley was anything like she described him, he was a man who compartmentalized every aspect of his life. *Rather like his daughter.* It would be interesting to discover whether he, too, closed doors on dark rooms and threw away the keys. The chances were high that he did. 'As far as Adam's concerned, Russell didn't exist,' Jinx had said.

'What happened to his mother?' Protheroe asked now.

'I don't know. He didn't have much to do with her after he married my mother. As far as I can make out, neither family approved of the marriage.'

'And the brother and sister? What happened to them?'

'They went back to London after the war, presumably to live with their mother. The only thing Adam has ever said

THE DARK ROOM

on the subject is that he's always regarded them as strangers because he and they grew up apart.'

'Does he still feel like that?'

She slipped down into the chair and laid her head against the back of it. 'He hasn't spoken to either of them for over thirty years. Uncle Jo emigrated to Australia and hasn't been heard of since, and Aunt Lucy married a black man. My father severed all his ties with her the day she walked up the aisle.'

'Because her husband was black?'

'Of course. He's a racist. Betty used to know Lucy quite well when they were all younger. She told me once that Adam tried to stop the wedding.'

'How?'

With shaking fingers, she lit a cigarette. 'Betty was very drunk. I'm not sure she was telling the truth.'

'What did she say?'

She took quick pulls on the cigarette, considering her answer. 'That Adam tried to scare Lucy's fiancé off with a beating,' she said in a rush, 'but that Lucy went ahead and married him anyway. It might be true. He really does hate black people.'

Alan watched her for a moment. 'How do you feel about that?'

'Ashamed.'

He waited. 'Because your father's a bully?' he suggested.

She could taste hot, sweet bile in her mouth and drew in a lungful of smoke to mask it. 'Yes – no. Mostly because I should have sought Lucy and her family out years ago and made a stand – but I never did.'

Veronica Gordon was right about the eyes, he was thinking. What the hell was going on inside her head that she could look so frightened and sound so composed? 'Why not?'

She turned her face to the ceiling. 'Because I was afraid the whipping-boys would be punished if I did.'

'Meaning your brothers.'

'Not necessarily. Any whipping-boy will do,' she said flatly. 'If I'd sought out my aunt, then Betty would have been taken to task because she knew Lucy as a child and would have been accused of being the instigator. But it's more often the boys than not.'

'Are we talking literally or metaphorically? Does your father physically beat your brothers?'

'Yes.'

'So was Russell another whipping-boy, do you think?' he asked mildly.

He caught her unawares and she stared at him in shock. 'My father didn't kill him,' she said, her voice rising. 'The police ruled him out very early on.'

'I was talking metaphorically, Jinx.'

She didn't answer immediately. 'I don't think you were,' she said, lowering her gaze, 'but it doesn't make any difference anyway. Russell was never punished for my short-comings.'

'No,' he agreed. 'I suspect you were punished for his.' He toyed with his pen. 'How much do you know about your mother? Why did both families disapprove of the match, for example?'

'Her people were middle class and my father's were working class. I presume it was straightforward snobbery on her side and inverted snobbery on his, and I don't suppose it helped that he made money out of black marketeering.' She was silent for a moment. 'I know he adored her.'

'Did he tell you that?'

'No, he never talks about her.'

'Then how do you know?'

'Because Betty told me. Her name was Imogen Jane Nicholls, she was the only child of a doctor, privately educated, and very much a lady, and he has photographs of her all over his office walls.'

He thought of the name on Jinx's file cover. Jane Imogen Nicola Kingsley. 'Do you look like her as well?'

'Of course I do,' she said with a kind of desperation. 'Adam set out to re-create her.'

He couldn't fault the desperation – it was there in her voice – but he doubted it had anything to do with her mother. 'Even your father can't perform miracles, Jinx,' he said with a touch of irony, as he watched the ash on her cigarette lengthen and curl. 'I suspect that little scenario is more in your stepmother's mind than his. We all need ways of coming to terms with a partner's indifference. None of us is immune from pride.' He nudged the wastepaper basket towards her with his toe. 'You should know that.'

The Vicarage, Littleton Mary, Wiltshire – 1.15 p.m.

Fraser watched Cheever's courteous and sympathetic handling of this devastated family with a far more willing admiration than he had felt for Maddocks yesterday. The Superintendent knew as well as he did that there were some strange undercurrents at work, but never for one moment did he pressure either of the Harris parents into saying what they were.

They drove in convoy back to Littleton Mary, with Mrs Harris and a motherly WPC in the leading car, and himself, Cheever and Mr Harris in the one behind. There was little conversation. The vicar clearly found talking difficult, and the Superintendent was content to leave him to his thoughts. Where 'initiative' was Maddocks's watchword, 'patience' was Cheever's.

In retrospect, of course, Fraser had to ask himself whether Maddocks's insensitive approach wouldn't have been more appropriate, for it was Cheever's willingness to take his time that gave rise to the events that followed. Maddocks would have squeezed every last drop of information out of them, irrespective of the trauma they were suffering, and Charles could not have conspired with Simon to keep the information about Meg and Russell's affair to themselves. But would justice have been better served, Fraser always wondered, if they'd known about it then instead of later?

As they drew up behind the other car in the vicarage driveway, Charles Harris touched a hand to his dog-collar as if seeking reassurance. 'Could I suggest that I have a quick word with Simon first?' he said rapidly. 'Just to explain why you're here, then perhaps you could talk to him outside, away from his mother? It's important you get a clear picture of Meg, and I'm afraid you won't get that if Caroline is listening.'

The Superintendent nodded. 'I'll ask WPC Graham to take Mrs Harris inside. Sergeant Fraser and I will wait here.'

It was five minutes before Simon emerged, his thin face

looking very drawn. He ushered them round the corner of the house to some chairs grouped about a table on the lawn. 'Dad's asked me to tell you about Meg,' he said, sitting down, 'but I'm not sure . . .' He took off his glasses abruptly to pinch the bridge of his nose. 'I'm sorry,' he said, struggling for composure. 'It's all been a bit of a shock.' He breathed deeply over the tears that were crowding his throat. 'I'm sorry,' he said again.

'That's all right, sir,' said Frank. 'Would it be easier if we asked you questions?'

Simon nodded.

'Your father says you worked in London for several years and saw more of Meg than they did. Perhaps you could tell us something about her lifestyle. Did she have many friends, for example? Did she go out a lot? Did she enjoy discos, pubs, things of that sort?'

'Yes,' said Simon, 'all of those. She loved life, Superintendent.' He wiped his eyes with the sleeve of his shirt, then put his glasses back on. 'She had a very happy personality, people always enjoyed being with her.'

Frank twisted his chair against the sunlight. 'That's how your mother described her,' he said, 'but your father seemed to have reservations. Why is that, do you think? Did he and Meg not get on?'

Simon's expression was unreadable because the sun was reflecting off his lenses, and Frank wished he'd had the sense to position him better at the beginning. 'No, Dad and Meg got on fine,' he said, but his tone was too flat and lacked conviction. He was silent for a moment. 'Look, perhaps it would be simpler after all, if I just told you what Dad's asked me to say. He's worried you've fixed on Jinx Kingsley as a suspect because of what happened to Russell.' He took off his glasses again and laid them on the table, fishing in his trouser pocket for a handkerchief to blow his nose. 'It's not much fun this,' he said by way of apology. 'I've been so angry with Meg for the last two weeks, and now – well, you never expect anyone to die.' He took a deep breath to steady himself. 'The irony is it's my job to comfort people in this position, tell them it's the whole history of their love that matters, not the two small weeks of anger.' He blew his nose. 'But it's only when you experience it yourself that you realize how patronizing that is.'

'We can only do our best, sir,' said Frank, giving the man's shoulder an awkward pat. 'In this job, we run up against it all the time. Such sadness everywhere and no easy answers.'

Oddly enough, Simon seemed to find this trite response rather comforting, perhaps because it proved to him that he wasn't alone in offering banalities by way of consolation. He rested his hands on the table and toyed with his glasses. 'The reason Dad didn't want Mum listening to this,' he said, 'is that she never really knew what Meg was like. She knew Meg had a lot of boyfriends but she assumed the relationships were fairly casual.' He corrected himself immediately. 'Well, of course, they *were* casual, but casual in Meg's terms, not in my mother's. I suppose you'd describe Meg as promiscuous, except that that gives a false impression of her because we tend to use it pejoratively only where women are concerned.' He gave an uncertain smile. 'I don't really know how to explain this to you without setting up prejudices in your minds. You had to know Meg. She was very innocent in an odd sort of way. She loved having fun.'

THE DARK ROOM

Fraser raised his head. 'It sounds to me as though you're saying she enjoyed sex, sir, but didn't want the commitment of a relationship. Is that so unusual these days?'

'No,' said Simon with relief, 'but I'm sure you can appreciate what my mother would think if she ever found out. She's very strait-laced.' He fell silent.

Fraser waited a moment. 'In fact, sir,' he said when Simon didn't continue and the Superintendent gave him the nod, 'your mother gives the impression that it's your father who's strait-laced. She refers to his preaching and the fact that Meg couldn't leave home fast enough to get away from him. She talks about the fact that they had arguments and that he was always lecturing her over the phone. She also knew about Meg's abortion, which your father clearly didn't. Are you sure she's as ignorant as you suggest?'

Simon nodded unhappily. 'Yes, but I'm afraid you'll have to take my word for it. Mum likes to think she knew what sort of life Meg led, but it's not true. In fact, Meg only ever lied to her because she didn't want to upset her.'

'So was the abortion a lie?'

'No, that did happen. But she didn't tell Mum about it until they had their row over Leo. It's one of the reasons I was so angry with her. If she'd only come down and talked to them in person, instead of giving them ultimatums over the phone about the fact that it was her life and she could do what she liked with it, then they might not have taken it quite so badly.' He raised his glasses off the table and swung them from side to side, watching the pendulum motion with absorbed fascination. 'She said a lot of things that I'm sure she regretted afterwards.'

Fraser glanced at the Superintendent before asking his next question.

'Are you saying her announcement about her relationship with Leo caused friction between your parents?'

Simon squeezed the bridge of his nose again. 'It's been a nightmare,' he said after a moment. 'I think the trouble was that Meg knew she was behaving badly so she set out to defend her position right from the word go. Dad, of course, homed straight in on her betrayal of Jinx, and Mum homed in on the fact that she must have been sleeping with Leo. If only she'd just apologized and left it at that.' He looked bleakly at the Sergeant. 'We never do, though, do we? It's human nature to justify ourselves.'

'What did she say?'

'I only know what she told me afterwards. She phoned me about lunchtime, but by then I'd had Mum on the phone in floods, so I was pretty angry as well.' He held the handkerchief to his eyes. 'We all said things we wish we hadn't, and now it's too late.' He breathed deeply through his nose to calm himself. 'As I understand it, she said Dad was a sanctimonious hypocrite who lusted after anything in a skirt, including her and Jinx, but hadn't got the balls to do anything about it, and Mum was a frigid prude who couldn't bear the thought of anyone enjoying sex. Meg said she'd told her about the abortion to prove there was at least one woman who didn't see babies as the only reason for having intercourse.' He caught the look of interest that flashed in Fraser's eyes.

'I'm telling you what she said, Sergeant,' he murmured tiredly, 'I'm not saying it's true. She was defending herself, so she went for their weaknesses. My mother is a prude, in so far as she deplores modern sexual practices, but she's not frigid. My father is extremely fond of Jinx because she shares his interest in the Classics, but he doesn't lust after her. If Meg had telephoned from France or if Jinx hadn't driven her car into a wall, the storm would have blown over in a day or two. As it was, my parents were left blaming each other for what they see as their fault – namely Meg's cavalier theft of her friend's fiancé, and Jinx's resulting suicide attempt. You really must understand what an impossible situation they found themselves in. Jinx's family wanted scapegoats – not unreasonably in the circumstances – but the only scapegoats available were my wretched parents. They've had to put up with some fairly strong abuse, so it's hardly surprising they feel responsible.'

Fraser nodded as he turned back through the pages of his notebook. 'Did you know about your sister's abortion before your mother did?'

'Yes.'

'When did she have it?'

'A long time ago. After she came down from Oxford. She was very much more careful after that.'

'Do you know who the father was?'

'No. I don't think she did either.'

'Did she tell you about it at the time?'

He nodded. 'I drove her to the hospital to have it done.'

'Did you approve?'

For the first time, Simon smiled. 'It didn't matter whether I did or I didn't.'

'But you must have had an opinion, sir.'

'Funnily enough, no. Where Meg was concerned, I never gave opinions. She wouldn't have listened to them.'

Fraser found the page he was looking for. 'You said: "It would be simpler if I just told you what my father wants me to say. He's worried that you've fixed on Jinx Kingsley as a suspect." Could you expand those remarks, sir?'

Simon nodded. 'Apparently my mother keeps accusing Jinx of murdering Meg and Leo, and he's afraid you'll believe her.' He looked enquiringly at the other man, but got no reaction. 'But Jinx wouldn't have done it. She and Meg were more like sisters than friends.'

'Even more reason to be angry, then, when Meg stole her fiancé,' suggested Fraser. 'Are you saying that wouldn't have upset Miss Kingsley?'

'She says not. I went to see her on Wednesday and she was very bullish about it, asked me to tell Meg she bore them no resentment and said she wished everyone would stop worrying about it.'

'Miss Kingsley's suffering from amnesia, sir. How can she know what she felt at the time?'

'I don't know, Sergeant, but I believe her and so does my father.' He leaned forward to emphasize his point. 'We've known her for years, and we can't accept she's a murderer. She certainly didn't murder Russell. She was with Meg that afternoon. Meg was her alibi.'

The Superintendent nodded thoughtfully. 'You said your father took Meg to task for her betrayal of Jinx. Am I right in thinking that's why you were angry with her as well?'

'Yes. Jinx didn't deserve to be treated so shabbily. She's been through hell one way and another, but she's never allowed it to sour her. She's very generous.' He jerked his head towards the parish church across the road. 'Helped Dad out with his steeple fund five years ago, persuaded her father to stump up for a Romanian orphans' charity I'm involved with. She's a very fine person.'

Frank smiled agreement. 'You have a high opinion of her.'

'Very.'

'Rather higher, perhaps, than you had of your sister? People who love having fun tend to be somewhat selfish and egocentric. Quite often, they're the black sheep of the family.'

Simon looked at him. 'Yes,' he said simply. 'Meg was certainly that.'

Chapter Thirteen

ALAN SENSED THAT Jinx felt she had revealed too much of herself. He wondered if this was his last chance to learn what he could about her. 'You told me your father wants you to leave, but you didn't say what you intend to do about it.'

She propped her chin on her hand and gazed at him with a troubled expression, but there was something studied about the whole gesture. 'I said I'd discharge myself back to Richmond and then take out an injunction to stop him ever interfering again unless he left well alone. Now I'm worried sick.'

He gave a surprised laugh. 'Why? I couldn't have advised better myself. You must be allowed the freedom to make your own choices.'

'I wish you'd try to understand,' she said helplessly. 'It's not my freedom that's likely to be curtailed, it's yours. If Adam thinks you suggested the injunction . . .' She gave a small shrug and didn't finish the sentence.

'You're worrying unnecessarily,' he said. 'What can he possibly do to me?'

'He hasn't built his empire on charm, Dr Protheroe. If

222

he's going to do something, he'll do it quickly. He won't want you putting any more unpleasant ideas in my head.'

'I can only repeat,' he said, eyeing her curiously, 'what can he possibly do to me?'

'That's what Russell said.' She stood up abruptly. She might have added – *and Leo, and Meg* – but she didn't.

Alan put through a telephone call to Matthew Cornell's father. 'No,' he assured him, 'Matthew's doing well. I wondered if I could pick your brains on an unrelated matter.'

'Go ahead.'

'What do you know about Adam Kingsley of Franchise Holdings?'

'I'm a criminal barrister,' Cornell reminded him. 'Not a stock broker.'

'Which is why I called you,' said Alan. 'I've been told he began life as an East End crook, and I wondered if there was any truth in it.'

'I see.' There was a short pause. 'All right, rumour has it he was active alongside the Krays and the Richardsons in the fifties and sixties, but kept a much lower profile and turned legitimate as soon as he could. He was never charged with anything because he adopted the Mafia *cuscinetto* system and erected buffers between himself and the violence his thugs meted out. But that is all hearsay, Protheroe, and not for public consumption. He's won damages in the past against two newspapers foolish enough to put that into print.'

Alan doodled on the pad in front of him, wondering how to frame his next question. 'How does he conduct business now?'

'Why? Are you thinking of investing in Franchise Holdings?'

'Maybe,' Protheroe lied.

'There's the odd hint from time to time that he's used unorthodox methods to acquire property and land in the London Docks, but it's pure speculation. I'd say he runs as clean a ship as the next man. Matter of fact,' he admitted, 'I've a small sum invested in him myself.'

'What about social skills? He was described to me as someone to be wary of in personal dealings. Would you agree with that?'

'What you'd expect from an East End boy made good.' Cornell sounded intrigued. 'I wouldn't want to get in too deep with him. Put it this way, he's not called the Great White Shark for nothing. If you work on the principle that he uses lawyers now as his buffers instead of hired muscle, then you'll probably have some idea of his *modus operandi*.'

'What does that mean exactly?'

'*Plus ça change, plus c'est la même chose.*'

'Are you saying: Once a Mafia boss, always a Mafia boss?'

An amused laugh floated down the line. 'No, Protheroe, *you're* saying it. I can't afford a slander suit.'

'Josh? It's Jinx. Are you busy or can you talk for a minute?'

'What is it?' He sounded hostile, she thought.

'Meg's dead.'

There was a silence. 'I know,' he said.

She was shivering with cold and her expression had a curiously vacant look, as if she were waiting for something. 'Who told you?'

'Simon rang,' he answered guardedly. 'They're both dead, Meg *and* Leo. How did *you* know, Jinx? Have you started to remember things?'

'No,' she said abruptly, 'I guessed. The police came here asking questions about them. What else did Simon say?'

'Nothing much, only that his mother's going out of her mind. She wants to know where Leo's parents live, so he called me.'

'Did you tell him?'

'I said I didn't know, so he's trying Dean Jarrett.'

It was her turn to hold the silence. 'You know quite well where they live,' she said at last. 'I remember telling you myself when Leo and I first got engaged. The wedding will be a nightmare, I said, Surrey gentry versus Hampshire parvenus, with each side trying to score points. And you laughed and asked which part of Surrey the Walladers came from. Downton Court, Ashwell, I told you.'

'I don't remember.'

He was lying, she thought. 'Why didn't Simon ring me?' Another silence.

'I'm sorry,' she said.

'What for?'

'Meg's death. She was your friend as well as mine.'

'Is that what you called to tell me?'

Her grip on the telephone was so brittle that her fingers hurt. 'I wanted to know what people are saying, Josh. Do Meg's parents think I killed her? Does Simon?'

'What makes you think they were murdered?' he asked.

'I'm not a bloody fool, Josh.'

'No one's saying anything,' he said. 'Not to me, anyway.'

She didn't believe him. 'Why are you afraid of me?' she

asked, addressing the fear she heard in his voice. 'Do *you* think I did it?'

'No, of course I don't. Look, I have to go. The police are due here any minute, and I'm trying to find out how the business stands with one partner dead. I'll ring back later when things calm down.' He cut the line and left her listening to empty silence. *Someone else she couldn't trust? Or someone as scared as she was?*

She replaced the receiver carefully, doubts seething in her tired brain. Was anything he said true? And why was he afraid of her? Because he thought her memory was coming back? She went to lie on the bed and stared at the ceiling, knowing that safety lay in remembering nothing, but knowing, too, that she must eventually remember something. However much her father might want what was locked inside her head to remain there for ever, she knew it was an impossibility. If Alan Protheroe didn't prise the truth out of her with his sympathetic existentialism, then somebody else would. And they wouldn't do it kindly either.

Tears stung her eyelids. Common sense told her it would be suicidal – she dwelt on that thought for a moment – to relay memories that no one believed. For this time there was no Meg to give her an alibi.

'There's a gentleman to see you, Dr Protheroe,' said his elderly secretary, popping her head round his office door. 'A Mr Kennedy. I told him you were busy but he says he's sure you can find time to talk to him. He's a solicitor, representing Mr Adam Kingsley.' She pulled a face. 'He's very insistent.'

Alan finished the notes he was writing. 'Then you'd better show him in, Hilda,' he said.

A small, thin man with spectacles and a pleasant smile entered the room a few seconds later and shook Protheroe firmly by the hand. 'Good afternoon,' he said, proffering his card and taking the chair on the other side of the desk. 'Thank you for seeing me, Dr Protheroe. Did your secretary explain that I'm here as Mr Adam Kingsley's representative?'

'She said something to that effect,' agreed Alan, examining the little man, 'but I can't imagine why Mr Kingsley feels he needs to send a solicitor.' *Jesus Christ!*

Mr Kennedy smiled. 'I am instructed to remind you of the assurances you gave my client when you undertook the care of his daughter.'

Alan frowned. 'Say again,' he invited.

The little man sat back in the chair and crossed his legs. 'Mr Kingsley is fond of his daughter, Dr Protheroe, and very concerned for her welfare. He asked you to take her in as a convalescent patient because, following the prolonged enquiries he made earlier this year, with a view to his wife becoming a patient at this clinic, he was satisfied that Jane would find the atmosphere here more congenial than the clinical surroundings of a hospital. In particular, he was keen to ensure that Jane would not feel pressured into taking part in any sort of psychiatric therapy that would remind her of her previous unfortunate experiences. To which end he asked you – as a doctor and not a psychiatrist – to take charge of her convalescence and leave her to recover at her own speed and in her own time.' He smiled his pleasant smile again. 'Would you agree that that is a fair summary of the faxed letter he sent you on the twentieth of this month?'

'I would, yes.'

'And is it equally fair to say that, in your telephone conversation with my client following receipt of his faxed letter, you made the very precise statement: "You have my assurance that your daughter will not be pressured, Mr Kingsley, and will certainly not be expected to engage in any form of therapy unless she chooses to do so."'

'I may have said something along those lines, but I can't vouch for the preciseness of the statement.'

'My client can, Dr Protheroe. He is a cautious man and insists on having tapes made of every conversation that relates to his affairs. That is word for word what you said.'

Alan shrugged. 'All right. To my knowledge, those assurances have been honoured.'

Kennedy removed a folded piece of paper from his pocket and consulted it. 'You sent my client a faxed letter last night in which you state: "One idea I'd like to discuss is the possibility of a joint session where, under my guidance, you and Jinx can explore any rifts that may have developed between you." May I ask if Miss Kingsley gave you permission to suggest this to her father? In other words, has she chosen to engage in such an activity?'

'Not yet. I thought it more sensible to seek his agreement first. There seemed little point in putting the idea to Jinx if her father wasn't prepared to take part.'

'Nevertheless, Dr Protheroe, simply by suggesting a form of therapy, you have gone against my client's express instructions to leave his daughter to recover at her own speed. It is also clear from other statements in your fax that you have been encouraging Jane to talk about events that Mr Kingsley asked you very specifically not to mention because he felt they would upset her.' He quoted extracts from the letter: '"She finds it difficult to talk about herself." "I have some problems understanding what compelled her to make an attempt on her life." "She retains a certain ambivalence following the death of her husband."'

Alan shrugged again. 'I don't recall your client instructing me to keep his daughter in solitary confinement, Mr Kennedy. Had he done so, I would most certainly not have agreed to take her.'

'You will have to explain those remarks, I'm afraid.'

'Jinx is an intelligent and articulate young woman. She is able and willing to participate in conversations. The only way to stop her talking would be to isolate her from everyone in the clinic. Is that what her father wants?' His eyes narrowed. 'To stop her *talking*?'

The little man chuckled. 'About what?'

'I don't know, Mr Kennedy.' He balanced his pen between his fingers. 'But then I'm not the one who's worried. Your client is.' *Who the hell was pulling the strings here? Adam or Jinx?*

'My client's concerns are entirely related to his daughter's welfare, Dr Protheroe. He believes firmly that any rehashing of the past will be to Jane's disadvantage, a point emphasized for him this morning when she threatened him with an injunction over the telephone. He feels, quite reasonably, that this abrupt return to her previous antagonism is due to your refusal to abide by his wishes.'

Alan considered that for a moment. 'Shall we get to the point?' he suggested. 'Is Mr Kingsley looking to control every minute of his daughter's life or does he want excuses not to pay?'

'I am instructed to remind you of the assurances you gave my client when you undertook the care of his daughter.'

'If you're referring to pressure and unwanted therapy, then there's no argument between us. Jinx has been subjected to neither.'

'Yet you state in your fax: "She finds it difficult to talk about herself."' He looked up. 'The clear inference is that you have sought to persuade her to do just that.'

'This is absurd,' said Alan angrily. 'I wrote to Mr Kingsley because I assumed he had his daughter's welfare at heart and, as Jinx's doctor, I believe it to be in her best interests to seek a rapprochement with her father. However, if his only response is to send a solicitor to spout gobbledegook, then obviously she is right and I am wrong. Her father is only interested in manipulating and controlling her, and little good can come from a meeting.' He squared the papers on his desk. 'Presumably there's some sort of implied threat in these repeated instructions of yours. Would you care to tell me what it is?'

'Now you're being absurd, Dr Protheroe.'

'This is all beyond me, I'm afraid.' Alan studied the solicitor with a perplexed frown. 'I really have no interest in playing games with my patients' well-being. If Mr Kingsley is seeking excuses not to pay, then I shall discuss the matter with Miss Kingsley herself. I have no doubts at all she will wish to honour the obligations her father entered into on her behalf. Please tell your client that I have strong reservations about his reading of his daughter's character. She is far less anxious than he appears to be about reliving her past experiences. In addition, I cannot agree with the police presumption that she attempted suicide.' He leaned forward. 'You may also tell him that, in my professional opinion, it is Mr Kingsley who represents the greatest threat to Jinx's peace of mind. There is an ambivalence in her attitude towards him which can only be resolved by a clearing of the air between them, particularly in relation to her husband's death and to what she perceives as Mr Kingsley's obsessive and continued need to interfere in her life. However, in the face of his obvious unwillingness to talk to her, a clean break by means of an injunction would seem to be the only alternative.' He placed his hands flat on the desk and pushed himself to his feet. 'Good-day, Mr Kennedy. I trust you will have the courtesy to convey *my* views with the same assiduous detail with which you have just conveyed your client's.'

The solicitor beamed as he, too, rose to his feet. 'No need, Dr Protheroe,' he murmured, patting his breast pocket. 'I have it all on tape. I believe I told you that Mr Kingsley insists on having taped records made of every conversation relating to his affairs. I know he will be interested to hear everything you've said. Good-day to you.'

The phone rang on Alan's desk ten minutes later, and he picked it up with ill humour.

'I've a Reverend Simon Harris for you, Dr Protheroe,' said Hilda. 'Do you want to speak to him?'

'Not particularly,' he grunted.

'He says it's important.'

'He would,' said Alan sarcastically. 'It'll be a red-letter day when someone doesn't think what they have to say is important.'

'You sound cross,' said Hilda.

'That's because I am.' He sighed. 'All right, put him through.'

Simon's voice came on the line. 'Dr Protheroe? Do you remember me? I'm a friend of Jinx Kingsley. I came to visit her on Thursday.'

'I remember,' he said.

'I find myself in a somewhat invidious position,' said the younger man in a voice that was clearly troubled. He paused briefly. 'Has Jinx told you that Meg and Leo are dead, Dr Protheroe?'

Alan raised a hand to his beard and smoothed it automatically. 'No,' he said.

'They were murdered, probably on the same day that she tried to kill herself.'

Alan stared across the room at a print of Albrecht Dürer's *Knight, Death and Devil*, and thought how appropriate it was that he should be looking at that. 'I'm so sorry, Mr Harris. You must be very upset.'

'We've not had much time to be upset,' said Simon apologetically. 'We had the police here until an hour ago.'

'I'm sorry,' said Alan again. 'What makes you think Jinx knows?'

'Her assistant told me.'

'You mean Dean Jarrett?'

'Yes.'

'How does he know?'

Simon sighed. 'Apparently the police visited her yesterday and she guessed something was wrong. She rang Dean during the evening and persuaded him to phone the Walladers for confirmation.' He paused again. 'She knew before we did, as a matter of fact. My parents weren't told

until ten o'clock last night and only made the formal identification this morning. My mother's very bitter about it.
She's blaming Jinx for Meg's death.'

Alan wondered what else his patient had withheld from
him. 'Why are you telling me this?' he asked.

Another hesitation. 'As I said, I find myself in an invidious position. My father, too.' He cleared his throat. 'It's
difficult to think straight when you're shocked – well, I'm
sure you know that —' He broke off abruptly. 'Sir Anthony
Wallader is going to *The Times* with accusations against Jinx
and her father, egged on by my mother. It's understandable.
They're both very upset, as you can imagine – well, of
course we all are.' He blew his nose. 'I've no idea how much
the newspapers are likely to print, but it could be very bad,
especially if the tabloids get hold of it. My mother's not very
well – she's . . . that is . . . Dad and I felt Jinx should be protected from the worst of it – it's little better than a kangaroo court – and I didn't know who else to phone. I thought
she'd have told you – about their deaths anyway.' His voice
broke with emotion. 'I'm sorry – I'm so sorry.'

Alan listened to the quiet tears at the other end of the
line. 'I wouldn't worry too much,' he said with a calm he
didn't feel. 'Jinx is an extraordinarily tough young woman'
– *even he hadn't realized till now just how tough* – 'and I'm
confident it's only a matter of days before her memory
returns in full and she's able to set minds at rest.' He
thought for a moment. 'Presumably we're talking about
speculation and not fact? If there were any evidence against
Miss Kingsley the police would have confronted her by
now. Am I right?'

Simon fought for composure. 'As far as I understand it,

yes, but we've been told very little. Sir Anthony's known since Saturday morning and he said that Leo had been bludgeoned to death . . . The same way Russell Landy was.'

'Does Jinx's father know Meg and Leo are dead?'

'I don't think so. Dad and I think their intention is to hit Jinx while she's vulnerable, but we can't see justice being done that way.'

Alan was curious. 'You're being very generous to her, Mr Harris.'

'Things aren't as straightforward as they might seem,' Simon said tightly. 'We're worried about my mother, and we don't want Jinx's suicide on our conscience. She'll be under a lot of pressure when the news breaks and what she's tried once, it seems likely she could try again.'

'Well, on that score at least I don't think you need worry,' said Alan slowly. 'If I had any doubts at all about her mental equilibrium you've just laid them to rest. Thank you for letting me know, Mr Harris.'

He said goodbye and replaced the receiver with a thoughtful frown. What on earth was going on here? Did Adam Kingsley know? Is that why he'd sent Kennedy? *God almighty!* Were he and the clinic being dragged into some sort of conspiracy to pervert the course of justice? 'SHI-IT!' he roared at Dürer's *Knight, Death and Devil*. Why the hell had he agreed to take the bloody woman in?

He sought out Veronica Gordon, the sister in charge. 'I've had it up to here,' he told her, chopping at his throat. 'I'm going AWOL for a few hours. If there's an emergency, get Nigel White to deal with it.' He thought for a moment. 'But if it's an emergency concerning Miss Kingsley, call me on the mobile. No,' he corrected himself, 'we'll go one step further where she's concerned. I want her checked every half-hour without fail. Got that? A physical check by you or one of the nurses every thirty minutes, and if you're worried at all, page me. OK?'

Veronica nodded. 'Any particular reason?'

'No,' he growled, 'just a safety precaution. Her father sent his blasted solicitor over to give me an ear-bashing, and he's put the wind up me. I don't want to be sued for negligence if she takes it into her head to do something stupid.'

'She won't,' said the woman with confidence.

'Why are you so sure?'

'I've watched her. Everyone does exactly what she wants, including you, Alan, and people like that don't hang up their boots lightly.'

'She's already had one go.'

'Balls!' said Veronica with an amiable grin. 'She may want her Daddy to think she did, but if it had been a serious attempt she'd be dead. My guess is there were a lot of hidden agendas at work when she threw herself out of her car, and a little fatherly sympathy was one of them. Mind you,' she added thoughtfully, 'she didn't research the science of movable objects hitting solid Tarmac very thoroughly. I'm not convinced severe concussion and amnesia were part of the original equation.'

Alan shrugged. 'It may not be part of the endgame either. You don't have to be Einstein to fake amnesia, Veronica.'

She looked at him in surprise. 'Are you saying she's a fraud?'

'Not necessarily,' he lied. 'I was merely stating a fact.'

'But why would she bother with anything so elaborate unless she had something to hide?'

'Perhaps she does.'

Fergus was leaning against Protheroe's Wolseley when the doctor emerged into the warm late afternoon and approached across the gravel. He gave a perfunctory nod towards the older man and ran a hand over the bonnet. 'I thought it might be yours,' he said. 'I noticed it when I visited Jinx the other day. Do you want to sell it?'

Alan shook his head. 'I'm afraid not. We've been together too long to part so easily.' He put the key into the lock. 'Have you seen Jinx, or are you on your way in?'

'Just waiting. She's wandering about the garden some-where. Miles has gone looking for her. Did Kennedy give you a roasting then?'

'Is that what he's employed to do?'

'It depends on Dad's mood. I told him you were pretty high-handed with me on Saturday, so I thought maybe he'd ordered his Rottweiler in to remind you who foots the bill. I also told him I reckoned you had the hots for Jinxy.' He peered at Alan out of the corner of his eye, judging his reaction. 'Dad was bloody cross about it, so I'm not sur-prised he sent Kennedy over.'

Alan gave a snort of amusement. 'I doubt you have the bottle to tell your father anything, Fergus.' He pulled the car door open. 'As a matter of interest, how did you know Kennedy was here?'

'I saw him leave.' He yawned. 'Miles wants to meet you. I promised I'd keep you here till he got back.'

'Another time perhaps.'

'No, now.' Fergus caught at his arm. 'We want to know what's going on. Does Jinx remember something?'

'I suggest you ask her.' Alan looked down at the restraining hand. 'You're welcome to come and talk to me any time you like, just so long as you make an appointment first. But at the moment' – he placed his hand over the young man's and prised it off his arm – 'I've more important things to do.' He smiled amiably and eased in behind the wheel. 'It's been nice meeting you again, Fergus. Give my best wishes to your mother and brother.' He shut the door and gunned the Wolseley into life, before spinning the wheel and roaring away down the drive.

When Sister Gordon did her rounds at nine o'clock that evening, she found Jinx standing by her window watching the remnants of the day burn to crimson embers. 'Isn't it beautiful?' Jinx said without turning round, knowing by instinct who her visitor was. 'If I could stand and look on this for ever, then I would have eternal happiness. Do you imagine that's what Heaven is?'

'I guess it depends on how static you want your Heaven to be. Presumably you've watched this develop from a simple sunset into glorious fire, so at which point would you have stopped it to produce your moment of eternal happiness? I think I would always be wondering if the moment afterwards had been more beautiful than the one I was stuck with, and that would turn the experience into a hell of frustration.'

Jinx laughed quietly. 'So there is no Heaven?'

'Not for me. Bliss is only bliss when you come upon it

unexpectedly. 'If it lasted for ever it would be unbearable.' She smiled. 'Everything all right?'

Jinx turned away from the window. 'Exactly the same as it was half an hour ago, and the half-hour before that. Are you going to tell me now why it's so important to keep checking on me?'

'Perhaps the doctor's worried that you've been over-exerting yourself. You put the fear of God into me this afternoon with that wretched walk. It was too far and too long.'

'It wasn't, you know,' said Jinx idly. 'I spent most of the time hiding.' She smiled at the other woman's surprise. 'I saw my brother coming and dived for cover in one of the outside sheds.' She glanced back towards the window. 'Dr Protheroe told me he was expecting a visit from my father,' Jinx lied easily. 'So do you know if Adam ever came? I thought he might pop in afterwards to visit me.'

'I believe his solicitor came,' she said, plumping up the pillows and smoothing the sheets, 'but I don't think your father did.'

Jinx pressed her forehead against the glass. 'Why hasn't Dr Protheroe been to see me?'

'He's taken himself off for a few hours' R and R. Poor fellow,' she said fondly, wishing as she often did that she hadn't saddled herself with Mr Gordon. 'He has a lot on his mind one way and another, and no one to share his problems with.'

Jinx wrapped her arms about her thin body to stop the shivering. *Did he have Leo and Meg on his mind? And was it Kennedy who'd told him?*

Sister Gordon frowned. 'You've been at that window too

long, you silly girl. Quickly now, into your dressing gown and into bed. No sense catching pneumonia on top of everything else.' She clicked her tongue sharply as she opened the dressing gown and slipped it over Jinx's shoulders. 'You were lucky that young couple arrived when they did on the night of your accident or you'd have started pneumonia then.'

'It was certainly convenient,' said Jinx impassively.

Tuesday, 28 June, Nightingale Clinic,
Salisbury – 12.05 a.m.

The Wolseley swung through the clinic's gates, its headlamps scything a white arc across the lawn. It was after midnight and Alan slowed to a crawl to avoid waking the patients with the crunch of wheels on gravel. He felt no relief about coming home, no sense of welcome at his journey's end, only a growing resentment that this was all there was. The temporary euphoria that a bottle of expensive Rioja over a meal of langoustines in garlic butter had given him had evaporated during his careful drive home to leave only frustrated depression. What the hell was he doing with his life? Where was the satisfaction in ministering to a clutch of rich bastards with over-inflated egos and no self-control? Why hadn't Jinx told him Meg and Leo were dead? And why couldn't he get the damn woman out of his mind?

He drummed an angry hand on the wheel, only to wrench it in alarm as the lights picked out the white flash of a face, inches from the nearside wing, disembodied against the blackness of the trees bordering the drive. *Shit!*

SH-I-IT! His heart set up a sturdy gallop as he slammed his foot on the brake and brought the crawling car to an almost instantaneous halt. Half-hourly checks, he'd said, and she was out here dodging bloody cars.

'Jinx,' he called, fumbling open the door and hauling himself out and upright with a hand on the car roof. 'Are you all right?'

Silence.

'Look, I saw you.' *God help him if he'd hit her.* He used the red light thrown by his rear lamps to scan the grass verge behind the car, but there was no huddled body there. 'I know you can hear me,' he went on, staring into the trees, searching for her. He walked round to lean against the passenger door. Sooner or later she would have to move and he'd see the flash of the white face again. 'I think you're a fraud, Jinx. The amnesia's crap and I don't believe for one second that you tried to kill yourself. It was a set-up, pure and simple, designed to get your father on your side, and it sure as hell worked, even if you probably did yourself rather more damage than you intended. So are you going to tell me what it's all about?' He waited. 'I should warn you I'm feeling pretty bloody ratty at the moment, and my mood isn't improved by hanging around in my own sodding drive because one of my patients wants to play silly buggers. But don't expect me to give up tamely and leave you here. You move one muscle, girl, and I'll catch you. So are you going to show yourself or are we going to wait this out till daylight? Your choice.'

There was a blur of movement, so quick and so close that he was completely overwhelmed by it. He lurched to one side but pain exploded in his shoulder as the solid metal head of a sledgehammer tore his arm from its socket. He ducked away from another arcing blow and scrambled round the bonnet of the car towards the open door of the driver's seat. With an instinct born of desperation, he threw himself behind the wheel and slammed the door. But as he reached across his chest to force the gear clumsily into reverse, the sledgehammer burst through the windscreen towards his face.

Amy Staunton looked at her watch. 'What's Dr Protheroe want half-hourly checks for anyway?' she grumbled. 'The girl's been fast asleep since ten o'clock.'

'Ours not to question why,' said Veronica Gordon. 'Ours just to do or die. Finish your tea. I can't see five minutes making much difference here or there.'

He didn't know if it was sweat or blood that was pouring down his face. As the car accelerated backwards, he only knew that he was in agony. With a sense of unreality he watched the figure – *a man* – vanish into the darkness before the Wolseley's back-end piled into a solid oak tree. *What the hell was going on?*

The door handle of number twelve rattled and the door was pushed half-open as the black nurse looked into the pitch darkness inside. She heard something and, with a start of fear, she felt about for the light switch. 'Are you all right, love?' She flooded the room with light, glanced at the bed where Jinx was threshing her sheets into a tumbled mess, then looked towards the french windows where the curtains flapped in the breeze. Tut-tutting impatiently, she crossed the room to close and lock the windows, then went to the bed and placed a gentle hand on the woman's forehead.

As though galvanized by an electric shock, Jinx sat bolt upright in the bed, mouth sucking frenziedly for air. *She couldn't breathe . . . Dear God, she couldn't breathe . . .* She clutched at her throat in a vain attempt to dislodge whatever was blocking her airway. *But it was earth, filthy acrid earth . . . and it was killing her . . . NO-O-O!* She flung herself off the bed and burst through the bathroom door, wrenching at the cold water tap in the basin and ducking her head under the icy water. She drew in breath on a gasp of shock and let the sweet, sweet water wash the taste of death away.

'Oh, good God, girl,' screeched the nurse, 'what's got into you? You being sick? What you been taking? What you doing with your clothes on? You was fast asleep last time I checked.'

Jinx slumped to the floor and stared at her from red-rimmed eyes. 'It was a dream, Amy,' she whispered. 'Only a dream.'

'Ooh, you're a wicked girl. I've never had such a fright in my life. You just wait till I tell Dr Protheroe. I thought you'd done for yourself good and proper.' She beat her chest. 'I could have had a heart attack. And why did you open your windows? Top panes only after nine o'clock, that's the rule. What you been up to?'

Jinx curled into a ball on the tiled floor. 'Nothing,' she said.

Bodies in Wood Identified

It was confirmed last night by Hampshire police that the two bodies discovered in Ardingly Woods near Winchester on Thursday have been identified as Leo Wallader, 35, of Downton Court, Ashwell, Guildford, and Meg Harris, 34, of Shoebury Terrace, Hammersmith, London. Police are treating their deaths as murder.

Information about the identity of the two victims came from Leo's father, Sir Anthony Wallader, 69, who is angry about what he calls police apathy over the affair. 'I identified my son's body on Saturday morning,' he claims, 'but have had no contact with the Hampshire police since. They tell me my son and his girlfriend were murdered some two weeks ago, yet there is no urgency to the enquiries. I have been contacted by Meg's mother, who lives in Wiltshire, and she is as upset by the police lethargy as I am. We feel it may have something to do with the fact that both sets of parents live outside the county. If this was a Surrey police investigation I would have more confidence.'

It is no secret that Leo Wallader was engaged to Jane Kingsley, daughter of Adam Kingsley of Hellingdon Hall, Hampshire, Chairman of Franchise Holdings, but the wedding was cancelled when Leo announced he wanted to marry Jane's friend, Meg Harris.

Subsequently, Miss Kingsley was involved in a mysterious car crash on a disused Hampshire airfield. Police believe this to have been a failed suicide attempt. Despite testing positive for alcohol when she was rescued from her car, Hampshire police have still failed to charge Miss Kingsley with any offence.

Jane Kingsley's first husband, Russell Landy, was clubbed to death 10 years ago with a sledgehammer but his murderer was never found. Hampshire police refused to comment on how Leo Wallader and Meg Harris died, but Sir Anthony said both victims had been brutally bludgeoned. 'It was terrible to see,' he said. 'I dread to think how Mrs Harris feels.'

'We have very little to go on at this stage,' said Det Supt Cheever of Hampshire police, 'but we are pursuing every lead we have. I am sorry Sir Anthony feels as he does but I can assure him we are leaving no stone unturned to discover his son's killer.'

Supt Cheever said he could not confirm that a sledge-hammer had been used to murder the couple. 'The bodies lay undiscovered for some ten days,' he said, 'and it is always difficult in those circumstances to be precise about how and when the victims died.'

The Times – 28 June

Chapter Fourteen

THE TWO CONSTABLES surveyed the shattered wind-screen and the crushed Wolseley boot with unfeigned disgust. It was parked forlornly by the front door where Alan had driven it when he realized that, without some very prompt action, his dislocated shoulder would require reduction under general anaesthetic at the nearest Casu-alty department. He had blared the horn with all the vigour of the angels and archangels sounding the last trump, and had sobbed with relief when the night security officer had emerged to rescue him, and Veronica Gordon, using strong hands and a steady nerve, had guided the bones back into place. Even so, it had been a close call. After fifteen minutes, the joint had been so swollen that the pain was unbearable.

'That's criminal,' said one policeman, lighting the damage with his torch. 'How many times did you say he hit it, sir?'

'Only once,' said Alan, cradling his left elbow in the palm of his right hand, unconvinced that the sling he was wearing was reliable. 'I smashed the back in when I was reversing away from him. I'm rather more interested in the fact that he had at least two swipes at me.'

'Still, sir,' said the other ponderously, 'he seems to have done more damage to your car.'

'Remind me to show you some pictures of dislocated joints thirty minutes after the event,' he said dryly, 'then tell me he did more damage to my car.' He led the way inside and into his office, padding wearily to his desk and hitching a buttock on to the edge. 'I suppose it's occurred to you he might still be out there.'

'Highly unlikely, sir, not with all the activity that's been going on.'

The police car had arrived within ten minutes of the 999 call and, following Dr Protheroe's description of events, namely that he had glimpsed a face in his headlights and had stopped to investigate, the policemen worked on the logical assumption that an intruder had come with the intention of burglary and the doctor had had the misfortune to get in his way. A thorough check of all the doors and windows, however, had failed to find any signs of a break-in.

'We can't fault your security, sir,' said the larger of the two constables with a perplexed frown, 'which makes me doubt this fellow had cased the clinic very thoroughly. If he was planning a burglary, he can't have known how difficult it was going to be to break in. So are you sure you didn't recognize him? Otherwise I don't understand why he bothered to attack you. He clearly hadn't committed a crime at that point, not unless he entered and left by the front door, which your security officer says is impossible because he's been at the reception desk since ten o'clock.'

'I'm sure. In any case I was beginning to think I'd made a mistake about seeing anyone at all until I felt the hammer brush my arm. I had no idea he was so close to me. I certainly didn't hear him, but, as I'd left the car engine running, that wasn't really surprising.'

'And you can't think of any reason why someone would want to attack you?'

Alan shook his head. 'Unless he knew I was a doctor and thought I had drugs in the car. I've been racking my brains but I can't think of anything else.' There would be time enough tomorrow, he thought, to decide whether it had been Jinx's face he had seen in the headlamps, or whether his imagination had put her there because she had been on his mind.

'An ex-patient, perhaps, who would recognize your car?'

'I wouldn't have thought so. It's one of the first things I make clear when they arrive. We have a limited supply of drugs on the premises and they're always locked away in that safe over there.' He jerked his head towards the solid Chubb in the corner. 'They certainly know I never carry anything in my car.'

The constable lowered himself on to a chair and took a notebook from his pocket. 'Well, let's get some details down. You say he ran away after smashing the windscreen, so you must have had a pretty good look at him then.'

Alan plucked a Kleenex from a box on his desk and dabbed at his face, which was still bleeding from where tiny shards of glass had embedded themselves in his skin. 'Not really. I was having a hell of a job trying to find reverse with my right hand, so I was concentrating on that.'

'Will you describe him for me, please?'

'He was a bit shorter than I am – say about five ten or eleven. I suppose you'd describe him as medium build – he certainly wasn't fat – and he was dressed in black.'

The policeman waited for him to continue, pencil poised over notebook on knee. When he didn't, he looked up. 'A slightly fuller description would be more helpful, sir. For example, what skin colour was he?'

'I don't know. I think he was wearing a ski-mask. All I saw was a man dressed in black from head to toe wielding a sledgehammer.'

'Fair enough. Then perhaps you could give me some details of his dress. What was he wearing on his top?'

Alan shook his head. 'I don't know.' He saw impatience in the constable's eyes. 'Look,' he said with a flash of anger, 'it's very dark. I get out of my car and the next thing I know some bastard is trying to make mincemeat out of me. Frankly, taking in the minutiae of his dress is the last thing on my mind.'

The policeman waited a moment. 'Except that you must have taken in a few more details when you were back in the car and he was running away.'

'It happened very fast. All I can tell you is that he was dressed in black.'

'It's not much to go on, sir.'

'I'm aware of that,' said Alan testily.

There was a short silence. 'Yet you're very sure it was a man. Why? Did he say something to you?'

'No.'

'Could it have been a woman?'

'Maybe, but I don't believe it was. Everything about him – body shape, strength, aggression – told me it was a man.'

'You wouldn't be so convinced if you saw some of the women we deal with, sir,' said the constable with heavy humour. 'There's no such thing as a weaker sex these days.'

Alan took a deep breath. 'Look, would it be a problem if we left all this till tomorrow? I'm pretty tired and my shoulder's giving me hell.'

The constables exchanged glances. 'I can't see why not,' said the one who had remained standing. 'The place seems secure enough and, without a good description, there's not much we can do tonight anyway. We'll have one of the plainclothes lads come and talk to you tomorrow. Meanwhile, sir, you might make a list of where you've been today and who you've spoken to.' He gave a courteous nod. 'It was a good bet that anyone coming back after midnight was more likely to be a doctor than a visitor or patient. So for what it's worth, I think your theory about drugs is the most likely explanation.'

Alan stopped at the nurses' room on his way to bed. 'Everything all right?' he asked.

Veronica Gordon, the only occupant, looked at his bloodied face. 'Are you trying to play the martyr?' she demanded. 'Is that why you won't let me do something about those cuts?'

'You're too ham-fisted, woman,' he growled. 'I'd rather do them myself, quietly and gently, in my own time. Any problems?'

'Good lord, no,' she said tartly. 'Why would there be problems when a house full of insecure drunks and drug addicts get woken in the middle of the night by security officers and policemen tramping about the gravel and shining torches through their windows? For your information, Amy and I are being run off our feet. She is currently responding to the three bells that rang just before you came in.' A light began flashing on the board at her elbow. 'There's another one. They're all too nosy for their own good. They want to know what's going on.'

'What about Jinx Kingsley? Are you still running the half-hourly checks?'

She swung the night register round for him to look at. 'Fast asleep, and has been since ten o'clock. Matter of fact, she's the only one who hasn't given us any trouble. Amy checked her just before you started blaring your horn but it's not recorded because we haven't had time, not with all the hoo-ha going on. I've popped my head in once since then, but she's out like a light. Do you want us to go on with it?'

'Yes,' he said thoughtfully. 'Just in case. It makes me feel easier, knowing where she is.'

It wasn't until after he'd gone that Veronica was struck by the inappropriateness of what he'd said. She intended to mention it to Amy Staunton, but it went out of her mind when the demands of another bell sent her off down the corridor. Had it not, and if Amy had been encouraged to tell her that Jinx was fully dressed, she, like Sergeant Fraser, often wondered afterwards how different the end result might have been.

Jinx's waxen cheeks lost their last vestiges of colour when Alan Protheroe entered her room before breakfast the following morning, his left arm supported in a sling and his face scarred with tiny cuts and scratches. 'Did Adam do that?'

He was visibly taken aback. Whatever reaction he'd

expected from her, it certainly hadn't been that. 'Why would your father want to break my windscreen?'

'He wouldn't,' she said rapidly. 'Forget I said it. It was silly. Is that what happened? Is that why the police were here last night?'

He smiled. 'There now, and I was reliably informed you slept through the whole thing.'

'I did.'

'Then how do you know the police were here?'

'Matthew told me. He came in half an hour ago.'

God damn bloody Matthew! He seemed to spend more time in this room than he did in his own. 'Did he say what it was all about?'

Jinx shook her head. 'He's on a trawl to see if anybody else knows.'

She was a great liar because she understood the importance of being plausible. 'I see.' He perched on the end of the bed. 'And you couldn't tell him because you don't know.'

She held his gaze for a moment before looking away. 'That's right.'

'The police think it was an intruder after drugs.' He examined her exhausted face. 'For someone who slept through it all, you don't look very rested.'

She forced a cheerful smile. 'It's my skinhead look. It doesn't do me any more favours than it does your average convict. But it's not really designed to, is it? Hair is the original fashion accessory.'

'Are you cold?' he asked her. 'You're shivering.'

'It's nerves.'

'Why are you nervous of me, Jinx?'

'I'm not.'

'Then what *are* you nervous of?'

'I don't know,' she said. 'I can't remember.'

He grinned broadly. 'I had a dream about you last night. I dreamt I was lying on my back on a cliff edge when a hand came up, grabbed my ankle, and started to pull me towards the brink. As I was sliding over, I looked down and saw your face staring up at me, and you were smiling.'

She frowned. 'Is that supposed to mean something?'

'Yes,' he said, standing up. 'It means you were pulling my leg.'

It was a Detective Constable Hadden of the Wiltshire police who took up where the two uniformed policemen had left off the previous night. He was a bluff middle-aged man who was there to pay lip-service to police procedure but without any obvious intention of pursuing the matter further. Rather to Alan's annoyance, he arrived with the newspaper which put paid, for the moment anyway, to Alan's attempts to substantiate what Simon Harris had told him over the telephone.

'Frankly, sir,' confided DC Hadden, pushing his ample bottom into the sculptured recesses of the leather sofa, 'I'm inclined to go along with the junkie theory, unless you've remembered anything overnight that points to something more concrete. You see our dilemma. We'd have more success looking for a needle in a haystack than scouring the countryside for this man you've described. It would be different if you could give us a name or if he'd stolen something –

there'd be a slim chance of tracing him through the goods – but as it is' – he shook his head – 'needle-in-haystack stuff, sir. I'm sure you understand the problem.'

'Then this list I made of the people I spoke to yesterday was a complete waste of time,' Alan snapped irritably. 'I could have had another half-hour in bed, which would have done me rather more good than attempting to assist the police in an inquiry they aren't even interested in.' He snatched the list from the coffee table and prepared to roll it into a ball.

'Now I didn't say that, sir,' said Hadden, holding out his hand for the piece of paper. 'We will, of course, look at any information you give us but the report of last night's incident emphasizes very strongly that you did not believe the attack was personal. Perhaps you've reconsidered?'

Alan shook his head. 'What I said was, I can't think of anyone who would want to have done it, but I did make the point that the man took another swing at me even after I'd shut myself in the car. If drugs were what he was after, why didn't he give up then?'

Hadden glanced down the list as he spoke. 'Because these types don't act logically, sir, as I'm sure you know. His mind was set on whatever you had in the car, so he smashed the windscreen to get at it. Hospitals lose thousands of pounds' worth of stock every week. Sooner or later, someone was bound to think a place like this was worth a hit.' He thumbed the corner of the page. 'Mr Kennedy, solicitor to Adam Kingsley,' he read slowly. 'Would that be Adam Kingsley of Franchise Holdings?'

Alan nodded.

The transformation from bored indifference to alert interest was startling. 'May I ask why his solicitor came to see you, sir?'

'Mr Kingsley's daughter is a patient here.'

'I see.' The detective frowned. 'Why send his solicitor? Is there some dispute between you?'

'Not that I'm aware of.'

'Then what did you talk about? Was it an amicable discussion?'

'Perfectly amicable. We discussed Miss Kingsley's progress.'

'Is that normal, sir? Discussing a patient's progress with her father's solicitor?'

'Not in my experience, no, but Mr Kingsley's a busy man. Perhaps he trusts his solicitor to keep confidential information confidential.'

The other man's frown deepened. Clearly, he found the episode as inexplicable as Alan had done. 'Have you met Mr Kingsley himself?'

'No. We correspond by fax and telephone.'

'So you can't say what sort of a man he is?' Alan shook his head. 'There's a Fergus Kingsley on your list. Would that be a relation?'

'The younger son. Miss Kingsley's half-brother.'

'And was your conversation with him amicable?'

He thought of Fergus's hand on his arm. The gesture had been annoying, but not hostile. 'Yes, it was amicable.'

DC Hadden folded the page and stuffed it into his pocket. 'You said your guy was carrying a sledgehammer. No question about that?'

'None.'

'OK.' He stood up. 'We'll see what we can do, sir.'

Alan raised an enquiring eyebrow. 'Why the sudden change of heart? Two minutes ago you were quietly going to drop the whole thing, now you are raring to go. What's Kingsley got to do with this?'

Hadden shrugged noncommittally. 'I seem to have given you a false impression, sir. The Wiltshire police take all assaults seriously. Presumably, if we need to come back to you, we'll find you here. You're not planning to go away in the next day or so?'

'No.'

'Thank you for your help. I'll be off then.'

Alan watched him leave, then, with a thoughtful frown, reached again for the newspaper. The piece about Leo and Meg was on an inside page and, when he read it, he understood why mention of sledgehammers in the context of the name Kingsley had galvanized so indolent a man as DC Hadden into activity.

Romsey Road Police Station, Winchester – 10.00 a.m.

An hour later and twenty miles away in Winchester, Frank Cheever listened to what his oppo in Salisbury told him over the telephone and smiled for the first time in twelve hours. It had been a bastard of a night, beginning with the call from *The Times* seeking confirmation of identity and continuing with a bombardment from other journalists demanding to know if the implications in *The Times* piece had any basis in fact. Sir Anthony Wallader, it seemed, had been very specific in his accusations against Kingsley and his daughter and, while none of the newspapers was foolish enough to print his statement verbatim, they had all followed *The Times*'s lead by mentioning Landy's death and quoting Frank's own refusal to specify whether a sledgehammer had been used. They had also flirted with Wallader's other accusation that Kingsley was using his influence to suppress the investigation in his home county of Hampshire, leaving their readers to tease out all the damning implications.

Frank's ears were still smarting from a deeply critical dressing-down by the Chief Constable for his failure to keep Sir Anthony and Mrs Harris informed of developments. Frank had pointed out, but to no effect, that Meg's body had not been formally identified until a few hours previously and that Sir Anthony's complaint to the newspapers was very specific, namely that Hampshire police had not immediately arrested and/or charged Adam or Jane Kingsley. The Chief Constable was unimpressed by such niceties of distinction. Frank should have addressed the Wallader and Harris concerns at the outset and never allowed this climate of distrust to develop.

'It must have occurred to you that the two sets of parents would get together. Why on earth didn't you go back to the Walladers the minute the Harrises had left? Of course they're going to suspect the worst if we can't be bothered to keep them informed. I'm organizing a press conference for this afternoon and I expect you to have pacified both families in the meantime. No one is to be left in any doubt at all that Hampshire police are pursuing this inquiry with vigour and commitment, irrespective of who may or may not be involved.'

Frank glanced at his watch as he replaced the receiver.

Sir Anthony and Lady Wallader were due in less than ten minutes. The Harrises had declined the invitation, but had agreed to see Detective Superintendent Cheever in their home at midday. The press conference was scheduled for three-thirty. He picked up the telephone again and ordered DI Maddocks into his office immediately.

'Sir,' said Gareth, presenting himself sixty seconds later, as anxious not to annoy the Superintendent as Frank was anxious not to further annoy the Chief Constable. The pecking order had been viciously active since seven o'clock the previous evening.

'I've had a call from Salisbury. Dr Alan Protheroe at the Nightingale Clinic was attacked last night with a sledge-hammer. He avoided serious injury by raising the alarm and attracting help but, and this is the interesting bit, Salisbury say Protheroe had a visit from Kingsley's solicitor yesterday afternoon. I want you to go to Salisbury, take Fraser with you, talk to Detective Superintendent Mayhew and a Detective Constable Hadden and then go on to the Nightingale Clinic to interview Dr Protheroe. Get me a complete run-down of his day, the names of everyone he spoke to and what was said. The solicitor's visit cannot be coincidence.'

Sir Anthony Wallader was in no mood to be placated. He denounced the Kingsleys as murderers, repeated his accusations of police lethargy, demanded to know why Russell Landy's death had gone unpunished, insisted that if the police had done their job over that, then Leo and Meg would still be alive. He seemed unable to contain his grief or deal with it, and three days had brewed in him an anger that needed to lash out at anyone who could be blamed for his loss. Lady Wallader, by contrast, sat with bowed head and said nothing.

Frank, too, sat in silence until the storm abated.

'Please accept my apologies for any insensitivity that I and my team have shown you and your wife, Sir Anthony,' he said quietly. 'Our difficulty was tracing Meg's parents and, as I'm sure Mrs Harris told you, it wasn't until yesterday morning that they were able to make the formal identification. Clearly, I should have telephoned you immediately afterwards to acquaint you with developments and I regret intensely that I did not.'

'At the very least, someone should have been sent to comfort my wife. Why wasn't that done? The Reverend Harris tells me you sent a policewoman to support *his* wife.'

'We did offer support and counselling, sir, but if you remember you said it would only make it worse to have strangers in your house.'

'Well, I'm not going to let it rest. I'm making an official complaint. In my view you should be taken off the case immediately and replaced with someone more competent.' Tears gathered in his eyes. 'My son has been murdered and what are you doing about it? Nothing. Any more than anything was done after Russell Landy's murder.'

'I do assure you, sir, we have done a great deal in the few days we've had. For example, we've located your son's London house where we expect to find most of his and Miss Harris's possessions.' He checked the time. 'A team of detectives was due in there this morning, accompanied by your son's solicitor. We have in addition requested the French police to enter his house in Brittany although, as it seems clear he and Meg died without ever leaving England, we are not hopeful of anything material coming back across the Channel. There is also the condominium in Florida, but, again, we think it unlikely that a search will bear fruit.' He paused for a moment, pretending not to see the hurt bewilderment on the older man's face. 'We are still trying to locate his two cars. His solicitor is sure that one of them, at least, is in the garage of the Chelsea house and he has given us the address of another garage in Camden which Leo rented for several years. Mr Bloom has agreed to take the detectives there after they have finished in the house. There are, in addition, two safety deposit boxes, which we will apply to search, and several bank accounts that may tell us something when we can gain access to them. I regret that these efforts had to be delayed until today, but we were only given Mr Bloom's name on Sunday afternoon. We contacted him yesterday and arranged for the searches to be made this morning.'

'But this is outrageous,' spluttered Wallader. 'We should have been told all this immediately.'

'In fact, this information was only confirmed for us late yesterday afternoon in a fax from Mr Bloom's office,' said Frank. 'It took some time to assemble because of the complexity of your son's affairs.' He folded his hands in front of him. 'I do regret the turn events have taken, sir. Please believe that Mr Bloom had agreed to accompany me to Guildford after the searches of your son's premises in order to clarify and explain what he knows of Leo's estate. Wrongly perhaps, I thought it would be more appropriate for you to hear the details from a solicitor. It seems your son had considerable assets which, from the little you were able to tell us on Saturday, I gather you and your wife knew nothing about.'

Lady Wallader looked up at Cheever. 'He had a flat in Kensington which he had to sell in eighty-eight to pay off his debts,' she said tiredly. 'He lost everything in the stock market crash and had to live in rented accommodation in Kew for five years until he met Jinx and moved in with her.'

Frank consulted the fax from Bloom. 'Would that be a flat in Kensington Garden Road?'

She nodded.

'It makes up part of his estate, Lady Wallader, together with three flats in Kew and two in Hampstead. His list of properties is as follows: a five-bedroomed house in Chelsea, which was let until April of this year, at which point he instructed Bloom and his agents to keep it vacant; the flat in Kensington, which is currently empty but with instructions to let; two flats in Hampstead, which are currently let; a three-storeyed house in Kew, which was converted to three flats four years ago, all of which are currently let; a house in Brittany, which is let during the holiday season when Leo himself doesn't require it; and a condominium in Florida, which is let year-round to holiday tenants. Off hand, can you remember where he said his rented flat was?'

'The Avenue, Kew,' she whispered.

'Tremayne, The Avenue, Kew?' he asked her.

'Yes.'

'He bought the entire property eight years ago for two hundred and eighty thousand pounds, Lady Wallader. Perhaps you misunderstood what he meant by rented accommodation.'

'No,' she said. 'He led us both to believe he was finding it difficult to make ends meet, but I knew he was lying. If I hadn't, I might have done what he asked and lent him some money.' She stared at him with red-rimmed eyes. 'Was it Jinx who gave you Mr Bloom's name?'

'Yes,' he told her.

'Does that mean she's better? I spoke to her stepmother on the telephone and she told me Jinx had lost her memory. I was very sorry to hear that.'

'I understand it's only partial amnesia, Lady Wallader. Two of my detectives spoke to her on Sunday, and most of what she can't recall relates to events in the two weeks preceding her accident.'

'How bloody convenient for her,' said Sir Anthony furiously. 'You realize she's probably lying.'

Frank ignored him. 'Did you like her, Lady Wallader?'

'Yes, I did,' she said quickly. 'But she was angry the last time we saw her and I guessed Leo was up to his tricks again. It's difficult to be objective about your children, Superintendent. For all their sins you go on loving them and, however much you wish they *would*, the sins don't go away.'

Her husband's hand descended on her arm in an iron grip. 'You're being disloyal,' he said angrily.

There was a short silence.

'I'm telling the truth, Anthony,' she said quietly. 'It doesn't mean I loved Leo any less. You know that.' She ignored his hard fingers digging into the flesh of her arm.

'The only truth that matters now is that your son was murdered,' he grunted. 'Do you want his murderer to get away with it?'

She looked at him. 'No,' she said, 'which is why it's important that the Superintendent knows the truth.'

'You're hurting your wife, Sir Anthony,' said Frank calmly.

The haggard face turned blankly towards him.

'Your hand, sir. I think you should remove it.'

Obediently, he unclenched his fist.

'Tell me why Jinx was angry the last time you saw her.'

'Oh, because she'd had enough of his lies and deceits,' said Lady Wallader matter-of-factly. 'Like every other girlfriend Leo ever had. In the end they all discovered that the charm and the good looks disguised a very selfish personality.' She glanced briefly at her husband. 'He couldn't share, you see, even as a child. He became quite violent whenever another child borrowed something of his, so in the end we took him to a psychologist who diagnosed a personality disorder. She told us there was nothing we could do about it but that he would probably learn to control his aggression better as he got older.'

'And did he?'

'I suppose so. He stopped using his fists, but I can't say hand on heart that he felt any less angry inside about having to share what he had. He was very immature.'

'Miss Kingsley described him as excessively secretive. Is that how he solved the problem, do you think? By refusing to divulge what he was worth.'

'Yes.' She gestured towards the fax. 'Well, clearly that's true. We had no idea he owned so many properties. I did recognize that he was much better off than he said he was, but not to this extent. I'm sure we must seem very gullible,

Superintendent, but life with Leo was so much calmer when he was allowed to keep his secrets.'

Frank waited a moment. 'You said Jinx had had enough, Lady Wallader. Does that mean it was she who called off the wedding?'

It was her husband who answered. 'No,' he said firmly. 'She was very abusive to us all, though to what purpose remains a mystery. At no point did she say she wouldn't go through with it. It was Leo who told her there wasn't going to be a wedding when she finally stopped shouting.'

'Did he explain why?'

'He said he'd been having an affair with Meg Harris and was going to marry her.'

'And what was Jinx's reaction?'

'Shock,' he said. 'It was the last thing she'd expected and she stared at him in complete shock.'

'Would you agree, Lady Wallader?'

She looked up. 'Yes,' she admitted, 'I would. She didn't say anything, but she clearly hadn't expected a response like that. I got the impression she was very angry but I think she was more angry with Meg than Leo. It's difficult now to say for certain. We were all very distressed and, frankly, Anthony and I were relieved when they left.'

'When was this?'

'It was the bank holiday weekend at the end of May.'

Cheever frowned. 'Yet, according to the evidence we have, the last thing Miss Kingsley remembers is saying goodbye to Leo on June the fourth when she set off to stay with her parents. Why was he still in her house a week after he said he was planning to marry her best friend?'

'We don't know,' said Sir Anthony. 'They left our house furious with each other, then Leo telephoned later that evening to ask us not to say anything to anyone until he gave us permission. But he didn't explain why and he didn't call until nearly two weeks later. It was the Saturday, June the eleventh, and he said he and Meg were making themselves scarce until the fuss died down.' His brows drew together in an angry frown. 'I accept Leo had his faults but he was a damn good catch for the daughter of an East End crook. My view is she wasn't going to let him go that easily. She flared up the May weekend for no good reason and then changed her mind. That's how I see it. Kept him with her till she went to Fordingbridge, then lost him back to Meg while she was away. I mean to say, if she was planning to back out of the whole thing, then why didn't she tell her father to send out cancellation notices during the week she spent at the Hall? That would have been the obvious time to do it. You see, it doesn't add up.'

'Yes,' said Cheever slowly, 'I see your point.'

Chapter Fifteen

WHEN ALAN PROTHEROE summoned Jinx to his office
to break the news of Meg and Leo's deaths, she drew away
from him into the corner of the wide leather sofa in his
office, a distant expression on her gaunt face. He wondered
if she was even listening or if, like so much in her life, she
was choosing to blank out what she didn't want to hear. She,
for her part, refused to be soothed by the sympathy in his
voice or the look of compassion in his eyes, both of which
she felt were false. Dr Protheroe was not a man to take on
trust, she thought.

'Bar the identities of the two bodies, I doubt many of the
other details in the newspaper are true,' he finished quietly.
'It reads to me as if Leo's father has made some sweeping
statements in a moment of grief which he will probably
come to regret, but I'm afraid we can expect another visit
from the police and I didn't want you to hear about this
from them.'

She favoured him with a tight little smile. 'I've known
since Sunday night. But you knew that already, didn't you?'

He nodded.

'Who told you?'

'Simon Harris. He phoned yesterday afternoon. He wanted to warn me that the story would break today.'

A look of relief crossed her face. 'Simon?' She searched his face. 'Why would he bother to do that?'

'I think he and his father feel this sort of treatment' – he tapped the newspaper on his lap – 'isn't justice. He talked about his mother and Sir Anthony whipping up a kangaroo court.'

'Caroline doesn't like me at all,' she said disconsolately. 'For some reason she's always blamed me for Meg's behaviour. She thinks Meg fell into bad company. I suppose she looked at Adam and decided like father like daughter.'

'It's not uncommon. We all blame other people for our children's failings.' He paused. 'Why didn't you tell me the police visit upset you?'

She rubbed her eyes. 'I don't trust the police,' she said, 'but it's a form of paranoia that I'm not particularly happy about. I might have been imagining things. There was no sense in worrying you unnecessarily until I knew for certain.'

'You could have told me yesterday.'

'Yesterday I was paranoid about what my father was planning.'

He raised his hands in a gesture of despair. 'How am I supposed to help you if you keep everything to yourself?'

'You're a very arrogant man,' she said without hostility. 'Hasn't it occurred to you that I might not *want* your help?'

'Of course,' he said curtly, 'but that doesn't mean I have to stop offering it. Do you think my other patients want my help any more than you do? They begin with good intentions but, within hours, most of them are climbing the walls to get out for their next fix. The only arrogance I see is on your side, Jinx.'

'Why?'

'You think you're clever enough to outwit me, the police and your father combined.'

She shifted her gaze back to his. 'I'm certainly contemptuous of fools who shut themselves away in their ivory towers and close their eyes to the madness outside,' she snapped. 'Russell was murdered. For ten years I avoided any sort of serious involvement. Then, when I thought the dust had settled, I let myself go and fell for Leo. Now he's dead, too, along with the only real friend I've ever had. So precisely what sort of help are you offering me? Help in remembering the deaths of my husband, my friend and my lover?' She looked very angry. 'I like it the way it is. I don't want to *remember* anything. I don't want to *know* anything. I don't want to *feel* anything. I just want to be allowed to take surrealistic photographs where all my repressed fears and desires jostle for expression in an idiosyncratic juxtaposition of purity and corruption.' She bared her teeth at him in a ferocious smile. 'And that's a direct quote from a review of my work in the *Sunday Times*. It's pretentious rubbish, but it sounds great.'

He shook his head impatiently. 'You know perfectly well it's not rubbish. I've looked at some of your published work, and that same theme appears over and over again.' He leaned forward. 'You seem to see the world in extraordinarily stark terms. Black and white. Good and evil. For every kindness, a cruelty; for every positive, a negative. Why are there no grey areas for you, Jinx?'

'Because perfection can only exist in an imperfect setting. In a perfect setting it becomes ordinary.'

'So it's perfection that fascinates you?'

She held his gaze for a moment but didn't reply.

'No,' he said, answering for her, 'It's *im*perfection that fascinates you. You're more attracted by the black than by the white.' He studied her face closely. 'The backgrounds to your pictures are always more compelling than the subjects, except in the few instances where you've turned the idea on its head by making ugliness the subject and beauty the setting.'

She shrugged. 'I expect you're right. Black humour certainly appeals to me.'

'As in *schadenfreude*?'

'Yes.'

'You're wrong, woman. You experience anguish on behalf of others while the only person you laugh at is yourself.' He quoted her own words back at her. 'My education was a waste of time. The *Sunday Times* writes pretentious rubbish about my art. I won't get out of bed in front of you because you'll turn me into a golfing club joke.' He paused. 'Are you laughing at Leo now? You should be if you enjoy *schadenfreude*. There's no blacker joke than the timely comeuppance of someone who's done you wrong.'

'I can think of several,' she said flatly. 'Like when you wake up one morning in a police cell and remember it was you who dealt the death blow. That's going to be a gut-wrencher when it happens. Ho! Ho! Ho! We'll all be splitting our sides.' She looked towards the window, cutting herself off, symbolically extending the space between them.

'I don't think that's very likely to happen.'

'Somebody killed them. Why shouldn't it have been me?'

'I'm not quibbling over whether or not you did it, Jinx. I'm quibbling with your waking up in a police cell one morning and remembering it was you. *That's* what's unlikely. Amnesia doesn't vanish overnight, so you'll know long before the police arrest you whether they've got good cause to do it.' He watched her. 'Have they?'

She continued to stare out of the window for several seconds before finally, with a sigh, turning back to him. 'I keep seeing Meg on her knees, begging,' she said, 'and last night I remembered going to her flat and feeling terrible anger because Leo was there. I have nightmares about drowning and being buried alive, and I wake up because I can't breathe. I can remember feeling strong emotions.' She fell silent.

'What sort of emotions?'

'Fear,' she said. 'It hits me suddenly and I start shivering. I remember fear.'

These revelations had come at him so suddenly that he wasn't ready for them, and he experienced a terrible sadness for she seemed to be remembering an overwhelming guilt. 'Tell me about Meg,' he prompted at last.

'She was begging, holding her hands out. Please, please, please.' Her eyelashes glittered with held-back tears.

'Was she begging from you?'

'I don't know. I just keep seeing her on her knees.'

'Where were you?'

'I don't know.'

'Was anyone else there?'

'I don't know.'

'OK, tell me what you remember about going to Meg's flat and finding Leo there.'

'I just had this image of Leo opening the door to me, and I knew it was Meg's flat because Leo was holding Marmaduke. Marmaduke's a cat,' she explained. 'The funny thing is I heard him purring, but the rest of it was completely static, like a photograph.'

'But you remember feeling angry with Leo.'

'I wanted to hit him.' She pressed her lips together. 'That's really what the memory *was*, not the picture so much as a sense of incredible rage. It came to me suddenly that Leo had made me furious and then I saw him in Meg's doorway.'

'Do you know when that was?'

She pondered deeply. 'It must have happened after June the fourth because that's the last thing I remember – saying goodbye to Leo. He came into the hall and said: Be good, Jinxy, and be happy . . .' She lapsed into another thoughtful silence.

'What did *you* say?'

'I don't know. I just remember what *he* said.'

He pulled forward a notepad and pen. 'Give me a run-down of the day before. What sort of day was that?'

She spoke with confidence. 'I was at work. We were doing some publicity shots of a new teenage band. It was tough to come up with anything original because they were deeply uninteresting and horribly pleased with themselves. Four clean-cut young men with flashing white teeth and hairless chests, who thought they were so pretty we could just take a few snap-shots and every pre-pubescent girl in the country would swoon.' She laughed suddenly. 'So I told

Dean to needle them a bit and, after three hours, we ended up with some brilliant shots of four extremely angry young men glowering into the lens.'

Alan chuckled in response. 'What did Dean say to them?'

'He just kept calling them "his pretty little virgins". They got pissed off very quickly, especially as we kept them hanging around for a couple of hours while we fiddled with lights and lenses. They really hated us by the end of it but we got some good pictures as a result.'

'So you developed the film straightaway?'

'No. We had some location work in the afternoon and we were running out of time, so we grabbed some sandwiches and left.' She paused in sudden confusion. 'I went straight home afterwards.' She stared at him. 'So when did I see those photographs?'

'Well, let's not worry about that for the moment. Was Leo there when you got home?'

'No,' she said slowly, 'but he wasn't supposed to be.' Her eyes lit with sudden excitement. 'I remember checking the rooms to make sure he'd really gone and then I felt a sense of absolute peace because I'd got the house to myself again.' She clapped her hands to her face. 'I remember. He wasn't there, and I was *pleased*.'

Protheroe wondered why she hadn't noticed the glaring inconsistency. *Or perhaps the inconsistency was part of the game.* 'So how did you celebrate?'

Her eyes gleamed with sudden amusement. 'I drank two pints of beer, ate baked beans out of a tin, smoked ten cigarettes in half an hour, watched soaps on the telly and had fried eggs and bacon in bed at half-past ten.'

He looked up with a smile. 'That's very precise.'

'I was making a statement.'

'Because they were the things Leo disapproved of?'

'A mere fraction of them. His view of how women should behave was modelled on his mother, and she's kept herself in clover by constant appeasement of a chauvinistic husband.'

He arched an interested eyebrow but didn't pursue the issue. 'So what did you watch on television?'

'Wall-to-wall soap. One after the other. *EastEnders. The Bill. Brookside.*' She smiled. 'Then I couldn't stand it any more, so I watched the news. Soap operas are pretty bloody boring when you haven't a clue what's going on.'

'Why didn't you watch *Coronation Street*?'

'It wasn't on.'

'Are you sure about that?'

'Positive,' she said. 'I went through the *Radio Times* and picked out the soaps deliberately. If it *had* been on, I'd have watched it.'

He stroked his beard thoughtfully. 'I'm not much of an expert, admittedly, but I'm sure *Coronation Street* goes out on a Friday, and you say you remember this as being Friday the third of June.' He eased gingerly out of his chair, his shoulder protesting at the movement, and went to the desk. 'Hilda,' he said into the intercom, 'can you rustle up a *Radio Times* from somewhere and bring it in? I need to know which days of the week *don't* have *Coronation Street*, but *do* have *EastEnders, The Bill* and *Brookside.*'

Her giggle rattled tinnily down the wire. 'There now, and I always thought you preferred the intellectual stuff.'

'Very funny. This is important, Hilda.'

'Sorry, well, I can tell you without the *Radio Times*.

Coronation Street is Mondays, Wednesdays and Fridays. *EastEnders* is Mondays, Tuesdays and Thursdays. *The Bill* is Tuesdays, Thursdays and Fridays, and *Brookside* is Tuesdays, Wednesdays and Fridays. So, if you don't want *Coronation Street* but you do want the others, then that means Tuesday.'

'Good lord!' said Alan in amazement. 'Do you watch them *all*?

'Most days,' she agreed cheerfully. 'Anything else I can help you with?'

'No, that's fine, thank you.' He returned to his seat. 'Did you hear that?' he asked Jinx. 'You appear to be remembering a Tuesday and not a Friday, and it does seem a little unlikely that Leo would have returned for breakfast immediately after he had packed his bags and gone.'

She stared unhappily at her hands.

'I wonder if you're quite as clear about Saturday the fourth as you think you are. You remember saying goodbye to Leo and you're very specific about the day and the date, but do you know why? What happened to fix Saturday the fourth in your mind?'

'It was in my diary for ages,' she said. 'Week at the Hall, beginning June the fourth.'

'And you were definitely leaving for the Hall when you said goodbye to Leo?'

'Yes.'

'So how many suitcases were you carrying?'

She stared at him in confusion.

'Did you have *any* suitcases?' he asked.

'I know I was going to see my father,' she said slowly. He waited. 'And?' he prompted at last.

'My bag was hanging on the back of the chair.' She stared

into the past. 'It's a small leather pouch on a long strap. I slung it over my shoulder and said, I'm off now.' She frowned. 'I think I must have put the suitcases in the car the night before.'

'Is that what you usually did?'

'It's the only thing that makes sense.'

'I wonder if it is.' He took a diary out of his jacket pocket. 'Let's work forwards,' he suggested, 'beginning with what you know to be true. Tell me about the first time you met Leo.'

The Vicarage, Littleton Mary, Wiltshire – 12.15 p.m.

Simon Harris answered the door and looked in some dismay at Frank Cheever. 'We – that is, my father and I —' He broke off as the sound of shouting erupted from the window to the right. 'My mother's not very well, I'm afraid. She can't really come to terms with what's happened. We'd like her to see the doctor but she won't have him near her. The problem is she's making some very wild accusations, and we're worried – well, frankly, she's accusing Dad of some terrible things and we – that is I —' He fell silent as Mrs Harris's voice rose to a scream, her words carrying clearly through the open window.

'How dare you deny it? Did you think I didn't know how you lusted after her? Did you think she wouldn't tell me what you did to her? She couldn't wait to get out of this house, couldn't wait to get away from you. You made her what she was and you dare to accuse her now of weakness. You disgust me. You've always disgusted me.'

Charles Harris said something in a murmur which wasn't audible.

'Of course I'll tell the police. Why should I protect you when you never protected her? You disgusting man.' Her voice rose to a scream again. 'CHILD ABUSER!' There was the sound of a door slamming, followed by silence.

Frank looked at Simon's shocked face. 'None of that would be admissible in court, sir. I couldn't possibly swear that it was your mother I was listening to and not a radio programme, so please don't worry unnecessarily. As you say, she's overwrought and we all say things we don't mean when we're angry.'

'But you heard it.'

'Yes.'

'It's completely untrue. My father has never abused anyone in his life, and certainly not Meg. It's my mother who has the problem.' Anguish pinched his already drawn face. 'This is so awful. I keep asking myself, why? What have we done to deserve it?'

Frank was spared an answer by the door opening behind Simon's back and his father putting an arm round the young man's shoulder and drawing him inside. 'Come in, Superintendent. You find us in turmoil, I'm afraid. Grief is often the most selfish of emotions.'

Nightingale Clinic, Salisbury – 12.30 p.m.

Alan smiled encouragingly as Jinx showed her first signs of faltering. 'You're doing very well. We can check all this with Dean later, but you've taken me up to Friday, the twenty-seventh of May without any hesitation at all.' He consulted his diary. 'The following Monday, May the thirtieth, was a bank holiday. Does that help at all? You're unlikely to have gone to work so maybe you took the opportunity for a long weekend away.'

'Friday was the last day of the *Cosmopolitan* fashion shoot,' she recapitulated slowly. 'Dean had tickets to a rock concert at Wembley and he had to meet his lover at five o'clock at the tube station, so he left me to develop the films. I wanted to get it done because . . .' She paused at the same place she'd paused before. 'I know it was urgent,' she said, 'but I can't remember why.'

'There were only four working days the following week because of the Bank Holiday Monday,' he pointed out, 'and you were spending the week after that at Hellingdon Hall. Perhaps you realized you were running out of time.'

She stared into the middle distance. 'Miles and Fergus came,' she said suddenly. 'It was after Angelica had left and they kept hammering on the studio door until I let them in. There was a cab-driver with them, demanding money. They were both pissed. They said they'd lost all their cash gambling, couldn't go home and needed beds for the night. I said why hadn't they gone to Richmond and waited for me there, and they said they had, but Leo had refused to pay the taxi fare and told them to come to the studio instead and make me pay for it. Which I did.' She took out a cigarette and lit it, watching the blue smoke spiral from its tip for a second or two before going on.

'I can remember now,' she said in a strange voice. 'I made them some coffee and told them to wait in the reception area till I'd finished what I was doing, but Miles was so drunk that he barged in on me in the dark room and let the light in.'

'What happened then?'

'The film I was working on was completely buggered, so I did what my father does and beat the shit out of him.' She gave a hollow laugh. 'I chased him into the studio and started hitting him with a plastic chair. I was *so* angry. And then Fergus came lurching in to find out what was going on, so I hit him as well. But the person I really wanted to have a go at was Leo. It was the last straw, sending them on to me when he knew I was up to my eyes in work.'

'How did he know?'

'Because when Dean left I phoned to tell him. We were going to his parents' for the weekend and he wanted to leave on the Friday evening. So I rang to suggest that he go on his own and leave me to follow on the Saturday, but he said he had things to do himself so it didn't matter.'

'And it was after the phone call that he sent Miles and Fergus on to you?'

She nodded.

'What happened then?'

'I made up my mind to call off the wedding. It was the money more than anything, the fact that he wouldn't pay their taxi fare.' Her lips thinned angrily. 'He'd been scrounging off me for so bloody long, and he wouldn't even pay one miserable taxi fare, and I thought, I'm mad. What the hell am I doing tying myself to this selfish bastard who doesn't give a toss for anyone except himself?' She looked at Alan. 'So I packed it in for the evening, got the boys into the car and went back to have it out with him. And he wasn't there.' She shrugged. 'So I ordered a pizza, made the boys eat some, and sent them to bed to sleep it off.'

There was a short silence.

'Weren't Miles and Fergus angry when you hit them?'

'I think they were too shocked.' She thought back. 'The funny thing is I lost my temper with Fergus the other day and I thought it was the first time I'd ever done it but it was nothing to the anger I felt that night. I remember screaming at them so much that I had a sore throat the next morning.' She smiled slightly. 'I didn't hit them very hard. It was the fact that I did it at all that shocked them. Miles burst into tears and said I was just like Adam, and I thought: For the first time I understand why Adam does it.'

'And why is that, Jinx?'

She looked at him. 'Because you're so bloody tired, you're working so bloody hard, you've tied yourself to a worthless parasite, and two immature drunks come along and ruin everything you've done because they think it's funny. I could have killed them all that night, every one of them. I got no sleep because I was so angry, and all I could think about was what hell the next week was going to be because I'd have to work late to catch up. And I kept worrying that the ruined film was the only film that was any good, and how was I going to explain to *Cosmopolitan* that we'd have to do the shoot all over again.'

'Did Leo come back that night?'

'If he did, I didn't hear him. I bolted the front and back door on the inside, so he couldn't get in.' She brushed imaginary fluff from her sleeve. 'He came back at lunchtime on the Saturday.'

'Were Miles and Fergus still there?'

She nodded. 'We were all in the kitchen when he came in through the back door. They couldn't go unless I lent them some money for the tube fare back to Miles's Porsche, which was parked outside a casino somewhere, but I was refusing to shell out any more. I said they could walk for all I cared, or phone Adam and explain what they'd been doing. He'd already told them that if they persisted with the gambling he'd cut them out of his will.' She closed her eyes and touched her fingertips to her eyelids as if she had a pain there. 'So Leo offered to drive them and they all left.'

There was another silence.

'And what did you do then?' asked Alan.

'I don't know,' she said. 'I can't remember anything after they left. I think I must have gone to sleep.' She lowered her hand and looked at him with a kind of despair.

The Vicarage, Littleton Mary, Wiltshire – 12.30 p.m.

They sat in the drawing room in deep discomfort. Caroline Harris was crouched on the sofa, misery etched into every line of her face. Charles sat as far away from her as he could, while Simon perched unhappily on a stool. Frank, over-heated and tired, was offered a deep leather armchair which hurt his back.

'We've located Leo's house in Chelsea,' he explained, 'and, according to the information phoned through before I left, there are several boxes and suitcases on the premises which appear to belong to your daughter. Preliminary searches have uncovered a photograph album which shows several snap-shots of Meg and Leo together, taken in July

1983.' He addressed his question to Mrs Harris. 'Were you aware they had known each other for at least eleven years?'

Her lips thinned to a narrow line. 'No,' she said.

'Was she a secretive person, Mrs Harris?'

The woman glanced spitefully at her husband. 'Not with me. She told me everything. It was her father she kept secrets from.'

'That's not true,' said Simon.

Frank glanced at him. 'You'd say she *was* secretive.'

'Very. She didn't want anyone to know anything about her life, least of all Mum or Dad. Particularly Mum, in fact. She knew how much Mum hated sex so she didn't tell her until recently how many men she slept with, and she only did that because she was angry.' He closed his eyes to avoid looking at his mother's pain. 'She loved sex, saw it as a healthy expression of life, love and beauty, and couldn't bear to have it treated as something dirty and disgusting.'

'You wanted her, too, Simon,' said Caroline in a whisper, 'just like your father. Never mind she was your sister. You think I didn't notice? I saw how you looked at her.'

A dull flush rose in Simon's face. 'It was you who made her uncomfortable,' he said quietly, 'not Dad. Everything she did was the opposite of what you've done. She got herself a decent education, she rejected God, she loved sex, she stayed single, she dived into London life to get away from the sterility of village rectitude. She experienced more in her thirty-four years than you will experience in a whole lifetime.' Tears glittered in his eyes. 'She didn't strangle life, she glorified every minute as if it were her last. I wish to God the rest of us could do the same.'

There was a desperate and terrible silence.

Frank cleared his throat. 'One of the photographs has a somewhat cryptic caption underneath it. It reads' – he consulted a notebook – '"Happiness AA". I'm told Meg is sitting in Leo's lap on a beach.' He looked up. 'Do you know what AA stands for? It seems unlikely that Automobile Association or Alcoholics Anonymous would fit the bill.'

Simon looked towards his mother but she had retreated into some internal world and was rocking herself tenderly on the sofa. 'After Abortion,' he said quietly. 'Married couples always talk about their lives BC – Before Children. Meg always referred to life after her abortion as double-A time. She said she'd never realized before just how awful it would be to have children and she thanked God she'd discovered early on that she wasn't cut out to be a mother.'

'Was Leo the father?'

'I don't know. She never told me who it was, and I didn't ask.'

'Did you know about Leo before your parents did?'

'Not by name. I knew she had a long-term lover who came and went between her other affairs. She was very fond of him, called him her old stand-by. I presume that was Leo if she'd known him eleven years.'

'Did she ever say why she didn't marry him?'

Simon shrugged. 'She said once that he was permanently broke, but the truth is I don't think she wanted to get married. She certainly didn't want children.' He glanced towards his father. 'She always felt that I fitted into our family better than she did, and she was afraid of bringing a child into the world who didn't belong. She said it wasn't fair.'

'It can't have been Leo,' said his father. 'Surely she

wouldn't describe a man with a house in Chelsea as permanently broke.'

Frank Cheever tucked his notebook into his pocket. 'In fact, sir, he had several properties both in this country and abroad, but no one knew about them, not even his parents. He made a habit of pleading poverty when, according to his solicitor, he was worth a very tidy fortune. Miss Kingsley describes him as a parasite who was obsessively secretive about money. His mother describes a disturbed young man with a pathological dislike of sharing. He wasn't a straightforward character by any means, so it's highly probable he did give your daughter the impression he had no money.'

'How very tragic.' Charles Harris looked distressed. 'One tends to think the type doesn't exist any more, certainly not amongst the young. I suppose we must blame Dickens for creating so extreme an example that the rest pass unnoticed.' He saw the Superintendent's perplexed expression. 'Scrooge,' he explained. 'Misers. People who need to hoard wealth but can't bring themselves to spend it. You come across them in the newspapers from time to time, old people who've died in shocking squalor only to leave a fortune behind.' He folded his hands in his lap. 'As I say, it's not something one associates with youth, but presumably a miser is a miser all his life. Poor Leo. What a sad, sad state of affairs.'

His wife began to scream. It was a piercing terrible sound that curdled sympathy and frayed nerves.

Nightingale Clinic, Salisbury – 12.45 p.m.

'Let's try a different tack,' suggested Alan. 'You said you and Leo were supposed to be staying with his parents for the weekend. Have you any recollection of doing that or was the whole idea abandoned when you decided you weren't going to marry him?'

Jinx's expression cleared. 'No,' she said, 'we did go. I had a row with them. I seem to have had rows with everyone that weekend.'

'It's not surprising. You were under a lot of pressure. The wedding was only a few weeks away and you were having second thoughts about going through with it.'

'But why did I go down there with him if I knew I wasn't going to marry him?' It was a puzzle, but not one she thought Protheroe could solve.

He recalled her acceptance of Matthew Cornell's invitation to lunch. 'Presumably they were expecting you, so perhaps you thought it was the polite thing to do.'

'Yes,' she said in surprise. 'I didn't think it would be fair to Philippa not to go.'

'Tell me about the row.'

'I remember it so clearly,' she said. 'It was after lunch on the Monday and I blew my stack when Leo asked his father for some money and Anthony said he was a bit short because he'd been forced to pay for some building work he'd had done.' She shook her head. 'The job had been completed six months before and he was angry because the builder had gone to a solicitor.' She pulled a rueful face. 'I'd been holding myself back for twenty-four hours, and I went berserk. I called him every synonym for skinflint I could think of, then turned on Leo and let rip at him. Poor Philippa looked mortified, and I was sorry about that because she'd always been so sweet to me.' She sighed. 'I wish I'd had the sense not to go in the first place. It wasn't a very dignified display. I kept spitting saliva all over the place because I couldn't get the words out fast enough.'

'Was that when you told Leo it was all off?'

A look of irritation crossed her face. 'I never got the chance. I just made an awful lot of noise, screaming and yelling and calling them names. I don't know what I thought I was doing really, except getting all the poison out of my system. It was Leo who said he wasn't going through with it.' She gave a small laugh. 'He said he'd been having an affair with Meg, and was planning to marry her instead.' She looked at him. 'I did tell you I wouldn't have wanted to kill myself over Leo and Meg. Do you believe that now? I can remember my relief when he said it. Thank God, I thought. I'm off the hook.'

'But it must have been a shock.'

'I suppose it was. I never thought she'd do it again, not after what happened to Russell.'

He was lost. 'Do what again?'

She looked at him rather blankly. 'It was history repeating itself,' she said impatiently, as if it was something he ought to have known. 'Meg was having an affair with Russell when he was murdered.'

Mystery surrounds murdered couple's relationship

Hampshire police revealed this afternoon that the murdered couple, Leo Wallader, 35, and Meg Harris, 34, had kept their eleven-year-old relationship secret from their families. 'It is not clear at this stage,' said Detective Superintendent Cheever, leading the investigation, 'why secrecy was important, but we hope that by publishing photographs of them someone may come forward who knew them as a couple.'

Further mystery surrounds Leo Wallader's estate, which has been valued at over one million pounds. 'He told friends and relations that he was in financial difficulties,' said Det Supt Cheever, 'and it came as something of a surprise to everybody to discover how much he was worth.'

Sir Anthony Wallader, Leo's father, who accused Hampshire police yesterday of lethargy, refused to comment on his son's financial affairs. 'My wife and I are too upset to talk to anyone,' he said. In the absence of a will, Sir Anthony and Lady Wallader, as next-of-kin, will inherit their son's fortune. Sir Anthony is believed to have a substantial fortune in his own right.

Det Supt Cheever agreed that Hampshire police were unhappy about the accusations of lethargy. 'We have been working very hard to find Leo and Meg's murderer,' he told journalists, 'but cases like this are never easy. The length of time that the couple knew each other clearly puts a different emphasis on what has happened here, and we need to establish why they felt it important to keep their friendship secret.'

He went on to say that he recognized the pressure both families were under and regretted any insensitivity Hampshire police may have shown. 'We have a tendency to assume,' he admitted, 'that the families of victims understand we are working hard on their behalf. Clearly this is not always recognized, and we will make sure there is no misunderstanding in future.'

Chapter Sixteen

ALAN PROTHEROE WIPED a weary hand across his face, then pushed himself out of his chair and wandered restlessly towards the window. Could he, hand on heart, say he believed anything Jinx told him? *When what she claimed to remember could be as fantastic as she chose because there was no one left to contradict her.* There were three dead people, and all three were intimately connected with this one woman. Logic dictated that she must know something about their deaths. Logic also dictated that her father knew something, or why had he put her in here with such very precise instructions concerning her care? Adam was as anxious as she was, it seemed, that her memories lie dormant.

'I'm not sure I can believe that,' he said with his back to her. 'You described Russell to me only a couple of days ago as possessive and jealous. You said your marriage was stifling. Now you tell me he and your best friend were having an affair. That doesn't quite square, does it?'

'Russell believed in double standards,' Jinx said reasonably. 'If he was capable of cheating the customs, do you not think he was equally capable of cheating his wife?'

'That's hardly an answer, you know. Obsession with one woman doesn't usually lead to philandering with others. Surely the two are mutually exclusive?'

'It depends what sort of obsession you're talking about. Russell was far more obsessed with himself than he was with me. I was little better than a trophy that he could show off to his middle-aged friends, the child bride who adored him so much she forsook fortune and fame to marry him. Meg was a different kind of trophy, the one that proved to him he was still sexually active and attractive at forty-plus. But we had no more value to him than the paintings in his collection. He liked owning things.'

He turned round. 'My problem is I have to take your word for that. Sadly for Russell, the dead can't speak for themselves.'

'Is there a reason why you shouldn't take my word?' She said it without hostility but there was anger in her eyes. 'Suddenly you're a policeman, yet ten minutes ago you only wanted to help.' She made as if to get up. 'This is just a professional exercise for you, and I'm hungry, anyway. I want some lunch.'

He refused to be intimidated. 'Don't be so childish,' he said sharply. 'Healthy scepticism and a wish to help are not mutually exclusive, Jinx. Arguably, the one strengthens the other. Convince the sceptic and you will have a stronger ally for the future. Perhaps if you changed your mind-set *vis-à-vis* the police in that area, you could shed your paranoia and make a positive attempt to help them find Meg and Leo's murderer. Or are you as disinclined to do that as you were to have Russell's murderer named?'

She looked at him with dislike. 'I'll phone Colonel

Clancey and ask him to post Russell's diaries and letters to you. I keep them in my bookcase at home. For what it's worth, the entry on the day we got married went like this: "Felt and looked great. Wore black velvet suit and white satin shirt. Speech afterwards was a triumph of wit and erudition. What a pity there were so few guests to enjoy it." I interpret that as self-obsession but then, admittedly, I'm an arrogant woman and I was put out that his bride didn't rate a mention.'

'Still, I'm surprised you didn't mention the affair before. It's a little odd, don't you think, that Meg should have slept with both Russell *and* Leo. Was she in the habit of stealing your men friends?'

'If you want to be strictly accurate about it, I stole them from her. She had a six-month fling with Russell, got bored with him and introduced him to me. She did the same with Leo, told me he was a business acquaintance and said he and I would get on like a house on fire. It was only later that I realized business acquaintance meant lover.'

'Didn't it upset you to get her cast-offs?'

'Everybody's somebody's cast-off. In some ways it's easier if you know your predecessor because then you know you're not competing with Superwoman.'

He resumed his seat. 'You're avoiding the question. Were you upset?'

'Only in retrospect. Meg was a great deal more attractive than I am and completely careless of other people's feelings, particularly men's. She had no qualms about taking up with someone, then dumping him two or three months later for somebody else. The trouble is, I'm less adept at that so I got lumbered with the jerks when it suited her.'

'But she took up with them again later when *that* suited her.' He shook his head in genuine bewilderment. 'If this is true, Jinx, then I can't understand why you describe her as the only real friend you've ever had.'

'I'm not doing this very well,' she said, surprisingly sanguine about his disbelief. 'You'd have liked Meg.' She marshalled her thoughts. 'Look, when I say I got lumbered with them that doesn't mean I hold her responsible for what happened afterwards. She kept telling me not to marry Russell, said I was mad to tie myself down at twenty-one, but by then it was too late. I couldn't just abandon him after what Adam had done, and that wasn't Meg's fault.'

Alan was highly doubtful that Meg Harris was a woman he would have liked. If Jinx had said one thing that was true, it was her admitted inability to make sensible decisions about her personal life, particularly where her choice of friends was concerned. She appeared to be completely blind to their character flaws, and he wondered if she realized that it was only the egocentric personality that seemed to attract her. Was this because she found it difficult to differentiate between self-centredness and self-confidence? She had so many mixed feelings about her domineering father that it wasn't surprising she found people impossible to read. 'I suppose it wasn't Meg's fault either that she had an affair with Russell after he was married?'

She looked at him for a moment. 'Not entirely, no. Presumably Russell had some say in it.' She shrugged. 'Anyway, they were very discreet. I didn't find out about it till after he was dead and by then it was water under the bridge.'

'Who told you?'

'No one. She wrote him some letters which he'd hidden

amongst a stack of old exam papers in the attic at Richmond. They were rather sweet,' she said, remembering. 'The sad thing is, I think she really did love him, but she couldn't bear the thought of being tied to one person. She was terrified of ending up in a country backwater like her mother and being the dutiful wife.'

'Did you ever talk to her about Russell?'

'No.'

'Why not?'

'I couldn't see the point.'

'Did the police know about it?'

'If they did they never mentioned it.'

'Why didn't *you* mention it?'

'Because I didn't find the letters until a year later and by then the case was effectively closed.' She plucked at her lower lip. 'I don't think you realize what it's like to be part of a murder inquiry. It's not a very comfortable experience. I'd have needed something much stronger than a couple of faded love letters to make us all go through that terrible mill again.'

He leaned forward. 'So for the next nine years you pretended nothing had happened and then you learnt about her and Leo and you were afraid history was about to repeat itself.'

She didn't say anything. Perhaps she realized how thin it all sounded, and how odd her own behaviour must seem in the circumstances.

'So what did you do, Jinx?'

'I thought it would be better if no one knew, so when we got back to London, I told Leo to phone his parents and make sure they didn't say anything until he gave them the go-ahead. I said I needed to speak to my father first.' She propped her chin in her hands and stared wretchedly at the carpet. 'But I can't remember if I spoke to Adam or not, so I don't know whether —' She broke off abruptly.

'You don't know whether you gave him a reason to have them murdered.'

53 Lansing Road, Salisbury, Wiltshire – 1.15 p.m.

WPC Blake inserted her foot in Flossie Hale's door and refused to remove it. 'I'm not going away until you talk to me,' she said firmly, 'so you may as well let me in.'

After a second or two the pressure against her foot lessened and the door swung open. Flossie regarded her without enthusiasm from a face rainbow-hued with healing bruises. She clasped an old candlewick dressing gown across her broad chest with a plaster-encased forearm, looking twenty years older than her forty-six years. 'What do you want?'

'Just a chat. How are you feeling now?'

'So-so.' She gave a wheeze of bitter amusement. 'Still a bit tender when I sit down, but I'm surviving.' She led the way into a tiny sitting room stuffed with overlarge furniture. 'You might as well take a seat,' she said ungraciously, propping her plump arms on a television set and leaning her weight on it. 'By rights I should be in my bed, but I can't say I fancy it much at the moment. I tried to persuade the hospital to keep me in a bit longer but they turfed me out for some old boy with piles.' She gazed disconsolately at the young policewoman. 'I suppose life's pretty grim for everyone these days.'

Blake nodded. 'It seems that way. I only ever hear hard-luck stories.'

'I wouldn't mind so much if I didn't pay my taxes. You're entitled to expect something for all the money you shell out.'

Privately, WPC Blake thought it highly unlikely that Flossie had ever declared an income in her life, but she nodded sympathetically. 'I agree with you, which is why I'm here. Part of what you should expect in a civilized society is peace of mind and safety, and until we find the man who assaulted you, I'm afraid you won't have either.' She ignored the expression of stubborn resistance that settled on Flossie's face and took her notebook from her handbag. 'You're not the only prostitute he's beaten up. There was another one three months ago and he was just as vicious with her. She says he paid her forty pounds. Was that what he paid you?'

'It may have been,' Flossie said grudgingly.

'She also said she thought he was expecting someone young and attractive and took against her when it turned out she was old enough to be his mother. Was that your experience?'

She shrugged. 'It may have been,' she said again.

'She advertises in telephone boxes and shop windows. I think that's how you get your customers, too, isn't it?'

'Maybe.'

'OK, well, I've done a bit of leg-work in the last couple of days around the girls who advertise the same way, and, while no one else seems to have suffered in quite the way you and the other woman did, three of them gave me a description of a well-spoken handsome young man who became aggressive during his climax.' She consulted her notebook. 'One described him as twisting his hand in her hair and almost pulling it out by the roots. Another said he hit her about the face with her own hairbrush, and the third said he pulled her wig off, then got so angry with her he stuffed it into her mouth. She said he apologized afterwards and paid her an extra ten pounds for her trouble.' She looked up. 'All three girls are in their twenties but they all agreed he had a thing about hair and hairbrushes. Does this sound familiar, Flossie?'

She sighed. 'Seems you've been working overtime, love. Go on then, what's the description?'

Blake read it out. 'Height, about five feet eleven. Slim, muscular build, with hairs down the centre of his chest. Good-looking, boyish face with dark blonde, slightly curly hair, possibly highlighted at the sides, and blue or grey eyes. No facial hair. One girl suggested he plucked his eyebrows because they were very fine and nicely shaped. Clothing varied between a dark suit and white shirt to Levi's and white T-shirt. They all described him as clean, well spoken and probably the product of a public school. Is that about right, would you say?'

'He looked as if butter wouldn't melt in his mouth, but, God, he was a vicious little brute.' She touched a hand to her bruises. 'I'll tell you something, he couldn't sustain himself for half a second. All the shouting and yelling and hitting he went in for was his way of pretending he could keep it up. It didn't occur to me the first time round – I mean, let's face it, you don't feel much when you've been on the game as long as I have. But the second time around he never even got it in he came so quick. And he didn't half punish me for that. It wasn't just that I was old enough to be his mother – though I guess that had something to do with it – mostly it was because he was inadequate.'

'Is there anything you can add to the description?'

She shook her head. 'Sorry. He was very good-looking, beautiful really, reminded me a bit of Paul Newman in *The Hustler*. Not that that'd mean anything to you. You're too young to remember it.' She paused for a moment. 'But there were some odd things he said. "It's not my fault, my father made me evil." That was one of them. And then when he was leaving: "I never had to kill a woman before."'

'Before what?'

Flossie regarded her morosely. 'I guess he meant he'd beaten up on lots of girls but that none of them had died.' She shivered suddenly. 'Gawd, he was mad, one of them split personalities. Looked like a little angel when he arrived and turned into a zombie with staring great eyes the minute he got a hard on. Bloody miracle he hasn't killed someone yet, that's my view.'

Blake agreed with her. 'Any idea how he got here? Car? Did he walk?'

'I don't know. I just wait for the bell to ring and let them in.' She frowned. 'Mind, he did have some car keys with him. I remember him fishing them out of his pocket when he left. He had a really nice jacket on, tight fit, padded shoulders, and he pulled his keys out and held them in his palm while he told me to keep my mouth shut.' She screwed her forehead in concentration. 'There was a black disc on the key-ring. It was hanging down between his fingers and I remember staring at it because I didn't want him to think I was staring at him.' Her eyes gleamed suddenly. 'It had an eff and an aitch on it in gold lettering, same initials as mine, which is why I noticed them. You know what? I reckon FH are the little sod's initials!'

Nightingale Clinic, Salisbury, Wiltshire – 1.30 p.m.

There was a tap on the door and Hilda poked her head inside. 'I'm sorry to bother you, Dr Protheroe, but there's a Detective Inspector Maddocks and a Detective Sergeant Fraser here. I've told them you're busy but they say it's too important to wait.'

'Five minutes,' said Alan.

The door opened wide before Hilda could answer, and Maddocks pushed past her into the room. 'It is important, sir, otherwise I wouldn't insist.' He stopped when he noticed Jinx. 'Miss Kingsley.'

Alan frowned angrily. 'Since when did being a policeman give you the right to barge, uninvited, into a doctor's consulting room?'

'I apologize, sir,' said Maddocks, 'but we've already waited fifteen minutes and we *do* need to talk to you rather urgently.'

Jinx stood up. 'It's all right, Dr Protheroe. I'll come back later.'

'I'd rather you stayed,' he said, looking up at her with a clear message in his dark eyes. 'I can't help feeling this is very poor psychology.'

'For whom?' she asked him, with a mischievous glint in her eye. '*Illi intus aut illi extra?*'

He dredged through his Latin for a translation. The insiders or the outsiders, he decided. 'Oh, *illi extra*, of course,' he said with a barely perceptible nod towards Maddocks. '*Caput odiosus iam maximus est.*' His odious head is already maximum size, was what he hoped he'd said.

Jinx smiled at him. 'If you recognize that, Dr Protheroe, then I don't think it's poor psychology at all. It means you hold the advantage. In any case, I really am starving so, with apologies for desertion, I think I'll go and find myself some lunch.' She gave him a brief nod then slipped past Fraser and Hilda, who were standing irresolutely by the door.

'All right, Hilda, thank you very much.' He gestured towards the sofa. 'Sit down, gentlemen.'

'May I ask what Miss Kingsley said to you?' enquired Maddocks as he took a seat.

'I've no idea, I'm afraid,' said Alan amiably. 'It was all Greek to me.'

'You answered her, sir.'

'I can run that stuff off by the yard,' he said. '*Vos mensa puellarum dixerunt habebat nunc nemo conduxit.* I haven't a clue what it means but it always sounds intelligent. What can I do for you?'

Maddocks, silently admitting defeat, eyed *The Times* which was folded neatly on the coffee table. 'Presumably you've read that?'

'I have.'

'So you know that Mr Leo Wallader and Miss Meg Harris are dead.'

'Yes.'

Maddocks watched his face closely. 'Does Miss Kingsley know?'

Alan nodded. 'I told her after I read it.'

'What was her reaction, sir?'

He stared the Inspector down. 'She was very shocked.'

'Did you also tell her that the man who attacked you last night was wielding a sledgehammer?'

Alan thought about that. 'I can't remember,' he said honestly. 'I mentioned the disturbance to all my patients this morning, but I really can't recall whether I gave precise details or not.' He eyed Maddocks with curiosity. 'Why?' he asked. 'Do you see a connection between the assault on me and the deaths of Mr Wallader and Miss Harris?'

Maddocks shrugged. 'We certainly find it interesting that Miss Kingsley and a sledgehammer appear to be the only common factors between three murders and a vicious assault,' he said bluntly.

'The third murder being Miss Kingsley's first husband.'

'Yes.'

'Well, I'm afraid I don't follow your logic. Let's say, purely for the purposes of argument, that there is a connection between the murder of Russell Landy and the murder of Mr Wallader, and that the connection is Miss Kingsley's attachment to both men. Marriage in the first instance and marriage plans in the second. And let's go on to say – again purely for the purposes of argument – that because Mr Wallader changed his mind and decided to marry Miss Harris instead, someone decided she also had to die. How does the assault on me fit into this hypothetical scenario? I have known Miss Kingsley as a conscious and functioning individual for a week. We have a doctor/patient relationship. I am neither married to her, nor engaged to marry her. I have not slept with her, nor do I have plans to sleep with her. I know none of her friends and she knows none of mine. She is a paying guest under my roof who is free to leave whenever she chooses.' His eyes narrowed in speculation. 'Have I missed something that makes this spurious connection even halfway believable?'

'Yes, sir,' said Maddocks evenly. 'Coincidence. It's not something that we, as policemen, can readily ignore. Our experience shows that where there's smoke there's fire.' He smiled slightly. 'Or, to put it another way, where there's Miss Kingsley there's also a sledgehammer.'

'Are you suggesting she wields the damn thing herself?'

'I'm not suggesting anything at this stage, sir. I am merely drawing your attention to the coincidence. You would be foolish to pretend it doesn't exist.'

'Well, it certainly wasn't Jinx who took a swing at me last night. She's not big enough or strong enough, and, judging by the build and the height, it was a man.'

'We understand you had a visit from her father's solicitor yesterday.'

'It wasn't him either, Inspector. He's a tiny little chap with dainty feet and hands. I'd have recognized him immediately, ski-mask or no ski-mask.'

Maddocks smiled. 'I was thinking more in terms of Mr Kingsley himself. Perhaps you said something to the solicitor that his boss didn't like?'

'I wouldn't know. I've never met Mr Kingsley so I've no idea what he looks like.' He thought for a moment. 'In any case, I'm sure it was a young man, and Mr Kingsley's sixty-six.'

'What about Fergus Kingsley? He's on your list.'

Alan nodded. 'Yes, he was about the right size. So was the waiter who served me at dinner, but my conversations with both were perfectly friendly and I can't see either of them taking the trouble to hang around the clinic waiting to belt me.' *But was that right? He had run up against Fergus twice now, and neither time had he felt comfortable with him.*

Maddocks saw the sudden thoughtfulness in Protheroe's expression. 'Tell me what you and Fergus Kingsley talked about,' he invited.

'Nothing very much. He was waiting beside my car when I came out. He expressed an interest in buying it, as far as I remember, then asked me to meet his brother. I explained I was in a hurry and suggested we leave it to another time. Then I left.'

Fraser looked up with a frown. 'But you weren't in a hurry, sir. According to the report we've seen, you decided to go for a drive and treat yourself to a decent meal because it's some time since you've had an evening off.'

Alan gave another amiable chuckle. 'So I made a polite excuse and left. Is that so odd? I'd spent a long time talking to his father's solicitor, I was hungry and I had promised myself a slap-up meal. At the risk of sounding churlish, I didn't particularly want to spend another half-hour making small-talk with a total stranger.'

'You've never met Miles Kingsley then?'

'No.'

'But both brothers have visited their sister here.' It was a statement rather than a question and Alan wondered how Maddocks knew.

'As I understand it, Miles came last Wednesday at about nine o'clock when I was off duty. Fergus came on Saturday.'

'So they both know their way around.' Another statement.

Alan frowned. 'Fergus spoke to Jinx in the garden, so presumably he could find his way back to the tree they sat under, and Miles, who saw her in her room, could probably find his way back there. Does that amount to knowing their way around? I wouldn't have thought so.'

'I was thinking more in terms of the layout of the driveway, sir.'

'Oh, for God's sake!' Alan snapped impatiently. 'Any moron can wait in the bushes near a gate in the hopes of someone driving in. You don't need to be acquainted with a place to follow a car going at five miles an hour, which is all I was doing because I didn't want to wake the patients by crunching the gravel.' He sighed heavily. 'Look, unless you've got something a little more concrete to put to me, I really can't see the point of continuing. My own view is that you should put your suspicions to Miss Kingsley herself, to her father and to her brothers.' He nodded towards *The Times*. 'In fact, *if*, as you are implying, there is such a strong link between all three murders, I share Sir Anthony's and Mrs Harris's surprise that you haven't done it already.'

'You're very defensive of this family, sir. Is there any particular reason for that?'

'Such as?'

'Perhaps you're more partial to Miss Kingsley than you pretend and perhaps that's why someone saw fit to attack you with a sledgehammer.'

Alan smoothed his jaw reflectively. 'But wouldn't I have had to have *told* someone I was partial to her to provoke such a response?'

'Not necessarily, sir. You looked pretty matey to me when you were spouting Greek at each other. Perhaps someone else sussed that your feelings aren't quite as reserved as you say they are.'

Alan's booming laugh brought a responsive twitch from Fraser's lips. 'I'm afraid I was teasing you, Inspector, when I said it was all Greek to me.' He stood up. 'I am doubtful, *ipso facto*, whether any conclusion you've drawn can be relied upon. Now, if you'll excuse me, I have patients to see.'

Outside, Maddocks scowled angrily as he reached into the car for the handset. 'Put me through to Detective Superintendent Cheever,' he grunted into the mouthpiece, 'and tell him it's urgent, girl. DI Maddocks, and I am at the Nightingale Clinic in Salisbury.' He drummed his fingers impatiently on the roof. 'Yes, sir. No, look, we've run into a spot of bother here. The doctor's playing hard to get and the whole set-up stinks. He and the girl were having a very cosy little chat when we arrived and our view is he knows a damn sight more than he's telling. Yeah, Fraser agrees with me.' He glared at the Sergeant, demanding support. 'No, I think we should talk to her now. We're on the spot, she's seen us and she knows Wallader and Harris are dead. If we leave it any longer she'll have a solicitor in tow guarding her interests. Matter of fact, I'm amazed her old man hasn't parked one here already, although maybe he's set the doctor up as watchdog.' His eyes gleamed triumphantly. 'Will do, sir.' He listened for a moment. 'Yes, got it. Letters from Landy ... abortion eighty-four ... Wallader or Landy the father.'

He replaced the handset and grinned at Fraser. 'We've been given the chance to show a bit of initiative, lad, so let's grab it with both hands. And whatever happens I don't want that arrogant jerk of a doctor around. So no by-your-leave on this, OK?' He nodded towards the path round the corner of the building that led on to the terrace. 'We'll go this way.'

Jinx was sitting in her armchair, watching the local news on the television, and didn't notice the two men approaching. She felt their shadows blot out the sun on the back of her shaven head as they stepped quietly across the threshold of her open french windows, and she guessed immediately who it was. Unhurriedly, she used the remote to switch off the television, and twisted round to look at them. 'There's a rule here that visitors seek permission before they impose themselves on patients. I don't think you've done that, have you, Inspector?'

Maddocks strolled in and perched himself on her bed as he'd done before. 'No,' he said bluntly. 'Does that mean you have objections to helping the police?'

'Several,' she said, 'but I can't imagine it'll make any difference.' She smiled coldly. 'Not to you anyway.' She glanced up at Fraser with a look of enquiry. 'It might make a difference to your partner.' She examined the younger, pleasanter face closely. 'No? Ah well, we can't all have principles, I suppose. It would be a dull, dull world.'

'You're very sharp for someone with memory loss,' said Maddocks.

'Am I?'

'You know you are.'

'I don't,' she said. 'I'm the first person I've ever met who's suffered from amnesia so I've no yardstick by which to judge it. However, if you're interested, you don't become a zombie just because a few days of your life are missing.' She gave him an amused smile. 'I don't suppose you remember every woman you've rogered, Inspector, particularly if you were tanked up when you did it, but it hasn't done you any harm, has it?' She reached for a cigarette. 'Or perhaps it has and that's why you accuse me of being sharp.'

'Point taken,' he said affably.

She flicked the lighter to the cigarette and eyed him through the smoke. 'Freud would have enjoyed that,' she remarked idly.

He frowned. 'What?'

She gave a low laugh. 'Your somewhat unfortunate remark following so closely on my description of your rogering habits. Freud would suspect that that's what your lady friends say to you at the moment *coitus* occurs.' She heard Fraser's snort of amusement. 'It's not important, Inspector.' She lapsed into silence.

Maddocks was not amused. 'We have a few questions to ask you, Miss Kingsley.'

She watched him but didn't say anything.

'About Leo and Meg.' He waited. 'We understand Dr Protheroe has told you they're dead.'

She nodded.

'It must have been a shock.'

She nodded again.

'Well, forgive me for saying this, Miss Kingsley, but the shock didn't last very long, did it? Your fiancé and your best friend have been bludgeoned to death with a sledgehammer, their faces smashed in just as your husband's was, and you're sitting here quite calmly, smoking a cigarette and cracking jokes. It's about the most unconvincing display of grief that I've ever seen.'

'I'm sorry, Inspector. Would it make you feel better if I did the little-womanly thing and wept for you?'

He ignored her. 'About as unconvincing, frankly, as this amnesia rubbish.'

'I'm sorry?' She compressed her lips into a savage smile. 'I'm afraid I've quite forgotten what we're talking about.'

Maddocks glanced at Fraser, who was grinning to himself. 'We're talking about the deaths of three people, Miss Kingsley, all of whom were closely associated with you and all of whom have been brutally murdered. Russell Landy, Leo Wallader and Meg Harris. In addition, we are talking about a violent attack on Dr Protheroe last night which, but for his own quick thinking, would have resulted in a similar bludgeoning to that received by your husband, your fiancé and your best friend. Presumably he told you he was attacked with a sledgehammer?' He flung the question at her, watching for a reaction.

'He didn't,' she said quietly.

'How do you feel about that?'

'Fine,' she said. 'I don't expect Dr Protheroe to tell me everything.'

'Doesn't the fact that a sledgehammer was used worry you just a little, Miss Kingsley?'

'Yes.'

'Then tell me now that you find the situation amusing, because I sure as hell don't, and neither do the two heart-broken mothers whose maggot-ridden children were dug out of a ditch last Thursday.'

She drew on her cigarette and stared past him. 'I'll tell you whatever you like, Inspector,' she said with an odd inflection in her voice, 'because it won't make any difference.'

She shifted her gaze back to him. 'You will still twist everything I say.'

'That's nonsense, Miss Kingsley.'

'*Experto credite*. Trust one who has been through it.' She flashed him a faint smile. 'You're no different from the last lot. They also wanted to prove my father was a murderer.'

Chapter Seventeen

FRASER MOVED INTO Jinx's line of vision. He pulled forward the second armchair and sat in it, hands clasped between knees, his face less than a metre from hers. *Grab the initiative, the DI had said.* And Fraser, at least, was intelligent enough to recognize that they wouldn't get anywhere with intimidation. But then, unlike Maddocks, he didn't feel he had anything to prove, not against women anyway.

'We really are trying to keep an open mind,' he assured her, 'but what we find difficult to ignore is the similarity in the method of killing and the fact that the three victims, although separated by ten years, were all known to you. We are not talking about passing acquaintances here, Miss Kingsley, we are talking about the two men who have probably been closest to you during your life and the woman whom your parents described at the time of your accident as your best friend.' He smiled ruefully. 'Do you see the problem we have? Even to the most impartial observer, your involvement with all three people would appear significant.'

She nodded. *Jesus wept! Did he think she was a moron?* 'I understand that. It appears significant to me, too, but for the life of me I can't tell you why. I've gone over it again and again and I keep coming up against the brick wall of Russell's murder.' She stubbed out her cigarette to avoid the smoke blowing into his face. 'The reason that was never solved is because the London police concentrated on me and my father. We were both ruled out of direct involvement because we both had alibis. I was then ruled out of indirect involvement because there was no obvious reason for me to want Russell dead. My father, on the other hand, had loathed him and made no secret of it, so the police convinced themselves that he'd ordered a contract killing and they abandoned the search for anyone else. But supposing they were wrong? Supposing my father had nothing to do with it, where is the significance then in my knowing all three victims?' She looked earnestly into his face. 'Do you understand the point I'm making?'

'I think so. You're saying that if someone else entirely killed Russell, then there may be an unknown link between the murders.'

'Yes, and if you make the same mistake the London police made, then that unknown person will get away with it again.'

'It's a little hard to accept, Miss Kingsley. We've been sent detailed accounts of the Landy case and there's no hint of a mystery person in the background.'

She shook her head vigorously. 'There *is*. I kept telling them about this artist Russell was rude to. He mentioned twice that he'd seen him hanging around the gallery, and he said if he came again he'd report him to the police. Then he was murdered.' She spread her hands in a pleading gesture. 'I am sure that's the man you should be looking for.'

'It was mentioned in the report but the view seems to be that, if the man existed at all, he was more likely to be your father's contract killer than a resentful artist. It would be different if you could have supplied the police with a description or a name but, as I understand it, you couldn't give them any information at all.'

'Because I didn't know anything. All I could tell them was what Russell told me. An artist came to the gallery with some bad paintings, Russell told him they were bad, the man became abusive and Russell ordered him out. He never mentioned it at the time, but he did tell me on two occasions later that he'd noticed a man watching the gallery and he thought it was this same artist.' She sighed. 'I know it's not much but no one was even remotely interested in following it up. They were all so hooked on my father having done it.'

'With reason, don't you think?'

She didn't answer.

'He made no secret of his dislike for your husband.'

'Oh, I know all the arguments. I listened to them often enough at the time. My father knew the right contacts in the underworld for a contract killing. He's ruthless, he's tough, he began life as a black marketeer, and he's thought to have made millions through dodgy business practices, although no one's been able to prove it. He has the credentials of a home-grown Mafia godfather, with the same blind loyalty to family, for whom the death of a hated son-in-law would be a natural way to solve a problem.' She smiled bleakly. 'I was even shown a psychological assessment of him, based on facts known to the police, in which he was portrayed as a psychopath with a phenomenal sex drive. This, apparently, was why he visited prostitutes because, as I was the real object of his desire, he was unable to satisfy his animal needs properly.'

Fraser waited for a moment. 'And you don't think any of that's true?' he prompted.

'I don't know,' she said honestly, 'but I don't see that it matters. The police squeezed that character assessment for all it was worth, but they still couldn't link Adam with Russell's death. Doesn't that mean Adam probably had nothing to do with it?'

Fraser shook his head reluctantly. 'It might mean he paid a great deal of money to put distance between himself and the murder.' But he, too, found the black saucer eyes in the white face compelling and he tried to soften the blow a little. 'That's not to say I've a closed mind on the matter, Miss Kingsley. It was a botched job for a contract killing. Russell was still alive when you found him, so his murderer was damn lucky to get away with it, and so was whoever hired him.'

Her tongue moistened her dry lips before, abruptly, she pushed herself back into her chair and clapped her hands over her nose and mouth. 'I should have thought about this a long time ago,' she said in a muffled voice. 'God, I've been a fool.' She took her hands away. 'My father's a perfectionist in everything he does,' she said, 'and so are the people he employs. None of them would have dared do a botched job. Adam would have skinned them alive.'

Fraser eyed her curiously. 'Meaning you think he was capable of ordering Russell's murder, but didn't in fact do it?'

'Yes.' She leaned forward again. 'Look, my father was in London that day, so his alibi always had holes in it. He wouldn't pay to distance himself only to end up being compromised. Plus, as you said, Russell was still alive when I found him and might have survived if I'd got there earlier, but Adam would never employ anyone who was so incompetent that the victim was still conscious an hour after he'd been attacked.'

'Perhaps the killer was interrupted?'

'No,' she said in excitement. 'Don't you see? If Adam had ordered the killing he would have given instructions for Russell to be killed anywhere but the gallery. He knew I had the only other key, so knew I was the most likely person to find the body, unless somebody happened to go round the back and saw the stock-room window had been smashed.' She saw his scepticism. 'Oh, please, Sergeant,' she begged him, 'hear what I'm saying. The police said Adam was so besotted with me that he became pathologically jealous of Russell. But if that were true, he'd have had Russell killed as far away from me as possible, certainly not left alive and bleeding to death where I would probably be the one to find him. The last thing he'd have wanted was for me to have a nervous breakdown and retreat into my shell. Don't you think?'

Fraser was impressed with this argument. 'Did you make that point to the London police?'

'How could I? I've only just thought of it. Look,' she said again, 'I know it seems odd, but when something that awful happens to you, you block it out as soon as you can or you go mad. Before my breakdown I never had time to think it through properly, there was the police, the funeral, the miscarriage . . .' She faltered slightly. 'And then when I came out of the hospital, I made up my mind to shut it away and never, never get it out again. It's only since my accident that it's started to come back. The nightmares, seeing Russell on the floor, the blood . . .' She faltered again but this time didn't go on.

Maddocks had listened to the exchange with growing scepticism but he spoke gently enough. 'The police weren't wedded to a contract killer, Miss Kingsley. They always recognized that your father might have wielded the sledgehammer himself. Let's say he went to the gallery, and he and Russell had a row. Do you think he'd care then whether you found the body or not? He'd be saving his own skin, and high-tailing it out as fast as he could.'

Jinx turned to look at him. 'You can't expect to have it both ways, Inspector. If Adam is the organized criminal you all claim him to be, then he would have arranged for the mess to be cleared up. And he wouldn't have left Russell alive.' She pressed her palm to her temple. 'He doesn't make mistakes, Inspector.'

'He beat a negro half to death,' said Maddocks idly, 'who went on to become your uncle. Perhaps that was another mistake. Perhaps he meant to kill him, too.'

Jinx dropped her hand into her lap and clasped it tightly over the other. She was feeling extremely unwell but knew Maddocks would exploit it if she said anything. She concentrated on Fraser, willing him to respond.

'Let's say you're right, Miss Kingsley,' the Sergeant said after a moment, 'and that there's another link between the three murders. Have you any idea what – or who – it might be?'

'The only one I can think of is Meg,' she told him gravely. 'She was as close to Russell and Leo as I was.'

Maddocks stirred again. 'Closer,' he said bluntly. 'According to some letters and diaries found in Leo's house, your friend Meg Harris was having an affair with your husband at the time of his death and also jumped in and out of bed regularly with your fiancé. One of them – and it's clear from entries in her diary that she didn't know which – was the father of a child she aborted shortly after Landy was murdered.'

There was a brief silence before colour flared in Jinx's cheeks. 'No wonder she was so upset when I lost my baby,' she said slowly.

Maddocks frowned. 'You don't seem very surprised about the affair.'

'I knew about that,' she said, 'but I didn't know she'd had an abortion. Poor Meg. She must have felt guilty if she thought hers had been Russell's child as well.'

'So this is something else you withheld from the London police?'

She held his gaze for a moment. 'How could I tell them something I didn't know? It was long after Russell was dead that I found out about the affair.'

'Ah,' he murmured, 'I think I could have predicted that. Did Miss Harris tell you?'

'No.' She repeated what she'd told Alan Protheroe, about the letters in the attic and her reluctance to re-open old wounds. 'But perhaps if I had said something, Meg and Leo would still be alive,' she finished bleakly. 'It's so much easier to be wise after the event.'

'Yes,' said Maddocks thoughtfully. 'Things do seem to take a very long time to germinate in your mind, don't they? Who else knew about this affair?'

'I don't think anyone did. I told you, they were very discreet.'

'Did you tell your father about it?'

'When I found out, you mean?' He nodded. 'There was no point.'

'Anybody else?'

She shook her head. 'Only Dr Protheroe. I told him this morning.'

Maddocks nodded. 'Did you and Miss Harris ever discuss Landy's murder?'

'Once or twice, before I went into hospital,' she said unevenly. 'We discussed it before, but never afterwards.'

'Did she say who she thought might have done it?'

She rested her cheek against her hand and tried to picture scenes in her mind. 'It's so long ago,' she said, 'and neither of us was very inclined to dwell on it, but I think she went along with the initial police view because that was the only one that was reported in the papers. A robbery that went wrong. As far as I know, that's what most people still believe.'

'So she never knew that both you and your father were under suspicion?'

She pretended to think about that. *Everyone knew, you bastard . . . every damn friend I ever had knew . . . why the hell do you think I've been so fucking lonely for the last ten years?* . . . 'I had to supply the police with a list of our friends, most of whom were Russell's, but Meg was on it as a friend of mine, and I do remember her telling me that the police were asking about the relationship between Russell and Adam.' She frowned suddenly. 'You know, I remember now. She did make one rather odd comment. She said: "They will keep asking for information but I'm sure it's better to let sleeping dogs lie. There's been so much pain caused already."'

'What did she mean by that?'

'At the time, I probably thought she was talking about Russell and Adam's relationship, saying she couldn't see the need to supply any more details. But now I think she might have been referring to her affair with Russell. I know the police dug very hard for evidence of something like that, on the principle he might have been killed by a jealous husband.' She paused for a moment. 'But she knew I didn't know about the affair, so perhaps she didn't want to hurt me unnecessarily by revealing it to the police.'

'It must have upset you when you finally found out about it,' said Fraser.

She turned to him with visible relief. 'I know it sounds callous, but in fact it made me feel better. Russell and I hadn't been getting on for months before he died, and I'd always felt guilty about it. It's awful to have someone die on you when you know you've made them unhappy. I kept thinking, if only I'd done this, or if only I'd done that' – she gave a troubled smile – 'and then I was let off the hook by a couple of love letters.'

Maddocks watched her performance with cynical objectivity. The story was too pat and too well polished and he saw Dr Protheroe's hand at work behind the scenes. 'So let me get this straight, Miss Kingsley,' he said acidly. 'Number one: at the time of Russell Landy's death, you and he were not getting on but you told the London police you were. Number two: you believed your father was capable of putting out a contract on your husband but defended him anyway. Number three: Russell and your best friend were having an affair but you knew nothing about it, and she did not reveal it to the police. Number four: she aborted the child she had conceived either by your then husband or the man who later became your fiancé, but neither you nor the London police were ever told about it. Number five: when you discovered your friend and your husband had been having an affair, you kept the information to yourself. Number six: your best friend, who'd had an affair with your husband and knew that your husband had been murdered, nevertheless proceeded to resurrect an old affair with your fiancé and so persuade him to abandon you for her. Number seven: he and she were subsequently murdered in an identical fashion, though in a different location, to the way your husband was murdered.' He arched his eyebrows. 'Is that a fair summary of what you've told us?'

'Yes,' said Jinx honestly. 'To my knowledge, that is accurate. Assuming the abortion and the way Meg and Leo were murdered to be true. Those are the only two things I didn't know.'

He nodded. 'All right, then I have one last question on the Landy murder before we talk about Wallader and Harris. According to the reports we have, you were ruled out of direct involvement because you had a cast-iron alibi. Who gave you the alibi?'

'It was Meg,' she said. 'I spent the afternoon and early evening with her and then she drove me to the restaurant for seven-thirty. I waited there about an hour and, when Russell didn't show, I took a taxi to the gallery. Isn't that in the report?'

Maddocks ignored the question. 'Wouldn't it have been simpler to phone the gallery?'

'I did. There was no answer. So I phoned home but there was no answer there either.'

'Then why assume he was at the gallery? Why bother to take a taxi there?'

'Because it was on the way home.'

'But you paid off the taxi before you went inside.'

'It was nine o'clock at night and the driver wouldn't let me leave the cab without paying. I think he was afraid I was planning to leg it down the nearest alleyway. He said he'd wait five minutes and if I wasn't back by then, he'd go. As it was, I was back within two, screaming my head off. The driver dialled nine-nine-nine while I sat with Russell, then he waited outside till the ambulance arrived. That's why the police had no trouble tracing him afterwards to support my story.'

Maddocks chuckled softly. 'You have an answer for everything, don't you?'

She studied him with a remarkably cool gaze. 'All I'm doing is telling you the truth, Inspector.'

'And let's face it, girl, you've had ten whole years to get it right.'

One of the security staff at the clinic, Harry Elphick, after learning about the assault on Dr Protheroe, made a detour on his departure to check the outhouses near the staff parking places. He remembered some weeks back seeing a sledgehammer in one of them, and it occurred to him that it might be worth a second look. He reasoned, quite logically, that the most likely person to take a swipe at Dr Protheroe was one of the more aggressive junkies in his care, and he went on to reason that, because the Nightingale was not a prison, then any observant patient had the same opportunities as he to notice the sledgehammer. Harry would have considered it naïve rubbish to assume that none of them would bother to attack Dr Protheroe because they knew he didn't carry drugs in his car. Harry, ex-Army and past his middle years, had little time for the sort of over-privileged dregs that Dr Protheroe treated, and it was with some satisfaction that he opened an outhouse door and, after a cursory search, found a sledgehammer with red Wolseley paint-work ground into its head.

'When did you first discover that Leo and Meg were having an affair?'

Jinx stared at her hands for a moment before reaching for her cigarette packet. 'When I came round a few days ago. My stepmother told me.'

Maddocks frowned. 'Are you saying that's the first you knew about it?'

She leaned back in her chair to light a cigarette. 'I don't know,' she said. 'I can't remember anything much from before the accident.'

'What *do* you remember?'

She stared at the ceiling. 'I remember saying goodbye to Leo at breakfast on the morning of June the fourth. I was coming down to Hampshire to stay with my parents for a few days.'

'That's a very precise memory.'

'Yes.'

'When did you find out they were dead, Miss Kingsley?'

She toyed with another lie, then thought better of it. She was too fond of Dean to drop him in this bastard's shit.

'Sunday,' she said. 'I knew you were lying about what had happened to them so I asked a friend to phone the Walladers. Anthony told him they were dead and the friend rang me back to tell me.'

'Which friend?'

'Is that important?'

'It depends whether you want me to believe you or not. This friend might confirm that you were genuinely shocked when you heard the news. Otherwise I'm having some difficulty trying to understand how a woman whose best friend and fiancé have been brutally butchered can retain such extraordinary composure.'

'My number two at the studio, Dean Jarrett.'

'Thank you. Were you upset when your stepmother told you Leo had left you for Meg?'

She shook her head. 'Not particularly. I was more relieved than upset. I think I made it clear to you on Sunday that I had severe doubts about Leo. I am sure in my own mind that I had no intention of marrying him, irrespective of whether he was having an affair with Meg.'

'Then why did you try to kill yourself?'

'I wish I knew.' She smiled suddenly. 'It seems very out of character for someone with extraordinary composure.' She flicked ash from her cigarette. 'So out of character that I don't think I did.'

'You were drunk and you drove your car at full speed towards the only structure of any substance on a deserted airfield. What other explanation is there?'

'But I didn't kill myself,' she pointed out.

'Because you were lucky. You were thrown clear.'

'Perhaps I *threw* myself clear,' she said. 'Perhaps I didn't want to die.'

'Meaning what, precisely?'

Her eyelashes grew damp but she held the tears in check. 'I don't know, but I've had far more time to think about this than I have about Leo and Meg, and it seems to me that if *I* wasn't trying to kill myself, then the only other explanation is that someone *else* was trying to kill me.' She abandoned any attempt to persuade Maddocks and turned instead to Fraser's more open face. 'It would be so easy. My car was an automatic. All anyone would have to do was aim it at the post, put it into *Drive*, wedge the accelerator at full throttle and then release the handbrake. If I was unconscious and belted in, I'd have been crushed in the wreckage. That might have happened, don't you think? It's a possibility, isn't it?'

'If you'd been belted in, how could you have been thrown clear?'

'Then maybe I wasn't belted in,' she said eagerly. 'Maybe the idea was to have me go through the windscreen. Or maybe I came round in time and released myself.'

He would have liked to believe her, but he couldn't. 'Then this hypothetical murderer would have seen what had happened and finished you off. He couldn't afford to leave you alive if he'd just tried to kill you.'

From her pocket she took the newspaper clipping that Betty had given her and pressed it into his hands. 'According to this I was found by a young couple. He wouldn't have had time to finish me off if he saw them coming.'

'Look, Miss Kingsley,' said Maddocks, 'I hate to be cruel,

but facts are facts. According to your neighbours in Richmond, this wasn't the first time. Your first attempt was on the Sunday. Whether you like it or not, indeed whether you remember it or not – and by your own admission you have a habit of blocking out anything that disturbs you – something so terrible happened that you primed yourself with Dutch courage and then had a second go at finishing it all.'

Something terrible happened . . . 'I've never been drunk in my life,' she said stubbornly. 'I've never wanted to be drunk.'

'There's always a first time.'

She shrugged. 'Not as far as I'm concerned, Inspector.'

'You had consumed the equivalent of two bottles of wine when you had your accident, Miss Kingsley. The bottles were found on the floor of your car. Are you telling me you can absorb that amount of alcohol without being what the rest of us would term drunk?'

'No,' she said. 'I'm saying I would never have *wanted* to drink that much.'

'Not even if you had done something you were ashamed of?'

She fixed him with her steady gaze. 'Like what?'

'Been party to a murder perhaps?'

She shook her head. 'Do you not see how illogical that argument is? As I understand it, Meg and Leo's bodies were found near Winchester, which means that whoever murdered them must have worked out some fairly complicated logistics. I can't find out from the newspapers whether they were killed in the wood or taken there after they were dead but, whichever it was, someone went to a great deal of trouble to get them there. But why would anyone go to those lengths if they were so ashamed of what they'd done that they then tried to kill themselves? It doesn't make sense. On the one hand, you're describing a very calculating personality who set out to get rid of two people; on the other, you're describing a weak personality who may have struck out in a moment of anger but was then so appalled by what he'd done that he tried to make amends by killing himself.'

'You really have given this a lot of thought, haven't you?'

The huge black eyes filled again. 'As you would have done, if you were in my place. I'm not a fool, Inspector.'

Maddocks surprised her by acknowledging this with a nod. It was on the tip of his tongue to say, 'Point taken,' but he checked himself in time. 'There's no logic to murder, Miss Kingsley, not in my experience anyway. It's usually the last people you'd expect who do it. Some of them show remorse early, some of them show it when they're convicted, and some of them never show it at all. Believe me, it is not uncommon for a calculating individual to plan a murder, carry it out, dispose of the body, and then have an attack of conscience. We see it over and over again. There's no reason why this case should be any different.'

'Then you might as well clap the handcuffs on me now,' she said, 'because I can't defend myself.'

Nothing would give me more pleasure, sweetheart. 'There's no question of that,' he said affably. 'As Sergeant Fraser said, we are pursuing various lines of enquiry, and this is just one of them. However, I'm sure you realize how important it is that you give us some indication of what went on in the two weeks prior to your accident and the deaths of Leo and Meg. Unfortunately, you seem to be the only person left who can shed any light on the matter.'

She drew on her cigarette with a worried frown. 'What about Meg's friends? Have you spoken to any of them? Surely they can tell you something.'

'Acting on the information you gave us, we spoke to Josh Hennessey yesterday. He told us that the first he knew about Leo and Meg getting together was a phone call from Meg on Saturday, June the eleventh. She told him your wedding was off, that she and Leo were leaving for France but that she would pop into the office before she left to bring him up to date with her side of the operation. She never showed and he never heard from her again. He also gave us the names of some of Meg's close friends. We spoke to a couple of them, Fay Avonalli and Marian Harding, and they told us the same story.'

'But didn't you ask Josh about her and Leo's relationship before that? I mean, he and Meg have worked together for years, he knows everything about her, so presumably he knew about the affair.'

It was Fraser who answered. 'He gave us the name of one man who featured seriously for two or three months at the beginning of this year, but he said Meg had hardly mentioned Leo at all, and he was surprised when she phoned to say they were planning to get married. He said Leo had been around for years, and they had an off-and-on relationship which resurrected itself whenever they were both at a loose end. But he'd never known them to stick together for more than a month or two because Meg always got so irritated with Leo's – he sought for a suitable word – 'selfishness. He said he told her she was mad to think it would be any different this time, and gave the relationship a month to run. He also told her she was a prize bitch and that the only reason she wanted Leo was because he was marrying you.' He smiled sympathetically. 'According to him, Meg was jealous of you. Apparently, she resented you inheriting Russell's money on top of the money you will inherit from your father. She said Jinx always lands on her feet, while she ended up in the cesspit.'

'Which is true in a funny sort of way. All Meg ever wanted was enough ready cash to give her the good times. She said it was so unfair that she had a vicar for a father when penury was the one thing she loathed. She couldn't understand why I didn't touch Adam for money at every opportunity.'

Fraser echoed Protheroe's scepticism of earlier. 'I'm surprised you liked her.'

'I don't have many friends. In any case, she was fun. I suppose it was a case of opposites attracting. I take life too seriously. She gloried in it. She's the only person I've ever known who lived entirely for the present.' A tear fell on to her cheek. 'I was far more jealous of her than she was of me.'

'So would you say your jealousy extended to anger over her stealing of your men friends?' asked Maddocks.

Jinx stubbed out the butt of her cigarette. 'No,' she said tiredly, 'it didn't. I'm sorry, Inspector, but I really don't think there's anything more I can tell you.'

Alan Protheroe was waiting by their car when they rounded the corner of the building. 'I trust, gentlemen, that you showed Miss Kingsley rather more courtesy than you showed me when you pushed your way into my office.' His eyes narrowed. 'I have extreme reservations about these bully-boy tactics of yours.'

'We had a little chat, sir,' protested Maddocks, 'which you could have joined at any time, had you or Miss Kingsley wished it.'

Alan shook his head in irritation. 'You're a type, Inspector, and it's not a type I admire or even believe should be in the police force. Do you really need reminding that Miss Kingsley was in a coma less than a week ago? Or that your colleagues at Fordingbridge believe she has twice tried to kill herself?'

'It's a funny business that suicide attempt.' Maddocks nodded towards Fraser. 'She told the Sergeant here she thought someone was trying to kill her. What's your reading of it, Doctor? Attempted suicide or attempted murder? Does Miss Kingsley strike you as the suicidal type? I can't see it myself.'

'But attempted murder *convinces* you?'

Maddocks grinned. 'I'd say that was a clutching at straws to lay the blame on someone else.'

'So what are you left with if it was neither?'

'A little piece of theatre, I think. She's one hell of an actress, this patient of yours, but then I'm sure you know that already.'

Alan nodded abruptly towards the front doors. 'One of my security staff has something to show you. My view is it should be handed to the Salisbury police, who I understood were dealing with the assault on me, but they appear to be passing the buck to you.' He led the way inside and gestured towards the sledgehammer, which was lying on top of the reception desk with a polythene bag neatly attached to its head. 'Harry Elphick,' he said, introducing the security officer. 'He found it in one of the outhouses. It has flakes of red paint on the metal which might have come from my Wolseley.'

Maddocks smiled appreciatively. 'Good man, Harry. What made you go looking for it?'

Harry, who prided himself on his judgement, recognized a good'un when he saw one. 'Well, sir, it was like this. Begging the doctor's pardon, I don't set as much store by the youngsters here as he does.' He launched into a rambling account of his reasoning processes, finishing with: 'So, as I always say, when you're looking for an answer, look for the obvious, and the obvious in this case is that one of the little tykes on the premises thought he'd chance his arm.'

Maddocks glanced towards Alan with a malicious smile. 'Or *her* arm,' he murmured. 'I hadn't realized until Miss Kingsley stood up in your room just how tall she is. Five feet ten would be my guess.'

Nightingale Clinic, Salisbury – 10.00 p.m.

Veronica Gordon heard the commotion from the front hall as she was sipping her cup of tea in the staff sitting room. She walked out and frowned angrily at the sight of Betty Kingsley trying to wrestle free of Amy Staunton. 'Black bitch,' Betty was shouting. 'Get your hands off me. I want to see my daughter!'

'What on earth is going on?' Veronica asked icily, laying a hand on the older woman's collar and yanking her back with surprising strength. 'How dare you speak to one of my nursing staff in those terms? I won't tolerate it, not from anyone, and most especially not from a drunk.' She looked very angry. 'What a disgraceful exhibition. Just who on earth do you think you are?'

Betty's face grew sullen as she shook the hand off. 'You know who I am,' she said aggressively. 'I'm Mrs Adam Kingsley and I've come to see my daughter.' But she was wilting visibly in the face of the sister's sobriety and superior aggression.

'That's out of the question,' Veronica snapped. 'It's ten o'clock at night and you're in no condition to talk to anyone. I suggest you go home and sober up, and come back again tomorrow morning in a rather more presentable state than you are in at the moment.'

Betty's eyes bulged in her powdered face. 'My husband's going to hear about this. You've got a right nerve talking to me like that.'

'What an excellent idea. Why don't we phone Mr Kingsley now? I'm sure he'll be delighted to hear that his wife has engaged in a drunken brawl with a nurse at the Nightingale Clinic.'

Tears coursed down the grotesque face. 'I need to see Jinx,' she wept. 'Please let me see my daughter.' But she seemed to realize that tears weren't going to win her any sympathy, so she took a deep breath, patted her hair and pulled her coat straight. 'There you are. That's better, isn't it? I won't cause no trouble, not if you let me see her.' She dabbed her eyes and fixed a pathetically roguish smile on her lips. 'Cheerful as anything. Don't take no mind of what I said earlier.' She patted Amy's arm. 'I didn't mean anything by it, dear. I've got a cruel mouth sometimes. Are you going to let me see Jinx? Please, it's that important.'

Veronica mellowed a little. 'What is so important that it can't wait till tomorrow, Mrs Kingsley?'

'Meg and Leo,' she said. 'Me and the boys read they'd been murdered but her Daddy's refusing to do anything about it. Seems to me someone should give the poor kid a cuddle, even if it is only me.'

Veronica agreed with her, and if she thought it a little odd that Betty had waited twelve hours and got herself drunk before she put the idea into practice, she didn't say anything. Instead she sent Amy down to find out if Jinx was still awake, before escorting Betty to number twelve and leaving the two women together with the door wide open. 'I'll be just along the corridor,' she informed them. 'You have fifteen minutes, Mrs Kingsley, and I do not expect to hear any raised voices. Is that understood?'

Betty waited till she'd gone then gave a disparaging sniff. 'She's a right bitch, that one.' She staggered to a chair and collapsed into it, staring morosely at her stepdaughter who was already in bed. 'I suppose someone's told you Meg and Leo are dead.'

Jinx hid her dismay. 'Who brought you, Betty?'

'I made Jenkins do it.' She waved a meaty hand towards the door. 'He's waiting outside.'

'Does Adam know you've come?'

'Course not.' She shook her head. 'He's in London. The shares have been sliding all day. He's trying to repair the damage.'

'I saw it on the news.'

'Oh, my, my. You're a cool one. Always were.' She blew her nose. 'D'you know why they're sliding? Because Leo's dead and Russell's dead, and fingers are pointing.'

Jinx watched her for a moment. 'It won't affect you or the boys,' she said calmly. 'The company's sound and Adam won't let the slide continue indefinitely. Your shares will go back up again, so you won't lose out.'

'And how's your precious Adam going to stop the slide?' she hissed, her little eyes like flints. 'You tell me that. There's me and the boys worrying ourselves sick, while you and your daddy behave as if nothing's happened.'

'If necessary, he'll resign.' A small frown creased her forehead. 'You know that as well as I do. It's what he's always said he would do in a crisis.'

'And where will that leave us?'

'With all the shares Adam gave you ten years ago.'

Betty took out a compact and floured her ravaged face. 'No,' she said tightly, 'it'll leave me with no home to call my own. It's not ours, remember, belongs to the company. An asset. That's what they call it, isn't it? Did you think of *that* when you brought this crisis on our heads? If your daddy resigns we lose the Hall. The boys'll be out of a job, and none of us'll have a roof over our heads. What've you got to say to that?'

'I'd say it means you've sold your shares and you're afraid Adam's going to wash his hands of you.' Jinx rested her head against her pillows. 'And about time, too. He deserves better than three dead-weights who know only how to drag him down. You should all be standing by him, instead of whingeing about what's going to happen to you.' She smiled to herself. 'Do you know what? When you came in, I

328

thought, my God, one of them has come to hold my hand. One of them has come to say, we believe in you, Jinxy. We know you must be going through hell, but we're here for you. What a mug, eh? Why on earth should I have imagined for one minute that you or your good-for-nothing bastards could change the habits of a lifetime?'

'Don't you call my sons bastards.'

'Why not?' said Jinx, pressing the bell beside her bed. 'It's what they are. You've never been a wife to my father.'

Betty's eyes filled with tears again. 'I hated you the first time I saw you.'

'I know. You always made that very clear.'

'You hated me, too.'

'Because you were so stupid.' She turned to Veronica Gordon, who had appeared in the doorway. 'My stepmother's leaving,' she said.

'I did my best,' said Betty. 'I wanted to love you.'

'No, you didn't. You wanted to displace me. Jealousy is a disease with you. You knew damned well that Adam loved me far more than he would ever love you.'

She smiled coldly, and Veronica found herself reassessing every opinion she'd ever had of the young woman. This was no dewy-eyed victim, she thought.

MEMO

From: Det Supt Cheever
To: CC
Date: Wednesday, 29 June, 1994
Re: Wallader/Harris

Detailed below is all relevant information, as of 09.00 hours today.

- Despite extensive enquiries, we can find no witnesses to an individual wearing bloodstained clothes in the vicinity of Ardingly Woods on 12/13/14 June. No weapon has been found. Reports of several cars in the area, but no effective leads. (NB: Forensic examination of Jane Kingsley's car reveals <u>no</u> bloodstains.)

- Wallader's and Harris's personal effects have been located at 35, Eagleton Street, Chelsea.

- Wallader's two cars have been located. One at Eagleton Street and the other in a rented garage in Camden. Harris's car was located in the street outside number 35. All three cars are undergoing forensic examination today, but a preliminary examination revealed nothing of significance.

- A reading of Harris's diaries, in conjunction with the evidence of friends and relations, suggests that Harris and Wallader had an ongoing, if spasmodic, sexual relationship for some 11 years. In addition, it is now

clear that Harris was sexually involved with Russell
Landy both before and during his marriage to Jane
Kingsley.

- There is evidence that Harris had an abortion in February, 1984, some five days <u>after</u> Landy's murder,
although it is unclear who the father was. Some indication that it may not have been Wallader <u>or</u> Landy.
Her diaries reveal a promiscuous personality, as borne
out by her brother's evidence.

- There remain question marks over the Harris family.
Clear indication of tension. Neither Simon nor Rev H
had much time for Meg, with both expressing prefer-
ence for Jane Kingsley (bizarre in the circumstances);
Mrs H, on the other hand, seems overly fond of Meg
and angry/jealous (?) of Jane.

- A twenty-five-year-old psychological assessment of
Wallader, supplied by his mother, describes a child
with a severe personality disorder.

- The Walladers mention an argument on Monday,
May 30, during which Leo claimed he planned to
marry Meg instead. He phoned later that evening to
warn his parents not to say anything until he gave
them the go-ahead. In the event, the go-ahead was
not given until Saturday, June 11, although Sir
Anthony and Lady W cannot account for the delay.

- Current estimate of Wallader's wealth, held in property, stocks and shares, and gold: £1.1 million.

According to his solicitor, Wallader consistently refused to make a will so there is none in existence.

- Harris informed her parents of events on Saturday, June 11. On the same day she also phoned her business partner and two friends with the information. We can find no one who was privy to the facts prior to Saturday, June 11. She told her business partner she would be in the office on Monday, June 13. (NB: Harris's diary entries are erratic. There are empty weeks, followed by a day, or days, fully recorded. There are no entries after Monday, May 18, and no mention of Leo Wallader, by name, since December, 1993, when she writes that after all these years she has finally introduced Leo to Jinx.)

- According to her partner, she did not visit her office on Monday, June 13.

- NB: Entry in Harris's diary, following Kingsley's marriage to Landy, reads as follows: 'Since becoming unattainable, Russell is so much more attractive.' Echoed, in April, 1994, by the following: 'Jinx tells me she is taking the plunge again. I knew I would live to regret that introduction.'

- According to Mr and Mrs Kingsley's statements of Tuesday, June 14 (following Jane Kingsley's accident), they were informed by telephone of their daughter's cancelled wedding on Saturday, June 11. This is supported by the evidence of Colonel Eric Clancey who stated, also at the time of the accident, that Jane

Kingsley told him about her changed wedding plans on June 11.

- The evidence of Mr and Mrs Kingsley (taken after the accident) is that Jane spent the week from Saturday, June 4 to Friday, June 10 at Hellingdon Hall. She appeared to be in good spirits, made no mention of the row with Leo and discussed preparations for the wedding as if it were going ahead.

- Jane Kingsley's own evidence in an interview conducted 28.6.94 is that she cannot remember anything since June 4. She admits to knowing about Harris's affair with Landy, though claims she only learnt about it <u>after</u> Landy's death. She claims not to remember being told about Wallader and Harris but this is disputed by the Wallader parents' testimony, which states Leo told her on the afternoon of Monday, May 30 (i.e. prior to memory loss from June 4). DI Maddocks is convinced she remembers more than she says, and this would seem to be borne out by the above.

- Miss Kingsley admits she believes her father could have ordered Landy's death but does not believe he did so. She can offer no evidence in support, other than her own conviction that he would not have allowed her to find the body. There is some merit in this argument if Kingsley is fond of her.

- A possibly related incident occurred at the Nightingale Clinic during the night of Monday June 27. Dr Protheroe, the clinic's director, was attacked by an intruder with a sledgehammer. Miss Kingsley has been a patient of his for some ten days, and in addition Dr Protheroe was visited by Kingsley's solicitor during the afternoon of June 27.

- Protheroe escaped relatively unscathed, however the weapon was found later in an outhouse at the Nightingale by a member of the security staff who states it belongs to the clinic. This is supported by preliminary forensic tests which have found <u>no</u> blood/hair/tissue on the hammer head but <u>some</u> paint from Protheroe's car, which was badly damaged during the assault. This would suggest his assailant was well acquainted with the layout of the clinic grounds and points to a past or present patient, or possibly a visitor. Protheroe described his attacker as male, 5' 10" or 5' 11" and of medium build. The assailant was dressed in black and wearing a ski-mask or similar.

- Miss Kingsley is 5' 10" and slim build. However (1) the attack was at night, (2) DI Maddocks is of the opinion that Protheroe is doing his utmost, for whatever reason, to protect his patient, (3) Miss Kingsley could have worn padding. One pointer that may be worth considering, assuming the incident to be related to the Landy/Wallader/Harris murders, is that Miss Kingsley is unquestionably weak following her accident and Protheroe had little trouble fighting off the attack. Dr Clarke does not rule out a woman being capable of the attacks on Wallader and Harris. In addition, the heel marks on the bank near where the bodies were found do seem to imply that a woman was present at the scene.

- Re: the Landy murder. Miss Kingsley's alibi for the afternoon and early evening of February 1, 1984, was suppli ed by Miss Harris. In light of the new evidence that Harris and Landy were having an affair, and that Miss Kingsley may have known about it, this alibi is not as straightforward as it appeared at the time. Worth a second look. NB: Harris's diary says nothing on the subject, indeed does not mention Landy's murder at all.

IN CONCLUSION:

1. Meg Harris clearly made a bid to win back both men after they had made serious commitments to Jane Kingsley. We only have Kingsley's word that she knew nothing about this and/or did not bear a grudge.

2. It appears Wallader and Harris did not reveal their proposed marriage plans until shortly before they were due to leave for the relative safety of France.

3. Jane Kingsley, too, saw fit to keep the secret.

4. Their killer probably drove them to Ardingly Woods in his/her own car.

5. On the most likely date of Wallader/Harris's deaths,

Kingsley drove her car at a concrete stanchion only some 20 miles from Ardingly Woods.

6. Shortly after Kingsley's admission to the Nightingale Clinic, Dr Protheroe was attacked with a similar weapon to Landy/Wallader/Harris.

The investigating team is concentrating its efforts on uncovering the movements of Wallader/Kingsley/Harris between May 30 and June 13. All relevant parties will be re-questioned with a view to establishing a timetable of events.

Yours   *Frank*

City worries about Franchise Holdings

There was a sharp drop in the value of Franchise Holdings (FH) Ltd shares yesterday, following the identification of one of the bodies found in Ardingly Woods last Thursday as Leo Wallader. Until recently, Wallader, a 35-yr-old stock broker, was engaged to Adam Kingsley's daughter, Jane, and the market has reacted to press speculation linking this murder to the murder of Kingsley's son-in-law, Russell Landy, ten years ago.

Concerns have been expressed for some time about who will succeed Adam Kingsley to the chairmanship, and it is these concerns that are fuelling the present crisis. Adam Kingsley has a reputation for hands-on management and, without his driving force, there are doubts about the future of Franchise Holdings.

A spokesman for the company said this afternoon that investors are being panicked by irresponsible press coverage. 'There is no question of Adam Kingsley stepping down,' he said. 'Our investors have done well by us and will continue to do well for many years to come.'

However, City analysts are more sceptical. 'Franchise Holdings is a one-man band,' said a source. 'If Kingsley goes, the collapse in confidence will be catastrophic. Frankly it will be a miracle if he can weather the present storm. The fear is that any investigation into Kingsley's affairs will uncover financial irregularities. The funding of some of his early acquisitions has never been adequately explained. It would be different if there was an obvious successor.'

Kingsley's sons, Miles, 26, and Fergus, 24, were expelled from public school for possession of drugs, and have been cautioned in the past for vandalism and theft. They are regulars at the various London casinos and at race meetings.

Adam Kingsley's daughter, Jane, 34, who owns and manages a successful photographic studio in South London, was married to Russell Landy for three years before his murder. Police have reopened the file since the death of her fiancé.

Chapter Eighteen

WPC BLAKE NOTED the thunder clouds on DC Hadden's face as he pushed past her and shouldered his way through the double-doors. 'What's up with Hadden?' she asked the sergeant as she leaned her elbows on the front desk.

'Politics,' he grunted, preoccupied with some notes he was writing. 'He reckons the DCI has given away the best case he's ever had.'

'Who to?'

'Hampshire police. He handed over a prime piece of evidence last night on the Ardingly Wood murders and Hadden's furious about it. Claims he's the one who cracked the case and now no one's going to credit him with it.'

'What was the evidence?'

'The sledgehammer that was used to attack the doctor up at the Nightingale on Monday night,' the sergeant told her.

Blake watched his busy pen for a moment. 'So what's the connection with Ardingly Woods? Sledgehammers come two-a-penny on building sites. What's so special about this one?'

'The dead man's fiancée is a patient at the Nightingale,

338

and she appears to be in the habit of losing husbands and lovers to death by bludgeoning.' He glanced up from his notes. 'Jane Kingsley, daughter of Adam Kingsley. It's been all over the newspapers for the last couple of days.'

'I've been busy.'

He pushed a tabloid towards her and stabbed a double column with his pen. 'Hampshire gave a press briefing yesterday. It's all there.'

Blake took the paper and read the piece rapidly. 'Well, I can see why Hadden's pissed off,' she remarked, laying it back on the counter. 'Who do you reckon did it?'

He shrugged as he signed his name. 'All I know is I wouldn't want to be employed by Franchise Holdings if they arrest Adam Kingsley. According to the business pages the shares are sliding already, and that's just on *fears* he might have been involved.' He straightened up. 'How are you getting on with the Flossie Hale assault?'

'Not bad.' She gave him a run-down of what she'd discovered. 'He was carrying a key-ring with a black disc embossed with a gold F and H. Flossie thinks they might be his initials but I'm not keen to put that in the description in case she's wrong. What do you think?'

He stared at her thoughtfully for a moment or two then picked up the newspaper and leafed through the pages impatiently, looking for the business section. Inset into the article on Franchise Holdings was a picture of the company's logo – entwined initials against a black background. He showed it to her. 'Something like that?'

'What are you, Sarge,' said Blake in amazement, 'a bloody magician?'

Nightingale Clinic, Salisbury – 9.30 a.m.

The floor around Jinx's feet was awash with newspapers when Alan Protheroe knocked on her door at nine-thirty. 'I ordered the lot,' she said with a weak smile. 'Have you seen what's happening?'

He nodded. 'I watched the breakfast news. The shares started sliding again as soon as the market opened.'

'Poor Adam, it's very unfair,' she said bitterly. 'They've been dying to cut him down to size for years and now they've been given the chance.' She clenched her hands in her lap. 'You know what makes me maddest of all? It's this garbage about no obvious successor. It's a cheap way to parade the family failings. Three of the present board are perfectly capable of taking over if anything happens to Adam, and the City knows it. There was never any question of Miles, Fergus or I stepping into his shoes. He wouldn't have it. He's worked too hard to watch his children destroy what he built.' She sighed. 'Well, we're destroying it anyway, between us. It wouldn't matter a tuppenny damn what I'd done if either Miles or Fergus could stand up and be counted.'

'What have you done, Jinx?'

'How about this for starters?' she said sarcastically. 'I managed to choose three murder victims as husband, fiancé and best friend. It does rather imply there's something rotten in the state of Denmark when three corpses litter the doorstep, don't you think?'

'Yes.'

There was a short silence. 'Do you know why I hated Stephanie Fellowes so much, and why I wouldn't engage in any of her psycho-crap?' said Jinx coldly. 'Because she couldn't believe I had nothing to do with Russell's death. Did she put that in her notes?'

'No.'

'Are you putting your scepticism in your notes?' *Would it hurt so much if she liked him less?*

'No.'

'But you are keeping notes?' He nodded. 'Then what are you writing about me, Dr Protheroe?'

'They're just private ones.' *The sexual fantasies of a man going mad from celibacy . . . OK, so Russell pressed the right buttons but did he turn you on? . . . What are you like in bed, Miss Kingsley? . . .* 'Yesterday, for example, I wrote: "It's a pity Jinx doesn't smile more. It suits her."'

She promptly frowned. 'Instead of saying "yes" just then, why couldn't you have said: The odds against you or your family being involved aren't good, Jinx, but they do exist? What makes you think I'm so fucking hard that I don't need reassurance, even if it is from a bastard like you?'

He grinned. 'Because you'd probably have torn strips off me for being patronizing. We both know you're not a fool and we both know you're up against it. All I can do, in the absence of something concrete to work on, is to point out the pitfalls. It's up to you how you choose to negotiate them.'

'It's patronizing to say smiling suits me.'

'It wasn't intended to be, but if that's how you choose to see it, then so be it.'

'I hate existentialism.'

'Sure you do,' he said. 'Which is why you're such a master of it.' He touched the newspapers with the toe of his shoe. 'What will happen to Franchise Holdings?'

'If they can't stop the slide, then Adam will resign,' she said matter-of-factly. 'He certainly won't stand idly by while receivers are sent in. In fact, if you've any spare cash, now's the time to gamble on some shares. They're a bargain at the moment. I guarantee the price will start back up again the minute the panic subsides.'

'What about the rumours of financial irregularities?'

'I'm betting there aren't any, or none that can be proved. Adam once said that if "Nipper" Read of Scotland Yard couldn't get anything on him then no one could.'

'Are you going to buy some shares?'

Her eyes gleamed wickedly. 'I already have. I phoned my stock broker this morning. He's selling everything in my portfolio to buy into Franchise Holdings.'

'What if you're wrong and you lose the lot?'

'It'll be in a good cause,' she said. 'At least I'll know I nailed my colours to the mast when it really mattered.'

'Is the motive really as pure as that?'

She looked at him suspiciously. 'What's that supposed to mean?'

'Veronica Gordon tells me your stepmother came last night. I just wondered if there was a little malice mixed in with the altruism.' Veronica had been shocked by Jinx's cruelty, far more than she had by Betty's drunkenness: 'I think I've underestimated her, Alan. My guess is, she's as ruthless as her father.'

'What sort of malice?'

'The sort that jumps up and down and says: Look at me, Adam, I'm supporting you. Look at her, she's not.'

Jinx lit a cigarette. 'Chance would be a fine thing, wouldn't it? Will I ever get the opportunity to do that? I don't remember Adam coming here, but perhaps that's something else I've forgotten.'

'Have you invited him?'

She gave her faint smile. 'I didn't invite Simon Harris, but he still came. I didn't invite Miles or Fergus, but they came. Why does Adam require an invitation, Dr Protheroe? Surely loving fathers visit their sick daughters as a matter of course.'

'Perhaps he's afraid of rejection, Jinx.'

'I doubt it. If he were, he wouldn't be so quick to reject everyone else.' She returned to his questioning of her motives. 'In any case, malice would be redundant where Betty's concerned. She's burnt her boats and she's drowning, and I'm not going to lift a finger to help her.'

Then why do you look so sad? he wondered.

14 Glenavon Gardens, Richmond, Surrey – 10.30 a.m.

The re-questioning of everyone connected with Jane Kingsley, Leo Wallader and Meg Harris was planned as a rolling programme throughout that Wednesday, with questions specifically geared to building a clear picture of their movements and whereabouts each day from the Bank Holiday Monday through to the evening of Monday, 13 June.

DS Fraser was assigned to London and interviews with the Clanceys, Josh Hennessey, Dean Jarrett, and Meg's neighbour Mrs Helms. He began with the Clanceys in Richmond, first explaining the purpose of the questions and then taking them back to Monday, 30 May, two weeks before Jinx's car crash. 'We understand from Leo's parents that he and Jinx returned to London some time during the late afternoon–early evening. Can you confirm that?' As he spoke, he tickled Goebbels's ears. The tiny little dog had stretched itself along his knees, chin hanging over the edge, and Fraser, thoroughly seduced, was grateful that Maddocks wasn't there to pour scorn on this simple affection.

Colonel Clancey pursed his ancient lips. 'I remember seeing Jinx on the Saturday morning but not on the Monday,' he said at last. 'I was in the garden and she came out to talk to me. She was hopping mad, far as I recall. Her two brothers were sleeping off hangovers upstairs, and Leo hadn't come home the night before. She asked me if I knew where he'd gone because they were supposed to be going down to Guildford together, and I said I hadn't seen him for a couple of days.' He glanced briefly at his wife. 'I also said,' he went on firmly, 'that she was making a mistake with Leo and she said, don't worry, Colonel, I've already come to that conclusion myself. Then she went back inside and a little while later Leo himself showed up.'

'You never told me you said that,' said Mrs Clancey.

'Thought you'd be angry,' he barked. 'You were always so keen on her marrying again.'

'Nonsense. It was you kept telling her she owed it to society to have babies. A woman like you with brains and initiative, you kept saying, you've got a responsibility to pass on the genes. Can't be doing with all these teenage nitwits producing hundreds while the clever people don't produce any. End up with idiots running the planet.'

Hastily, Fraser forestalled the development of this argument. 'When did you next see either of them?'

'I saw them leave together on the Sunday morning,' said

Daphne helpfully. 'Jinx was wearing a baseball cap because Leo would insist on driving his car with the top down, and I remember thinking how much prettier she'd look in a straw bonnet.'

'Why was she going away with him if she'd already decided he wasn't for her?' asked Fraser thoughtfully.

'She has lovely manners,' said Mrs Clancey.

'The Wednesday after,' said the Colonel baldly, who had been thinking hard. 'We were in the garden, six o'clockish, G&T time anyway, and Jinx came down the path from the garage' – he gestured towards the window – 'runs along the fence, don't you know? She was happy as a sandboy, singing her head off, and I called out: "Who's won the jackpot?" And she popped her head over the top and said: "How's tricks?"'

'Yes,' agreed Daphne, 'and I said: "You're obviously looking forward to your week in Hampshire," and she said: "Got it in one, Mrs C. A change is as good as a rest."'

Fraser waited for a moment while Goebbels turned on his back and offered his tummy for scratching. 'Was that all?' he asked, crooking a sly finger and plucking at the golden fur.

They nodded simultaneously.

'You didn't ask her about Leo and how the weekend went?'

The Colonel looked offended. 'Good lord, no,' he said. 'None of our business. Doubt she'd have told us anyway. Private sort of person, Jinx.' He scowled at Goebbels, whose erect penis was showing pinkly through his fur. 'Filthy little beast. Kick him off if it upsets you.'

Fraser, who hadn't noticed, smiled weakly and un-crooked his finger. 'Did you see Leo that day?'

'No. Matter of fact' – the Colonel paused for thought – 'I don't recall seeing him at all after the Saturday morning. Hadn't really considered it, to tell you the truth, but now you ask . . .' He looked enquiringly at his wife. 'Do you remember seeing him?'

'For me it was the Sunday,' she reminded them.

The Colonel snorted impatiently. 'Afterwards, woman, afterwards.'

'Well, I wouldn't expect to see him, not as a general rule,' she said, addressing her remarks to Fraser. 'He never went out of his way to be particularly pleasant. The odd "good morning" once in a while, and that was the most one could expect. I think he resented us because we'd known Russell and he was afraid we were making comparisons, but we didn't like Russell very much either, and it was a bit of a disappointment to find Jinx had picked the same type again.'

Her husband fixed her with a basilisk glare. 'The question was, you silly old thing, did you see him after the Sunday?'

She smiled absentmindedly. 'I don't think I did, no.'

'Not even during the week Jinx was away?' Fraser prompted.

'Definitely not,' barked the Colonel fluffing his moustache, 'but then he wasn't supposed to be there. Jinx popped in on the Friday night – that'd be June the third – to say *she* was off to Hampshire in the morning and *he'd* be spending the week in Surrey. She said not to bother about watering the house plants but yes, please, put some water on the garden when I had the hose running. Back the next Sunday, she told us.'

Fraser frowned and leant down to flick through some

papers he'd placed on the floor beside his chair. 'I was under the impression she came back on the Friday, June the tenth.'

'Well, yes, matter of fact she did. Not that we knew until the next morning. Came looking for me on the Saturday – that'd be the eleventh – and said: "Guess what, Colonel, the wedding's off as of last night. The bastard's jilted me, and the only bugger is he beat me to it."' He pursed his lips again and frowned. 'And let me tell you, Sergeant, she was pleased as punch about it, looked as if a weight had been taken off her shoulders. Then she went back inside to phone her father, telling me to keep my fingers crossed that he wouldn't make her pay for the cost of the cancelled wedding.'

'According to her parents, she came home earlier than she'd planned after a phone call on the Friday afternoon. When she got here, she caught Leo packing his belongings, at which point he told her he was going to marry her best friend and left. The implication was that he had been here all the time.'

'No,' said the Colonel stoutly, 'and I'm damn sure he didn't put in an appearance on the Friday either. I was in the front garden all afternoon so I'd have seen his car.'

'Are you sure about that?'

'I certainly am. We have a strict routine. Tuesdays and Fridays, the front garden; Mondays and Wednesdays, the back; Thursdays, shopping. Never varies.'

Fraser glanced towards Daphne Clancey, who nodded. 'Never varies,' she agreed. 'I blame the Army for it.' A sly smile crept around her mouth. 'I blame the Army for a lot of things.'

Fraser chewed the inside of his lip in thought. 'Why

didn't you tell the Richmond police this when they interviewed you after Jinx's accident?' he said.

'Because they were only interested in why Jinx would want to kill herself,' the Colonel pointed out. 'So Daphne told 'em Leo jilted her and, before I could explain that she didn't seem too unhappy about it, Daphne starts weeping and wailing about the incident on the Sunday. False conclusions being drawn all over the place, if you ask me.'

'What's your explanation for the incident on Sunday, sir?'

'It was an accident,' he said. 'Door blew shut. Goebbels was on to it like a shot. Me, too, for that matter. Hauled her out of the garage and she was right as rain in no time.'

'The silly old fool nearly killed himself,' said Mrs Clancey fondly. 'Jinx is no lightweight in all conscience.'

Fraser nodded again. 'Did she give you an explanation after you got her out of the garage?'

'Just agreed it must have been an accident,' said the Colonel, 'then begged Daphne to stop fussing. "I'm all right," she said.'

Fraser had observed the outside of the garage when he arrived. Like the Clanceys', which was separated from it by a narrow pathway beside the four-foot wall that divided the properties, it was part of a two-storey side elevation at the rear of the house with access from inside. The front doors faced each other under discreet porches halfway between the corners of the houses and their garages, leaving an enviable stretch of ground between the gates and the front elevations. Jinx's was full of shrubs and small trees, masking the ground floor of the house from the road; the Clanceys' was rather more formal with rose beds around a small area of lawn. After all, thought Fraser, it wasn't surprising Tuesdays and Fridays were given over to its care. A view of the back garden through their sitting-room window showed an area of equivalent size.

'Did Miss Kingsley drive off in her car after you rescued her?' he asked Colonel Clancey.

'Not immediately.'

'But she did go out?'

He nodded. 'She made a phone call first, then shooed us out, saying she was fine.'

'Who was she phoning?'

'No idea. Made the call from her bedroom. Whoever she was going to visit, presumably, needed to explain why she was delayed.'

'Do you think it was wise to let her drive in the circum-stances?'

'Matter of fact, no, but there wasn't much we could do to stop her.'

'Did she come back later?'

The Colonel looked at his wife. 'Couldn't say, to be honest, but I would imagine so. She wasn't one for staying out.'

Fraser tugged one of Goebbels's ears. 'So were the garage doors bolted or unbolted when you went to see why Goebbels was barking?'

'Unbolted,' said the Colonel.

'Oh, Eric!' scolded his wife. 'Where's the sense in lying? It won't help Jinx. They were bolted,' she told Fraser. 'Eric looked through the garage window, saw what

349

was happening, and came to me for the spare key. Frankly, it's a mercy she hadn't bolted the front door as well, otherwise he'd have had a terrible job getting in.'

The old man pushed himself out of his chair and moved across to gaze out over the garden. 'Known Jinx since she first moved in here with Russell,' he said shortly. 'Thirteen, fourteen years, give or take a year. She's a fine woman, a little remote, perhaps, too independent sometimes, thinks she can do anything a man can do, then finds she's not as strong as she thought she was – rescued her once from under a bag of cement because it was too damn heavy for her.' He paused on a low chuckle. 'Wedged under it like a great floundering crab – haven't laughed so much in years.' He paused again. 'Saw her through that terrible business over Russell, watched her put her life back together again and make a success of her photography. And with no help from her father, I might add. She wouldn't have it. "I'll make it on my own, Colonel, or not at all." That's what she said.' He turned round with his beetling white brows drawn together in a ferocious frown. 'Woman like that doesn't commit suicide, or even think about doing it. And if she did, she'd do it right. She'd have run a hosepipe from the exhaust and plugged the gaps in the window where it came in. Wouldn't rely on the fumes in the garage to kill her.'

'Perhaps she wanted to be rescued,' suggested Fraser.

The Colonel snorted derisively. 'Then she'd have wept her heart out afterwards and told us how unhappy she was,' he argued. 'Seems to me, the important question is why. Before anyone knew Leo and Meg were murdered, the police latched on to Jinx's unhappiness at losing Leo as the reason. Two suicide attempts when you're depressed make some sort of sense.' His eyes narrowed. 'But what's your thinking now that you know Leo's dead? You suggesting she knew about the murders and tried to kill herself afterwards?'

Fraser thought about this for some time, his eyes searching the old man's face closely. It was a good point, he admitted to himself. There was an inherent paradox if the first suicide attempt happened before Meg and Leo were murdered, because it was a peculiarly complicated psychology that led you from suicidal despair to murderous anger and back to suicidal despair again.

He cupped his hands around the little dog, turned him over and set him on his feet on the floor, then he picked up his notes and sorted through them. 'I spoke to her yesterday,' he told them. 'She talked about her car crash, said she didn't think she'd been trying to kill herself.' He isolated a page. 'She said: "It seems very out of character." Then she went on: "If I wasn't trying to kill myself, someone else must have been trying to kill me."' He looked up. 'Did you see anyone come to her house that Sunday? Did you hear anyone? Did you notice anything when you let yourself in through the front door?'

Colonel Clancey shook his head regretfully. 'No,' he admitted.

Fraser felt oddly disappointed. 'OK,' he said, 'then let's move on to Monday, June the thirteenth.'

'*I* did,' said Mrs Clancey, with a faraway look in her eyes. She drew them back from whatever memory she was observing to gaze with fixed concentration on the Sergeant. '*I* did,' she repeated. 'How very strange, I'd forgotten all about it. I was so worried about Eric having a heart attack

351

when he was pulling Jinx out of her car that it quite went out of my head.' She leaned forward, her pale old eyes suddenly alight with excitement. 'Goebbels went into the house with Eric,' she said, 'and I could hear him barking his little head off. Well, of course, I thought he was with Eric, but the next thing I knew he was rushing up the path from the back garden, barking and snarling as if he were looking for someone. Well, you know the noise dogs make when they're after an intruder. He must have jumped out of the window in the drawing room, and *that* means,' she said firmly, 'that someone had jumped out before him, probably when Goebbels first raised the alarm. Certainly the drawing-room window was open when we took Jinx inside. I closed it myself when she was making her phone call.'

'Well done, old thing,' said the Colonel approvingly. 'Bound to be what it was all about. Some bastard was trying to do away with her. Nothing else makes sense.'

'Then why didn't Jinx tell you that?' said Fraser reluctantly. 'She wasn't suffering from amnesia then.'

'Made a big fuss of Goebbels, you know, after I told her he was the one who alerted us to what was happening. Nearly squashed the poor little bugger.'

'Still . . .' The whole scenario was idiotic, Fraser told himself, but he felt drawn to continue. 'Look, you don't put a conscious person in a car and start the ignition in the hopes of them being silly enough to sit there until they die. She'd have to be unconscious.'

'She said her head was hurting.'

'Then someone must have hit her first. So why didn't she report it to the police?'

There was another silence.

'Because,' said Mrs Clancey stoutly, 'she knew the person very well and couldn't believe they had meant to hurt her. No harm had come to her, after all, and Eric went on and on about it being a silly accident. It's human nature to assume the best, you know.'

'*Or*,' said Colonel Clancey reflectively, 'she had more important things to do than answer police questions. As I said, very independent woman, Jinx. Probably thought she had the situation under control. I mean, who was the telephone call to? Seemed perfectly straightforward at the time, but now – well worth looking into, I'd say.'

Fraser made a note. 'When did you next see her?'

The old man looked at his wife. 'I don't remember seeing her again. The next we knew the police were banging on our door on the Tuesday, telling us she was in hospital.'

Fraser eyed them both thoughtfully. 'Your neighbour tried to commit suicide and you didn't check up on her?'

'Suicide wasn't mentioned until the Tuesday,' said the Colonel sharply. 'Far as we knew, it was a silly accident. Kept an eye out, naturally, but there was nothing untoward happening. Weren't going to make a nuisance of ourselves when the poor girl probably felt like a prize ass.'

Harris and Hennessey, Soho, London – 12.30 p.m.

Josh Hennessey, who, despite his threats on Meg's answer-phone to withdraw from the partnership, was still working to keep the business alive, greeted Sergeant Fraser with little enthusiasm. 'I've already told you everything I know,' he said, ruffling his hair into a crest and staring sourly at the man in front of him.

Fraser explained the purpose of his visit. 'If you have a business diary,' he suggested, 'it might speed things up a little. I need as accurate a timetable of Meg's movements as possible.'

With bad grace Hennessey took a book from his desk drawer and rustled through the pages. 'OK, these are Meg's appointments. Monday, May thirty: nothing. It was a bank holiday, Tuesday, May thirty-one: blank. But it's crossed through with a blue pencil so that means she'll have been working in her office.'

'Do you remember her being here, sir?'

'No,' said Josh curtly. 'It was three weeks ago and Meg and I have worked together for years. How am I supposed to remember one day amongst thousands? In any case, if I was out I wouldn't have known.'

'Were you out?'

He glanced at the diary. 'According to this I was in Windsor, recruiting.'

'Are the blue lines reliable? Would she cross a day through even if she hadn't been in the office?'

'Yes, if it suited her.'

'Go on.'

'Wednesday, June one: ten o'clock, Bill Riley, 12 Connaught Street. All day meeting. Thursday —'

'One moment, sir,' Fraser broke in. 'Did she keep that appointment?'

'It's crossed through which, in theory, means it was dealt with.' He shrugged. 'OK, yes. Considering the amount of time I've spent since on that one customer, she was probably there until midnight sorting out his personnel problems.

Mind you,' he admitted grudgingly, 'it's keeping us afloat at the moment. Precious little else is.'

'Fair enough. Thursday,' he prompted.

'Thursday, June two: blank in the morning, meeting with bank manager at three-thirty. Both crossed through.'

'Would that be the partnership's bank manager or her personal bank manager?'

'Probably the partnership's. We've been through a rough patch during the recession and Meg has fairly regular meetings with the bastard who holds our loans. *Had*,' he corrected himself bleakly. 'I keep forgetting she's dead. Friday, June three: blank but crossed through. Monday —'

'I'm sorry to keep interrupting, sir, but have you any idea what she did over the weekend of the fourth and fifth?'

'We had a business relationship, Sergeant, as I explained the last time I spoke to you. What she did at weekends was a closed book to me, unless it involved the partnership. Monday, June six: ten o'clock, Bill Riley again. Crossed through. Tuesday —'

'Perhaps it would be easier if I just made a photocopy,' said Fraser. 'I suspect it's a waste of both our time to go through it like this if there's nothing you can add to the written entries.'

Hennessey pushed the book across the desk. 'There's nothing. I checked after the last time you lot came, and bar a couple of meetings with Riley and the bank manager's demands for a business plan on the tenth, she seems to have spent most of that week skiving. You're farting about in cloud-cuckoo-land, frankly, if you think there's anything I can tell you.'

'You're being very unhelpful, sir,' said Fraser mildly. 'Do you not want your partner's murderer found?'

Josh reached for a pack of cigarettes at the side of the desk. 'I thought I'd kicked this fucking habit until all this happened. Now I'm back with a vengeance.' He lit a cigarette and tossed the match into an ashtray, gazing moodily at the twists of smoke that rose from the spent head. 'I don't know what I want, Sergeant. Meg was a good friend. Jinx is a good friend. Heads you win, tails I lose.'

'Why do you say that?'

'Because I can read,' said Josh curtly. 'The newspapers are full of it and, unless they're way off beam, you're aiming to arrest Jinx or her father because of the way Russell died.'

'Did you know Russell?'

'Not very well. Jinx brought him to the office a couple of times when Meg and I were still with Wellman and Hobbs.'

'Did he ever come to see Meg without Jinx?'

Josh shook his head. 'Not that I remember.'

'Did you know she was having an affair with him?'

Josh drew heavily on his cigarette. 'Not at the time. I heard about it afterwards.'

'Who told you?'

Josh didn't answer immediately. 'I don't remember,' he said flatly. 'Either Meg or Simon, I should think.' He seemed to make up his mind. 'It was Meg. She was really cut up about Russell's death, kept bursting into tears for no apparent reason, so I asked her why and she told me.'

Fraser didn't believe him. 'I think it was Miss Kingsley who told you.'

Josh looked at him for a moment. 'I don't remember,' he said again. 'It was a long time ago.'

Fraser gave a pleasant smile. 'It's not particularly important, but we're trying to tie up a few loose ends. Can you recollect how soon after Russell's death she told you?'

'Look, I haven't said it was Jinx, OK?' Fraser was fascinated by Hennessey's hands, which seemed to have a life of their own, twitching, plucking, always fidgeting.

'Understood. Can you remember when you first heard about it, sir?'

'I think it was after she lost the baby.'

'Thank you,' said Fraser easily. 'I don't need to keep you much longer. I'd be grateful if we could just run over the last conversation you had with Meg, which I believe was the telephone call to your home on Saturday, June the eleventh. According to what you told us before, she said Leo and Jinx's wedding was off, that she was going to marry him instead, that they were leaving for France on the Tuesday but that she would pop in before then to bring you up to date with office affairs.'

'That's right.'

Fraser consulted the business diary. 'Yet, according to this, she returned to the office on the Friday afternoon following an appointment with the bank manager. So why didn't she tell you then? That's a bit odd, isn't it?'

'Too bloody right, it's odd,' he growled. 'Dammit, I get this phone call out of the blue saying she's pissing off to France, leaving me to hold the fort till she gets back. I gave her absolute hell and told her I'd swing for her if she didn't get in here and sort her desk out before she left.'

'So it was your idea and not hers that she come in on the Monday?'

Josh frowned as he thought back. 'Probably. I was damned angry about her leaving me in the lurch without any warning. Who the hell's going to have confidence in a business where one partner buggers off at the drop of a hat? I sank every cent I own into this sodding venture.' He shook his head. 'Does it make a difference?'

'It might,' said Fraser. He paused to think about it. 'Perhaps you made her feel guilty enough to keep them hanging around longer than they meant to.'

'I don't get it.'

'Meg made all her phone calls on the Saturday morning,' said Fraser slowly. 'I wonder if the idea was to make the announcements and then leave for France immediately. Let's face it, she knew better than anyone what had happened to Russell Landy.'

'Are you saying they'd still be alive if I hadn't laid a guilt trip on her?' asked Josh harshly.

'I don't know, sir. I think we need some idea of where they were on the Monday before we come to any conclusions. I mean, it's you who put pressure on them to delay their departure.' Fraser looked at the other man closely before continuing. 'And as things stand, I only have your word for it that she and Leo didn't come here as promised.'

Chapter Nineteen

Wednesday, 29 June, 53 Lansing Road,
Salisbury, Wiltshire – midday

FLOSSIE HALE EXAMINED the newspaper clipping of
the Franchise Holding emblem. 'Oh, yes,' she said, 'no question, that's the key-ring all right.' Next she turned her attention to the grainy faxed photograph of Miles and Fergus
Kingsley in the members' enclosure at Ascot and, after a
brief hesitation, planted her finger on a face. 'That looks like
him, but it's not a very good picture, is it, love? I don't recall
his hair being as dark as that. The jacket's similar.'

'What about the man next to him?'

She held the page away from her, half-closing her eyes,
as if looking at an impressionist painting. 'The trouble is
you don't look at their faces much, not when they're punch-
ing you. You're too scared. Yes,' she said with sudden decision, stabbing at Miles again, 'that's him all right. Little
bastard. I said butter wouldn't melt in his mouth. Who is
he then?'

'His name's Miles Kingsley.' WPC Blake retrieved the
photograph and tucked it into her bag. Samantha Garrison
had also picked out Miles and, if neither woman had been
quite as decisive as Blake would have liked, she put it down
to the poor quality of the photocopy and postponed her

niggling concerns over whether or not this could ever result in a successful prosecution. If Flossie had been more co-operative at the start, allowed them in to dust for finger-prints or let them take swabs, they would have had something more concrete to work on.

'Well, I don't understand it,' the older woman was saying. 'How'd you turn what I told you into a blooming photograph of someone with the initials MK?'

'Just luck, Flossie. He's a bit of a playboy, this creep. If you're interested, the photograph was faxed through to us from *The Tatler*. You got done over by one of society's best. His dad's a multi-millionaire.'

Flossie shook her head. 'It makes you wonder what the world's coming to. What's he doing trawling Salisbury for cheap old tarts like me if he can afford the high-class ones in London?'

Blake couldn't answer that.

The Studio, Pimlico, London – 1.00 p.m.

Dean Jarrett was effusively helpful. 'Well, of *course*, dear,' he told Fraser, ladling out the charm while sussing him coolly from the corner of his eye. He thought this police-man looked less of a homophobe than most, might even, if the friendly smile was anything to go by, be tolerably sympathetic towards Jinx and her bizarre entourage at the studio. Certainly, he had taken Angelica's pink hair in his stride and appeared unfazed by Dean's flirting. 'I can give you a blow-by-blow account of everything Jinx did from Tuesday the thirty-first until Friday the third. But after that it's a complete no-no, I'm afraid. She was at Hell Hall the next week, and we didn't hear a dicky bird out of her – didn't expect to, of course, because she was on her hols – and then she did a vanishing trick on us. Angelica phoned and phoned on the Monday, when she was supposed to be here, and all she got was Jinx's answerphone.'

'That would be the thirteenth of June?'

'It would. And then, on the Tuesday, we heard the awful news that the poor mite was unconscious in hospital somewhere. I suppose you've seen her. Is she all right?'

His face contorted itself into a moue of concern, and Fraser nodded reassuringly, even if he did find the expression less than sincere. 'She seems fine. A bit hazy about what happened, but otherwise very alert and very composed.'

'Isn't she *amazing*?' said Dean. 'Quite my most favourite lady.'

'Yet you haven't been to see her,' said Fraser dispassionately, 'or not as far as we know. Is there some reason for that?'

The moue vanished abruptly. 'Yes, well, unlike the Josh Hennesseys and Simon Harrises of this world, who both tell me they've inflicted themselves on her, I prefer to wait for an invitation. Imagine the awfulness of feeling like death and having well-meaning friends impose themselves on you. Jinx is a very private person. Half the time I think she's completely ignorant of how much we all adore her, the other half I retreat into my little shell because I'm afraid the truth is we bore her rigid.' He sighed. 'In any case I didn't know where she was for ages. Her brute of a father wouldn't tell me.'

'Still, I'm surprised she wasn't worried about the studio.'

Dean gave a squeak of distress. 'How crushing you are, Sergeant. Don't you feel the poor darling has rather more pressing concerns at the moment than leaving her business in the hands of the second best photographer in London?'

Fraser's lips twitched. 'What did you think of Leo?'

'He was absolutely *dire*. A real leech, but could Jinx see it? Well, you know what the trouble is, she's blinkered when it comes to a pretty face. Falls for the outside, and forgets that what's underneath is more important. It's her father's fault. He looks like an old vulture and he's always been so damn distant with her that she assumes a pretty face means a pretty personality.' He rolled his eyes to Heaven. 'I hate to say it, because he's a very rude man, but I actually think Adam Kingsley is probably worth ten Leo Walladers. If the number of phone calls he's made, checking up on me and Angelica, is anything to go by, he cares about Jinx a great deal more than she's ever given him credit for. My *God*, if we'd thought about letting things slide – which we haven't – he'd have been round here tearing our innards out.'

Fraser grinned. 'You've met him then?'

'I was introduced the first time he paid one of his terrifying visits,' said Dean with a shudder, 'as was Angie. But as I'm gay and she's black, it was hardly the social event of the century. He washed his hands afterwards in case he'd caught something. On all subsequent visits, he has grunted rudely in our direction and swept through to talk to Jinxy in private.'

'Why are his visits terrifying?'

'Because he insists on bringing his tame gorilla with him.' Dean rolled his eyes again. 'Says he's the chauffeur but since when did chauffeurs need fifty-four-inch chests? The man is there to make mincemeat of anyone who dares say boo to the boss.'

'That's not so unusual these days, you know. A body-guard-cum-chauffeur. Most millionaires have them. You said Mr Kingsley's distant, but would you also say he's fond of Jinx?'

'Yes, in a brooding sort of way. He never touches her, just sits and stares at her as though she were a piece of Dresden china. I get the feeling he can't really believe she's his. I mean he's common as muck, after all, and she's such a lady, and the only other two children he had are A-one arse-holes.' He thought for a moment. 'Fond isn't the right word. I think he idolizes her.'

'How does she feel about that?'

'Loathes it, but then you have to understand that he's not idolizing Jinx, he's idolizing the person he thinks she is. I mean, you'd have to be mentally deficient to see Jinx as Dresden china. A piece of good solid Staffordshire pottery that bounces when you drop it and retains its integrity through a thousand washes, that's a better analogy.'

'Why doesn't Jinx put him straight?'

'She's tried, dear, but there's none so blind as those who will not see. She was going to marry Leo Wallader, for God's sake. What better demonstration could there be of flawed judgement and appalling taste? Not that her father could see it, of course. Leo had blue blood in his veins, so he must have been a cut above the rest of us.'

Fraser smiled. 'Tell me about Tuesday, May the thirty-first,' he invited.

'That was a very busy day. We had a teenage band here all morning who thought they were the bee's knees. Their record company wanted some publicity shots and it was like drawing blood from a stone to get them to do anything other than simper into the lens.' He thought for a moment.

'OK, in the afternoon we did some location work round Charing Cross station for a television company. Atmospheric stills for a documentary on homelessness. We clocked off about six, because Jinx wanted to get home in reasonably good time.'

'Did she say why?'

He shook his silver head. 'But she was in a brilliant mood all day and, when I asked her if we could thank Leo for it, she said: "In one respect, I suppose you can." So I said: "Don't tell me, darling, he's finally come up trumps in the rogering department." And she said: "Don't be absurd, Dean, Leo would need to be face down on a mirror to do that." And I thought, thank God, she's finally seen the light, but, for once, I was far too tactful to say it.'

Fraser grinned again. 'Wednesday, June the first,' he prompted.

'Let me think now. All right. I spent the morning developing and printing contact sheets. There was some undeveloped film left over from the previous week, and the two projects from the previous day. Jinx caught up on a mound of paperwork in order to clear it before she went on holiday. Wednesday afternoons are always reserved for portrait work, and I think we had five or six families that day. Then we grabbed supper at about half-six, before going back to Charing Cross to finish the location work there. They wanted twilight and night-time shots as well, so we didn't clock off that day until about ten-thirty.'

'And how was her mood on Wednesday?'

'The same. Happy, sunny, brilliant. Angie and I were quite persuaded she'd given Leo the boot, but she didn't say she had, so we guessed she was hanging fire till she could tell her old man during her holiday. You've got to realize we'd been walking on egg shells for God knows how long. The mere mention of Leo's name brought glowering looks and an abrupt change of conversation. Then suddenly, out of nowhere, she's her old sweet self again.'

'And you put that down to the fact that she'd decided not to marry him after all?'

Dean nodded. 'More than that, sweetheart, I put it down to the fact that he wasn't *there* any more, and certainly not in her bed. For the first time in weeks, she actually *wanted* to go home. Take the Thursday. She had me working like a slave all morning and, come the afternoon, she suddenly looks at her watch and says: "Do me a favour, Dean, and mind the shop. There's a few things I need to do at home, and tomorrow we're out all day." You could have knocked me over with a feather. She'd been avoiding the place like the plague ever since Leo got his knees under her table.'

'Why?'

Dean tut-tutted impatiently. 'Because she realized she couldn't stand him, of course, but she didn't know how to admit it. Her father's fault again. He'd really gone to town on the wedding preparations, invited half of Surrey and Hampshire, and Jinx was too embarrassed to say anything. I mean, there were a couple of Cabinet ministers coming, and you don't tell them to bog off without a few qualms, do you?'

Fraser chuckled. 'I've never had the chance. Could be fun, though.' He paused. 'It makes sense if he wasn't there. She and he had a blazing row on the Bank Holiday Monday, and the logical thing would have been for him to move out immediately.' Pensively, he pulled at his lip. 'But she claims he was there on the following Saturday morning, June the fourth, when she left for Hellingdon Hall, remembers their farewells as fond ones.'

Dean shrugged. 'Then Leo must have undergone a character transplant in the meantime. I swear to God, if the sight of blood were a little less sickening, I'd have bopped him on the nose several times. He was a complete slime-ball.'

'So what are you saying?'

'That Jinx is telling fibs about the fond farewell.'

'You think they had a row?'

'No. I'm guessing she didn't want anyone to know he'd gone, so pretended fond farewells that never happened. I mean, if we always had to tell the truth about our relationships, we'd be wobbling jellies with no self-esteem. I lie all the time about mine – keep some lovers going long after they've deserted me.'

'It's a pity you didn't tell the police all this at the time of her accident,' said Fraser in mild reproof.

'Well, I would have done, if they'd been remotely interested in anything prior to Friday, June the tenth, but all they wanted to know was had we seen or heard from her since her return from Hampshire. I did say that we were a teensy-weensy bit surprised to hear she'd only cancelled the wedding on the Saturday after she got back from Hell Hall, when we were sure she'd made up her mind two weeks earlier, but they said it was Leo who had jilted *her*, and as I couldn't prove any different, there wasn't much more to be said.'

'OK, then there's just Friday the third left to cover. Anything unusual happen that day?'

'Just a wall-to-wall fashion shoot in London's Docklands. We began at eight-thirty and went right through to seven o'clock in the evening without a break. Jinx dropped me off with all the cameras and equipment at the studio around seven-thirty, blew me a kiss and said: "It's all yours for a week, so be good." And I haven't seen her since.'

'Have you spoken to her?' asked Fraser idly.

'Just once, on the telephone.'

'When was that?'

'Sunday night.'

'Who called who?'

'She called me.'

'At home?'

Dean nodded.

'It must have been important then,' said Fraser.

'Oh, it was,' said Dean. 'It was my thirtieth birthday and she knew I'd have died a *thousand* deaths if I hadn't spoken to her, never mind she's flat on her back in hospital and suffering galloping amnesia.' He beamed engagingly. 'As I said, she's quite my most favourite lady.'

Fraser flicked over a page or two of his notebook. 'Odd,' he said. 'According to her, she asked you to phone the Walladers to find out whether Leo and Meg were dead. She never mentioned your birthday. Can *anything* you've said be relied upon, sir?'

Romsey Road Police Station, Winchester – 1.00 p.m.

The call from Salisbury came through to the incident room as Detective Superintendent Cheever was briefing the team he'd picked to conduct interviews at Hellingdon Hall that afternoon. He listened for five minutes, with only the odd interjection to show he was interested, then he said: 'And the prostitute is certain of her identification?' A longish pause. 'You've got two of them who swear it's him. Yes, we're planning to interview the whole family this afternoon. No, he's never entered the frame at all.' Another long pause. 'Because he was sixteen when Landy got done, that's why. OK, OK. We all know ten-year-olds do it now.' He compressed his lips into a thin, frustrated line. 'Well, how quickly can she get here? Half an hour. Yes, all right, we'll hold on. Yes, yes, yes. We've had cars stationed outside since yesterday afternoon. The whole family's there, including Kingsley. He drove back from London this morning.' He listened again. 'No, we won't steal her blasted thunder.' He slammed the phone on to the rest and glared at the assembled detectives. 'Damn!' he growled.

'What's up?' asked Maddocks.

'Miles Kingsley has been beating up on prostitutes in Salisbury. The DCI there says he has all the hallmarks of a classic psychopath.'

'Where does that leave us?'

Testily, Cheever fingered his bow-tie. 'High and dry for the moment. They're sending a WPC over with what she's managed to get on him. I suggest we put everything on hold till she gets here.' He steepled his hands in front of his face. 'This is what's known as a spanner in the works, gentlemen. Why in God's name should Miles Kingsley have murdered his sister's husband, fiancé and friend? Can any of you make sense of that?'

'You're jumping the gun, sir,' protested Maddocks. 'So the bastard beats up on prostitutes, that doesn't make him a killer.'

'You still favour Jane for the murders then?'

'Of course. She's the only one with a motive for all three.'

'And her father, knowing what she's done, protects her?'

'That's about the size of it. After Landy's death, she's bundled off to a psychiatric unit while Dad takes the flak himself because he knows the Met will never be able to prosecute him. This time, she's shoved into the Nightingale, following a fake suicide, and we're told, hands off, because she's got amnesia. Meanwhile Dad's solicitor is busy on a crisis limitation exercise with the clinic's administrator. She's guilty as sin. Her father knows it and so does Dr Protheroe.'

'That's a hell of a conspiracy theory and it's full of holes, anyway. If the doctor's protecting her why did she go for him on Monday night?'

'Because she's off her bloody rocker, sir.'

'She's a psychopath, in other words.'

'Sure she is.'

Frank lowered his hands and smiled sarcastically. 'The Met said her father was a psychopath. Salisbury say her brother's a psychopath. You say she's a psychopath. It's beginning to look like an epidemic, and I don't buy that, Gareth.'

Maddocks shrugged. 'What would you buy, sir?'

'One psychopath, maybe, but not three. I suggest two of them have been tarred with the brush of the other.'

The announcement that Adam Kingsley had resigned in favour of his number two, John Normans, was released through Franchise Holdings' London headquarters at twelve o'clock. At one o'clock on the BBC television news, video footage of the gates of Hellingdon Hall formed a backdrop to the news story. 'Adam Kingsley reached his decision this morning amidst the peace and quiet of this palatial eighteenth-century house on the edge of the New Forest, although it is unlikely he will be here for very much longer. Hellingdon Hall is a registered asset of Franchise Holdings and sources say it will be sold off to recoup some of the losses of the last few days.'

Incident Room, Romsey Road Police Station,
Winchester – 1.45 p.m.

The message over the radio crackled with excitement. 'Listen, sir, a Porsche, registration number MIL 1, has just left Hellingdon Hall by the tradesman's entrance, and it's piling off up the road at about a hundred miles an hour. We're following but it's definitely not old man Kingsley. Do we go back to the Hall or do we continue?'

'Who's your back-up?'

'Fredericks at the trade entrance, and half a dozen uniformed local chaps at the front gate, keeping the paparazzi in order. But the place has been dead as a dodo all morning, sir. This is the first action we've seen.'

'All right, continue,' said Frank Cheever, 'but don't lose him. It's probably Miles Kingsley, and I want to know where he's going. Fredericks, are you hearing me? Stay alert, and if anyone else comes out notify me immediately. Understood?'

'Will do, sir.'

The first radio burst back into life. 'He's turning on to the A338, Guv'nor. Looks like he's heading for Salisbury.'

43 Shoebury Terrace, Hammersmith,
London – 2.00 p.m.

Fraser's last port of call was Meg's neighbour in Hammersmith, Mrs Helms. She greeted him with surprising warmth, rather as she might an old friend, and took him into the front room. 'My husband,' she said, waving her hand towards a pathetic husk of a man who was sitting with a blanket across his knees and gazing forlornly on to the quiet street. 'Multiple sclerosis,' she mouthed. She raised her voice. 'This is Detective Sergeant Fraser, Henry, come to talk to us about poor Meg.' She went back to her whisper. 'Just ignore him. He won't say anything. Hardly ever does these days. It's a shame, it really is. He used to be such a busy little soul.'

Fraser took the armchair that Mrs Helms indicated and, for the fourth time that day, explained the purpose behind his questions. 'So, have you any idea what Meg did over the bank holiday weekend?' he asked.

She greeted this with a girlish squeal. 'I couldn't begin to say,' she declared. 'Goodness me, I can't even remember what *we* were doing that weekend.'

Fraser glanced towards her husband, thinking that if his mobility was as poor as it appeared to be, then the chances of them *not* being there were fairly remote. 'Perhaps you had family come to visit?' he suggested. 'Does that jog any memories? Meg wouldn't have been at work on the Monday.'

She shook her head. 'Every day's the same. Week days, weekends, holidays. Nothing varies very much. Now, if you could tell me what was on the television, that would help me.'

Fraser tried a different tack. 'It's a fair bet that Leo was here during the nights of Friday, May the twenty-seventh, possibly Monday, the thirtieth, and very probably Tuesday, the thirty-first. In fact, he may well have been in residence for the rest of that week *and* the week after. Does that help at all? In other words, did you notice him around more than usual? Before when I spoke to you, you said there was a lot of coming and going shortly before they left for France.'

'Well, I certainly noticed he was in and out rather more often than normal, but as to whether he was living with her . . . ' She shook her head. 'Dates don't mean anything to me, Sergeant. And how on earth would I know if Leo stayed on a particular night? Frankly, Meg's love-life was of no interest to either of us, and why would it be? We've enough troubles of our own.'

Fraser nodded sympathetically. 'Leo had two very distinctive Mercedes convertibles, one black with beige leather upholstery, and the other white with burgundy seats. We think one or other would have been parked outside whenever he was there. Do you remember seeing either of them at any point in the two weeks before they left for the holiday in France?'

She gave her girlish squeal again. 'I wouldn't know a Mercedes from a Jaguar,' she said, 'and I never notice cars, full stop, unless they're blocking my way. Dreadful invention.'

Fraser gave a quiet sigh of frustration. Mrs Helms's epitaph of a few days previously – *she never gave us any trouble* – came back to haunt him afresh. What a pity, he was thinking, because if she *had*, then Mrs Helms might have taken a little more notice of her. He looked disconsolately towards her husband. 'Perhaps Mr Helms saw something?' he suggested.

She shook her head vigorously. 'Wouldn't notice a double-decker bus if it was parked in his lap,' she said *sotto voce*. 'Best not to bother him, really. It makes him anxious if he's bothered.'

But Fraser persisted, if only to reassure himself that he had left no stone unturned. 'Can you help me, Mr Helms? It is important or I wouldn't press the point. We have two unsolved murders, and we need to establish why and when they happened.'

The thin face turned towards him and regarded him without expression for several seconds. 'Which day was the second?'

'Of June?'

The other nodded.

Fraser consulted his diary. 'It was a Thursday.'

'I had a hospital appointment on the second. I came home by ambulance and the driver noticed the Mercedes. He said: "That's a new one, not seen that here before," and I told him it belonged to downstairs and had been there two or three days.'

Fraser leaned forward. 'On and off or permanently?'

'It was there each night,' he managed with difficulty, 'but not always during the day.'

'Can you remember when it left for good?'

It was clear he had difficulty articulating words, and Fraser waited patiently for him to resume. 'Not sure. Probably when they went to France.'

Fraser smiled encouragingly. 'And would you be able to say which day that was, Mr Helms?'

The man nodded. 'Clean sheets' day. Monday.'

'Goodness me,' said Mrs Helms, 'do you know he's right. I'd just stripped the beds when Meg came with the cat food. Dumped the sheets in Henry's lap while I went out to talk to her. There now, and I'd quite forgotten.'

'That's grand,' said Fraser. 'We're making real progress. Did they leave together in the Mercedes?'

Mr Helms shook his head. 'I didn't see. Anthea pushed me and the sheets into the kitchen.' There was a look of irritation in his eyes and Fraser thought, you poor bloody sod, I bet she sorted the sheets on your lap as if you were a mobile laundry basket.

'Did you happen to notice when Meg's car went? It's a dark green Ford Sierra. We've found it since in a street in Chelsea.'

'The Friday evening. Both cars went. Only the sports car came back.'

With both Meg and Leo in it?'

'Yes.'

'Which makes sense. They were clearing the decks before they left on holiday.' He drummed his fingers on his knee and addressed his next question to Mrs Helms. 'Did Meg give any indication on the Monday that they had postponed their departure for any reason?'

She pulled a face. 'Not really. She just rang the doorbell, thrust the key and the food at me and said they were off to France. Very odd, I thought.'

'Did anything else strike you as odd?'

'Not really,' she said again. 'She hadn't done her hair, and her eyes were rather red, so I thought she might have been crying, but I put it down to a lover's tiff.'

'Anything else?'

'Well, saying Marmaduke had to be kept a prisoner in the hall was a bit odd. She'd never done that before. Poor little fellow, it's no way to keep a cat.'

Fraser frowned and flicked through his papers. 'Last time we spoke,' he murmured, isolating a page, 'you said Meg was insistent that Marmaduke shouldn't go into any of the rooms.'

'That's right.'

'But just now you said she wanted him kept prisoner in the hall.'

'Well, yes. Same difference.'

'Can you remember her actual words, Mrs Helms?'

'Oh lord. It's nearly three weeks ago.' She screwed her face in concentration. 'Let me see now. It was all over in half a second. "You remember I said we were going to France, Mrs Helms?" That's how she began. Well, of course, she'd never said anything of the sort but I was too polite to say so. "And you promised you'd look after the cat?" she said next. Which annoyed me because I hadn't. I'd have said so, too, except she shoved the key and tin at me, and never gave me a chance to answer. "The cat's imprisoned and will want to get out. Please be careful how you open the doors. I don't want any more damage done." And that was all she said. And that's what I've done, though for the life of me I can't imagine why it was necessary. Damage never worried her before.'

'She said "the cat" and not Marmaduke?' The woman nodded. 'And you were outside on the doorstep?'

'That's right. She wouldn't come in.'

He pictured the little porch under the basement steps and realized then what had happened. Someone had been down there, listening, he thought. He tapped his pencil against his teeth. For Leo, read lion, read cat. 'Leo is imprisoned. Please be careful. I don't want any more damage done.' *Jesus!* What despair Meg must have felt, knowing her only chance resided in this irritatingly stupid woman. But if he were honest, would anyone have understood so cryptic a message?

'OK.' He turned back to Mr Helms. 'What did they do on the Saturday and Sunday. Do you know? Did you notice anyone coming to the door?'

His mouth worked. 'Her friend came,' he blurted. 'The tall one. Saturday night.' He raised a weak hand and dropped it on to his thigh. 'Banged on the door. Said: "You must be mad. What the hell are you doing?"'

'Was it a woman?'

'Yes.'

'Jinx Kingsley?'

'Tall, dark. Drives a Rover Cabriolet. JIN 1X.'

'When did she leave?'

But Mr Helms shook his head. 'Anthea likes television. I'm not allowed to sit here all the time.'

'I should think not,' said his wife sharply. 'The neighbours would get quite the wrong idea if you did. They'd say I was neglecting you.'

Fraser flicked the man a sympathetic glance. 'Not to worry,' he said. 'Did you happen to notice any other visitors?'

But Mr Helms had told him all he could.

'We're on our way now,' said Detective Superintendent Cheever on a mobile link to his colleague in the Wiltshire police. 'It looks as if he's heading for the Nightingale. Got that. You'll send back-up to the clinic? Agreed. We'll only talk to him about the murders after you've charged him on the assaults. No, Adam Kingsley's on hold at the moment. I'm more interested in hearing what Miles has to say.'

Nightingale Clinic, Salisbury, Wiltshire – 2.30 p.m.

Miles stormed through Jinx's open french windows and flung himself into the vacant armchair with the sullen expression of a thwarted five-year-old. 'I suppose you've heard what he's done?'

'You mean his resignation?'

'Of course I mean his resignation,' he said in a mimicking falsetto. 'What the hell else would I mean?' He drummed his feet on the ground. 'God, I'm so angry. I don't know which of you I'd rather strangle at the moment. You realize you've buggered everything between you?'

'No,' she said calmly, lighting a cigarette. 'I can't say I do realize that. What exactly is buggered, Miles?'

'FOR CHRIST'S SAKE!' he yelled, his eyes narrowing to unattractive slits. 'We've lost everything, the house, everything.'

She gazed at him through the drifting smoke. 'Who's we?' she murmured. '*I* haven't lost anything. The shares have risen ten points since Adam resigned, which means I've already made a tidy paper profit on my morning's investment alone. I hope you're not going to tell me you sold your shares, Miles. When Adam gave them to us, he said: Sell everything else but don't sell these. You should have had more faith in him.'

'I had to,' he said through gritted teeth. 'Fergus, too. We

borrowed money on the back of the damn things and the bastard we were in hock to made us sell out to cover the debts.'

She shrugged. 'More fool you.'

He was as tightly strung as a new bow. 'Oh, Jesus, if you knew how much I hated you – it's all your fault this has happened . . .' His voice carried a tremor of despair.

She arched a sardonic eyebrow. 'How do you make that out?'

'Russell – Leo – they were both shits.'

'What's that got to do with anything?'

'If you'd picked someone halfway decent, we wouldn't be in this mess.'

She watched his knuckles turn white as he gripped the arms of the chair. *After all, what did she really know about this brother of hers?* 'You were only sixteen when Russell was murdered,' she said slowly. 'Betty swore you and Fergus were at the Hall all day.'

He stared at her with hot, angry eyes. 'What the hell are you talking about?'

'I thought – never mind.'

'You thought I did it?' he sneered. 'Well, sometimes I wish I had. The old man would have bent over backwards for me after that. I'd have done it for free, too, because I'd have enjoyed doing it. I loathed Russell. He was almost as arrogant and patronizing as you are. He surged out of his chair in one violent movement and trapped her in hers by leaning over and gripping the arms. 'It cost Dad a packet to get rid of him, you silly bitch, and another packet to do for Leo and Meg. And now Fergus and I are in the shit because of it. The police are parked all round the Hall, just waiting to arrest him, and the minute they do, Mum, me and Fergus will be out in the sodding street. We're wiped out – don't you understand? Mum, too – she sold her shares months ago. There's nothing left.'

'You've still got your jobs,' she said, gazing steadily up at him so that he wouldn't guess how frightened she was.

He threw himself petulantly back into his chair, his anger spent. 'God, you're so naïve,' he said. 'John Normans won't keep us on. We're only there because of Dad. *You* know that. Everybody knows it. Christ, it's not as though either of us is even needed. All I have to do is make sure the site security contracts are kept up to date. Any moron could do it.' He banged his fist against the chair arm. 'I get a moron's salary because of it. Do you know what I do? I engage the night watchman and put my signature to the standardized contract that comes off the sodding word processor.'

'Then why aren't you doing it now?' she asked him. 'Surely this is the time to prove that you're worth keeping.'

His anger flared again. 'You stupid, patronizing BITCH!' he screamed. 'IT'S OVER! Dad's made sure you're OK, because you're his fucking darling, but he's dropped all the rest of us in it. Can't you get that into your thick skull?'

She blew a stream of smoke towards the ceiling and watched the patterns it made in the draught from the open windows. 'How do you know Adam had Russell killed?' she asked quietly.

'Who else could have done it?'

'Me,' she suggested.

Miles looked amused. 'Little Miss Perfect. Come off it, Jinxy, you haven't got the guts.'

'And you think Adam has?'

He shrugged. 'I *know* he has.'

'How?'

'Because he's bloody vicious, that's how. Look at the way he treats me and Fergus.'

She formed her lips into an approximation of a smile. 'I want proof, Miles, not impressions. Can you *prove* Adam had Russell killed?'

'I can prove he *wanted* him killed. He said afterwards that Russell had got what was coming to him. Your precious husband was shafting your best friend. Dad hated him for it.'

'What did he say when he heard about Leo and Meg?' Even to Jinx her voice sounded strangely remote.

Miles shrugged again. 'That he hoped your memory loss was permanent, then he shut himself in his office and called his solicitor. He's paranoid about you starting to remember things, so we reckon you saw something you shouldn't have done.'

She stared at the opposite wall. 'You said it cost him a packet. How much exactly?'

'A lot.'

'How much, Miles?'

'I don't *know*,' he said sulkily. 'All I know is it comes damned expensive.'

She shifted her gaze lazily to look at him. 'You don't know anything, do you? You're talking about what you *wish* Adam had done, not what he actually did. I suppose it makes you feel better to think of your father as a murderer.' She laughed suddenly. 'You know, I really feel quite sorry for you. Presumably you've spent the last ten years justifying all your shabby little deceits against Adam's guilt, so how the hell are you going to cope when it turns out he's whiter than white?' A movement at the windows caught her eye and, as she looked enquiringly towards the two uniformed policemen blocking the light, there was a peremptory knock on the door behind her. She frowned as WPC Blake walked in uninvited. 'Can I help you?' Jinx said politely, looking beyond her to Superintendent Cheever, Maddocks and Alan Protheroe, who were standing in the open doorway.

Blake glanced at her briefly before transferring her attention to the brother. 'Miles Kingsley?' she asked.

He nodded.

She proffered her warrant card. 'WPC Blake, Wiltshire police. Miles Kingsley, I have reason to believe you can assist us in our enquiries into the grievous bodily harm and indecent assault of Mrs Flossie Hale on the evening of the twenty-second of June last, at number fifty-three, Lansing Road, Salisbury —'

'What the hell are you talking about?' he broke in angrily. 'Who the fuck's Mrs Flossie Hale? I've never even heard of the bitch.'

Chapter Twenty

LITTLE LORD FAUNTLEROY, thought Blake, was a good description of Miles Kingsley, with his clean-cut face and his wide-spaced blue eyes. They weren't the sort of looks that attracted her – she preferred her men rougher and tougher – but she could imagine Flossie finding them appealing. 'She's a prostitute, Mr Kingsley. She was brutally attacked on the evening of the twenty-second. She has identified you as her assailant, as has Mrs Samantha Garrison, another prostitute, who suffered a similar assault on March the twenty-third.'

He frowned angrily. 'They're lying. I've never been to a prostitute in my life.' He rounded on Jinx. 'What the hell's going on? Is this something Dad's set up?'

'Don't be an oaf,' she snapped. She looked at the policewoman. 'How could they identify him? Did the assailant give a name?'

Blake ignored her. 'I think it would be better if we discussed the whole matter at the police station. Mr Kingsley, I am requesting you to accompany me —'

'Look, you sour-faced cow,' said Miles, surging aggressively to his feet, 'I don't know what your game is —'

'Sit down, Miles,' hissed Jinx through gritted teeth, grabbing his arm and forcing him into his chair again, 'and keep your mouth shut.' She took a deep breath. 'You say you have reason to believe my brother can assist you, so please will you explain what those reasons are. In particular, how both women came to identify their attacker as my brother.'

Blake frowned. 'I'm not obliged to explain anything, other than to say we have a positive identification of the man two women say attacked them. We would like him to answer some questions on the matter and to that end we are asking him to accompany us to the police station. Do you have a problem with that, Miss Kingsley, bearing in mind the assaults were serious enough to put both women in hospital?'

'Yes,' she said curtly, 'I think Miles should refuse to go with you. You obviously have nothing more concrete than this inexplicable identification or you'd have come with an arrest warrant.' She glanced at Maddocks. 'My guess is, you're trying to pick us off one by one to answer questions on Meg and Leo's murders. I'm even doubtful if these prostitutes exist.'

Miles sneered. 'That's the stuff, Jinxy. Give 'em hell.'

The young policewoman eyed him curiously for a moment then addressed herself to his sister. 'I'm Wiltshire police, Miss Kingsley, and I've spent the last week investigating the attack on Flossie Hale. She's forty-six years old. She sustained severe injuries to her head, face and arms and, but for her own courage in getting herself to hospital, would have died in her bed. She has identified your brother as the man who injured her. I will admit that the publicity surrounding the death of your fiancé and your best friend led indirectly to her identification of him, but

MINETTE WALTERS

that's as far as the connection goes. I am not interested in you or your relationship with the Hampshire police. I am merely interested in preventing any more women suffering as Flossie did.'

'OK,' said Miles cockily, leaning back in his chair and stretching his legs in front of him, 'then arrest me. You won't get me any other way. Have you any idea what sort of fuss my father's likely to kick up about this? Sacking will be the least of your worries once his solicitor gets on to it.'

Jinx pressed fingers to her throbbing head. 'Shut up, Miles.'

'No, I bloody well won't,' he snapped, whipping round to look at her. 'You bug me, Jinx, you really do. You can say anything you like because you're so fucking clever, but not stupid Miles. He's got to sit here with his mouth shut.' He slammed his fist into his palm. 'Jesus, I wasn't even in Salisbury on the twenty-second and I can prove it.'

'You visited your sister here at nine o'clock last Wednesday night, Mr Kingsley,' said Maddocks bluntly. 'Last Wednesday being the twenty-second of June, and the Nightingale Clinic being in Salisbury. Both your sister and the staff on duty will testify to that. Mrs Hale was attacked at eight-fifteen, which would have given you plenty of time to sort yourself out before you presented yourself here.'

His face took on a pinched look. 'OK, so I forgot. It's no big deal. I drove straight here from Fordingbridge. My mother and brother will swear I was at Hellingdon Hall till eight-thirty.'

Blake looked at Jinx. 'Is that what he told you when he got here?'

She didn't answer.

Miles darted her a frightened glance. 'Tell them I told you.'

'How can I? I don't remember you saying it.'

'The nurse said it when she brought me in. Here's your brother from Fordingbridge. You must remember that.'

'I don't.' She could only remember him saying he'd been gambling that night. *But had he?*

'Oh shit, Jinxy,' he begged, 'you've got to help me. I swear to God I never hurt anyone.' He reached out a hand and clutched at her arm. 'Please, Jinx, help me.'

Meg is a whore . . . please . . . please . . . please . . . help me, Jinx . . . such fear . . . oh God, such terrible fear . . . 'I'll talk to Adam and ask him to send Kennedy out,' she said shakily. 'Just don't say anything else till he gets there. Can you do that, Miles?'

He nodded and stood up. 'As long as you don't let me down.'

Blake put a firm hand on his arm and steered him towards the windows. 'This way, Mr Kingsley. We've a car waiting outside.'

'What about my Porsche?'

She held out her hand. 'If you'll give me your keys, I'll have one of these officers drive it for you.' She nodded towards the two Salisbury policemen. 'He can follow along behind us.'

Miles fished them out of his pocket and thrust them into her palm with bad grace. She looked at the fob – a black disc with gold lettering – then led him away.

With shaking hands, Jinx reached for her cigarette packet off the arm of her chair, then retreated to the dressing table and its firm, supportive edge. She looked briefly towards Alan Protheroe, who was leaning against the wall by the door, then turned her attention to Frank Cheever. 'I recognize you from the television,' she told him, lighting a cigarette with difficulty. 'You gave a press conference the other day, but I'm afraid I can't remember your name.'

'Detective Superintendent Cheever,' he told her.

She glanced at Maddocks. 'Then you're here to talk about Leo and Meg?'

Frank nodded.

'And you think Miles might have done it because of what happened to these wretched women?'

'It's a possibility.'

She nodded. 'In your shoes, I'd probably say the same.'

'And if the roles were reversed and *I* were in your shoes, what would I say then?'

She stared at him rather strangely for a moment. 'I think you'd be too busy stifling the screams inside your head to say anything at all.'

Frank watched her. 'Are you well enough to talk to us, Miss Kingsley?'

'Yes.'

'You don't have to,' said Alan sharply. 'I'm sure the Superintendent will give you time to recover.'

That amused her. 'They kept telling me that when Russell died. It meant I could have ten minutes to compose myself before they started in again.' She took a pull on her cigarette. 'The trouble is, you never recover from something like that, so ten minutes is just time wasted and, as I need to phone my father, I'd rather get this over and done with as quickly as possible.'

'Please,' said Frank, gesturing towards the telephone. 'We'll go outside while you do it.'

She shook her head. 'I'd rather wait till you've gone.'

'Why?' asked Maddocks. 'The sooner your brother has a solicitor with him the better, wouldn't you say?'

'Oddly enough, Inspector, I'd like to work out what I'm going to say first. My father will be devastated to hear his son's been accused of a brutal sex attack. Wouldn't yours? Or is that something he's come to expect from you?' She turned abruptly to the Superintendent again. 'Miles didn't kill Russell, so if the same person went on to kill Leo and Meg, then it wasn't Miles.'

'Do you mind if we sit down?' he asked.

'Be my guest.'

The two policemen moved across to the chairs, but Alan remained where he was. 'Why are you so sure he didn't kill Russell?'

She thought deeply for several seconds before she answered, and then she did so elliptically. 'It's rather ironic, really, considering I've just told him to keep quiet until he has a solicitor present. You see, I'm not convinced solicitors always give good advice. I consulted one after Russell was murdered,' she told them, 'because it became clear to me that I was at the top of the list of suspects. He persuaded me to be very circumspect in how I answered police questions. Do not volunteer information, keep all your answers to the minimum, avoid speculation, and tell them only what you know to be true.' She sighed. 'But I think now I'd have done better to say everything that was in my mind because all I achieved was to raise the level of suspicion against my father.' She fell silent.

'That's hardly an answer to my question, Miss Kingsley.'

She stared at the floor, taking quick, nervous drags at the cigarette. 'We were talking about Russell's death before you came in,' she said suddenly. 'Miles told me he's always believed my father was responsible, which means he and Fergus could indulge in petty deceit after petty deceit without a second thought. Nicking twenty quid off the gardener or forging their mother's cheques counts for nothing against the enormity of murder.' She looked up. 'But what Miles believes – indeed what anyone believes – is confined by his own prejudices, and in this instance it is very important that you understand how desperate my brother has always been to feel superior to his father.'

'Does he have proof of your father's complicity in your husband's murder?'

'No, of course he doesn't, because Adam wasn't involved.'

'But presumably you can't prove that any more than your brother can prove he was.' He smiled without hostility. 'Truth is a disturbingly elusive phenomenon. All I, as a policeman, can do is accumulate the available facts and weigh them in the balance. In the end, I hope, truth carries weight.'

'Then why do so many policemen only hear what they want to hear?'

'Because we're human and, as you said yourself, belief is confined by prejudice.' He gestured towards Maddocks. 'But I think we're both professional enough to stay objective about what you tell us, so I hope that gives you the confidence to speak out.'

She drew on her cigarette and gazed steadily at Maddocks. 'Would you agree with that, Inspector?'

'Certainly,' he said, 'but you're asking for miracles if you expect us to take everything you say on trust. For example, explain this to me. How come you never resorted to petty theft as a way of getting back at your father? Surely I'm right in thinking you, too, have always believed he was guilty of Landy's murder? What was *your* revenge, Miss Kingsley?'

'Rather too subtle for you to understand,' she said curtly before returning to her previous point. 'If you're willing to be objective, then why were you so dismissive of everything I told you yesterday?'

His smile didn't reach his eyes. 'I don't recall being dismissive. I do recall challenging some of the statements you made. But then you're a suspect in this case, too,' he pointed out, 'which means that anything you say will be subject to scrutiny. Is that unreasonable, do you think?'

'No, but I'd be interested to know if you've pursued any of the suggestions I made to you. For example, have you looked for another link between the three murders? Have you examined the possibility that someone was trying to kill me on the day of my accident?'

'These things take time,' he said. 'We can't work miracles, Miss Kingsley.'

'But are you even *trying*, Inspector?' She turned to Cheever. 'Is anyone?'

The Superintendent, who was ignorant of both suggestions because they had not been relayed to him, answered honestly. 'Not to my knowledge, no, but if you can persuade me they are worth pursuing, then I shall certainly do so. Why do you think someone was trying to kill you?'

She glanced towards Protheroe, seeking support, but he was staring at the floor. 'Because of a series of negatives,' she said flatly. 'I'm not the type to kill myself. I didn't want to marry Leo. I never get drunk. I didn't kill Russell, so can't imagine I'd have killed Leo or Meg either. And the car crash clearly wasn't an accident. I can't think of another explanation for what happened to me bar attempted murder. And I keep thinking, what if I *had* died? Would you have looked for anyone else in connection with Leo and Meg's deaths? Wouldn't you all just have said to yourselves: That explains everything, she must have killed Russell as well?'

'Do you remember anything at all about the crash, Miss Kingsley?'

She looked away. 'No,' she said, her face devoid of expression.

He studied her for a moment, unsure if he believed her. 'Well, I'm quite happy to go through all the documents relating to it to see if there's anything we've missed, but I should warn you I'm not very optimistic. Even if you're right, I don't see how we'll ever be able to prove it.'

'I realize that, but the important thing is that you don't dismiss it as a possibility. You must see what a different light it sheds on the whole thing. I keep coming back and back to it in my mind. If someone tried to kill me, then that means *I* – she pressed her hands to her chest – 'must know who murdered Leo and Meg, even though I can't remember it. And it also means that *that* someone is the missing link, because whoever the person is probably murdered all three.' She regarded him anxiously. 'Do you follow?'

'Oh, yes,' he said, 'I follow very well. It's an interesting hypothesis, but it doesn't help us very much unless you can suggest a name.'

And if I suggest a name, what then? Do you have any proof, Miss Kingsley? 'What good is a name if I can't give you any evidence?'

The Superintendent shrugged. 'It would give us a starting point.'

But she was only interested in the endgame and she doubted whether the police could ever deliver a result. *Truth is a disturbingly elusive phenomenon . . . presumably you can't prove that . . . policemen accumulate the available facts and weigh them in the balance . . . what was your revenge, Miss Kingsley?*

'Yesterday,' Maddocks reminded her, 'you argued that it was Meg who linked the three murders.'

'And I still believe that's right,' she said, turning back from long corridors that led nowhere. 'Look, I spent all last night thinking about it.' She drew on her cigarette before stubbing it out in the ashtray. 'I haven't been sleeping too well,' she explained. 'I don't blame you for seeing my relationship with Russell and Leo as the focus for what's happened, but Meg's relationship with them was just as strong. Last night, I kept coming back to the thinking at the time of Russell's murder, which was that my father killed him because he didn't like him. I remember one of the policemen saying to me: Whoever killed him hated him because it was done with such rage. And that set me wondering if the rage was jealous rage.' She gave her troubled smile. 'But not jealousy over me,' she said. 'Jealousy over Meg.'

There was a short silence.

'We've read her diaries,' said Frank Cheever. 'At a rough estimate, she slept with fifty different men in the last ten years. Even by today's standards, she would be described as promiscuous.'

'Only because she had a very hedonistic view of sex. Why say no, if you both want to do it? In some ways she had a very masculine approach to life. She could love them and leave them and never turn a hair while she did it.'

'But surely you must see the flaw in your argument? If someone was so jealous that they were prepared to kill her lovers, then we should have fifty corpses on our hands instead of two.'

It was Alan Protheroe who answered. He had stood with bowed head, listening intently to Jinx's reasoning, but now he looked up. 'Because Russell and Leo were the only two lovers she really cared for,' he pointed out. 'By the sound of it, the rest meant nothing at all. Jinx told me the letters Meg wrote to Russell were very moving, and the newspapers talk about an eleven-year relationship between her and Leo. If someone else was in love with her, then it's those two men who represented the threat, not the fifty or so others who came and went as regularly as clockwork.'

'Why kill Meg as well?'

'For the same reason jealous husbands kill their wives when they find them *in flagrante delicto* with other men. On the face of it, it's illogical. If you love a woman enough to be jealous, then how can you summon the hate required to kill her? But emotions are never logical.'

'Then why wasn't she killed when Russell was killed? Why only kill her over Leo?'

Alan shrugged. 'For any one of twenty reasons, I should think. A desire to give her a second chance. A belief that

Russell was a sort of Svengali who'd influenced her against her will. Simple logistics – she wasn't with him the day of the murder. Myself, I'd probably pick the Svengali option because that would explain why she had to die this time. If she'd known Leo for eleven years then it must have been clear to anyone who knew them both that she was an equal party to all decisions made. You need to find out who else knew about the affair with Russell. Isn't that the key?'

DI Maddocks cleared his throat. 'I could almost buy this theory if it wasn't for one small snag. Like Superintendent Cheever says, we've read her diaries, or what there is of them, and nowhere is there a mention of another man who lasted longer than three or four months. So who is this mysterious lover? You knew her better than anyone else, Miss Kingsley. Do you know who it is?'

'No,' she said, 'I don't.'

Maddocks was watching her carefully. 'So give us a handful of likely candidates, and leave us to ferret out what we can.'

'Ask Josh,' she said, evading the question. 'He knew her men friends far better than I did.'

'We'll do that. Did he also know her women friends better?'

'Probably.'

'Did she have many?'

Jinx frowned, unsure where he was leading. 'A few close ones, like me.'

'That's what I thought.'

She flicked him a puzzled glance. 'Why is it important?'

He quoted her own words back at her. '"Why say no if

you both want to do it? Meg had a masculine approach to life.'" He held her gaze. 'I wonder if this jealous lover was a woman, Miss Kingsley.'

Canning Road Police Station, Salisbury – 3.30 p.m.

Blake showed Miles into an interview room. 'You can wait here till the solicitor comes, although I may have to move you if the room's needed by someone else.'

'How long are you planning to keep me here?'

'As long as it takes. First we wait for the solicitor, then we ask you questions. It could be several hours.'

'I don't have several hours,' he muttered, glancing at his watch. 'I need to be out of here by five at the latest.'

'Are you saying you don't want to wait for the solicitor, Mr Kingsley?'

He thought rapidly. 'Yes, that's what I'm saying. Let's get on with it.'

Nightingale Clinic, Salisbury – 3.30 p.m.

'Which way?' asked Maddocks as he turned out of the clinic gates. 'Salisbury CID or back to Winchester?'

'Stoney Bassett airfield,' grunted the Superintendent. 'Young Blake will keep Miles on ice till we get there. Let's face it, he's not going anywhere in a hurry.'

Hellingdon Hall, Fordingbridge, Hampshire – 3.30 p.m.

Betty put down the extension in her bedroom and dragged herself to her dressing-table stool, pools of sweat gathering under her arms and drenching her corset at the back. She thrust her fat face at the mirror and desperately applied powder in an attempt to repair the ravages of time and her husband's neglect. She listened for his footsteps on the stairs, knowing that it was over. This time there would be no reprieve for her or the boys. As usual, she turned her resentment on the first Mrs Kingsley, whose ghost had defied every attempt she had ever made to lay it. It wasn't fair, she told herself. All right, so no one had ever promised her a rose garden, but no one had warned her that marriage to Adam would be a bed of thorns either. 'Hello, Daddy,' she said with desperate gaiety, as the door was flung open, 'it's been a bugger of a day one way and another, hasn't it?'

Stoney Bassett Airfield, New Forest,
Hampshire – 4.15 p.m.

They stood on the bleak, heather-strewn plain where broken Tarmac runways, covered in weeds, were all that remained of the wartime airfield. 'What are we looking for?' asked Maddocks, careful to keep his tone neutral. He could happily have kicked his boss from here to eternity. Like Fraser yesterday, a few clever words and a troubled smile had made him doubt the girl's guilt and, for the life of him, Maddocks couldn't see how she did it.

Frank pointed to the concrete stanchion which reared up like a single broken tooth some yards from where they were standing. 'We'll start there,' he said. 'Presumably, that's what she drove at. How wide would you say it was?'

'Nine feet square,' guessed Maddocks.

'Interesting, don't you think?' murmured Frank.

'Why?'

'I thought it was much narrower. You've seen the photographs. The car appeared to be wrapped around it like a metal fist.' He cocked his head from side to side, studying different angles. 'It must have impacted on one of the corners and the arc lights threw everything else into shadow.' He moved forward to prowl around the structure.

'What difference does its size make?' asked Maddocks, following him.

The Superintendent squatted down to examine an area of gouged and heavily scarred concrete on both faces of one corner. 'If you were driving at a nine-foot-wide wall with the intention of smashing into it, wouldn't you head straight for the middle? Why aim for one end?'

There was shattered glass from the windscreen still littering the ground, and intermittent tyre traces to a point fifty metres back where the car had obviously been sitting until, at maximum revs, she had released the brake to hurl it and herself at the concrete structure. Frank spent ten minutes walking back and forth across a broad expanse of area around the stanchion, then he returned to stand and gaze at the burnt rubber marks where the tyres had spun before biting into the Tarmac. He crouched down and followed the line the car had taken. 'She was absolutely square to the middle of that wall when she set off,' he said, 'so how come she ended up wrapped around the right-hand corner?'

'Hit a pot-hole and lost control?' suggested Maddocks.

'Except there isn't anything big enough, not on this stretch. That's what I was checking for. She could have driven at any of the three sides that face on to the Tarmac but she chose the one with the best approach. If she was intent on killing herself, then there was nothing to stop her driving in a dead straight line.'

'She changed her mind at the last minute,' said Maddocks. 'Didn't fancy it so much when she saw the wall rushing towards her and tried to pull out of it.'

'Yes, that's a possibility.' He turned with his back to the wall and surveyed the area that would have been behind the car. 'Why didn't she start further off and use the greater distance to build up her speed? Why sit here and rev up the engine?'

'Because it was dark and she needed to see the wall.'

'It was ten o'clock on one of the longest days in the year. She could have seen that thing two, three hundred yards away.'

'All right, then, she parked herself here, sat staring at the wall while she drank herself stupid, then suddenly made up her mind to do it. Look, sir, I know what you're getting at. You're saying that attempted murder isn't out of the question. Someone got her drunk – though I have to say that's a mystery in itself – picked the best piece of ground for the car to stay in a straight line, made it near enough to the stanchion to preclude too much divergence from the track, stuck her unconscious in the driving seat, put the car into *Drive*, wedged the accelerator flat down with one of the empty bottles, and released the brake. At which point, brave Miss Kingsley comes out of her drunken stupor, sees what's happening, tries to steer clear, realizes she can't make it so throws herself out of the open door.' He gave a sour smile. 'Apart from the fact that you'd do yourself a hell of a lot of damage, leaning in to release the handbrake of a car on full throttle, why on earth didn't he finish her off when she threw herself out?'

'You wouldn't use the handbrake,' said Frank, 'you'd use the foot brake with some sort of brace – a piece of two by four, maybe – a sledgehammer, even' – he lifted a teasing eyebrow – 'between the metal frame of the seat and the pedal, with a rope attached. Then you'd wedge your throttle and use the rope to yank the brace away. The other alternative would be to chock the tyres and not use the brakes at all.' He gestured towards the ground. 'But I think it'd be obvious if chocks had been used.'

'And the fact that he didn't bother to finish her off?' muttered Maddocks sarcastically.

'Perhaps he thought he had,' said the Superintendent mildly, 'or perhaps he didn't have time to check.' He was silent for a moment. 'Would you care to explain to me why this little exercise is making you so angry?'

'Because she's guilty as hell, sir. The whole thing was a set-up to get her old man's sympathy. I can't see it makes a blind bit of difference which approach she chose, how far away she was when she started, whether chocks were used, or when she was found. She was in control of the car from the moment she set off.'

Frank scuffed his foot over the broken surface of the Tarmac. 'She could have torn the skin off her face throwing herself out of a speeding car on to this. Why not choose something less painful?'

'Because she likes drama,' said Maddocks dismissively. 'Anyway, she didn't tear the skin off her face. She's not going to be permanently disfigured once her hair grows and the bruises fade. All things considered, she came off very lightly.

Too lightly for attempted murder or genuine suicide, wouldn't you say?'

Canning Road Police Station, Salisbury – 4.45 p.m.

'Look,' said Miles angrily to the two police officers sitting opposite him, 'how many times do I have to tell you? I've never been to a prostitute in my life. Why would I need to? Jesus, I had my first lay when I was fifteen.' He banged his fist on the table. 'I don't know any Flossie Hale and I don't know any Samantha Garrison, and if I wanted to shaft a forty-six-year-old – which I bloody well don't – I could shaft Dad's housekeeper for free. She'd probably pay me if I asked her. She's had the hots for me for years.'

'You have a very high opinion of yourself, Miles,' said the Sergeant.

'Why shouldn't I?'

'No reason, except that men who talk big tend to be better in theory than they are in practice.'

'What do you expect me to do? Burst into tears and say I'm so fucking inadequate I need to pay some old slag to give me a good time? Do me a favour.'

'Is that what you'd do if you felt you were inadequate?' asked Blake.

Miles shrugged and lit a cigarette.

She turned to the tape-recorder on the table. 'Mr Kingsley's response was a shrug.'

'Like hell it was,' said Miles furiously. 'Mr Kingsley's response is, I'm not fucking inadequate so I wouldn't fucking well know what I'd fucking do if I was.' He yelled into the microphone. 'Have you fucking well got that?'

'Calm down, Miles,' said the Sergeant wearily. 'You'll break the machine if you keep shouting at it. Why don't you just tell us where you were and what you were doing on the night of the twenty-second?'

'You've asked me that same sodding question a hundred times and I've given the same sodding answer a hundred times. I was at home till eight-thirty, when I left to visit Jinx.'

'And we don't believe you. Tell me, will the randy house-keeper lie for you, the way you claim your mother and brother will?'

'I never said they'd be lying.' He looked at his watch. 'Oh God! Look, I've got to get out of here. Are you going to charge me or not? Because if you're not, then I want out.'

'Why? What's happening at five o'clock that's so important?'

'I owe money, you moron,' said Miles through gritted teeth, 'and I need to buy a bit more time. That's what's happening at five o'clock. Why the hell do you think I went to see Jinxy? OK, so we shout at each other a bit but she's always come through in the past.'

There was a tap on the door and a second WPC looked in. 'I've got a Mr Kennedy out here, Sarge. He says Mr Kingsley's his client.'

'Show him in. Tape stopped at four fifty-one p.m.'

Kennedy looked at Miles with dislike, refused the chair that was offered him and, instead, placed two photographs on the table. The first showed Miles entering a hotel foyer, the second showed him getting into his Porsche. 'My client's sister informs me that you are enquiring into an assault on a prostitute in Lansing Road, Salisbury, at around eight o'clock on Wednesday, June the twenty-second. Is that correct?'

'Yes,' agreed Blake.

Kennedy tapped the photographs, indicating the printed times and date in the bottom right-hand corners. 'My client, Miles Kingsley, entered the Regal Hotel, Salisbury, at five-thirty p.m. on Wednesday, June the twenty-second. He returned to his car at eight forty-five p.m. that same evening and drove to the Nightingale Clinic to visit his sister. While at the Regal he spent three and a quarter hours in room number four-three-one, leaving it only once to meet a man in the lobby.' He placed another photograph on the table, of Miles, head down, talking to someone whose back was to the camera. 'That was at seven o'clock. He remained with this man for three minutes before visiting the gentlemen's lavatory in the lobby. He returned to room four-three-one at seven-fifteen. He was followed, photographed and watched from midday until midnight on June the twenty-second by one Paul Deacon, who can be contacted on this number and at this address.' He placed a card beside the photographs. 'I trust this clears my client of any suspicion in connection with the assault in Lansing Road.'

Blake looked from the photographs to Miles's drained, white face. 'It would certainly seem to,' she agreed.

Kennedy smiled coldly at his client. 'Your father's outside, Miles. I suggest we don't make him wait any longer than we need to.'

Miles shrank into his seat. 'I'm not going,' he said. 'He'll kill me.'

'Your mother and Fergus are with him. I'm sure they'll

both be very pleased to see you.' He gestured towards the door. 'Your father's most aggrieved by all of this, Miles, and he gets very angry when he's aggrieved, as you know. You wouldn't want your mother and brother to bear the brunt of his anger, would you?'

Miles looked terrified. 'No,' he said, lurching to his feet. 'It was my idea. Mum and Fergus were just trying to help. I thought, if we put the shares up as collateral, we could get out from under once and for all. So it's me he should blame, not them.'

Blake watched the young man pull the remnants of his courage together and thought he was braver than she'd given him credit for. But what the hell sort of man was Adam Kingsley to inspire such fear in his twenty-six-year-old son?

Chapter Twenty-one

DR PROTHEROE STOOD in Jinx's open doorway, watching her. She was speaking on the telephone, body rigid with tension, fingers clenching the receiver, shoulders unnaturally stiff. Her father, he guessed, for he doubted anyone else could elicit so much nervous energy. He remembered another woman standing in just this way, listening to a voice at the other end of the line. His wife, hearing her own death sentence. *I'm so sorry, Mrs Protheroe. How long? It's difficult to say. How long? Twelve months – eighteen, if we're lucky.*

Jinx watched him while she spoke. 'What's wrong?' she asked as she replaced the receiver.

He shook his head. 'Nothing. I was thinking of something else. Bad news?'

'No, good,' she said dispiritedly. 'They've let Miles go.'

'With or without charges?'

'Without.' She climbed on to her bed and sat cross-legged in the middle of it. 'Kennedy was able to prove he was somewhere else.'

'You don't seem very happy about it.'

'Adam was on his mobile. I could hear Betty crying in

403

the background. I think the sword has finally snapped its thread.'

'Are we talking about the sword of Damocles?'

She nodded. 'Adam's had it hanging over their heads for years. The trouble is . . .' She lapsed into one of her silences.

'They were too stupid to realize it,' he suggested.

She didn't say anything.

'So what was Miles really doing that night?'

She pressed her hands flat on the counterpane, then released them, apparently intrigued by the depressions they'd made. 'Cocaine,' she said suddenly. 'In between gambling his nonexistent fortune away. He and Fergus are in hock up to their eyeballs.' She was silent for a moment, stroking and pummelling the bed. 'Adam paid off fifty thousand pounds on their gambling debts in March, and he said if they ever gambled again he'd throw them out and disinherit them. He's had them watched for the last four weeks.'

Alan took up her favourite position against the dressing table. 'Why?'

'Because Betty sold the last of her shares halfway through May and he guessed it was to cover their losses.'

'So why didn't he make good his threat then?'

She smiled rather grimly. 'I imagine he wanted to know who he'd be dealing with when the boys failed to pay up.'

'They're over twenty-one,' said Alan dispassionately. 'He's not responsible for their debts.'

'You're back in your ivory tower again,' she said, two spots of angry colour flaring in her cheeks. 'Do you honestly believe anyone would bother to take Adam Kingsley's sons to the cleaners if they didn't think they'd get their money? You've seen what Miles is like. Now imagine what he and Fergus will have said about Adam and Franchise Holdings while high on cocaine. There'll be a video some-where full of damaging allegations.'

Alan folded his arms. 'He can't have a worse press than he's had in the last couple of days, so what does it matter what your brothers might have said?'

'It would have mattered four weeks ago,' she said through gritted teeth. 'Four weeks ago he was planning a society wedding and he couldn't afford any scandal, not if his precious Jinx was to have her day. Miles was right. It *is* my fault. If I'd had the sense to tell them I didn't want to go through with the bloody thing, well . . .' She fell silent again.

He watched her for a moment. 'As a matter of interest, why didn't he kick them out at twenty-one and tell them to fend for themselves?'

She didn't answer immediately. 'Because they'd have done this, anyway,' she said at last. 'If he'd turned them loose, he'd still be expected to pay their debts. I think he hoped that by keeping them close he could check their worst excesses.' She bent her head so that he couldn't see her expression. 'They've always wanted to throw his money in his face the way I do, but get-rich-quick schemes were all they could think of.'

Was that her subtle revenge, he wondered, pissing pub-licly on what her father valued most, his self-made wealth?

'He's making good his threat now,' she went on flatly. 'He's going to turn them off without a penny and divorce Betty.'

'Do you blame him?'

'No.'

'What will happen to them?'

'I don't know. I doubt he can leave Betty penniless because the courts won't allow it' – she pressed her forehead into her clasped hands – 'but I'm not sure about Miles and Fergus. He says he doesn't care any more.'

She was more upset than he would have expected. If she had any love for her stepmother and her two brothers, she had always hidden it well. 'There is a bright side,' he said after a moment. 'If your father's had them watched for the last four weeks, then one thing you can be sure of is that neither of them is guilty of the murder of Leo and Meg, or for that matter responsible for the attack on me.'

'I never thought they were,' she muttered at the bed.

'Didn't you?' he said, injecting surprise into his voice. 'They've always struck me as likely candidates. They're self-centred, not overly bright and very used to getting their own way, usually through you or their mother. I can imagine both seeing murder as a solution to a problem.'

'It never occurred to me,' she said stubbornly.

Of course it didn't, because you've always known who the murderer is. 'I wish you'd tell me why you don't trust me,' he said, in a carefully impassive voice. 'What have I ever said or done to make you feel you can't?'

She rested her chin on her hand and regarded him as impassively. 'How do you know it wasn't me who attacked you?'

He took the sudden switch in his stride. 'It didn't look like you.'

'Matthew says it was dark, the person was dressed in

black and the only description you could give was five feet ten and medium build.'

'How does Matthew know what I said?' asked Alan.

'Everyone knows.'

'Veronica Gordon,' he murmured. 'One of these days that woman's going to talk herself out of a job.' He watched her curiously for a moment. 'Look, there are plenty of compelling reasons why it couldn't have been you. You're too weak to wield a sledgehammer. You've no reason to want to attack me. You didn't know when I was coming back, and I'd ordered half-hourly checks to be made on you before I left. If you'd been out of your room, Amy or Veronica would have noticed.'

'Except that I *was* out of my room.'

He made no attempt to pretend surprise.

'After Sister Gordon did her nine o'clock rounds,' she went on, 'Amy took over. I was in bed with my light out the first time she came. The second time, I was in the bathroom in darkness, and she didn't bother to check whether the pillow I'd stuffed down the bed was me or not. After that, I got dressed and went outside. I was wearing black jeans and a black jumper. I'm five feet ten, and before the crash I weighed nine stone, so my clothes can easily take some padding.'

'Go on,' he said.

'I wanted to know why Adam had sent Kennedy over, so I thought I'd waylay you. I waited under the beech tree until I was so tired I couldn't wait any longer, then I went back to bed and fell asleep with my clothes on. I was having a nightmare when Amy found me. I'm amazed she didn't report it. She was scared stiff I'd been doing something I shouldn't and might be held responsible.' She examined his face. 'Or perhaps she did report it and you haven't told me.'

He shook his head. 'No.'

'Then obviously she trusts me more than she trusts you, Dr Protheroe.'

He lifted an eyebrow. 'Is that what this was? A lesson in who's trustworthy and who isn't?'

'More or less,' she said, refusing to look at him. 'You already knew I was outside – Matthew heard you calling my name – but you've never mentioned it, not to me anyway.'

Damn Matthew to hell and back! He was going to shred the little toe-rag the first chance he got. 'Only because I realized I'd made a mistake. I thought I saw you at the side of the road as I drove in but, as it wasn't you who attacked me, I saw no point in mentioning it. Does that set your mind at rest?'

'No,' she said bluntly. 'You talk about trust as if it can be had for the asking. Well, it can't, not when you're up to your neck in it. All I know for certain is that my father's paying you to look after me, that for some reason he sent his solicitor over to talk to you on Monday afternoon, and that shortly afterwards you ordered half-hourly checks on me before disappearing.' A glint – *of humour?* – appeared in her eyes. 'Then, when you finally reappear, you're attacked with a sledgehammer and the police come down on me like a ton of bricks.'

Thoughtfully, he scratched his beard. 'You've run those facts into a related sequence when my interpretation is there's no relation between them at all.'

'Why did Kennedy come and see you then?'

'Assuming there were no hidden agendas at work, to remind me that I promised your father you wouldn't be subjected to therapy you didn't want. Kennedy taped our conversation and, as I haven't heard anything since, I've concluded that I said the right things in response and not the wrong things.'

'What did you say?' she shot at him.

'I suggested it was Adam and not you who didn't want you remembering anything.' He noted her alarmed expression. 'I also said he'd misread your character entirely and that he was worrying unnecessarily about any rehashing of Russell's murder because you didn't share his anxieties on the subject. Mind you, at that stage I was unaware that Meg and Leo were dead, or that you knew about it.' Her alarm deepened. 'If I had, I'd have been even more forceful in my remarks on his misreading of your character because I've never met anyone, man or woman, who is as self-reliant as you are.'

She plucked at the counterpane. 'It's something you learn very quickly when you find yourself on the wrong end of a murder inquiry,' she said. 'You never stop watching your back.'

'Yet you're so adept at getting everyone else to watch it for you,' he said mildly. 'Amy, for one; Matthew, for another.'

She smiled grudgingly. 'Poor Amy is watching her own back. She's terrified of getting the sack, but you can't use what I've told you as an excuse. You're my doctor and everything I've said was said in confidence.' She changed tack. 'According to Matthew, the police think the sledge-hammer that was used to attack you belongs to the clinic. Is that right?'

'What a mine of information that young man is.'

She ignored that. 'Is he right?'

'Yes.'

'Is there any doubt about it?'

'I don't think so. One of our security officers went looking for it because he knew we had one. It was abandoned in an outhouse with paint from my Wolseley on the head.'

She sat in deep thought for several seconds. 'Could your security officer have been mistaken?' she asked suddenly. 'I mean, it seems such an odd thing to leave to chance. How could he rely on a sledgehammer being here?' She searched his face eagerly. 'He must have brought one with him. It doesn't make sense otherwise.'

He found himself moved by the terrible yearning in her amazing eyes. Were Matthew and Amy as easily moved? 'Meaning there's another sledgehammer out there somewhere?'

She nodded.

'OK. If it's there, I'll do my best to find it, but wouldn't it be easier just to tell me who *he* is?'

Her face took on a closed expression. 'Whoever hit you.'

He straightened with a sigh. 'No, Jinx, it was whoever tried to kill me. *You're not the only one watching your back at the moment.* 'Think about that.'

Matthew Cornell was lounging against the front porch, smoking a cigarette, when Alan went outside. Alan toyed with the idea of tearing his arms off, then abandoned it as a non-starter. All in all, he was growing increasingly fond of his ginger-haired convert.

'How's it going, Matthew?'

'Pretty good, Doc. How's the shoulder?'

'So-so.' He eased the muscles gently. 'Could have been a lot worse.'

'Yeah. You could be dead.'

Alan watched him out of the corner of his eye. 'Any ideas who might have done it? One theory is it was a junkie after drugs.'

'That's not the way I heard it.'

'Is it not?'

'There's only one person in the frame and it sure as hell isn't a junkie.'

'You mean Miss Kingsley.'

'She's the only one with sledgehammers in her background.' He ground his cigarette out under his heel.

'Except she doesn't fit the bill. It was a man I saw in my headlights.'

'You sure, Doc? You've got a loud voice and I was sitting by my window Monday night, having a quiet smoke. I didn't get the impression you thought it was a man.'

'And you told her all about it the next morning.'

Matthew grinned at him. 'Didn't seem fair not to. It's a mean old world, Doc, and how was I to know you weren't going to tell the police? I knew she was out there. She lit up her face every time she had a fag. I was watching her for about an hour before you came back and got clobbered. You should remember where my room is, upstairs on the corner, with windows facing both ways.'

'Are you saying you saw everything that happened?'

'Not everything. I watched Jinx for a while, then some time later I heard you calling and looked out the other window. I saw your car parked, then – wham! – your wind-screen exploded and I saw a silhouette against your head-lights as you roared backwards and piled into the tree.' He lit another cigarette. 'I thought, shit, what the fuck is going on and what the fuck do I do about it? And by the time I'd made up my mind, all hell was breaking loose. You were driving up to the front door, blaring your horn, and all the lights were coming on. So I reckoned I'd keep my head down and see what panned out.'

'Thanks very much,' said Alan tartly. 'I could have been dead by the time you came to a decision. You're required to act in good faith, you know, not stick your head in the nearest bucket.'

He grinned again. 'Yeah, well, I thought it was only your windscreen that'd been smashed, not your shoulder, and no one dies of a broken windscreen. You should have lights along the drive, then maybe I'd have seen a bit more.'

Alan glared at him. 'So all you saw was a silhouette,' he growled, 'and you don't know any better than I do who it was.'

'That's about the size of it.'

'Are you planning to elaborate, or is that all I get?' he said curtly. 'It may have escaped your notice, but I suffered an unprovoked attempt on my life two nights ago and I'm not keen for a repeat experience.'

Matthew blew a stream of smoke into the air. 'It was hardly unprovoked, Doc. The way I remember it, you were threatening to stay there all night till Jinx showed herself. You're too convincing, that's your trouble. The bastard believed you.'

Alan had forgotten that. 'So what was he doing there?'

412

'Waiting.' He flicked him a sideways glance.

'What for?'

Matthew shrugged. 'For whatever he came here to do.' He saw thunder clouds gathering on the doctor's face. 'Look, Doc, I can guess, same as you can, but that's not to say either of us'd be right. Personally, I can't see that scarecrow in number twelve murdering anyone, therefore there's some maniac wandering around out there, trying to shove the blame on to her. Strikes me he'll be shitting bricks in case she spills the beans, so my guess is he was waiting to have another go at her.'

Alan considered this for a moment. 'That can't be right. You said she was out there for an hour and you saw her face every time she lit a cigarette. If you saw her, then he must have seen her, too, so why not finish her off then?'

Matthew looked down the drive towards where Alan had stopped his car on Monday night. 'Because he didn't expect to find her outside. She'd have screamed her head off if he'd crept up on her under the tree.'

'Not if he'd hit her from behind. She wouldn't have had time to scream. *I* didn't.'

'Jesus, Doc,' said Matthew severely, 'you don't have much imagination, do you? He wasn't going to make it look like murder, not after he went to so much trouble to fake suicide last time. He was going to trap her in her room, slit her wrists or string her up from the bathroom door, and you'd have had a suicide on your hands next morning, and the cops would have rubbed their hands and closed their files. My guess is, he's been waiting for days for an opportunity to slip inside and do the business, but he's up against it here. He probably didn't reckon on so many people being on the premises at night. You've got good security, Doc, but then you need to with the sort of fees you charge.' He grinned. 'There are too many rich bastards in here who'd do their nuts if intruders could walk in and out as they pleased.'

'Why did he have the sledgehammer if he didn't plan to hit her with it?'

Matthew shook his head in exasperation. 'You're no psychologist, are you? It's the tool of his trade, Doc, and the rule is, you carry the tools with you just in case. Look at the Yorkshire Ripper, he carried his hammer and chisel with him wherever he went. You should study a bit. This guy's an organized nutter, and your average organized nutter doesn't go out unprepared.'

'Except we're not talking about a serial killer.'

'You reckon? Three murders look like a series to me.'

'Come on, Matthew, there was ten years between them, two of the victims were men and one was a woman, and all three victims were linked to Jinx Kingsley. That's not a typical pattern for serial killing.'

'Not yet maybe,' said Matthew, 'but I'd say his control's really slipping now, wouldn't you? There were nine years between Jeffrey Dahmer's first and second murders, then in the next four years he committed another fifteen. Will you still be saying this guy isn't a serial killer when the next poor sod gets bludgeoned to death?' He saw Alan's scepticism. 'Anyway, who's to say what he's been doing between then and now? I'll lay money on the fact that he's found some other way to work out his aggressions. You should talk to my Dad. He's represented creeps like this at trial. They're bloody clever and bloody manipulative, and I'll tell you this for free, if I were Jinx, I'd have amnesia too.'

'All she has to do is give his name.'

'Which means it'll be her word against his. Get real, Doc. She's number one suspect, so it stands to reason she's going to try and throw suspicion on someone else. That's the name of the game as far as the police are concerned. She needs proof, and my guess is, there is none. I'd say she's desperately buying time at the moment until she can remember something that will nail the bastard.'

'She couldn't be any worse off than she is now.'

Matthew flicked his butt on to the drive. 'You're forgetting she's been through this once with Russell. She already knows what happens when no one's convicted of a crime. The victim's nearest and dearest live with the guilt for ever and tear each other apart in the process. Suspicion's an evil thing, Doc. I know. I've been there. My old man's accused me of some terrible things in the past, not because he knows I've done something, but because he's *afraid* I've done it.'

'So has she told you who it is?'

'There'd be no point. What could a junkie do? It's her father she needs to tell. He's the only guy with the clout to sort this bastard out once and for all.'

Alan frowned at him. 'You haven't suggested that to her, have you?'

'Jesus Christ! Do me a favour!'

'You have to act in good faith, Matthew, and that usually means acting within the law.'

Matthew grinned. 'I know what good faith is, Doc.'

But did he?

The Nightingale employed two gardeners, who were packing up for the evening and who both agreed there had been a sledgehammer in the tool sheds prior to the assault on the doctor. 'I used it myself a week or two back,' said one. 'When I was replacing the fencing posts near the bottom gate.'

'Do you remember where you put it when you'd finished?' asked Alan.

He nodded towards the younger man. 'Tom here took it back on the trailer, same as always.'

Alan turned to the lad. 'Do you remember which shed you put it in?'

There was a moment's silence. 'I didn't put it nowhere,' said Tom, shuffling feet that were too big for him. 'I borrowed it out to my dad to do some building work back home. There weren't no harm. We've only used it here once in six months, and Dad's looking after it like it were his own.'

Romsey Road Police Station, Winchester – 7.15 p.m.

Frank Cheever found the note from his secretary when he returned to his office later that evening, following a fruitless trip to Salisbury after his bird had already flown. 'We couldn't hold him,' said Blake. 'And, if you're interested, the solicitor gave us another photograph as he was leaving.' She handed it over. 'I think it was meant for you and not for us. He said to remind anyone who was interested that it takes a minimum of five hours to drive from here to Redcar, and another five hours to drive back again.'

The Superintendent looked at a picture of Miles and Fergus laying bets on a racecourse. The time was 3.10 p.m.; the date was June the thirteenth and the venue, according to a handwritten piece on the back, was Redcar in Cleveland. 'How did Adam Kingsley know Meg and Leo were murdered on the thirteenth?' he grunted suspiciously. 'We don't know for sure ourselves when they died.'

'Because the thirteenth was the day his daughter faked her suicide,' said Maddocks impatiently.

'*Dr Protheroe phoned,*' said the note. '*The sledgehammer found at the Nightingale Clinic on Tuesday is not the one Harry Elphick saw before the assault. Dr Protheroe has interviewed the gardeners and has established that the clinic's hammer has been on loan to a Mr G. Stack for the last two weeks and is still in his possession. Address: 43 Clonmore Avenue, Salisbury. He suggests this rules Miss Kingsley out of suspicion as far as the attack on himself is concerned and further suggests that you test the sledgehammer in your possession for Leo's and Meg's blood. If it proves positive, he believes this will absolve Miss Kingsley of their murders. There is* no *way (he asked me to underline 'no' twice!) she could have brought the murder weapon with her to the Nightingale as she was semi-conscious when she arrived by ambulance and has not left the premises since. (Dr Protheroe insisted on the following PS) Why am I expected to do DI Maddocks's work for him? I am tempted to say that, had the matter been left to the Salisbury police, the above facts would have been unearthed yesterday afternoon.*'

Frank tossed the note to Maddocks. 'Well?' he demanded.

Maddocks read it with a frown. 'Not my fault, sir. I can only pursue one line of enquiry at a time.'

'Meaning what precisely?'

'Meaning that you never gave me the chance to follow

up. The weapon was handed over to us yesterday afternoon, sir, and I've been chauffeuring you all today. Anyway,
Bob Clarke's already given it a clean bill of health. There's
no blood on it, only paint.'

'Well, it's a pity you didn't establish ownership yesterday afternoon,' said Frank sharply. 'It might have saved us
today's wasted exercise.'

'Hardly, sir,' said Maddocks with careful emphasis, 'you'd
have been even more inclined to pursue Miles Kingsley if
you knew the hammer had come in from outside.' He
looked at the note again. 'I'd like to know what set Dr
Protheroe asking questions of the gardeners. He was listening when Elphick told me he'd seen the sledgehammer
before and, believe me, it didn't occur to him any more
than it did to me or Fraser that the old boy had got it
wrong.' He put the paper on the desk. 'What's the betting
the girl put him up to it after you and I left this afternoon?'

'What are you suggesting now? Some sort of conspiracy
theory?'

'I'm just commenting on the way we're being drip-fed
information that seems to suit a certain party.'

Frank folded himself into his chair and reached for the
telephone. 'Find out if DS Fraser's back and send him down
to my office.' He leaned back to look at Maddocks. 'Go on,'
he invited.

The DI shrugged. 'It's gut instinct. She's our murderer.
You see, I've always wondered how I'd do it if I ever wanted
to get rid of someone. The received wisdom is you keep it
simple, engineer a reasonable alibi and deny everything,
but she couldn't do that because of Russell's murder. The
police were bound to draw parallels, and whatever method

she used to do away with Leo and Meg, she would still be in the firing line.' He stroked his jaw. 'So she's done what I would have done. She's made herself the obvious suspect by tying Leo's and Meg's murders to Russell's ten years ago, and my guess is she's just waiting for the right moment to prove beyond a shadow of a doubt that the alibi Meg Harris gave her then is rock solid. Which will leave us floundering because we've bust a gut to tie the three murders together.'

'Are you saying she didn't murder Russell but did murder Leo and Meg?'

Maddocks nodded. 'Yes. Look, you've read the Met reports. Landy's murder was a contract killing, carried out by one Jason Phelps on the instructions of Adam Kingsley. There was never anyone else in the frame. All this garbage about Adam not allowing Jane to find the body comes from her, and, dammit, she's had a hell of a long time to come up with excuses. She says herself that her brothers have always believed her father was responsible, and that's pretty obvious, frankly, from the way they behave. You don't grow up normal if you think your father's a ruthless murderer. And look at the wife. Drunk as a skunk by ten o'clock in the morning according to Fordingbridge. We're talking major family breakdown here, and the idea that the daughter's immune from the madness is crazy.' He paused to collect his thoughts, nodding briefly to Fraser as he entered the room. 'I think she's telling us the truth about Russell. At the time of his death, I think she knew nothing about his affair with Meg. I also think she knew nothing about the murder and was genuinely shocked by it. But I'd argue that ten years of living with the knowledge that her father ordered it and got away with it has left her as damaged as she claims her two brothers to be.'

Nightingale Clinic, Salisbury – 7.15 p.m.

Sister Gordon was insistent. 'Doctor's orders, Jinx. He wants you moved to a room upstairs.'

'Why?'

'Good grief, girl,' she said irritably, 'do you question everything? How would I know? As usual, no one's bothered to tell me anything.'

Jinx glanced towards her french windows. 'I'd rather be in a room I can get out of if I have to.'

'Yes, well, perhaps that's what's worrying the doctor,' said Veronica tartly, who had been putting snippets from the rumour factory together with Alan's peculiar remark on Monday night and his sudden decision to move Jinx to a room upstairs. 'I expect he'll feel safer knowing you've only got one exit.'

Romsey Road Police Station, Winchester – 7.25 p.m.

'There's a chance she did know about Meg's affair with Russell at the time of the murder,' said Fraser slowly. 'According to Hennessey, she told him about it after she lost her baby but, if you remember, *her* story was that she found some love letters in her attic a year later.'

Maddocks put his hands on the Superintendent's desk and leaned forward belligerently. 'I'm sure that's not the only lie she's told us. I swear to God, sir, she's leading us all by the nose.'

'Why would Meg Harris give her an alibi?'

'Because she convinced her she was innocent. Dammit, she's all but convinced you and you hardly know her.'

'Five minutes ago you were arguing she didn't kill Russell.'

'Five minutes ago there was no evidence she knew about the affair, but you'll never get a better motive for murder than straightforward jealousy. Dammit, everything else I said stands. Even better if it was precious Jane who got away with Russell's murder, she could tie the other murders to it and say: "But the Met have proof I wasn't involved. They know it was my father."'

'There's still no evidence she knew about the affair *before* the event,' Fraser pointed out. 'If Hennessey's telling the truth, then we only have hearsay evidence that she knew about it at the time of her miscarriage, and that was two weeks *after* the murder.'

'Is there any reason to think he isn't telling the truth?' asked the Superintendent.

Fraser shook his head. 'No, but I wouldn't want to rely on him in a witness box. He's pretty hyped up at the moment, swings from anger against Meg for leaving him in the lurch, through anguish when he remembers she's dead, to a sort of sullen protection whenever Miss Kingsley's name is mentioned. I think he thinks Jane is responsible, but I also think he blames Meg for provoking her into it. My guess is he was fond of them both and doesn't know who to blame.'

Frank drew a doodle on a pad in front of him. 'How fond?'

'He's known them both a long time.' He consulted his

notebook. 'He was working with Meg at a company called Wellman and Hobbs when Jane was married to Russell.'

'I meant, was he sleeping with either of them?'

Nightingale Clinic, Salisbury – 7.30 p.m.

Fergus shouldered his way into Jinx's new room and stood aggressively over Matthew. 'I want to speak to my sister,' he said, jerking his head towards the door.

Matthew leaned forward to stub out his cigarette in the ashtray on the coffee table. 'I assumed the whole point of your being given another room was to stop aggressive visitors barging in,' he told her. 'I'll bet it was that old fool Elphick who told him where you are.'

'You heard me,' said Fergus. 'On your bike.'

Matthew ignored him. 'Is he dangerous, or are you happy to speak to him in private?'

'I think I'm safe enough on my own.'

'I'll be down the corridor. A good scream should fetch me back.' He raised his skinny frame off the bed and squared up to Fergus. 'I hope you're going to behave like a gentleman, Mr Kingsley.'

'*Piss off*,' said Fergus.

Matthew smiled gently before bringing his knee up with the speed of an express train into the young man's crotch and pushing him backwards against the wall. 'Never judge a book by its cover,' he murmured. He cocked a finger at Jinx. 'Sorry, but your brother's a creep. I'll see you around.'

Jinx waited till he'd gone, then looked down on the slumped, defeated shoulders of her baby brother. 'Where's Miles?' she asked him.

'Outside in the car,' he said tearfully. 'Dad gave him a hell of a beating then threw us out.'

'What about Betty?'

'She's in the car as well,' he said shamefacedly. 'Look, I know it's a lot to ask, but we need a place to stay. We've pooled our petrol in one car, and we've enough to get to Richmond. Miles and Mum said you'd never agree but, well . . .' He flushed. 'Well, I said you might and it was worth a try.'

She let him stew in his own discomfort for several seconds. 'I'll crucify you all if you do a damn thing in that house I don't like,' she said crossly. 'That means no mess, no gambling, no drugs, no drunkenness, and you bend over backwards to be nice to the Clanceys. Do you understand?'

He nodded. 'We'll need a key.'

'Try saying: Thank you, Jinx, you're a sodding brick. We owe you one.'

'Thank you, Jinx, you're a sodding brick. We owe you one.' He smiled sheepishly. 'We'll still need a key.'

'The Clanceys have one. I'll phone them and ask them to give it to you when you arrive. There's probably enough food in the freezer to keep you going till I get back.' She glared at him. 'And you're not to run up phone bills. And you're not to tell Adam where you are. I won't have my house turned into a war-zone. Got that?'

'Sure.' He rose. 'I knew you'd be OK about it.'

'It won't be for ever, Fergus.'

'I know. Hey, we'll take care of the house, I promise. I'll make sure Miles and Mum behave. And no phone calls. We'll lie low till you get back.'

She nodded.

He paused by the door. 'To be honest with you, I wasn't really sure you'd say yes. You're not so different from Dad, you know. I guess you were right the other day. You got the good genes and we got the bad ones.' He checked himself in case she changed her mind. 'But, look, I'm grateful. You won't regret this, honestly.'

She smiled suddenly. 'I know I won't. I'd have had far more to regret if you hadn't asked me, Fergus. I was really afraid this afternoon that I was never going to see any of you again.'

He looked surprised. 'Why?'

'I didn't think you'd bother with me if Adam chucked you out.'

'That's what we thought about you,' he said. 'I guess we never learnt to trust each other. That's pretty sad, really. I mean, if you can't trust family, who the hell can you trust, Jinx?'

Chapter Twenty-two

SUPERINTENDENT CHEEVER GAVE a small shake of his head as he replaced the receiver. 'They've tailed Fergus's Porsche, containing Fergus, Mrs Kingsley and Miles, from the Nightingale Clinic to Jane's house in Richmond,' he told Maddocks and Fraser. 'The old boy next door has just let them in, switched on the lights and left. They've got several suitcases between them, and as many boxes stuffed with bits and pieces as they could cram into the Porsche. According to the tail, they look like staying for the duration.' He tapped his pen thoughtfully against his teeth. 'That's interesting, don't you think?'

Maddocks prowled irritably towards the window. 'It's all over the news that Kingsley Senior's about to lose Hellingdon Hall, so I guess he's told the three of them to bugger off. She's given them a roof over their heads. What's so odd about that? She's their sister.'

'I said interesting, not odd,' snapped Frank, pulling off his bow-tie and slapping it on the desk. He unbuttoned his shirt collar and ran his finger round the inside. 'Obviously Jane's family doesn't share your low opinion of her. Would you move into her house, believing what you do about her?'

'Miles and Fergus lived under their father's roof long enough, believing he was a killer. Same difference, wouldn't you say?'

'No.' Frank jabbed his finger angrily at the air. 'There's no comparison. If Kingsley's responsible, then he's kept a healthy distance between himself and the killings. If the daughter's responsible, then she's done them herself and she's bordering on the insane. So I repeat, would you move into her house if you had doubts about her?'

Fraser cleared his throat. 'Look, sir, with the best will in the world this isn't getting us anywhere. The truth is we need more evidence or it'll be a re-run of the Rachel Nickell murder inquiry, or the Russell Landy one, if it comes to that.'

'Jesus, Fraser,' said Maddocks, rounding on him furiously. 'How the hell did you pass your sodding sergeant's exams?' He raised his hands to Heaven. 'More evidence, he says. Where do you expect us to find it, for Christ's sake? We've put everything under the microscope – Ardingly Woods, Leo's possessions, Leo's house, his cars, his garage, Meg's possessions, her flat, her car, Jane Kingsley's car. Zilch. Zero. Nothing. We've got a heel mark on a bank which may or may not have been made by a woman's shoe, and we might be able to argue that, because Miss Kingsley's clothes were disposed of by the hospital after the accident, some of the blood on them might have been Leo's and Meg's.' He paused to draw breath. 'It's not much, I agree, but what we have in abundance is circumstantial evidence pointing in one direction, and one direction only. Towards the woman who had both motive and opportunity. I say we go with that and persuade her to talk.'

'Explain why the blood on her clothes failed to get into her car,' said Frank. 'Bob Clarke's team have taken it apart and there's not a spot in there, not even her own.'

'She was wearing a jacket when she was found. She put that on over her bloodstained clothes when she got into the car.'

'That's fantasy, not evidence. Explain how the sledge-hammer got to the Nightingale Clinic on Monday night.'

'It was a set-up, courtesy of her father. Get me off the hook, Daddy, and Daddy obliges. Fake attack on Dr Protheroe with pristine sledgehammer and finger points to an outsider being involved.'

Frank jerked his chin at Fraser. 'Your turn,' he said curtly.

They'd been round this circle a hundred times already and, with a sigh, Fraser set out on it again. 'OK, the DI reckons she's manipulating events because she's guilty. I think she's manipulating them because she's innocent and scared. I'm guessing Leo left her on the night of Monday, May the thirtieth, to move in with Meg and I'm also guessing that she didn't give a shit about losing him. What concerned her was how her father was going to react. I think she was terrified of him because she shared her brother's view that he'd had Russell murdered. But no one could prove it, so she did her best to keep her distance from him and cut him out of her life. All she achieved in the process was to ratchet up his rather peculiar obsession with her. Dean Jarrett describes Adam as sitting staring at her as though he couldn't believe she was really his. My guess is, she became so paranoid about it that she persuaded Leo and Meg to leave for an indefinite stay in France in case her father reacted badly to the news of Leo's desertion.'

Frank drew a Cupid on the pad in front of him and stabbed an arrow through its heart. 'Except that the ideal time for them to go was June the fourth, the day she went down to stay at the Hall. Why wait till the following weekend?'

'Because they didn't share her paranoia. Look, as far as they were concerned, Russell was killed by a burglar.' He glanced at Maddocks, saw his sardonic smile. 'We're talking about two very egocentric personalities here, and that's on the word of their own families. Self, self, self, in other words. Leo thought principally in terms of money and possessions; Meg thought principally in terms of money and sexual gratification. Do you seriously believe either of them would dwell on the death of Miss Kingsley's husband? Meg was probably upset for a while but, as I recollect, her diary recorded her going to bed with a complete stranger less than a month later, and there's no evidence Leo even *knew* Russell. Frankly, if they ever thought about him at all, it was almost certainly in terms of a burglary gone wrong.'

He went on. 'The only one haunted by the wretched man's death was his widow, but even she got over it eventually. Sure, she's kept herself to herself rather more than most, but she's made an independent life, refused any help from her father, who she suspects is a murderer, and she's come out on top at the end of it. Then the nightmare starts all over again. She embarks on another attempt at marriage, only to find that Leo's no different from Russell and that she's making another mistake.' It was his turn to smile maliciously at thrice-married Maddocks. 'Which isn't so unusual in all conscience. People tend to be attracted by the same type every time. What is unusual is that her first marriage ended in murder instead of divorce, and Meg was involved with both men.'

'So she goes ape-shit and kills for a second time,' said Maddocks.

'You still haven't explained why they didn't leave on the fourth,' Cheever reminded him wearily.

'Because they couldn't go until the eleventh, sir. Meg had a business to keep afloat and Leo had investments to look after. The eleventh was the earliest day they could leave.'

'You're guessing again.'

'Yes, but it makes sense. Look, Jane is privately convinced her father had her husband killed, probably because the police profile persuaded her. She may even suspect he knew about the affair with Meg, which would have given him a motive. But when she tries to convince Meg and Leo, they're highly sceptical. However, they feel guilty enough about their own affair to humour her. They agree to keep the whole thing under wraps until they can leave for France – and that probably suits them anyway, because they know they'll be castigated when the news leaks out. Meanwhile, Jane has to face the week in Hampshire with her family. If she doesn't go, questions will be asked. If she does, she has to pretend the wedding's still on. So she pretends. She returns to London on the Friday for the mythical row when Leo tells her he's going to marry Meg, all three make their phone calls on the Saturday morning and Meg and Leo scarper.' He paused. 'That was the plan, anyway.'

'Then Josh Hennessey persuades Meg she's being a first-class bitch and they delay their departure till the Monday,' Frank said, driving another arrow through his Cupid's heart. 'Which brings Jane scurrying round on the Saturday night, asking them why the hell they're still there.'

'It's as plausible as the Guv's scenario, sir.'

'What about the business in her garage on Sunday?' demanded Maddocks. 'How does that fit in?'

'How does it fit in with *your* scenario?' countered Fraser.

'It was a fake, like the second one. The more attempts she made, the more protective her father would become.'

'With respect, Guv, that's bullshit,' snapped Fraser. 'Like Colonel Clancey said, if she wanted people to believe it was suicide, then she'd have wept all over him and his wife. Plus, she's done her damnedest to persuade us since that she's not the suicidal type. It doesn't add up. And another thing. You keep harping on about this protection her father's supposed to be giving her. Well, where the hell is it? He's not been near her. He's far more interested in salvaging his precious business.'

'He's paying four hundred quid a day to a corrupt quack to let her pretend she's an amnesiac. I tell you, if we could get her in here for questioning, she'd spew the lot before you could say Jack Robinson.'

Frank listened to this heated exchange with ill temper. 'I'm going home,' he said abruptly. 'We'll pack it in and sleep on it.' He started to lift his jacket off the back of his chair, then paused. 'Why did she tell Fordingbridge that the last thing she remembered was saying goodbye to Leo on the fourth of June if he wasn't even in her house?' he demanded of Fraser. 'And don't tell me she was manipulating events when she was semi-conscious, because I'll hit you from here to Salisbury and back if you even try.'

'No, sir, I'm not.' He glared at Maddocks, who was smirking. 'Look, there's no question she was concussed and there's no question, either, that she thought the accident happened on the fourth. I'm sure, to that extent, her amnesia was genuine. It may still be, for all I know. But I've done a bit of reading, and I'm guessing that story's what's called confabulation. In other words, she made it up. It was the story she was going to tell her father when she saw him on the fourth, the one she probably rehearsed all the way down in the car and then delivered convincingly. Leo's fine. I kissed him goodbye over breakfast. He sends his regards. The fact that it wasn't true is neither here nor there. It remained in her memory as something that happened because she knew that's what she had to say to her father when she saw him.'

'So her father's our murderer?'

'I'd say it's a probability, sir.'

Frank stood up, thrusting his arms into his jacket sleeves. 'You're right about one thing, Sergeant,' he said acidly. 'This is a carbon-copy of the Landy case. We have the same two suspects, and no likelihood of bringing a prosecution against either of them unless someone finds me some evidence.'

Thursday, 30 June, Hawtree Estate, Winchester – 3.30 a.m.

The child's screams rent the air as they had done every night for the last two weeks. In the kitchen, Rex started barking. 'CINDY!' yelled her mother, thrusting her arms into her dressing gown and storming across the landing to throw open her daughter's bedroom door. 'I've had enough.' She seized the child and shook her furiously. 'Either you tell me what this is all about or I'm taking you to the doctor. Do you hear me? DO – YOU – HEAR – ME? I can't stand it any longer.'

Nightingale Clinic, Salisbury – 6.30 a.m.

Alan Protheroe slept badly that night. At six o'clock he finally gave up the struggle, rolled out of bed with a groan, dressed and went for a jog in the grounds of the clinic. It had rained during the night and the grass was sodden under his feet. Water oozed through the fabric of his trainers, his cheek hurt where the shards of glass had cut the skin, and his shoulder ached with every step he took. *What the hell was he doing?* Jogging was for masochists, not for cynical middle-aged doctors who knew that death was as random and unfair as Government health policies.

With a sense of relief at a decision made, he hobbled to a bench on the terrace and sat down to view the misty landscape. Far away, beyond the clinic boundaries, low hills rose purple against the pale summer sky. Closer in, the majestic spire of Salisbury's beautiful cathedral showed above the myriad greens of the tree-tops. He viewed it, as ever, with weary pessimism. Perhaps it could survive the terrible encroachment of man and man's devices, but he doubted it.

'You look very thoughtful,' said Jinx, slipping on to the seat beside him.

She was dressed in black with a dark woollen hat pulled low over her forehead. He studied her wet shoes for a moment before nodding towards the spire. 'I was pondering man's destruction,' he said, 'and whether when it comes to it, as it surely will, he will destroy himself or his artefacts first.'

'I don't suppose it matters much,' she said, following his gaze. 'Nature will overrun whatever we leave behind, so our artefacts will cease to exist whether we destroy them or not.'

'It's rather depressing, isn't it?'

She laughed. 'It won't happen if man learns to live within his means, and if he can't learn, then he doesn't deserve his place on the planet. I have no sentimental attachment to mankind as a species. On the whole, I'd say we're one of the nastier by-products of natural selection.' She pointed to the trees around the boundaries. 'They do nothing but good. We do nothing but harm.'

'They have no choice,' said Alan.

'Yes,' she said slowly. 'Free will is a bugger, isn't it?'

They sat in silence for a while.

'Nice hat,' said Protheroe finally.

'Matthew lent it to me to keep my head warm.'

He decided not to ask her if she had had it on Monday night. 'Where have you been?' he said instead.

'Walking.'

'You're very brave. According to Matthew, the place is crawling with would-be killers. I can't believe he hasn't alerted you to that threat when he took so much trouble to alert me.'

She nodded. 'Has he also told you about the fox in the trap, the one that was biting its own leg off to try and escape?'

'No.'

'It died of fright. I don't want to die of fright.'

'So you went for a walk to prove you're not afraid.'

'Yes.' She flicked him a quick glance, then resumed her

433

study of the cathedral spire. 'But I couldn't sleep anyway. Matthew's bath wasn't very comfortable.'

'They rarely are,' he murmured. 'Is there a particular reason why you were trying to sleep in Matthew's bath?'

'Of course there was. I'm not in the habit of doing anything without a reason.'

'Are you going to tell me what it was?'

'His bathroom door has a lock on it.'

'I see.'

Another silence.

'So where was Matthew?'

'Probably in my bathroom, unless he was brave enough to sleep in my bed.'

He waited. 'Are you going to explain,' he said at last, 'or am I expected to go on racking my over-tired and rather addled brains?'

'I'm his surrogate fox. He's become very bossy in the last couple of days, and I blame existentialism for it. He thinks assuming responsibility means taking control.' She turned to look at him and her quiet laugh fanned the hairs on his cheek.

Oh, God, he thought, *think of ice-packs, Protheroe. She's a patient, for Christ's sake.*

Stoney Bassett Airfield, New Forest,
Hampshire – 7.30 a.m.

There was a roar of sound as the car, which had been parked in the same place since dawn, sped across the Tarmac and smashed on full throttle into the scarred concrete pillar. There was no survivor. Nor was there a convenient courting couple to effect a rescue. The car burst into flames almost on impact, probably because it was packed with open petrol cans, and by the time a passing motorist saw the smoke and called the fire brigade, the only occupant – the driver – was dead.

Romsey Road Police Station, Winchester – 9.00 a.m.

'You'd better read this,' said Frank, poking a statement across his desk with the tip of his pen. 'A Mrs Hanscombe and her daughter Cindy came in at four o'clock this morning to get Cindy's worries off her chest. Apparently, she's been having nightmares for two weeks and her mother felt the sooner she came clean, the sooner the family would get a decent night's sleep.'

It was Tuesday, June 14th. Me and Bobby Franklyn found the bodies after we'd done it in the woods. I ran away from Bobby and slid down this bank. I was that scared. Rex, my dog, had dug in the ditch and I saw this dead person. I think it was a man. Bobby said he'd stick me in there with him if I ever said a word, but I can't stand it no more. I keep dreaming the man's going to get me. No, I didn't know the ditch was there. I dug my heel in to stop myself sliding. I was afraid Bobby would catch me at the bottom. I hate Bobby Franklyn. He's no good at anything. I'm twelve years old. Yes, he knows that.

Signed: *Cindy Hanscombe*

Parent's signature: *P. Hanscombe*

Maddocks read it slowly. 'So where do we go from here?' he asked.

'We go back to the beginning,' said the Superintendent. 'I want a second search made of Ardingly Woods, and I want all the water dragged within a mile radius. I also want the statements of every sighting in that area on June the thirteenth re-examined and, if necessary, we go door-to-door again to jog memories. There's a sledgehammer and some bloodstained clothing out there somewhere, and I want them found.'

'What about the Kingsleys, sir?'

Frank nodded towards the door. 'You heard me, Inspector. We start again and, this time, we do it the hard way.'

Canning Road Police Station, Salisbury – 10.30 a.m.

'Flossie is adamant the key-ring had the Franchise Holdings emblem on it,' protested Blake. 'She says it was identical to the one Miles was carrying.'

'She also said Miles was the man who assaulted her,' the Sergeant reminded her. 'She's hardly the most reliable witness, is she?'

'I accept that, but she insists the two men were not dissimilar, and there must be something in that or she and Samantha would have blown me away when I showed them the photograph.'

'What's your point, Blake?'

'There's got to be a Franchise Holdings connection or why would he have a key-ring?'

'Come on! The bastard's married to someone who works there. He was given it during a promotion. He found

it in the street. It's a big organization, Blake. You'll be interviewing people into the twenty-first century.'

'Not necessarily. I thought I'd give it one shot and if that
doesn't work I'll abandon it.'

He looked at her suspiciously. 'Jane Kingsley, I suppose.'

'She's on our doorstep, Sarge. We'd be mad to miss out.'

Nightingale Clinic, Salisbury – 11.30 a.m.

Jinx was standing by her window when Blake tapped on her
open door and pushed it wide. 'I saw you arrive,' she said,
without turning round. 'I thought Miles was in the clear.'

'He is, as far as I'm concerned. I can't speak for my colleagues, though,' she said honestly. 'I'm afraid he's quite
likely to face gambling and narcotics charges as a result of
the information your father's supplied.'

Jinx turned round. 'I suppose that means you've been
given the name and address of anyone Miles has been in
contact with in the last four weeks?'

Blake nodded. 'I'm afraid so. A Mr Paul Deacon came
in this morning at our request and supplied us with copies
of everything he had, including photographs.'

'So Fergus is implicated as well?'

Blake nodded.

Jinx smiled rather bleakly. 'I should have expected it,
really. My father wouldn't miss an opportunity like that to
get the blood-suckers off his back.' She flopped into an
armchair and lit a cigarette, proffering the pack to the
policewoman. 'Do you smoke?'

'No thanks.' Blake took the other chair. 'I could be speaking out of turn, Miss Kingsley, but a prosecution isn't always

a bad thing. It depends on your brothers. It might be just the sort of shock they need to pull themselves together.'

Jinx sighed. 'You're wasting your time if you've come to talk to me about Miles and Fergus. I truly do not know anything about what they've been doing and I don't want to know. As far as I'm concerned it's a closed book.' *You're not so different from Dad . . . as far as Adam's concerned, Russell never existed . . . it's a closed book . . .*

'I haven't. That's a different case now, and I'm not involved with it.' She took a photograph of a Franchise Holdings key-ring out of her handbag and showed it to Jinx. 'Do you recognize this?'

'Yes.'

'Could you tell me what it is?'

'You know exactly what it is. It's Miles's key-ring. You took it off him yesterday.'

'How do you know it's Miles's?'

Jinx touched a spot on the black embossed disc in the photograph. 'The diamonds are in different places. It's how we tell them apart. It was my stepmother's idea. Think of the disc as a watch face with the Franchise Holdings logo the right way up. Adam's diamond's at two o'clock, mine's at four o'clock, Betty's is at six o'clock, Miles's at eight o'clock, and Fergus's at ten o'clock. That's the one you took off Miles yesterday.'

Blake couldn't hide her surprise. 'We thought it was a bit of glass. It must be pretty valuable then.'

Jinx smiled. 'I think each one cost about three thousand pounds. The disc is jet and the letters and rim are gold. Betty commissioned them two years ago from a jeweller in London for her and Adam's twenty-fifth wedding anniversary. She said it was something we should all celebrate.' The smile became rueful. 'It was a nice idea until Adam saw the bill. After that all hell broke loose.'

'Presumably there's a cheaper version in plastic which your father's employees use?'

'I suppose there may be. I've never seen one, though. Betty always told me she thought this up for herself. She wanted something unique to the five of us.' She frowned suddenly. 'Why do you want to know?'

Blake debated with herself. 'Oh, what the hell!' she said suddenly. 'I guess Flossie got it wrong again.' She sighed as heavily as Jinx had done. 'One of the reasons we thought your brother was involved in the assault on Flossie Hale was because she said her attacker had a key-ring just like this. She remembered it because the initials were the same as hers, and when we showed her the Franchise Holdings logo, she identified it immediately. So we then showed her a photograph of your two brothers, and she picked out Miles. I accept she made a mistake over that, but she was adamant this morning that this, or one exactly like it, is the key-ring the man was carrying.' She shrugged. 'I'm sorry. It looks like I've wasted your time.'

'Have you made that public?' asked Jinx, in a detached tone of voice, as though she didn't care what the answer was.

'About the key-ring? No. It's been a low-priority investigation because the prostitutes didn't want to talk.'

'What are the chances of this man still having the key-ring on him?'

'Pretty good, I would think.'

Jinx closed her eyes suddenly, and Blake thought she saw tears on the lashes. 'I gave mine away,' she said in an unsteady voice. 'I didn't think there was much to celebrate, not after my father lost his temper. In any case, he paid for it, and I made a vow a long time ago never to accept anything from him again.' She pressed her fingertips to her eyelids before lowering them to look at the young policewoman. 'The irony is, when I gave it away, I said I hope it brings you luck.' She ran her tongue round dry lips. 'But I think the luck must have stayed with me.'

'Who did you give it to, Miss Kingsley?'

'A vicar. He's Anglo-Catholic and he said the F could stand for Father. Father Harris. He has a parish in a village called Frampton. He's better looking than Miles,' she said in a strained voice, 'but they aren't unalike. Simon's thinner and not so dark. His sister confused them once so you mustn't blame the prostitutes for getting it wrong.'

Blake listened to the tremors in her voice. 'Would the sister be Meg Harris? Your friend who was murdered?'

'Yes.'

'Did this Simon have something to do with that?'

Jinx's eyes grew huge. 'I think I'm going to be sick,' she said. 'I'm so sorry.'

Blake moved her feet rapidly as vomit sprayed across the carpet.

The Vicarage, Frampton, Hampshire – 12.25 p.m.

Blake drew to a halt beside the other police car and switched off her engine. 'What's going on?' she called to a uniformed copper by the front door. 'Is the vicar in there?'

'Not as far as I know.'

'Do you know where he is?'

'Last I heard, he was stinking to high heaven of roast pork on Stoney Bassett airfield.'

To whom it may concern:

I don't believe in God but I have stood with the Host in my hand every Sunday and professed belief on behalf of others. I wonder sometimes if it would have been different if I had believed, but I don't think so. If God exists, He had no power to change what He had ordained, that I must be brother to Meg. There is no greater torment than to love a woman you can't have.

People will say I am mad. Perhaps I am. Yet it's a strange madness that brings meaning to the actions men say are wicked and confusion to those they condone. They say I'm a good priest, yet I stumble in black night before the altar of God's flesh and blood, and only see clearly when Man's flesh and blood is warm between my hands. Then I understand that sacrifice is necessary if the dark rooms of the mind are to be cleansed, for purpose takes over and what I do becomes inevitable. I am alive. I see truth.

It starts again CONFUSION
___

Meg became a WHORE *but I knew why and forgave her. She said, better a generous whore than a spiteful wife. She was open and honest and hid nothing from me. There was no* love *only physical gratification and excitement, until*

SECRECY

terrible uncertainty   where is god   god sleeps   but not Russell. Russell laughs and his laugh breaks into my head, smashing my brains   smashing   smashing   Meg loves russell simon hates god

Remembering is painful. I understand why Jinx prefers to forget. I have always hated Jinx. She made Meg jealous. What were Leo and Russell to my sister till Jinx made them desirable? Nothing. Little men of little worth, unJinxed. She turned them into gods and sent them back to Meg. With Jinx there is always

secrecy & SPITE unJinxed Meg is an honest whore

confusion *again. Awful, terrible   danger   danger   danger forget, forget   whores   young whores   old whores You're wicked where's my hairbrush naughty boy   smack smack   I hope that hurts   don't you look at your sister like that again wicked*

wicked   wicked

GOD the father made simon dEVIL

Where are they? Not in Hammersmith. The birds have flown because Jinx made them   it was a SECRET but simon made Jinx tell

kill kill kill   no WEAPON

god loves Jinx   miracles for her not for simon

she is SAVED

she follows simon to leo's house and simon says gods will be done amen

But why does god save Jinx? Three times simon tried to kill her and three times god saved her. He didn't save Meg or Leo. They tried to save themselves with

lies

you don't want the cat to die, Simon   you love the cat   let me go to hammersmith and feed the cat   let the cat live   the cat's imprisoned

she means leo   leo's imprisoned in simon's boot   dead already

like jinx imprisoned in a box in chelsea, buried alive in her coffin, dead if Meg disobeys

no one sees no one hears   she begs for life   too late   too late

please SIMON pretty please simon simon says NO

forget forget forget forget forget forget forget forget forget

simon says sorry

Epilogue

Friday, 1 July, Nightingale Clinic,
Salisbury – 11.00 a.m.

DETECTIVE SUPERINTENDENT CHEEVER and DS Fraser waited in silence while Jinx read the letter that Simon Harris had left behind on his desk before setting out to take his own life. It was a chilling document, not least because the sickness it revealed was echoed nowhere else in his house, except, perhaps, in a single cassock which, although it had been cleaned, still showed positive where blood had splattered the front. Despite this and the letter, however, there was considerable unease about Simon's suicide, particularly in respect of the open petrol cans that had turned his car into a fireball, destroying all chance of forensic analysis, and the extraordinary order in his life that was in such contrast to the apparent disorder in his mind.

The police had not been able to discover a single parishioner in Frampton who found their vicar's homicidal tendencies even halfway credible. 'He was a sweet man.' 'Nothing was ever too much trouble for him.' 'Father Harris wouldn't hurt a fly.' 'He was the hardest working priest we've ever had.'

There was circumstantial evidence to show that he had been absent from the vicarage from lunchtime on Sunday,

12 June, to the morning of Tuesday, 14 June, but it hardly stood up to close scrutiny. 'I noticed Simon's car wasn't outside on the Sunday or Monday night,' said his next-door neighbour, 'but he used to park it in his garage sometimes, so it may have been in there. I don't remember seeing him after morning service but that wasn't unusual. We're busy people and we don't keep track of each other's movements. The car was certainly there on Tuesday morning. I had a form for him to sign and I had to walk round it to reach the front door. No, I didn't notice anything odd about him. He was in his usual good spirits.'

Caroline Harris, quite destroyed by the disasters that had overtaken her family, swore that Simon had been with her and Charles on the Sunday and Monday night. She also claimed that he had been staying with them on June the twenty-seventh, when Protheroe was attacked. But when her husband was asked later to corroborate these stories he shook his head. 'No,' he said quietly, 'I'm afraid neither is true.' He had read his son's letter without obvious emotion and handed it back to Cheever with a request that his wife should never see it. 'I blame myself,' he said. 'I should have realized how damaging it was to grow up in a house where the sexual act was viewed as something degrading and disgusting. Selfishly, I thought it was only I who was affected but, clearly, Meg confused it with love and Simon confused it with hate . . .'

To begin with, Flossie Hale and Samantha Garrison were doubtful that Simon was the man who assaulted them. 'He didn't wear glasses, you see,' said Flossie, studying the photograph of the earnest young vicar, 'and he was better looking.' But when shown a snap-shot of a younger smiling

Simon minus spectacles and in casual clothes, they were more confident. 'Little Lord Fauntleroy,' said Flossie triumphantly, 'and he's not so different from the first one I picked out either. Same eyes. It's the innocence. Gawd, I'll remember never to be taken in by pretty blue eyes again.'

DI Maddocks was liaising with the Metropolitan police in an attempt to discover whether any London prostitutes had suffered similar assaults to Hale's and Garrison's during the five years that Simon had worked there. If they could establish a prolonged pattern of criminal assault on prostitutes, it would ease police doubts over the meagre evidence pointing to Simon's involvement in the murders of Landy, Wallader and Harris. For, as Maddocks said to Cheever when he'd read Simon's letter: 'Someone beat the crap out of him to make him write this, sir. It's got bloodstains on it.'

Frank watched Jinx lower the letter to her knees. 'As you see, Miss Kingsley,' he said, 'there are one or two questions left unanswered. We're still looking for the weapon, but there was a cassock in his house that appears to have bloodstains on it. However, it will be some time before we can say definitely that the blood was Meg's and Leo's. The likely scenario is that he removed the cassock after he killed your two friends, which would explain why we had no reported sightings of someone wearing bloodstained clothes. We believe he probably used the same method to kill your husband, donned his cassock in other words, to keep the blood off his clothes.' She looked paler and more drawn than ever, he thought, and the hand that held the letter shook violently. 'I don't wish to upset you further, but we would be grateful for any details you can give us.'

She glanced towards Alan Protheroe for support, then nodded.

'Perhaps we could begin with Saturday, the eleventh of June, the day you phoned your father to tell him the wedding was off. Do you remember that day, Miss Kingsley?'

'Most of it, yes.'

'Do you remember going to Meg's flat in the evening and being angry when she or Leo opened the door to you?'

Jinx nodded.

'Could you tell me about that? We assume they were supposed to be long gone, so what made you think they were still there? Why did you go?'

'To collect Marmaduke and take him home with me,' she said simply. 'I couldn't believe it when I saw Leo's car parked outside. I was furious.' Tears welled in her eyes. 'I'd gone to so much trouble and they just thought I was being paranoid.'

'So you had a key to Meg's flat?'

She shook her head. 'I was supposed to collect it from the neighbour. But I could see Leo in the sitting room, so I hammered on the door instead and let rip at them.' She dabbed miserably at her eyes. 'I wish I hadn't now. It was the last time I really spoke to either of them and I was so bad-tempered. You see, I knew they were in danger. I had this feeling all the time that something terrible was going to happen.'

Frank waited a moment till he felt she was back in control of herself. 'What happened then?'

'Meg gave me this big spiel about Josh and how badly she was behaving towards him. She said it was my fault, that

I was using Russell's murder as a stick to beat her and Leo with because I wanted to make life as uncomfortable for them as I could. We really did have an awful row.' She looked at her hands. 'Well, that's not relevant any more. I bullied them into going to Leo's house in Chelsea until Monday. I said, at least they'd be safer there than in Hammersmith because I was the only other person who knew the address.'

'Did they go?'

'Yes.'

'What time was that?'

'I think it was around midnight. Meg insisted on leaving the flat spick and span so that prospective purchasers wouldn't be put off when they went round it.'

'So she was selling it?'

'Yes,' said Jinx again. 'I was going to put it with an estate agent as soon as they left for France. That was part of the deal. Meg's business needed an injection of cash, and I promised to try and raise it through the sale of her flat if she and Leo would agree to make themselves scarce for a while. The plan was for me to explain it to Josh after they'd left . . .' She faltered. 'But Meg got cold feet when she spoke to him on the phone on Saturday and decided to postpone the trip so she could tell him in person.' She licked the tears from her lips. 'Josh threatened to pull out of the partnership unless she gave him a few guarantees about her commitment, and they'd been going through such a rough patch recently that she believed he'd do it unless she took the trouble to calm him down.'

Frank studied her bent head curiously. 'I have some

problems understanding why they were prepared to go along with all the secrecy, Miss Kingsley, particularly if, as you say, they thought you were being paranoid.'

She stared at him rather bleakly for a moment. 'Meg had done the dirty on me twice. She was in no real position to argue. In any case, Leo was on my side. He was cock-a-hoop about being in France when the news broke. The last thing he wanted was to face the embarrassment of a cancelled wedding. He'd have gone immediately if Meg had been free to leave.'

'Why wasn't she?'

'She had a client she didn't want to lose, and a couple of meetings with the bank manager. She said he'd pull the plug on the business if she tried to cancel them. The earliest she could leave was the eleventh.' She fell silent.

'Then she reneged at the last minute?'

Jinx nodded. 'She only agreed to go along with it in the first place because Leo was in favour, but the minute Josh came down on her like a ton of bricks she dug her heels in, kept calling me neurotic and absurd.' The tears ran down her cheeks again. 'I think she wanted to say she was sorry afterwards, but she was too afraid of Simon to look at me. It was very sad.'

'I understand.' He waited again. 'So they left for Chelsea at about midnight on the Saturday? Are you sure they went there?'

'Oh, yes. I followed them. Leo parked in the garage, and I watched them both go inside. Then I went home.'

'What about the cat? What happened to him?'

'We stuck with the original plan, but delayed it until Monday. We left poor old Marmaduke in the hall with some food and the cat tray, but he was only going to be there for thirty-six hours at the most. I would collect the key from the neighbour, rescue Marmaduke, and explain about the flat going on the market. Meg was supposed to call them the minute she got to France, tell them I was kosher and ask them to let me in.'

'But why was it so necessary to keep Mr and Mrs Helms in the dark?' asked Fraser. 'You can't have suspected them of being involved in Russell's death.'

'Of course not.' There was a long silence. 'I thought it was my father we needed to be afraid of,' she said at last, 'and I couldn't be sure how much he already knew about Leo and Meg's affair. I know he found out about Meg and Russell because Miles told me afterwards. That's one of the reasons I thought he might have had Russell killed.' She rubbed her head. 'Leo swore his parents wouldn't have said a word to anyone, but' – she raised her hands in a small gesture of helplessness – 'Adam has a way of finding out. If Mr and Mrs Helms knew anything in advance, they would tell the first person who asked them. In fact, Meg said it was worse, that Mrs Helms wouldn't wait to be asked, she'd stand on the street corner and broadcast it to the world.'

'Why weren't you worried about Leo parking his car in Shoebury Terrace if you thought your father was having him and Meg watched?' asked the Superintendent.

She lifted her head to look at him and for the first time he understood some of the agonies she had been through. 'I was. I tried to persuade him to leave it in Richmond but he wouldn't go along with it. He said that was taking the whole thing to ridiculous lengths. But, you see, I knew what had been done to Russell and they didn't. I spent a nightmare week at the Hall, worrying myself sick. I made Leo phone every day to let me know they were all right and to make my family think everything was normal. Then he phoned on the Friday afternoon to say they were leaving first thing the next morning, and it was safe to come back and make the announcements. And I thought, thank God, it's all over. I've made a complete idiot of myself, but I don't care.' She held a handkerchief to her eyes. 'I can't explain it because I don't believe in second-sight or precognition, but I knew the minute Leo told me he wanted to marry Meg that they were going to die. It was like having cold water thrown over me.' She looked wretchedly towards Alan. 'So I put two and two together and came up with Adam and, if I hadn't, then maybe, just maybe, they'd still be alive.'

'No,' he said. 'It would have made no difference. At least Adam was a terrifying enough prospect to force them to listen to you. They'd have been dead a week earlier otherwise.'

She held out Simon's letter. 'Except that I made them keep the secret,' she said, 'and that's why he killed them. It was the secrecy that made him do it.'

'No,' said Alan, who had read the letter before he took the two policemen to Jinx's room. 'He was a very disturbed man, Jinx. It was his illness that made him do it, and nothing you could have done would have stopped that.'

'The doctor's right, Miss Kingsley,' said Superintendent Cheever. 'The only person who might have guessed that Simon murdered Russell was Meg. She was closer to him than anyone else, in all conscience. If it never occurred to her to be afraid of him, then there's no reason why it should have occurred to you.' He paused. 'Did she ever show any fear of him?'

'Not in the way you mean. She's been afraid *for* him as long as I've known her. If only Simon were more like me, she always said, he'd be OK. She was worried that he was becoming a bit of a loner. He never seemed to have any friends. I remember her saying once, he never plays at anything except being a priest.'

'Didn't it occur to her he might be ill?'

Her expression clouded. 'She asked me once if I'd noticed anything odd about him, and I said: What sort of thing? I think he pretends, she said. I'm sure he hates our parents, Mother in particular, but he never says anything unkind about her or to her. I'm the exact opposite. I'm always rude about her because she's a square peg in a round hole and won't do anything to change it, but I'm actually quite fond of the old bag, and all right, Dad's a sanctimonious old buzzard, but I wouldn't have him any different.' She pressed her lips into a thin line to stem her tears. 'She wondered if I'd ever got the impression that Simon hated them but, as I never had, she let it drop. I know she always thought he was far too withdrawn, but I think she put that down to religious fanaticism. I'm sure it never occurred to her that he had anything to do with Russell's death.' She laced her fingers nervously. 'Well, it never occurred to anyone.'

'That's very clear, thank you. Let's move on. Tell us about the Sunday afternoon and this incident in your garage. What was that all about? Presumably the reference he makes in his letter to the birds having flown, and the phrase "it was a secret but Simon made Jinx tell" had something to do with it?'

Her hands began to tremble so violently again that she

gripped them in her lap until the knuckles shone white. 'It's what he says. I told him where they were. He knew they'd left Hammersmith, you see, because Meg didn't answer the phone.' She stared at Cheever in desperation. 'It was – he thought they'd gone to France – but he made me – I was the only one who knew.' She brought herself back under control with an effort. 'He came after lunch to apologize for what Meg had done,' she managed. 'He said he'd prayed for me during services that morning but realized prayers weren't enough and he needed to come and commiserate in person. So I laughed' – her voice broke again – 'and said there was nothing to commiserate about. I said if anyone needed commiseration it would be poor old Meg in a few months' time when she discovered she'd tied herself to a mean, self-serving bastard.' She swallowed painfully. 'I shouldn't have laughed. I think he guessed I'd known about it for a while. He was so angry – kept talking about secrets – called Meg a whore . . .' She tailed off into a long silence.

'What did he do then?' asked Frank gently.

She shook her head.

'I think it might be easier if I tell you,' said Alan. 'When the news came through yesterday that Simon was dead, Jinx told me as much as she could remember of what happened.' He squatted down and pressed a warm, protective hand to the nape of her neck. 'Would you like me to do that, Jinx?'

She looked into his face, for a moment, then looked away again. Why couldn't he see what he was doing to her? She was far too emotionally disturbed to survive an Alan Protheroe undamaged. She wished he would take his hand away. She wished he would go to the other side of the room. *Oh, God, she wished . . .* 'If you're allowed to,' she said curtly.

The Superintendent nodded. 'I have no problem with that, Doctor.'

Alan straightened. 'Then I think it's important you understand how terrifying it is to be confronted with an individual whom you've known for years as a mild-mannered non-entity, but who, without any warning at all, becomes dangerously psychotic. This was Jinx's experience that Sunday afternoon. It's difficult to say what Simon's diagnosis would have been if he'd ever been examined, but it seems clear that he was suffering from some very extreme paranoid disorder, probably of a sexual origin, either centred on his mother or his sister, or both. I think this hatred he had of God may well have been a more general hatred of any dominant male figure because he seems to have seen the sexual act as a degenerate exercise. Only whores enjoyed it, therefore for a man to enjoy it he must either employ whores or make respectable women miser-able.' He looked enquiringly at the Superintendent. 'Which may have been something his mother instilled in him. If she persuaded him that nice women found sex disgusting, then he would have had a very ambivalent attitude towards it in later life, particularly if his adored sister flaunted her libido while he curbed his by choosing voluntary celibacy within the Anglo-Catholic church.'

'His mother clearly has problems in that area but I doubt she set out deliberately to destroy her son.'

'I'm sure she didn't, and I'm sure there were other factors involved. For example, he hated being laughed at. That seems to have been one of the triggers of his paranoia.

It may have been why he chose to enter the church, because he was more likely to be taken seriously inside it than he was outside. Another clear trigger was secrecy. As long as he knew what was going on, or thought he did, he could keep his paranoia under control, but the minute he discovered he had good reason to be paranoid, then the control deserted him. It's interesting what close tabs he kept on everything. Jinx says he used to phone her or Josh quite regularly, and I suspect he continued to do that after Meg and Leo were dead. He certainly phoned me to try and find out what information I had.' He rubbed his shoulder thoughtfully.

'One of the complicating factors of a paranoid disorder,' he went on, 'is that, while it may impair your functioning on certain levels, particularly where relationships are concerned, your thinking remains clear and orderly and you can function normally within your job and the wider social environment. Which is why I told you it was important to recognize what Jinx was suddenly faced with that Sunday, and equally important that she recognizes it, too.' He looked down at her bent head. 'She's been terrified of Simon ever since she started to remember what happened, but I'm afraid she feels she didn't do enough to protect Meg and Leo. Isn't that right, Jinx?'

She didn't answer, and Fraser, for one, thought he was being surprisingly insensitive.

'She went into the kitchen to make some coffee, and she thinks Simon must have hit her on the head while she was doing it, but she doesn't remember the blow. What she does remember is coming round to find herself lying on the floor with her hands tied to her feet behind her back. Simon then put a polythene bag over her head and said he would smother her if she didn't tell him where Meg and Leo were. She couldn't breathe and she believed him. So when he took the bag off her head, she told him the Chelsea address. The next thing she remembers is being pulled out of her car by her neighbour. She didn't know how long she'd been there, how long it took her to clear her head, or find the number of Leo's house in Chelsea, but by the time she phoned to tell Meg that Simon had just tried to kill her, Simon was already there. Am I right so far, Jinx?'

Silence.

'She was given a straightforward choice,' Alan went on. 'Simon said: Leo is in the same position you were in. In other words, he will be dead of asphyxiation in two minutes. Meg is tied up but can speak into the phone if I hold it to her mouth. If you do what I tell you, they will live. If you don't, they will die.' He brushed the back of her head with his fingertips. 'She chose to help them live. She clung, as we would all have done, to the Simon she knew best. The vicar, the man who loved his sister, the man to whom she'd given her expensive key-ring for luck. It was her tragedy, and Meg's, that they had only ever known and learnt to trust Simon's false self, while his true self, the damaged self, had remained hidden. We all protect parts of ourselves – God knows it's not unusual – but for most of us, the hidden self isn't dangerous.'

Jinx wiped her tears away. 'I should have told Colonel Clancey. He's always been the best friend I've ever had.' She sucked in her anguish on a sob. 'I know some people think he's eccentric and stupid, and they make fun of him behind his back, but he would have made it all right.' Her mouth worked as she sought for words. 'I did it all wrong. I told the Clanceys everything was OK when it wasn't. I thought, if I just do what Simon says – because, you know, we used to play that game all the time, Simon Says. But it was just arrogance – I thought I knew the right thing to do.'

Fraser glanced at Protheroe for a permission he didn't need. 'It's not arrogance to believe a threat, Miss Kingsley, particularly if you knew what Simon was capable of. I'm no expert admittedly, but it sounds to me as if you acted out of love, and I'd say that does you credit.'

Alan nodded. 'He said there wasn't much traffic because it was a Sunday, and that she had twenty minutes to drive her car to Leo's house in Chelsea. If she wasn't there in twenty minutes, he'd know she'd spoken to the police and he would kill Meg and Leo. Then he put Meg back on.'

'And Meg asked you to do as he said?'

Jinx nodded.

'What happened when you reached the house?'

Alan took over again when she didn't say anything. 'She saw Leo briefly through an open doorway. He was lying on the floor and, from the way she describes him, he had probably died of asphyxiation before she got there, so whatever was done to him afterwards was done to disguise that fact. At least she gave Meg a chance to live by arriving when she did. Simon promised he wouldn't hurt them because he never killed women. All he wanted to do was talk. He sat them beside each other against the wall, tied their hands and feet in front of them, and talked for hours. So long, in fact, that Jinx felt he was beginning to calm down.'

'And?' asked Frank Cheever, when neither of them spoke.

'Meg offered to have sex with him,' said Alan into the silence. 'She thought that's what he was after. It probably was, but he didn't want to be reminded of it.' He shook his head. 'To be honest, I shouldn't think it mattered a damn what Meg said. Whichever role she chose – sister, mother, lover, friend – he would still have gone off the deep end.' He glanced at Jinx's fluttering hands. 'But there's nothing Jinx can tell you about what happened to Meg and Leo after that,' he went on. 'Simon went berserk at that point, grabbed Jinx by the ankles to pull her away from Meg, then put a polythene bag over her head and taped it to her neck. All she remembers is Meg screaming and drumming her heels on the floor before she lost consciousness.'

There was another silence. 'Can you tell us what happened to you, Miss Kingsley?' asked Frank. 'Or would you prefer Dr Protheroe to do it?'

Her huge eyes searched his face, looking for understanding. 'I truly don't remember very much,' she said unsteadily, 'except that I woke up at some point. There was a hole in the bag where my mouth was and, because my hands were crammed up under my chin, I was able to make the hole bigger. But that's all I could do. I was wedged into a sort of box and every time I tried to move it was so painful I gave up.' She plucked at her lip. 'I thought he'd buried me alive, and I just wanted to die.' She paused, lost in some private hell. 'Then the engine started and I knew I was in the boot of my car. The funny thing is, I felt better knowing that. It didn't seem so frightening.' She gave an odd little laugh. 'But he was so angry,' she said. 'He kept kicking me and saying, get up, get up. He couldn't understand why I wasn't dead. You should be dead. You should have died in your garage and you should have died in your boot. Why does God love you?'

'Where was that?' asked Frank.

She looked at him blankly. 'I don't know. Somewhere outside. I woke up and I was lying on the ground, but I couldn't move because I was so stiff. There was a black dustbin bag round me and it smelt because I'd' – she glanced at Alan – 'I think I must have been in it for hours.'

'So do you know what time it was?'

'No, but it was getting dark.'

'Do you remember him giving you something to drink?'

'I think so. He talked about sacrifices,' she said in some confusion, 'and Jesus.'

'Which is probably when you drank the wine, although if you'd been there for hours then you were probably very dehydrated, and I doubt you drank as much as your blood sample implied. What happened next?'

She stared down at the letter, which she'd abandoned in her lap. 'I don't remember anything else.' She crumpled the photocopy into a tight ball. 'I don't remember anything else,' she said on a rising note of alarm. 'I think I remember him putting me into the car seat, but after that – I don't remember anything else.'

'That's fine,' said Frank with a smile of encouragement. 'I think we can work out the rest. You obviously have a very strong will to live, Miss Kingsley. I envy you your courage, and whichever guardian angel is watching over you, because I can't believe that courting couple arrived by accident.' He watched her for a moment. 'Dr Protheroe tells me Simon came to visit you the day after you regained consciousness. Did you know then that he was responsible?'

'No.'

'When did you remember?'

She kept her head down. 'Yesterday morning,' she said, 'when the policewoman asked me about the key-ring.'

'Not before?'

She didn't say anything.

'Did you tell your father that Simon had murdered Meg and Leo, Miss Kingsley?'

Her head snapped up, eyes huge with surprise. 'No, of course I didn't. Why would I do that?'

Cheever nodded. 'Your brothers? Your stepmother?'

'No.'

Alan Protheroe frowned. 'Why do you ask, Superintendent?'

Frank Cheever gave a small shrug. 'Just tying up loose ends, Doctor. We don't want accusations floating around afterwards about the' – he sought for a word – '*convenience* of Simon Harris's suicide. One might almost say the poetic justice of how he met his end. Our problem is there's only this letter and the bloodstains on the cassock linking him to the murders and, as the cassock had been cleaned recently, it may not produce the material evidence we're looking for. We assume Simon took Leo and Meg in his own car to Ardingly Woods but, as it was completely burnt out yesterday, we're very doubtful of being able to prove anything from a forensic examination. We've also examined your car, Miss Kingsley, and I have to tell you there's nothing to show you spent twelve to eighteen hours in the boot.'

'There wouldn't be,' said Alan. 'Not if he wrapped her in black polythene before he put her in there.'

'I accept that, but it's a problem nevertheless. It would've helped if you had been able to identify him as your attacker.'

Alan nodded towards the crumpled photocopy in Jinx's hands. 'But you've got a written confession. Doesn't that count for anything? Presumably you've verified that it's Simon's handwriting?'

'Certainly we have, but the original is being tested at the moment for the blood and mucus stains on it. We believe Simon was bleeding from his nose when he wrote it. And that means he may have been coerced into doing it.'

'By whom?'

'We don't know, sir, which is why we're interested in finding out when Miss Kingsley began to remember and whether she told anyone about it.' He glanced at Jinx. 'It would be very unfortunate if doubts about Simon's guilt began to circulate.'

Alan rubbed his jaw aggressively, his fingers rasping through the thick stubble. 'Are you suggesting Jinx is lying about what happened, Superintendent?' he demanded. 'Because if you are, then I begin to understand why she has such a low opinion of Britain's policemen. Goddammit, man, imagine if the murdering little bastard was still alive, and she tried to tell you he was guilty. She wouldn't stand a chance. You'd still be sitting there smugly, giving us this garbage about lack of evidence. Well, thank God she didn't remember before is all I can say, because she'd have been signing her own death warrant by naming him. He was obviously a psychotic with paranoid delusions, but he was quite clever enough to convince you of his innocence while he did away with the woman he held responsible for his murderous binges.'

Cheever shrugged. 'You've encapsulated our dilemma rather well, sir. Personally, I have no doubts that Miss Kingsley is telling the truth. I am also hopeful that we will find other prostitutes in London who will identify Simon Harris as the client who assaulted them, which, in turn, will point to a pattern of serial criminal behaviour. However, in the short term, we have a rather timely suicide on our hands which, in view of Harris's undoubted cleverness, to which you yourself referred, and his past determination to throw the blame on Miss Kingsley, raises rather too many doubts for comfort. I am sure Miss Kingsley does not want this story to run and run, any more than we do' – he turned his attention to Jinx and held her gaze with his – 'so anything she can tell us now that will result in the coroner bringing in an unequivocal verdict of suicide would be helpful.'

Jinx nodded. 'I understand,' she said, glancing towards the open notebook on Fraser's lap. She thought for a moment. 'I did not remember anything until the policewoman asked me about the key-ring yesterday, then it all came back to me in a rush and I was violently sick, as she will testify. I have been told since that Simon had been dead for some hours before I gave her his name. Because I did not remember who tried to kill me, I could not tell anyone who it was. Dr Protheroe, whom I trust implicitly and whom I would have told had I been able to remember, will testify that at no time did I ever give him a name or even hint at a name. Had I been able to remember, I would, of course, have told the Hampshire police. From the outset of the investigation they have made it clear to me that, while I was a suspect, media speculation would not be allowed to cloud their judgement. As a result, I have always had confidence in Superintendent Cheever and his team and have given them all the time and assistance I could.'

She looked enquiringly at Frank, saw the tiny encouraging lift of his eyebrows and went on. 'I believe Simon, through his telephone calls to my friends, my doctor and my relations, learnt that the Hampshire police had refused to take anything at face value and realized he would be arrested the minute my memory returned. I have known him a long time, and knew him to be very fond of his parents. It is my own conviction that he would have done anything to avoid putting his mother and father through the trauma of his trial, and I am saddened but not surprised that he took his own life.'

'I doubt he'd want his colleagues or his parishioners to be subjected to that sort of trauma either, do you?' Cheever prompted.

'I knew him to be a very dedicated clergyman,' she resumed obediently, 'who must have been appalled, when lucidity returned, to realize that the burden of his guilt would fall on the people who loved him. He was an ill man, not a bad one.'

Cheever held out his hand to her as he stood up. 'It's hardly appropriate to say this, Miss Kingsley, but I've enjoyed crossing swords with you. I'm only sorry we had to meet in such tragic circumstances. You may be required to appear at the inquest but, if you give your evidence there as clearly as you've just given it to us, there shouldn't be a problem. In my experience, a little generosity goes a long way. Suicide is always easier to accept if there's a good reason for it.'

'I know,' she said, shaking his hand. 'If Simon had made

my car crash look like an accident, then I'd have been a little more worried. You see, I could always accept I might have killed Meg and Leo. They really did behave like bastards. I just couldn't accept I'd kill myself.'

His eyes twinkled. 'So you weren't quite as indifferent as you led us to believe?'

'I have my pride, Superintendent.' She smiled suddenly. 'After all, I am Adam Kingsley's daughter.'

Fraser turned the car into the main road. 'So what's the verdict, sir?' he asked. 'Do you still reckon she got her old man to take Harris out?'

'I do,' said the Superintendent mildly. 'She was afraid it would be her word against Simon's, didn't trust us to believe her, so turned to her father to sort something out.'

'Well, I'm not so sure. She strikes me as being dead straight, sir.'

'But, as she said herself, Sean, she's Adam Kingsley's daughter.'

'With respect, sir, I don't see what difference that makes.'

'You would, if you'd ever met the breed.' Frank looked out of the window on to sunlit countryside. 'They're effective. They get things done.'

'They weren't too effective when Landy was murdered.'

'People rarely are when they're at cross purposes.'

'How come?'

'I suspect *he* became convinced that she killed Russell, and *she* became convinced that he did. If they both learnt about the affair afterwards, then they both knew there was a motive for the other one to commit the murder. Divided they fell, united they stand.'

'It seems odd that Miss Kingsley didn't tell the police, though. You'd think she'd want her husband's murderer punished, and, let's face it, it's not as though she's very fond of her father.'

'You think so, do you?'

'She certainly doesn't go out of her way to express affection for him.'

Cheever smiled but kept his thoughts to himself.

'So are you going to charge Adam Kingsley with Simon's murder, sir?'

The Superintendent closed his eyes and let the sun warm his face. 'I don't think I heard you right, Sergeant. Did you say something about a murder?'

'Isn't that what you reckon . . .' Fraser broke off.

'Yes?'

'Nothing, sir.'

Nightingale Clinic, Salisbury – 12.45 p.m.

Matthew Cornell opened his eyes to find Alan Protheroe looming over him where he lay sprawled on a bench in the clinic gardens. 'Hi, Doc.' He shielded the sun's glare with a raised hand, then swung his legs off the seat and sat up, lighting a cigarette.

Alan lowered himself on to the vacant piece of bench. 'The police have come up with a bizarre theory about Simon Harris's suicide,' he said in a conversational tone. 'They seem to think Jinx might have given his name to her father in order to have him dealt with once and for all.' He glanced sideways. 'However, she's persuaded them that she didn't remember anything until yesterday morning, which means neither she *nor* any of her friends here could have passed the information on to Adam Kingsley.'

Matthew looked straight ahead. 'Why are you telling *me*?'

'Because I know how you like to keep abreast of the facts.'

The young man turned to grin at him. 'Plus, as an existentialist, you want to be sure I continue to act in good faith. Isn't that right?'

'I couldn't have put it better myself, Matthew.'

'Well, I reckon good faith is all about justice.' Matthew turned the cigarette between his fingers. 'Have you ever wondered what a murderer's victims would demand if their voices hadn't been silenced? At the very least they would ask to be heard as loudly as their killers, wouldn't they?'

'There's a difference between justice and revenge, Matthew.'

'Is there? The only difference I see is that justice comes damned expensive. If it didn't, my father couldn't afford to keep me here.'

Half an hour later, Alan stood with Jinx at her window and watched a tall, well-built man in an immaculate suit emerge from the back seat of a Rolls-Royce. 'Your father?'

'Yes.'

'You've never explained why you call him Adam.'

'What makes you think there is an explanation?'

He smiled. 'Your expression every time the subject comes up.'

She watched the tall figure disappear from view into the building. 'I wanted to punish him, so I did what God did and cursed Adam for allowing his wife to seduce him.' She turned to Alan. 'I was seven years old. I've called him Adam ever since.'

'You were jealous of Betty?'

'Of course. I didn't want to share my father with anyone. I adored him.'

Alan nodded. 'In spite of everything, I suspect you still do.'

'No,' she said, 'I'm long past adoration. But I do admire him. I always have done. He achieves while the rest of us get by.'

'Well, I hope you recognize that he's making the first move,' said Alan casually. 'Will you be generous to him?'

'If I'm not, the clinic won't get paid.' She smiled slightly at his expression. 'Don't go sentimental on me, Dr Protheroe. The one thing you can be sure of is that my father will never change. He'd sue if he thought you'd deliberately poisoned my mind against him.'

'So what happens now?'

'I'm discharging myself. I'm not your patient any more. I think we say goodbye.'

'Where will you go?'

'Back to Richmond.'

'Does your father know Miles and Fergus are there?'

'Not unless they've told him.'

'If they need a good barrister, then don't forget Matthew's father. I'm told he's one of the best.'

Jinx smiled and tapped her pocket. 'Matthew's given me his card. I thought I'd use the gains I've made on the Franchise Holdings shares to pay his fees. Matthew says they'll be exorbitant.' She shrugged. 'Then, with luck and a little emotional blackmail, I may persuade Adam to acknowledge Betty and the boys again once it's all over.'

'You don't think it might be better to let Miles and Fergus fight this battle alone?'

'Probably.'

'Then why don't you?'

'Because they're my brothers,' she said, 'and their mother's the only one I've ever known. It's worth another try, don't you think?'

'It depends whether you believe in the triumph of hope over experience.'

'I do. Look at me. Look at Matthew.'

He nodded. 'Matthew's very fond of you, Jinx.'

'Yes.' She listened for footsteps approaching down the corridor. 'But only because I have the same black eyes as his dying fox. He wants to train as a vet when he leaves here. Has he told you that?'

Alan shook his head.

'He's a sucker for wounded animals. People, he can take or leave.'

'He's not so different from you then.'

She gave a little jump as Adam's footsteps sounded at the top of the stairs. 'On the whole,' she said in a rush, 'I'm not quite so prepared to leave them as I used to be. Perhaps my judgement's improving.'

'That's good.' He smiled down at her. 'The Nightingale's achieved something then.'

'Except that I don't think it was the Nightingale.' She crossed to the door and stood with her back to it. 'I don't always look like something the dog threw up, you know. You'd be amazed what a little hair does for me.' She hesitated.

'I – er – I suppose you wouldn't like to look me up in a month or two when I'm more presentable?'

He shook his head. 'Not really.'

She blushed with embarrassment. 'It was just a thought, Dr Protheroe. Rather a stupid one. Sorry.'

There was a loud knock on the door. 'Jane, are you in there? It's your father.'

Alan lowered his voice. 'The name is Alan, Jinx, and who the hell needs hair? I only ever fantasize about bald women.'

Another knock. 'Jane? It's your father.'

Her eyes gleamed. 'I'll be with you in ten minutes, Adam,' she called. 'There's something I have to do first. Can you wait in the foyer for me?'

'Why can't I wait in there?'

The Nightingale's administrator lifted an eyebrow. 'I'll be psychotic in two months,' he murmured. 'It does a man no good to keep his feelings zipped up as tightly as this. I'm in considerable pain here.'

Jinx was shaking with laughter as she quietly locked the door. 'It's a woman's thing, Adam,' she called to him in a quivering voice. 'You'd only be embarrassed.'

'Oh, I see. Well, no rush,' said her father gruffly. 'I passed Dr Protheroe's office on my way in. I'll have a word with him while I'm waiting.'

'You do that,' she said, wiping the tears from her eyes. 'You'll like him, Adam. He's your sort of man. Straight as a die and larger than life.'